Coming of the Shadow

MORGANNA CUMMINGS

COMING OF THE SHADOW

CHRONICLES OF THE GUARDED REALM:
THE SHADOW WARS

OTHER REALMS PRESS

For my Mother

Contents

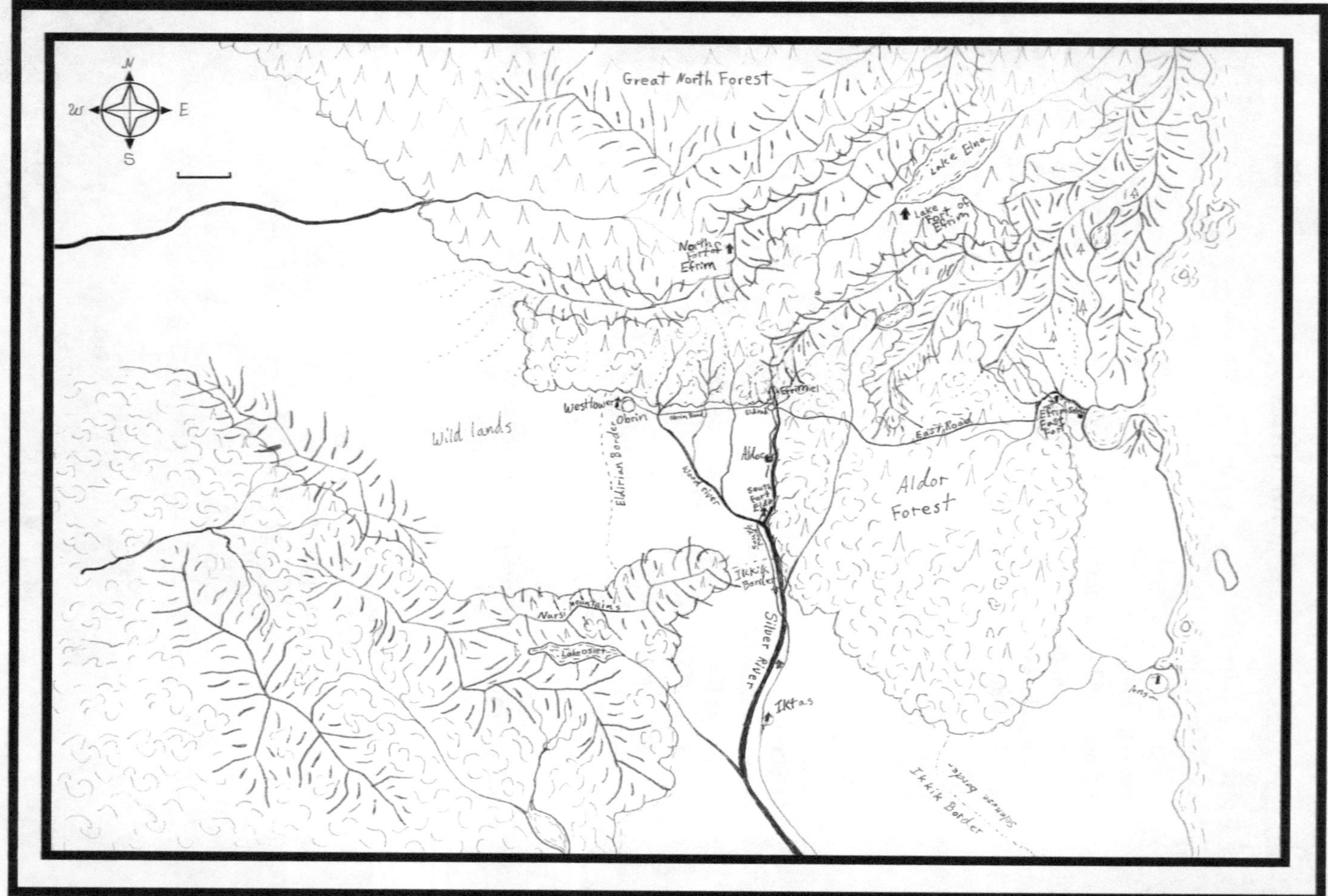

N
W
E
S
Great North Forest
Lake Elna
Lake Fort of Efrim
North Fort of Efrim
Efrimiel
Westtower
Obrin
Obrin Road
Eldrin
Eldirian Border
Wood River
Aldo
South Fort Elari
East Road
Efrim's East Fort
Aldor Forest
Ikkik Border
Narsi Mountains
Lake osier
Silver River
Iktas
Ikkik Border
Solenese border
Anga
Wild lands

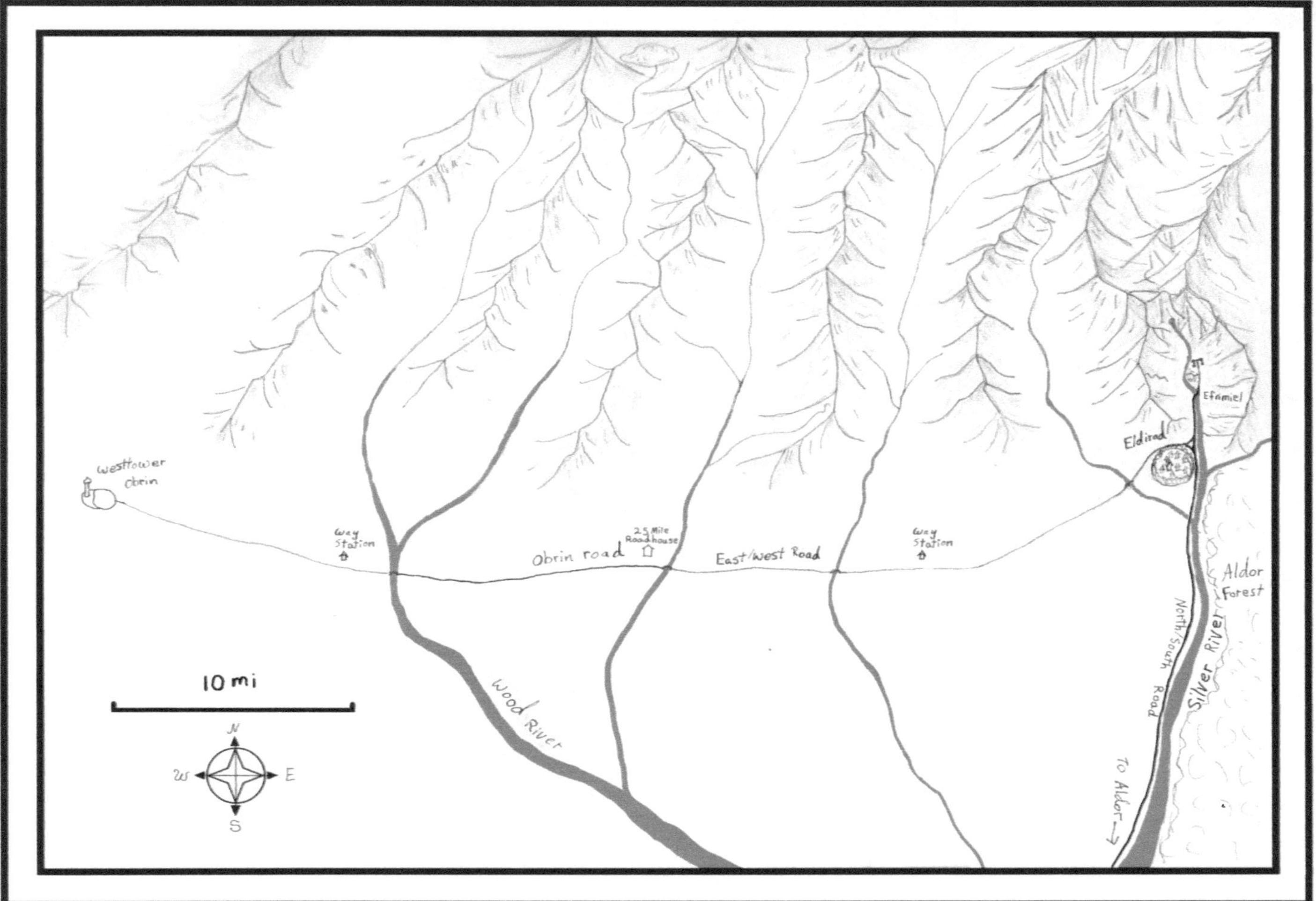

Westtower Obrin
Way Station
Obrin road
2.5 Mile Roadhouse
East/West Road
Way Station
Wood River
Eldirad
Efamiel
North/South Road
Silver River
Aldor Forest
To Aldor →
10 mi
N
W
E
S

Chapter 1

An Opportunity

12-22 July, Year of the Alliance (YA) 1121

South Fort of Eldir

"Aren't you coming in?" Elisabeth called, as she rested her arms on the rocky riverbank. Only her broad, muscular shoulders and the straps of her white bra top showed above the water.

Tatyana looked up from her book, squinting at the sunlight that was sparkling on the water behind Elisabeth's head and making the drying wisps of her golden-brown curls glow about her face. Tatyana was leaning against a huge linden tree with her book in her lap and her glossy black hair piled on top of her head. The sleeves and cuffs of her light cotton tunic and trousers were rolled up, and she was barefoot.

"You make studying impossible. I'll come when I finish my chapter."

"Hurry up and we can have a race."

Tatyana sighed as Elisabeth splashed back into the river. Why must Elisabeth always have someone to compete with? It seemed sometimes to Tatyana that winning was all Elisabeth cared about. Perhaps that wasn't fair. Being a warrior in the national guard was Elisabeth's whole ambition. She didn't have the Healing gift like Tatyana and Helen and so had no need to spend time studying books of obscure herbs and ancient magical techniques. Tatyana wished she was on duty with Helen. Helen was Elisabeth's older sister, and she and Tatyana had been best friends since they were little girls.

Tatyana forced her eyes back to the page. It was an interesting book, but rather dry, and the warm day made her tired. She slipped in a silk bookmark and stood. It never hurt to do more training, and the river looked inviting. She shed her outer clothes leaving only her sturdy linen bra top and undershorts. Then she ran and dove in. The water felt wonderful.

She turned her face into the current and swam as hard as she could. Having made six or seven yards, she turned and swam rapidly downstream. It felt like soaring, like being a hundred times more powerful than she really was. A boulder stood a hundred yards past the spot where the two rivers met, and she could see Elisabeth sitting on it, looking at her.

Tatyana caught herself on the rock and pressed all the way into a handstand, her lithe, slender body sparkling and dripping in the sun. Then she lowered herself gracefully to sit beside Elisabeth. She smiled as she looked around.

The southern fort was a sturdy, elegant building of white stone on the triangle of land where the Silver and Wood Rivers met. To the east, the forest was lush and shady, and the grass all around was thick with flowers. It was a lovely place to be stationed in high summer.

Tatyana, Elisabeth, and their companions were guards on duty, watching over the trade road to the kingdom of Ikkik in the south, but it was an easy job. All it really meant was being there for two weeks, training hard, and occasionally performing customs duty for merchants coming up the road from the south. Then they would return home to the capital city of Eldirad, where they would train three hours in the morning and have afternoons free to pursue other crafts or be the homemaker while their spouses had more time for their profession. Common soldiers only had to go out to border duty two weeks out of eight so long as they kept up morning training. Guardians went out two weeks out of four. Captains had a choice. Super-dedicated captains with dreams of guardianship, like Tatyana and Elisabeth, always took the four-week schedule, but Helen had never done more than the required two weeks out of eight.

The training of the Eldir guards, and their allies the Efrim, was far superior to all their neighbors, and everyone knew it. Their terms of trade were fair, and so any form of aggression was rare, and always brief. The Eldir guard hadn't had to fight a real battle since Tatyana's grandmother was a little girl. Still, the guards were important. As Tatyana's father said, a nation had to have a skilled standing army in order to always have peace.

Tatyana swung a foot over the side of the rock and into the water. "It does feel rather good," she said. Her voice dropped and her exquisite features grew grave. "But it won't help me when Grandmother asks what I've learned."

"You already got your healer's badge when you came of age. Why do you still have to study?" Elisabeth sounded relaxed and as if she thought Tatyana's worry foolish.

Tatyana was a little ruffled but tried to sound light. "Grandmother's never satisfied, even now that I'm a woman. She never will be, I suspect, at least not until I'm queen. That is, if I ever make guardian. I can't even be crown princess if I don't make guardian."

Life was perfect: training, working in the hospital, going to the theatre when she was home, and being with her family and friends. But Tatyana wanted more than anything to serve her people as their queen. She was the oldest child of the royal house, and in Eldir, that meant the crown would go to her first if she could earn it. She had been raised with those expectations and trained for it all her life. She had passed the test to be a captain at her coming of age, but being a princess didn't make advancing to the rank of guardian any easier. To earn that title she had to prove herself and earn the respect and confidence of a great many people. A respect no king or queen of Eldir could rule without. But how could she earn that respect when everything was so peaceful?

Elisabeth's intense light-gray eyes were fixed on the water. "I keep trying to beat Margaret in mock battle and to win in fencing matches and all that," she said. "I took Sarah and Jacob's watches in the lookout tower last week, but it doesn't seem like enough. I want to do more. I would do anything to be a guardian."

Tatyana nodded. Margaret was the guardian in charge of their post on this rotation, and Tatyana and Elisabeth had often been stationed under her since they became captains. It was pretty impressive that Elisabeth sometimes succeeded in beating her in mock battle, but it was just like Elisabeth to think throwing energy at it would do the trick.

"I'm not sure that's what a guardian should say," Tatyana said softly. Guardians were supposed to be selfless protectors. They were not just the highest rank of the army like an Efrim general.

"I don't know. Of course, in storybooks heroines always save people from terrible fates or ferocious creatures, but I'm not saying I want any of that. I just want to be famous, to go down in history as a great warrior. Being a guardian would be enough I think, so long as I could make a name for myself."

Tatyana was conflicted enough about her own desire to win the title, but Elisabeth's bare ambition bothered her. She was about to say something when a shadow passed before her eyes. She froze. For a moment she saw something dark and terrible standing behind, almost over, Elisabeth. It was huge, with many legs and glowing red eyes. Then it was gone, and she saw only Elisabeth's eager face and realized she was still talking about the fame she would win.

Tatyana felt shaken. She stood and looked away to hide her face. The Sight, along with the Healing gift that usually came with it, was the greatest magical power of the Eldir. It was inherited and uncommon, but it always ran in the royal line through a blessing of the magic. It came in varying degrees of strength, and Tatyana's was a fairly strong gift—or curse, as the case may be.

The part of the gift she could control was useful. She could feel if those closest to her were in pain or danger and then go to them in spirit with what was called the Sending. She could even speak to them if they had the Sight, too, although that was a stretch for her level of the gift, and at her strongest she couldn't manage more than a word or two. However, the other side of the power was prophecy: vague dreams and strange momentary visions, unreliable, often at the worst moments, and, in her experience, always troubling.

Tatyana shook herself. "You want to race me upstream to the cherry with the crooked trunk?"

Elisabeth cut short in the middle of whatever she had been saying. "Are you all right? Are you even listening to me?"

"Sorry. I'm fine. I just thought you wanted to race."

"Well, yeah."

"Let's go then."

They stood side by side on the rock and Tatyana counted them off. They dove in together and swam as hard as they could. The river current was strong, and the experience of going upriver was very different than going down. It was a fight, but they enjoyed it, and it helped Tatyana put her fears away. They neared the tree and pushed even harder.

Elisabeth reached forward, swinging herself up onto the tree a second before Tatyana touched it.

Half an hour later, after a spirited game of water tag with some of their fellow guards, they headed back to the fort. Elisabeth walked casually, dripping, and carrying her clothes under one arm. She was an imposing woman of mixed Efrim and Eldir blood, something that was relatively rare even after a thousand years of close alliance. The broader build of her Efrim blood was very pronounced, but she also had the height of the Eldir who tended to be a few inches taller than their Efrim neighbors. This made her an exceptionally large woman, and she was lean and muscular with a powerful stride.

Tatyana put her clothes back on for the walk to the fort even though the water soaked through them and made them stick to her skin. An inch taller than Elisabeth and just as strong, she had a very different build. She was slim and narrow about the shoulders even for an Eldir, in spite of her well-muscled arms, and had a very curvy feminine figure. She had only been a young girl of sixteen when she first noticed boys looking at her, and while they were polite enough about it, she didn't like it much. It didn't help that she had a beautiful face too, with an alabaster complexion, full lips, and long-lashed gray eyes.

They grabbed towels in the bathing room and went upstairs to the women's dorm to change into dry clothes. Tatyana sighed in annoyance as she went to get her duffel and found several wilted flowers and two notes on her cot.

"I do wish boys would leave me alone." Tatyana said, putting on a dry bra top.

Elisabeth shrugged into a purple tunic. "I'm glad nobody gets all silly over me. I'd probably give them a good shaking to knock some sense into them."

Tatyana smiled. "Maybe that's why they don't."

"Maybe." Elisabeth was unconcerned.

Tatyana took the towel off her head and let her hair fall down her back as she slipped on her tunic and trousers. After a minute she said, "It's our turn to make dinner tonight. I know that isn't a way to prove we're great warriors, but if we make something nice at least the rest of the company may be pleased with us."

"Yeah. I suppose so. Do you have any ideas?"

"Well, we could make a meat pie, but I think it's too hot. What about chicken and dumplings, and some green beans? My mother makes dumplings better than me, but I have her recipe. It's a really good one. We made it for the ambassadors from Selna last week." Tatyana liked cooking, and it was a comforting prospect to settle down to the everyday task of preparing dinner even if here it was for almost two hundred warriors rather than her family.

"All right, but we need to think of something. Not for dinner. I mean something we can do to prove ourselves."

"It would be nice," Tatyana conceded. "But I don't see what." She paused. "We should ask Margaret how she became guardian."

"Let's. Do you know how your father got it?"

"There was a fire in the forest of Aldor near the town. Father was a captain on forest patrol and saw it and organized the firefighting. They had it out in three hours. He burnt his hand rather badly, but that night the warriors voted him guardian." Tatyana sighed. "He was young, just turned thirty." Tatyana gave an impatient tug at her embroidered belt. An Eldir came of age at thirty, so it was the youngest anyone could receive a title. Her father had become crown prince within three months; and it had already been two years since she came of age.

Elisabeth stuffed her duffel under her bed with more than necessary force. Then she smiled. "I guess life is just too good for people who want to be heroines, but I'm sure we'll find a way. Let's go make dinner."

* ✶ ✶ ✶ ✶ ✶ *

The next day, after a long training session in the sunny meadow north of the fort, they found a moment to ask Margaret their question. The rest of the soldiers had gone to jump in the river, and the two captains were left alone with the guardian to clean up.

Tatyana spoke first. "Lady Margaret, can I ask you a question?"

"Why of course. What's the matter?" Margaret looked from Tatyana's grave face to Elisabeth's eager one. "Both of you, is it?" She smiled and picked up a pile of jump ropes.

"Yes." Elisabeth clattered shields into a crate, looking up at Margaret. "You see, we wanted to ask how you became a guardian."

Margaret put the ropes in a bag and then looked from one to the other. Elisabeth's light gray eyes were bright and eager. Tatyana's face was hard.

"Do you girls remember the grand tournament twenty-one years ago to celebrate year 1100 of the alliance? You would have been little..."

"Yes. I remember. I was eleven." Tatyana put a lance on the rack, but her steel-gray eyes were unfocused, seeing only memories. "I watched all the competitions, and then Sebastian and I competed at home. We weren't much good, but it was fun."

The celebrations had been glorious. She didn't remember well, but it all seemed like a swirl of silk and lanterns, feasts and warriors in shining mail with jeweled swords. The alliance with the Efrim was a very close and special one, nothing like the treaties with other nations. The two nations had been very different when the Eldir came out of the north, but they saw similarities at once. Both nations were tall, strong, powerful people, and much longer lived than their neighbors. Their cultures and magic gifts were different, but they got along and traded knowledge and skill. The alliance was so important both nations counted their years from the time they met.

Elisabeth bounced from one foot to the other, her eyes still on Margaret. "I remember the great battles they staged in the palace courtyard at Eldirad. It was the most spectacular thing I had ever seen, and I wanted to be in it. Did you win your guardianship in the contests?"

"Yes." Margaret smiled, a faraway look in her eyes, and stood still gazing over the meadow in the direction of Eldirad. Then she looked at the young women beside her. "We have tournaments like that every so often, but that was the only one I've been in. It was a truly grand thing. I was a captain, and just thirty-two like you, Tatyana. King Edward and Lady Clara put it on together with Queen Evelina and Commander Louranin of Efrim, and all the soldiers of both armies competed."

"There was every kind of event, wasn't there? I remember the fencing, and high jumping I think." Elisabeth stood still with a bag of heavy balls forgotten in her hands.

"Oh, yes, all the usual events. But the best part was the group sword fighting tournament. Every captain and guardian had a team, and generals of course."

Both nations had captains as their lower rank of commander, but although the ancient Eldir tongue had mostly faded into the modern Efrian language both societies now spoke, the Eldir had never adopted the Efrian word 'general' for the higher commanders. Eletrian, or guardian, was one of the few Eldir words that remained other than technical terms associated with medicine and woodworking. The Eldir maintained that it meant something quite different than general, although the rank was equivalent.

"Is that where you won your title?" Tatyana asked.

"Yes. I came in second in the tournament behind Commander Louranin. I even beat King Edward, Prince Peter, Clarissa, and Henry, who were the only other guardians then. That very night I was awarded my stars." Her face was shining with more than the sweat of the hot day. She shook her head. "It was grand. I don't know why we don't do it more often."

"I wish we would," Tatyana said softly.

"Why can't we?" Elisabeth asked. "I want to compete. Surely it's time."

"You should talk to King Edward about it. I'd be happy to second you," Margaret said.

"I will." Elisabeth looked at Tatyana.

Tatyana nodded. "Yeah. I'll talk to Father about it as soon as we get home."

* ★ ★ ★ ★ ★ *

Two days later, the warriors were all sitting around the big table in the kitchen eating dinner. The windows were all open to let in a breeze, and people were talking and laughing. The day's mail carrier had arrived on a fresh horse from Aldor and was passing letters around the table. He handed one to Tatyana, and she broke the seal eagerly, recognizing the loopy, elegant hand of her brother at once. He was currently on guard duty at Westtower, the westernmost guard station of the Eldir that watched over the protectorate village of Obrin. The letter began by describing a game of bat ball she rather wished she had been a part of. He said he missed her and he thought their team would have won if she had been there to pitch for them.

Then he went on:

> *My dear sister, I have some real news for you today. I had to tell you at once.*
>
> *Last night when I was on watch I spotted a group of wandering ruffians sneaking in the dark through the scrub-land beyond the Westtower wall. I ran and woke those on call for my watch and we waited where they couldn't see us. When they tried to get in towards Obrin we jumped out. They fought, but we disarmed them pretty quickly and chased them off. Nobody was hurt on either side, but they were pretty scared I think. Anyway, this morning Prince Peter called me into his house and told me the warriors in the garrison had all voted me guardian the night before. So there you have it. I will get my stars as soon as I go home for Father to bestow them. I*

didn't think I really did anything special, but I can't refuse. I have always felt my duty to serve my people. Prince Peter wants to retire, so I will be prince of Westtower before the summer's out. I always hoped to earn the title, but I have to admit I have mixed feelings about it now. It will be hard to move out of Eldirad.

Tatyana forced herself to swallow a bite of bread. She should be glad; she was proud of Sebastian, of course she was... but he was her little brother, and he was a guardian already, only two months after his coming of age. His quiet humility bugged her, perhaps all the more because she knew it was genuine. He was prince of Westtower. That was great. It was his to earn as the second child of the royal house, but if she didn't make guardian soon... Father wouldn't retire for nine years, but he would want to designate an heir. What if he made Sebastian crown prince? Her right as the elder meant nothing if she didn't win guardian. Any guardian could be prince or princess of Westtower if there was only one guardian of the royal house.

She folded the letter and forced herself to finish her dinner, avoiding the curious looks sent her way. She knew it was no real disgrace to be the oldest and not become queen. Her aunt Amanda was the firstborn and chose not to be queen, but that was different. She had never even trained as a warrior. She had decided she wanted to be a potter instead. Tatyana wanted so badly to serve her people. It was her greatest desire in life, something she had worked for since she was a little girl. But what if she wasn't good enough?

She was quiet that evening. She sat by the fire with a book, as she often did, but she didn't read it much. She kept thinking about the letter, her hopes and fears, and the frightening visions she had seen.

✶✶✶✶✶✶

That night, Tatyana had another dream: *She was looking down from an eagle's eye view on her country, and the Efrim land and the forests and rivers beyond. Everything was green and lush and beautiful. Then, to the north, the trees of the mountain forests began to blacken. A blight, or desolation, crept over forests and mountains leaving nothing living in its wake. It was coming closer and closer to the mountain forts north of Efrim, and then it came and washed over the land.*

She was standing on the steps of the royal house in Eldirad now and the blackness was getting thicker and thicker. Her friends were disappearing into the mist. Helen and Elisabeth were gone, Clarissa was swallowed by the mist. Joseph and Sebastian vanished beyond dark curtains, and then she could no longer see Analisia or Aranin either. Faintly she could see people around her and they looked thin and haggard. She still saw her parents, but try as she might, she could not reach them.

She woke soaked in sweat, but shivering in the warm summer night. She wanted it to be an ordinary bad dream, but every detail was crystal clear. She had felt the stones of the palace steps under her feet and smelled the bitterness of the black mist. She told herself she was just anxious, and rolled over, but it did no good. Lying to herself wouldn't change anything. It was another Sight dream, and not all that unlike one she had a year ago. Only this one was worse. Longer, more darkness, the starving faces of her people. She squeezed her eyes tight shut against the tears that forced their way onto her cheeks.

Perhaps it wouldn't happen, one never knew, and yet something was certainly coming. Sight dreams always meant something. The Sight had been warning the rulers of the Eldir of danger and giving vague glimpses into the future for thousands of years. One couldn't always trust it, but no wise person ignored it. How could she even care about who became ruler at a time like this? Perhaps she was just being selfish, and yet... and yet, her people needed her more than ever now. How could she let them down by not being good enough?

"Is that you, Tatyana?" Elisabeth's voice asked close by.

Drat it. Why did she have to be awake?

"Are you all right?"

"What are you talking about," Tatyana murmured, trying to sound sleepy. "What are you awake for?"

"Oh, I was just thinking about the tournament."

"Yeah?" Tatyana didn't feel like hearing about it, but she wasn't going to admit to Elisabeth how frightened she was or any of her conflicted feelings over Sebastian's letter. She wouldn't understand, but she would think she did, and that was worse.

"I just can't wait. I'm sure it's time to do another one. How can new warriors come up in the ranks without tournaments like that? And I know if I only have the chance to prove myself people will see I can be a great warrior. I want to be respected—the kind of person people will turn to."

"Oh, you will be," Tatyana muttered. Elisabeth's eternal confidence made her angry, and for a moment she wanted to tell her about the monster she had seen behind her that day on the rock. She wanted to see if she could frighten her. Could anything shake that confidence? She hesitated, but then she didn't say it. A suspicion that Elisabeth would just laugh it off or think it exciting held her back. She thought bitterly that Elisabeth didn't understand Sight dreams, or fear.

"Hey, what's this?" Elisabeth had come over and was pointing at the letter that showed pale in the starlight against the dark wood of Tatyana's nightstand. "Bad news?"

"No. Sebastian just got named guardian." Tatyana didn't look at Elisabeth.

"Oh, I see, so you're jealous that he got promoted before you?"

"No, not really..." How could she ever explain? "I'm proud of him, really. I just worry I may not get to serve my people." She wasn't sure how to put her feelings into words. It wasn't really about glory. It was about living up to expectations and hopes. It was about being there so people could count on her, and about making her family proud.

"Well, we will have a tournament soon," Elisabeth said cheerfully. "Then we can prove ourselves."

Tatyana bit her lip and straightened up in bed. "I hope." She looked down at her hands in her lap in the faint starlight. Then she looked up at Elisabeth. "No. I will not hope for anything. I will do my best and abide by the result."

Elisabeth grew grave and was silent a minute. Then she whispered,

"That is how a guardian should feel. I don't deserve it half as much as you if I can't feel that way too."

Tatyana refrained from telling any of her fears in the letters she wrote over the next week, and she spoke of it to no one. She tried to think of other things. The next day she finished a letter to Princess Analisia full of cheerful gossip about the fort and the games in the river, as well as questions about the books she was reading, and the last theatre production. Then she wrote to Sebastian congratulating him on his title. She did look forward to being home in time to see him receive his stars, but most of all she wanted to talk to her father and Helen.

* * * * * * *

The sun was setting when the company reached the city of Eldirad; its last rays shone on the white stone, silver, jewels, and carved wood of the people's houses and made the fields of green wheat and vegetables around the city glow. It was a soft, beautiful evening, so peaceful that all her dreams seemed almost silly. The company dispersed as they entered the town, and Tatyana made her way alone towards the royal house. Unlike in Efrim, Eldir tradition had very little pomp around the royal family. It was considered wrong for a person of authority to have anything better than those under them, and the king's family lived much like everyone else, except on ceremonial occasions. The royal house was larger than most because they had to entertain ambassadors, but it was nothing like the Efrim palace.

Tatyana went in through the kitchen door on the side, instead of the big walnut front doors, just in case there were diplomats in the living room. The kitchen was large, bright, and airy with the windows open, and her mother—Lady Clara, the queen consort—was washing dishes. She wore a blue apron over her knee-length summer dress, and her long raven and silver hair was braided and wound on her head to keep it out of her way. Her soft, slate-gray eyes lit up when she saw Tatyana, and her smile was warm and beautiful.

After the usual greetings and mundane questions about life on both sides while she had been gone, Tatyana went upstairs to see her father.

She knocked on his door and went in. He looked up and smiled when he saw her. He was a tall, athletic man of slender build, with touches of silver in his long ebony hair. His smile lessened as he walked towards her, and his sea-gray eyes grew softer, searching her face.

"Something troubles you, my dear?" he said gently, taking her hand.

"Yes, I... I don't know how to say it exactly."

"Please tell me all about it." He sat down on the edge of the big bed, and she sat beside him.

"Oh, Father, there are so many things. I have had more Sight dreams, and I'm worried about our people." She dropped her voice even lower. "I'm worried I will fail them."

Edward was silent for a long minute. He took her hand. "I'm worried, too," he whispered. "All we can do is our best." He looked up into her face and smiled a little. "But if you are worried because Sebastian got his stars first... you know it was only chance that gave him the opportunity. I am very proud of him, but I'm sure you would have done the same. You have time yet."

"I know... and I was thinking, I mean when I was talking to Elisabeth and Margaret, we thought about the last tournament, and it seemed it might be time. Bring new people up in the ranks."

"It's a good idea. There are many young warriors who haven't had the chance, and with Henry retiring, and Prince Peter, we only have three guardians even after Sebastian is official. Besides, you deserve the chance to show the people what you can do."

"I will do my best. I don't know if I'm good enough, but I feel like my people need me."

"I believe in you, my dear. I cannot give you the title, but I look forward to bestowing it."

She smiled and squeezed his hand. "Thank you," she whispered.

"I don't know what is special about the year 1121, but we'll think of something. Perhaps it could have something to do with Sebastian's crowning, or perhaps just that it has been twenty-one years since the last one."

"Works for me."

"I'll go talk to Louranin, and I think I will have to get an audience with Queen Evelina in person for this." He made a slight face. Evelina's traditionalist Efrim views made her and Edward's relationship very stiff, but there were some things that had to be handled between the actual rulers.

"I'll help if you like," Tatyana offered without much conviction. Evelina was a good person, but Tatyana didn't agree with her principles and hated her treatment of her son. The idea of going with her father and sitting there while Evelina addressed all her questions to her, with the faint chill of disrespect to her father that implied, made her uncomfortable and a little angry.

"No. It's better if I go alone," he said. There was a pause.

"It should be a nice party for all the people, make them happy..." she didn't say 'before whatever it is comes,' but her voice dropped and quavered slightly.

Edward nodded. "I am really worried. Something Helen said the other day when she stopped by... Do you want to tell me what you saw?"

She described the vision from the river and then told him about the nightmare in every detail. "Our people looked hungry and scared," she concluded. "And... and everyone was going away from me." Her voice was shaking and there were tears in her eyes again. Telling it brought back all the fear and uncertainty she had been trying to repress while at the fort.

Edward was silent for a long time, but he put a strong, protective arm around her. She buried her face in the shoulder of his soft linen tunic and cried. After a while, she felt a little comforted, straightened up, and looked into her father's face.

"What are we going to do? The Sight is so confusing, and I don't want to frighten people, but surely we must do something."

He cleared his throat, and when he spoke his voice was husky. "I don't know what we'll do. It is hard to tell with the Sight, but whatever threatens us, it seems like a food shortage is involved, or at least could be. The hungry people you saw... and I had a dream with a shock of wheat turning to black dust last week."

"We should store food just in case, shouldn't we?"

"Yes, I think we should. I'm not sure how to take action without alarming people, but maybe the tournament would be just the thing to distract them."

✳✳✳✳✳✳

Prince Aranin of Efrim was riding his gray horse up the valley road with his company on his way back from a two-week stay at the eastern fort. The fort was a nice enough place, but he was very glad to be home. He looked up at the cherries hanging from the trees over his head and picked one without stepping out of line. Then he saw a field, one of the ball fields, off to his right. A group of two dozen men and women, mostly young and some only youths, were playing kick ball. He watched with a smile. They played kick ball and bat ball at the fort, of course, as well as fencing, and running, jumping, and wrestling, and just about any other athletic sport one could think of, but it wasn't the same. The fields at home were nicer and, most important, when he played at home Analisia was always there. After just a moment his eyes were attracted to a young woman of medium height, her caramel colored curls unsuccessfully tied back with a bit of ribbon.

"Analisia!" he called.

She stopped running and looked towards him. She had a small, somewhat turned-up nose and clear lake-blue eyes just like his. Her face lit up. "Someone cover for me," she called over her shoulder as she ran towards him.

He stopped his horse and jumped off as she came up, panting. She wore a short-sleeve top and trousers cut off at the knee. One of her knees was scraped. Her round, rosy face was glowing with delight and dripping with sweat. She ran into his arms.

"Oh, I'm so glad you're home," she exclaimed, releasing him. "You look stronger."

16

Aranin laughed. "General Kalsian works us really hard." He paused, looking down. It had never seemed right that he and his twin sister should be separated, and even after four years it was still strange to be coming home to her. Until he apprenticed they had done everything together. He had to go to the city school while she had tutors, but he had stayed in much longer than boys usually did, partially so they could still do homework together. Being away from her so much had been the hardest part of his tough decision to join the guard. "I brought you a present." He fumbled in one of his saddlebags and pulled out a book with an attractive picture of a fantasy creature with bird wings and the body of a deer. "I know you wanted something new in Selnese, to practice, and I thought you'd like it. Happy birthday."

She beamed. "I love it, thank you. I have your present in my desk. We had the most wonderful party. I will have to tell you all about it. There was a ball, and a huge chocolate cake. We danced in the courtyard so lots of people could come. I asked Yeven to dance with me one dance." She blushed.

Aranin swallowed a trace of sadness. He liked Yeven. He was the son of a leather worker who made beautiful things, and he and Aranin had been the only boys in the art class at school, or in either of their classes at graduation. They were friends, but he didn't like thinking of Analisia getting a sweetheart. She would in time, of course, but he wanted his sister to himself as long as possible. Sometimes he was jealous of Yeven because his mother and grandmother had been willing to teach him the family trade even though he was a boy. Of course he was an only child, but most Efrim probably would have taken an apprentice instead. At the same time, it was brave of him to apprentice in a women's profession and Aranin had to admire that.

"I can imagine you together," he said after a little while. "What colors did you wear? I could paint it perhaps..."

They walked slowly down the road together while she told him in detail all about the party.

"I wanted Mother to wait until you got home, but she wouldn't hear of changing the date," she concluded.

"Of course not. A national festival like the princess's birthday cannot be postponed. It doesn't matter. The party wasn't for me."

"I would have thought it was. I would have made them let you sit with me to cut the cake."

He smiled.

"I got Mother to promise to do another little party tonight for you."

"Thank you. You know she's doing it for you, though."

"That's not true. She loves you too."

He shrugged. "I suppose so." They walked in silence for a few minutes.

"Did you do any painting?" she asked.

"Some, in the evening mostly. We train so much during the day, and then there is the harbor to explore. I wish you could see it too."

"So do I." She looked wistful for a minute. Then she smiled. "Mother will take me the next time she goes on a diplomatic mission, I think, or maybe I could even go with one of the ambassadors sometime."

"You can, but it would be more fun together." Aranin sighed. His father came from a line of generals and had always said it was the only profession where a man could make a mark. Sometimes Aranin wished he had been brave enough to go against tradition and the expectations of his father and join the bookmakers' shop as an illustrator. Then he could have stayed home with Analisia and done the work he dreamed of. But he wanted to serve his people too, and he wanted to make his father proud. He liked the training for the most part, and getting to see other places, although he had been terribly homesick at first. It might even have been fun if Analisia could have come too, but in Efrim the crown princess wasn't allowed to be a warrior. The years of Eldir influence had changed things in Efrim a little. Other women could be soldiers if they wanted, and there was at least some small chance for men in skilled professions, but traditions were stubborn things. "Oh well. Someday, when you are queen, and if I can be good enough, maybe I will be high commander like Father and we can work together again."

"Of course we will." She gave his hand a quick squeeze and smiled. Her hand was small and soft in his large, hard one. "Now Aranin, I have something I just have to tell you."

"What?"

"There's going to be a festival and tournament in Eldirad on the equinox." She skipped a little in excitement. "King Edward came and talked to Mother about it last week, and then when Father came home he went to see Edward in Eldirad and talk about it too, since it is going to be mostly for the soldiers. I wish I could compete, but Mother says I can help her officiate."

"Nice." He wasn't sure what he thought of the idea, but he couldn't help smiling as he watched the eagerness on her face.

"Mother and I will be judges and such for some things, us and Elder Queen Josephine and Grandmother. There are going to be banquets too, and at least one ball, and I can do that of course. And I get to watch... but you can be in it, I'm sure. There are going to be all sorts of competitions..." Her smile faltered, and she said in a graver tone. "You will have to do it for both of us. I'm going to be counting on you."

Aranin looked down at his big soft leather boots on the paving stones. The fingers of his free hand fussed with the strap of his pack. "I'm not sure I'm good enough for that. I mean, I'm only an apprentice, I'm only twenty-six..."

"So? I'm sure they will let the apprentices be in it too. You don't have to win... just make me proud." Her eyes sparkled like sunshine on water. "Or, if you think you're too slow, we could trade places and I'll run the foot race for you."

They both laughed. There had been a time, until about twenty when she started to develop as a woman and he got taller and more like a man, when they looked so similar they could play tricks like that. But those days were long past now. Not even their faces looked that much alike anymore except for their eyes and noses. He had lost much of the softness in his face and his jawline had become clear and square, while her face remained round and soft, making her look younger than he was.

"I wish you could," he said. "I bet you are still faster than me, although I've been practicing." He said it to make her smile, but he knew it wasn't true anymore. She was no longer his athletic equal. That fact saddened him. It wasn't that he was four inches taller now. No, he had been training hard the last four years in the guard, and her rosy face was just a touch rounder than the last time he had seen her. Her figure was still athletic, but where her arms and legs showed they were soft. Her face was flushed, and the stray hair on her forehead wet with sweat. They shared a broad build, as well as their caramel colored curls and blue eyes, but her muscles didn't show much and, although Aranin was a bit more graceful and less bulky than his father, he had gained the broad, heavily muscled shoulders common among Efrim male warriors.

"Sure you have, and I spend too much time reading, or studying... but still..." She grinned. "I'll race you any time."

"I don't feel like racing. Besides, I have to walk my horse home." He looked around for a way to change the subject. "I'm sure there are tons of things you haven't told me. I want to know everything. What have you been reading?"

That got her started, and they talked about books the rest of the way to the palace.

Chapter 2

Dreams and Premonitinos

1 August 1121 (ten days later)
to 14 September YA 1121

Westtower: Eldirad

THE GOLDEN LIGHT of the August sunset flooded into the tower room from the large western windows that looked out over the wild land beyond the wall that protected Obrin. Helen stood looking out, enjoying the peaceful beauty. It seemed like a propitious day. She was glad today had been chosen for Sebastian's crowning as prince of Westtower. She had come from the city with the royal family and his best friend Joseph for the ceremony, but Edward, Clara, and Tatyana were already in the house of the prince, where they would spend the night. Joseph had excused himself a few minutes before. Sebastian and Helen were alone in the lookout room at the top of Westtower.

"Helen?" Sebastian's voice was hesitant.

She turned to look at him. He stood a few feet away beside the table in the center of the room. He had taken off the silver circlet he had been given at the ceremony and fingered it absently. His large, beautiful, slate-gray eyes were fixed on the sunset, but didn't seem to see it.

"What is it?" she asked.

He looked at her now. "I have something to ask you." Color rose in his cheeks.

She felt excitement flutter through her body and knew her own color was rising. Since she was the older child in her family, and Sebastian was the younger, Helen could have asked him at his coming-of-age last spring, except for the possibility he would become prince of Westtower. The younger child of the royal house could join their spouse's family like anyone else if they didn't earn the title of Westtower, but if they did, they must remain in the royal house. Helen had believed he would earn it, and so she had waited. Now it was his place to ask, instead of hers.

"Of course, anything," she said.

"I know you have many things to keep you in Eldirad," he said in a soft, grave voice. "You are a captain, and there is your family, and the hospital, and your studies... I am going to miss being in the city with all our people and everything happening, but I can come visit often once I appoint a captain to be in charge when I'm not here, and it is nice out here. There will be time for my miniature houses, and reading... and your sewing. We could have a nice little garden, and take picnics... I mean, I understand if you want to stay in the city, but my duty is to this place now. I must keep the guard tower and do my best to be a prince to the people of the protectorate of Obrin. I'm tied to this place for something like forty years, until the next prince is crowned." He paused and his voice grew very soft. "But I can do without the rest of the city. If... if you would come... and be my consort, I would be the happiest man alive."

She smiled, and her bright gray eyes filled with tears. She had some slight misgivings, the nagging fears of Sight dreams boding of some kind of duty that lay before her. Sight dreams were not always clear, but they always meant something, and that worried her. Still, just now, that concern seemed very small and distant, and as she felt his strong, slender hand in her small hard one and looked up into his face, all doubt melted away.

His long raven hair shimmered in the golden light and his eyes were very tender. She opened her mouth to speak, and a shadow passed before her eyes, between them. For a moment she saw his face through the shadow, and it was very different. His fair complexion, a little ruddy from the sun, was white. His fine, high cheekbones stuck out painfully, his smooth rounded cheeks were hollow, and his eyes sunken and shadowed. Darkness, fingers of shadow, seemed to coil around him, pulling him away from her.

The shadow passed as quickly as it came, and his handsome face was not changed, but his slate-gray eyes had darkened and his thick black brows drawn together in concern. She realized she had pulled away from him. Shaken, she turned to the window and put her head in her hands, her fingers pushing into her straight black hair. Her gift of the Sight had never seemed so much like a curse.

Prophecy was such a messy, vague business. What could this one mean? Even after years of making a study of the Sight and historical dreams, there was no way to be sure. Could it be telling her that if she married Sebastian right away she could protect him from whatever that shadow was? She wanted so much to believe that, but the timing was wrong. If the vision was telling her anything it seemed to be trying to stop her from getting married. Was it a premonition that if she neglected the duties in Eldirad and Efrim that other dreams had hinted at, she would doom him to this?

"What's the matter, dearest?" Sebastian's voice was soft and strained and he laid a hand on her shoulder. "You can say no, if you must, or if you aren't sure... I'll wait as long as you wish."

"It isn't that," she whispered, turning to him. "It's... it's the Sight, and I'm just so confused." She lay her head on his breast and felt the soft, cool silk of his tunic against her cheek. He put his arms around her. She wanted to stay there forever. She let her arms slip around his lithe, strong body and clung to him.

He held her in silence for a few minutes. "You do want to get married then?" he asked in a shaky voice. Then said, "I'm sorry. I shouldn't ask that."

"I love you, Sebastian," she whispered. "So much. I'm just afraid there is something I must do, that something is going to happen..." She couldn't say more. It was all so vague and confusing, and everything she saw was frightening. She released him, and they stood side by side looking out the window.

"You don't want to tell me what you saw?" His voice was soft and almost succeeded in being steady. He understood Sight visions, although his gift was very slight, but that didn't take away the pain.

"No, not yet."

"I won't ask anything more then," he said so low she barely heard him.

She looked up into his face. The flush was gone from his cheeks and his eyes had a sad, pained look that hurt her heart. Softly she slipped her hand over his on the windowsill.

✦✦✦✦✦✦

Helen saw the village of Aldor in the South, and then she was standing on a white wall looking out into a forest of sickly trees. Her sister, Elisabeth, was beside her. A shadow was all about them. She couldn't see, but she still knew she was holding Elisabeth's hand, and as they both held tight the shadow slowly began to fade. The scene switched and she saw the city of Eldirad silent, draped in mourning. Buildings were broken, trees dead. She saw her own house. The door broken down and blackened, the garden dead. A thin child in the street was weeping.

Helen woke with a start. She was in a bed in one of the tower dorms. Her heart pounded against her ribs. The city in mourning... dead, starving. She couldn't let that happen. Perhaps what they needed were better healers? Perhaps there would be a sickness, or people would come home badly wounded? Maybe it was a crop failure, or even an attack on the city itself. That didn't seem possible, but broken buildings...? If her house was destroyed where were her parents? And Elisabeth... she felt that she had to do something with Elisabeth.

She got up and walked silently down the stairs and out into the peaceful, starry night. She walked through the fields where the grain was drying. Then, near the inner village wall, she let herself out through the gate and walked into the forest. At last, her ruffled spirit began to settle. She wished she didn't have to be saddled with these premonitions, but she couldn't ignore them. Whatever the vision of Sebastian had meant, she felt that the dream had told her that there was something she had to do with Elisabeth and that perhaps there was something she could do as a healer to help her people and her city. None of the visions might come true, and she prayed they were only meant to warn her. This, too, could be warning her not to marry yet. It was no use trying to convince herself it was a normal dream. She went back and let herself in at the gate, locking it behind her.

"Is that you, Helen?" It was Sebastian's voice from the wall.

She had walked back to within a hundred yards of the tower and his sharp eyes had caught her even in her gray cloak. It must be the deepest part of the night, for Sebastian always took the most disliked hour of guard duty. As a prince in Eldir society that was only natural. The hardest task in a company went to the captain, the hardest in a kingdom to the ruler.

She took a deep breath and decided she was ready to talk to him again. "Yes," she said. She walked over and climbed the steps to the wall where Sebastian was sitting in the starlight on one of the crenellations.

"It's a very beautiful night," he said with an obvious effort to sound easy.

"Yes," she returned without feeling. She sat beside him. "I had another Sight dream." He was silent and she went on. "I have made up my mind for now."

He stiffened a little. "And?"

"There is something that needs me." She fought to keep the fear and confusion out of her voice, and kept it low and grave. "I don't understand it. I want to be here with you, but I think I need to stand by my sister, that there is something we are destined to face together. I don't understand any of it, and I hope I'm being foolish, but I can't say when I'll be free to get married." She could feel the tension in his body even though they weren't touching. His head was down, and he was very silent. She knew she had hurt him, and that felt like a knife to her heart, but she didn't know what to say.

After a moment she said, "I... if you need me... if you call, I will always come with the Sight." True love, whether platonic or romantic, was a very strong connection, and she could go to him as easily as to her parents or sister. His gift was too weak to use Sending, but it was enough for him to be able to hear her.

He managed a slight smile. "That's something... And I mean, if something really threatens our land, then neither of our happiness can be on this side of it." There was a quaver in his voice. "I know that, but everything seems so peaceful now, perhaps it is something smaller you must do, something on guard duty, or some new breakthrough in healing from your studies..."

"We will pray together that whatever it is it will soon pass." She tried to believe it would. She caught her fingers fiddling with her cloak pin and forced her hands to stay folded in her lap. She couldn't bear to tell him everything she had seen. She didn't want to frighten him as badly as she was frightened.

"We'll hope," he whispered. His voice was husky and so low she hardly heard.

✶ ✶✶✶✶ ✶✶

"Sebastian told me you have been having more dreams," Edward said softly as he handed Helen the other end of the measuring string.

"Yes." She took the string and measured the first marker line for the long jump. It was a few days after the crowning. Several people were working on the setup for the competitions in the fields just outside the city of Eldirad, but Edward and Helen were somewhat apart from the others. Helen kept her eyes on the marker tiles.

"You know I understand," he said very low.

She looked up.

Edward was a handsome man with the same high cheekbones and long, slightly curved nose of his son. His sea-gray eyes looked sad and stormy, but his expression was gentle. His right hand, scarred red from that fire years ago, set the marker, but he didn't seem to see it. "I mean why you didn't say yes to Sebastian. I'm sorry. I looked forward to having you be my daughter, and he takes it very hard, but I think he understands too."

Helen smiled faintly. "Thank you. I'm not sure I really understand. I just worry... I am so confused... but there is something."

"Yes. There is. If only we knew what." Edward walked to the other side of her to place the next marker tile. "Did Tatyana tell you about her dream back in July?"

"Yes, some of it at least. I think she might be right about it being some kind of blight or crop failure..."

"I have been thinking about that," Edward said. "I had a dream that seemed to point that way too, and Mother has had a couple. I want to commission a new storehouse. A good big one, but I don't want to alarm people. Do you suppose there is any way we could get the farmers to grow extra grain without scaring them? I mean, I could just ask them to, and I suppose they would, but they would want to know why, and I am so unsure..." His voice trailed off and he sat on his heels staring off into the distance.

"Maybe I could talk to my mother," Helen said. "She might take the challenge, and she could maybe get others excited about it. That's the kind of person she is, not a leader exactly, but..."

"Yes, she has such a hopeful, friendly way," he said with a faint smile. "That's a good idea. Perhaps we could have a kind of contest for farmers like the warriors are doing, only it would have to last a year, and there could be a prize for whoever grew the most."

Helen smiled. "That's a great idea. I'll talk to Mama about it when I find the right moment."

"Thank you. See what she thinks before I tell anyone else." He looked down and realized he had fussed with his piece of chalk until it broke. He smiled wryly and put one piece in his pocket. "I wonder if that will be enough... or if I'm just getting paranoid..."

She didn't reply for a few minutes. They set the rest of the distance markers and went to put a taut ribbon on the ground for the jump line. "I don't know," she said at last. "Sometimes I feel like I'm going crazy..."

"I don't believe that," he said.

She smiled faintly. "Thank you, I guess... Anyway, my last dream, well, it seemed almost like the city itself had been attacked by someone."

His face went a shade paler, and he looked up at her. "A real enemy? You mean an army?"

"I don't know, but there was destruction." Her voice faltered ever so slightly, and she couldn't say more.

He nodded. "The other day when I was walking down the street towards the river, I saw this wave of darkness come flooding up out of the forest towards the city. I know dark in visions can mean a lot of things. I thought maybe Ikkik has some nasty allies we never heard of and they're going to attack. The king of Ikkik is a heartless rotten potato, but I've never seen a sign he could be a real threat. Maybe it's someone else altogether. That doesn't seem likely either, but I feel uneasy, like a cloud hangs over us. I wish we had a wall. I never would have thought that before, but somehow, the city feels exposed."

"I know what you mean," she said. "But people will never like that. No one would be willing to imagine that defenses of the city itself could ever be needed."

"I know, and I pray to the Stars they're right. I wouldn't want to convince them, and I don't want my people to think I'm losing it or becoming paranoid. That won't do for a king, and yet... well, it's my duty to protect them."

"I don't suppose there's any way we could convince them a wall is just pretty?" Helen said without much hope.

✶ ✶ ✶ ★ ✶ ✶ ✶

Helen was working in the kitchen garden with her mother. It was an afternoon near the end of August. She sang along to an old Efrim folk tune while she pulled weeds from the lettuce bed, but she kept seeing Sebastian's face downcast in the moonlight, or when they had said goodbye the next morning. He had spoken almost cheerfully, but his face stayed grave and his eyes on his boots. She knew he was sad, and Edward had said as much, too, but what could she do?

"You never told me what happened at Westtower," her mother said softly after a silence.

"Sebastian was crowned. The people seemed happy. It was a beautiful day." Helen's tone was flat.

"So Sebastian didn't...?"

Helen swallowed. She loved her mother dearly, but it was hard to talk to her about Sight-related things. Yevenia was a warm, open, friendly person in a quiet, hospitable way, but she had little need for the wider world. Helen often worried that she had disappointed her when she decided to join the guard. Her mother had hoped she would be a farmer like her. Farmers provided food, and nothing was more important than that. It was a highly respected profession, especially for one with the Efrim magic gift with plants that Helen had inherited from her mother. Farmers got anything they wanted from the craftsman of the city and were paid by the crown so they could buy trade goods. They worked hard and were useful, and they had everything they wanted. It was a good, respectable life. Her mother had been proud of her for studying healing too, but the guard she thought silly.

"Yes, he did," Helen said after a long, heavy silence. She sat back on her knees in the dirt and looked at her mother.

"But, my dear?" Yevenia, too, sat up on her heels, her long golden braid shining in the warm sun and her soft brows furrowed with concern. "I thought that's what you wanted. I was sure you said... and the way you two look at each other..."

"Yes, it was." Helen looked back at the weeds and her voice went very low. "But I saw a terrible vision right when he asked me, and then that night I had more dreams. I just don't feel like I can get married yet. There is something I have to do first." There was a faint quaver in her voice, and it grew a little husky. "I am afraid I made him really sad, and that makes it so much harder..."

Yevenia was silent a moment. She rose and came over to kneel beside her daughter. "I don't pretend to know much about prophecy," she said softly. She put a hand on Helen's shoulder. "You have to do as you think best, but that's no reason you can't show him he is still your boy. Perhaps you could give him a little gift? Or take him flowers? Or just ask him to dance with you at the balls we will have at this festival? Make sure he knows how hard this is for you. Maybe you would want to be engaged? Sebastian is such a nice gentle boy, and you have always seemed so fond of each other."

"Oh, we are," Helen whispered. Then she smiled and gave her mother a hug. "I'll think about it and try to do something for him."

They finished the lettuce in silence. Yevenia stood up to stretch her back and Helen looked up at her. Yevenia wasn't a tall woman, especially living among the Eldir, but she was strong and stocky with a kind smile and friendly dark blue eyes.

"Mama," Helen said hesitantly. "There's something I have been wanting to talk to you about. It is sort of a Sight thing, but it is also about farmers."

"What is it?" Yevenia ran her hands along a tomato vine, and it grew greener beneath her touch.

"You see, everyone I know who has the Sight, except maybe Sebastian... but anyway, Edward, Lady Josephine, Tatyana, Father, and I, we have all seen something that makes us think some kind of famine may be coming. It could be war, or plague, or a blight on the crops of some kind, or really bad weather, but Edward has been working with an architect on plans for a new storehouse and wondering the best way to get the farmers to grow some extra crops without alarming anyone."

"There sure aren't signs of bad weather coming any time soon. I like to think I can grow in any weather, but that may not be true of others, and things happen. I don't mind growing an extra field or two if King Edward sees fit to make a new storehouse."

"We thought maybe we could make a contest out of it, kind of like the tournament for warriors, only for farmers to see who produced the most storable extra food by next summer. To make it fun."

"People might like that. I'm not sure it would be fair if I compete with a bunch of Eldir farmers who have to do it without magic, though." Yevenia smiled. "I'll be happy to rise to the challenge either way. However big he wants to make that storehouse, I'm sure we can fill it up in a couple years with no trouble."

"Perfect. I knew you would help."

"Why, of course. A farmer works the land and sees no one is hungry, and they're rather foolish if they don't listen to the advice of people with the Sight when it comes to their work."

About ten minutes later, Elisabeth came home. Her jaw was set hard, her thick eyebrows drawn slightly together, and her naturally ruddy cheeks were unusually flushed. Helen and her mother looked at each other, and Helen rose to follow her sister. She went into the house, washed her hands, and took off her muddy shoes. Then she started looking. It was not long before she found Elisabeth sprawled on her bed in their room. She entered silently and put a hand on Elisabeth's shoulder.

"What's the matter, Elisabeth?" Helen's voice was very gentle.

Elisabeth sat up and wiped her eyes on her sleeve. "I was trying to get people for my team in the tournament," she mumbled, looking away.

"And you didn't get the people you wanted; is that it? You haven't been home very long."

"I picked out exactly who I wanted, spent hours on it, and then today I asked six of them and they all denied me." Elisabeth looked up into Helen's hard, calm face. Her voice rose, her face flushed, and her light gray eyes flashed fire. "No one wants to be on my team. I'm sure John and Rebecca Bluebell, were lying to me. They were hoping someone they liked better would ask, but they hadn't actually promised yet!"

Helen didn't contradict her. It was no good. Elisabeth's Sight gift was so slight as to be nearly useless, but she could tell when someone was lying. Instead, Helen looked into Elisabeth's eyes and held her gaze. "You are a good captain, a very good captain, and you and I are not the only people who know that. There have been smaller contests like this before, at festivals and in training, and you have often won. The warriors that were on your teams on those occasions know how well you lead them, even if no one else does."

"But no one wants to be on my team." Elisabeth tried to look away, but Helen held her with her eyes.

Elisabeth had more innate power than anyone else Helen knew, or at least anyone she had seen angry, but the fire in her eyes was no match for the steel in Helen's. Elisabeth might push other people around, but it didn't matter that Elisabeth was six inches taller and much broader built —Helen could always stare her down.

"That's not true." Helen's voice was stern and even. "You shouldn't say things that you know aren't true. You asked six people and conclude that no one wants to fight with you. Did it ever occur to you that the rest of the commanders of Eldirad are thinking of their companies, and they are all likely to have the same ideas of who the best warriors are and choose the same people? Those same six may have been asked by all the guardians and half the captains in the realm, and so they choose their favorite, either through allegiance or friendship or the first to come."

"I suppose you're right." Elisabeth broke away from Helen's gaze and looked down at her big, calloused hands. The fire went out of her voice as well, and it was quiet and grave. "But then who should I ask?"

"Ask people who know you well, people who have served under you and know your skill. I would be glad to be in your company if I wasn't supposed to make one of my own." Helen smiled a little ruefully. "I don't have anyone in my company yet either, if that makes you feel better."

Elisabeth smiled then and reached out and caught her sister's hand. "Thank you, Helen. I suppose I've been foolish."

"That's all right. I just don't care as much as you, about this…" Helen looked down for a moment. Then she looked up and smiled. "We can go out looking for warriors together if you like. When they see the choice between the two of us, you'll be certain to get first pick."

✦✦✦✦✦✦

"Lisi, you should use a compass, you can't make proper circles that way."

"Why don't you draw them, then?" Analisia said crossly, dropping her pen. "You're the one who is so good at everything."

Aranin looked up, startled, from the seemingly endless pile of entry slips registering the various commanders of the two countries, and the even more endless badges that he was making for each team. He couldn't imagine why anyone would think he was good at everything, or anything really. Analisia and Tatyana were among the very few people who would even treat him as remotely equal. "Where did that come from? I only told you to use a compass. No one can draw a target without one."

"Here, you can borrow mine." Tatyana pulled a compass from her pocket. "Catch."

Analisia turned instinctively and caught it in both hands. She stood, biting her lower lip, and her cheeks flushed a little. "Thanks," she said in a low voice. Then she added, "I'm sorry, Aranin, but these stupid targets go on forever. Why do we need so many, anyway?"

Tatyana sucked the thumb that she had just hit with a hammer. "The horseback archery competition wouldn't be much fun if there were only two or three targets, and we don't want them in the same place over and over."

Aranin glued a piece of ribbon to one of the wooden badges he had painted earlier, wondering how to cheer his sister up. "You want to ride the course against me when we get it finished? That would make it more fun, right?"

Analisia blushed and nodded.

Tatyana stopped hammering on the target stands and looked up. "I'll time you."

Analisia smiled. "Thank you. That would be fun. I guess I'm a little sad that I don't get to compete with the rest of you." The competitions were only for warriors, and Analisia had never wished so much that she had been allowed to join the guard with Aranin.

"I'll fence with you any time you ask," Tatyana said with a kindly smile.

"You'd beat me so easily. I'm not even a warrior, and you're a captain, and you're so much older... I probably wouldn't even be good practice."

"Nonsense. I'd be happy to."

Aranin was grateful to Tatyana for saying that. He could see she was humoring Analisia, in the kind, big-sisterly look in her eyes and the way she moved her hands, but it was faint. Analisia didn't notice. Analisia had shown talent with the sword since she'd talked Tatyana into teaching her when she was fifteen, but even so she was no match for Aranin now that he was an apprentice, let alone Tatyana. Still, he knew Tatyana would make it even.

Aranin looked down and smiled at the purple pansy he was painting. There were a lot of them, but it was fun, and he was really happy he had been asked to do them.

He hadn't made a big deal about competing to Analisia. It was hard to talk to her about it when he knew she wanted to and couldn't, but he was very proud that his father had asked him to be in his company for the tournament. There were so many warriors and, as high commander, Louranin could have anyone he wanted. There was no reason he need take any apprentices, and yet the very night after Aranin came home his father had asked him. He could remember every detail. He had been reading in his room when Father came in and asked to talk to him.

Louranin was a big, burly man, powerfully built, with a strong, straight nose and intense blue eyes in a hard, square-jawed face. He had innate power, too, and a gruff, hard manner, and even now that Aranin was fully grown he still felt like a nervous little boy in his presence. "I want to put you on my team, my son," Louranin had said. Just like that. Of course Aranin had thanked him and promised several times that he would do his best. He had been dazed after Father left, and he still couldn't believe it. Aranin had been an apprentice four years, but he still had four more before he'd be a man and a full warrior, and he'd always felt like he was a bit of a disappointment to his father. Yet, Father had asked him. Aranin was proud and also terrified. He wasn't sure he could fight with so many people watching him, and it would be horrible if he messed up for Father.

"Can I make all the targets in different colors?" Analisia asked.

"I don't see why not. It just makes it more challenging if they aren't always the same," Tatyana said with a smile. She swung the hammer again, the beam slipped, and she hit her finger yet again. "Ow." Her lips went thin. She held her finger in her other hand, whispering a soothing charm. "I'm no good at this."

"Why don't you help me paint targets?" Analisia said, holding out a paint brush.

"All right, I think Joseph's coming home with Margaret's company this afternoon, maybe he'll do it." Tatyana put the hammer on the table and joined Analisia. "I'm going to start with one in six shades of green. That should be hard, especially if we put it in a tree."

There were a couple quick steps in the lane and a tall, lean young man in the simple tunic and trousers of a returning guardsman vaulted over the gate into the yard with the easy grace of a cat.

Joseph beamed at them each in turn. "I think I heard my cue, ladies and gentleman. Carpenter at your service." He bowed so low he fell over and did a roll forward, landing in a straddle with his chin in his hands, looking up at them. His silver-gray eyes danced with fun, and he shook his messy chocolate-brown hair out of his flushed oval face.

Analisia laughed and Tatyana and Aranin smiled.

"Do you really have that good of timing?" Tatyana asked, her large steel-gray eyes twinkling too.

"Oh, maybe not quite." He shrugged and got to his feet. "I was going to come see how things were going, and when I heard you complaining about carpentry I waited, hoping to get a cue."

"Well, you got it. I have smashed my fingers enough times."

Joseph picked up the hammer and skillfully pulled out the bent nail. Then he smiled at Tatyana. "I shall endeavor to be the savior of your thumbs, my illustrious princess," he said in a grandiose tone, holding up the hammer like a sword and striking a pose of ostentatious pride that was a very good imitation of a certain class of illustrations of heroes.

Tatyana and Analisia laughed, and Joseph let down the pose, laughing too. Aranin watched with amusement and didn't drop his eyes to his work until Joseph had actually started on the target stand. For all his silliness, Joseph was a careful and skillful set designer, and his hands moved with ease over the wood and nails. Aranin respected him for that, even if he was a little too goofy for his taste sometimes.

"Can my badge be one of those cute cartoon puppies you used to draw on your slate?" Joseph asked ten minutes later. "Something like this?" He put his hands up like paws, cocked his head sideways, and grinned.

Everyone laughed.

In a few quick strokes with a bit of charcoal Aranin made a sketch. He held it up. "Like this?" He kept his voice serious, but a smile tugged at the corners of his mouth. The sketch was of a puppy with large floppy ears and a silly grin, begging on its hind legs.

Joseph beamed. "Perfect."

There was another long, industrious silence. A lark was singing in an apple tree over their heads and a soft breeze blew through the private back garden of the royal house. It was a lovely late-summer afternoon. A few insects chirped in the bushes, and more birds sang from other trees around them. The air in the shade was mild and comfortable. Only Joseph's hammer broke the peace of the nature sounds.

"Tatyana," Aranin said as he added careful details to the image of a golden deer on the badge for Elisabeth. "What would you want to have on the badges for your team?"

Tatyana frowned a little and paused with her paintbrush hovering in midair. "I don't know... I suppose Father should have the Royal Star, and

Sebastian the Golden Lily now that he's prince of Westtower, but for me..." She stared at her work without seeing it. "A white rose, maybe, to symbolize eternal devotion." Her voice dropped and she said, "I may never be queen, but I will always serve my people." There was a slight break in her voice, and Analisia heard it.

"Oh, Tatyana, of course you'll be queen. You're the noblest person I've ever met, and you work so hard."

Tatyana smiled weakly. "Thanks, you flatter me. I do try as hard as I can, and we will see if that's good enough. If it isn't, well then..." Her voice trailed off. Then she added, "Since he got his guardianship, I keep dreaming that Sebastian is king. I don't know why. I suppose I'm just nervous about the tournament." She dipped her brush into the paint a little too forcefully.

"Don't worry, Tatyana," Joseph said with a smile. "We all know you can do it."

"Of course we do." Analisia looked up at her friend with shining eyes full of confidence. Then she dropped her eyes back to her paints. "And you know, when you do become queen, it will mean a lot more than it will for me. I mean, sure, if I was stupid, or terribly shy, my mother could have found a cousin, or second cousin or someone that would do it. At least she didn't do that, but I don't really have to do anything to become queen."

"You have to care about your people the way your mother does," Tatyana said softly. "You have to study a lot and put up with ambassadors and that sort of thing."

"Yeah, and follow a lot of rules," Analisia muttered. "But there's no test. No one has to vote me worthy, and so how do I know if my people respect me or not?"

"You will be able to tell, and I'm sure they will. You will be a good queen."

"Thank you." Analisia washed her brush. "I'm going in to ask Lady Josephine for some water, do you want some?"

They all said they would, and she ran off towards the house. Joseph was sawing a board. Tatyana worked on her target in silence, and Aranin started on the white roses thinking about the nobility in Tatyana's desire to serve her people. "I know," he said slowly, "in Efrim a prince is nothing. No duties, or opportunities. It is only an honor in name, and not much of one at that, but whenever I'm with you and Sebastian I start feeling like I have some kind of duty I should be doing for my people."

A trace of a smile came to Tatyana's lips. "Why not? I know our cultures are different, but there are lots of men and women in both our countries who feel the need to serve their people, and growing up in the royal house, how can you help but feel it more deeply?"

Aranin expertly dabbed a little paint to create the shadow of the curving inner petal of a rose. "The funny thing is I mostly feel it when I'm with you, not at home. I mean, Father is proud of coming from a long line of generals, and he wants me to make a name for myself in the army. But I cannot say I care about that, although I try my best not to be a disappointment. Mother talks to Analisia about duty all the time, but never to me. I don't know... Father pressures me, but you make me feel the nobility of it. Make me feel why I'm doing this."

21 September, YA 1121: Eldirad

Helen was in the fields by the road, helping her mother dig potatoes and keeping a bit more than one eye on the road to Westtower. It was the evening before the tournament, and the sun was setting in a glory of rose and gold.

"You missed three in this hole," her mother said close beside her.

"Oh, sorry." Helen blushed a little and looked down at her work, picking several fine large golden potatoes out of the crumbly dirt.

When she glanced up again there were horses on the road in the distance. She looked at her mother. "Do you mind too much if I go to meet them now?" She stood, already dusting off her hands.

Her mother smiled her gentle smile. "No, dearie. I'll just finish this up."

Helen didn't wait to say more. She left her trowel on the ground and ran towards the approaching horses. They were coming at a trot, and it was only a minute before she reached them. Sebastian saw her coming and swung down from his horse at the side of the road. The others waved as they trotted on towards the city, and Sebastian walked towards her with his arms out and a timid but hopeful expression on his face.

She felt so much love for him, and regret for making him sad, her heart seemed like it would burst. She ran into his arms, and he picked her up around the waist and spun her in a circle. He set her down on her feet and they held each other close for a minute. Then she released him.

They both looked down and their cheeks flushed a little.

A single tear shone on his cheek, and there was a slight smile on his lips. He held her hand tight. "I'm home for a whole week, anyway," he whispered after a moment. He shook off the tear and grew paler and graver, his eyes on his boots.

She looked up into his handsome face. Right now, her fears seemed very far away, and a little foolish. She was so tempted to ignore them and be happy. She longed to see his eyes light up the way she knew they would if she told him she had changed her mind. Yet she knew she couldn't. She made herself smile. "We will make the most of every minute of it," she said with conviction.

He smiled, too, just a little, and dropped a hesitant kiss on her cheek. "Yes, my dear." He put a hand out to catch his horse's reins before he wandered off. Then he added, "I pray to the Stars that I won't have to fight you in the tournament."

"Yes, me too." She took his free hand and they started to walk towards the city together.

As they walked past the fields and came in among the houses of the city they felt a little more comfortable. Helen's shoulders relaxed and Sebastian smiled more. He led his horse along beside them as they talked about the tournament and which of their friends they thought were training hardest for different competitions.

"I believe Elisabeth and Tatyana both have their hearts set on the team event," Helen said as they turned up the street towards the royal house.

"Yeah, last time I saw Tatyana she hardly talked about anything else, except the long forest run... she has a chance at that one. She's swift as a deer."

Helen nodded. "I think Elisabeth would give almost anything to win the singles sword fight competition too."

"Joseph keeps talking about looking forward to the archery contests, but I think Tatyana's the one for that. He might just be joking since he played an archer in the last play they did. Although, I think he's serious about wanting to win something. In his last letter he had half a dozen different possibilities, mostly real long shots, but you know..." He laughed slightly. "He told me Jane was teasing him to win, and I think he meant it. Said she promised not to make fun of the national guard for at least a year if he would win her one of the silver pins being made for the champions to wear at their wedding." The energy in Sebastian's tone broke off and the last word was said very low.

Helen swallowed and couldn't make herself speak for a minute. Joseph and Jane had been betrothed for a year; she had asked him the day he turned thirty, and they were getting married next month. It would be a pleasant party, and Helen was happy for Joseph. Jane was a nice, cheerful person. She was a skilled actress and musician and very loyal to Joseph, if a little too chatty for Helen's taste. All the same, it would be really hard, especially for Sebastian, to see his best friend married right now. "I'll be cheering for him," she said weakly.

Sebastian didn't speak. They said goodbye at the entrance to the royal stable and Helen walked home slowly, not seeing the bustling town around her. She felt tormented, her heart so heavy it weighed her down. If only it didn't have to be this way.

Chapter 3

The Tournament
22-25 September, YA 1121

Eldirad

At eight o'clock in the morning, the Efrim party approached Eldirad and children waiting on the road ran ahead into the city shouting with excitement. The Efrim marched into the square led by three beautiful women on fine white horses. In the center was Queen Evelina, wearing a long, soft aqua-blue silk gown covered in pearls. She was not an especially tall woman, curvy and a little plump, but she held herself with imposing dignity. The Efrim crown of pearl, silver, and diamond worked in large white flowers glistened in her golden-brown hair. At her right hand was the crown princess Analisia, bare headed and dressed in pink silk with a white flower pin matching those in the Efrim crown at her throat. On the left rode the retired queen, Tinianna, in a lavender gown with jewels shimmering in her white hair. The warriors came next. Men and a few women in sparkling mail vests, very much like those the Eldir warriors wore, with the emblems of their houses in embroidery and jewels on their belts and sword scabbards. Louranin, as prince consort and high commander of Efrim, rode at the head of the warriors, and behind him came the generals, the captains, and the common soldiers.

From where Aranin rode at the back with the other apprentices he couldn't even see his father, let alone the royal party, but he could see the Eldir royalty gathered on the steps above to greet them. This was one of those few occasions when the royal family of Eldir stood apart. They all waited on the royal house porch to meet their guests in their finest silk embroidered shirts and dresses. Edward looked very royal, with the seldom-worn crown of stars in his dark hair, and Sebastian stood beside him wearing the silver circlet of the prince of Westtower and the Golden Lily on his breast. On one side of them stood Clara and Tatyana, both very beautiful in fine silk gowns, and on the other, the retired queen Josephine and her consort.

The Efrim civilians coming just behind the apprentices were talking and laughing, and there was gayety in the air. As they entered the big square before the royal house steps there were cheers and greetings from the Eldir warriors and the crowds of Eldir civilians, in silk and satin festival clothes, sparkling with jewels. Aranin saw Helen and Elisabeth standing with Joseph and Jane and waved. They all waved back.

Edward raised his hands, and silence fell over the crowded square. He made a short speech to welcome the Efrim. Evelina mounted the steps to stand beside Edward, and together they pronounced the week of competition open.

Everyone gathered in an empty flax field as soon as the competing members of the Eldir royal family had changed into warrior dress and the Efrim had put their horses out to graze, and the competition began with throwing and jumping contests. Joseph came in third in the high jump, and he was so pleased that he took Jane and waltzed her around the field until they were both giggling like a couple of little children.

* * * ★ * * *

Elisabeth stood with several of her friends by the palace steps, cheering for the young Eldir man who had won the long jump. The cheers died and he bowed and retired. Then Queen Evelina stepped into his place. The warm early afternoon sun turned her hair to gold with touches of silver and sparkled on her crown and dress.

"Warriors and people of both nations," she said in a voice that rang over the hushed square. "The time has come to begin the team battle competition that will be a centerpiece of the games for the rest of the week. I have here two baskets. The names of all the leaders of both nations have been written on folded slips of paper, which have been divided at random. I will draw a name from the blue-and-gold basket and ask that person to step forward. He or she will then have the opportunity to draw the name of their opponent from the green-and-silver basket and read it aloud."

In spite of the warm sun, Elisabeth felt a chill run down her spine, and her stomach tightened. So much depended on this first pairing. If she got one of the very best and lost... well, there was a second chance, but not a third, and besides it would be so embarrassing and demoralize her company. She stood with Helen and Tatyana, but she didn't say anything while she waited. There was a tension in the air. The hopes of so many young commanders rested on this first choice.

Sebastian was called up. He pulled a name and let out a small exclamation of dismay. "Joseph White-lily," he read out.

Joseph made a face of wide-eyed, comical dismay. "No, I can't do that," he said, comedy changing to true concern.

"How can I compete against my best friend?" Sebastian said in a soft, pained voice as he rejoined the others. "It's one thing when it doesn't matter, but one of us has to lose the first round."

"Would you rather play against me?" Tatyana gave him a sly smile as she was called forward to pull a name.

"No, that would be even worse." Sebastian's cheeks went red.

Tatyana read aloud the name, "Adrianna Pine." Then she returned to her friends. "At least she's only a captain," she said with a smile.

Elisabeth heard her name called. Going forward, she reached her hand into the basket and closed her eyes. She took a piece of paper. It felt like it should be so much more than that. Then she read it and her stomach did a flip. She didn't know the man personally, but she knew he was a general of Efrim. She announced her choice and walked back to the group, while a man named Aldinen drew Helen. She watched her sister's face, but Helen made no expression at the news.

"Do you know him?" Elisabeth asked as they walked off together.

"Not well. He's a captain," Helen said with a slight shrug.

"Tinukal's a general." Her voice dropped and there was a touch of frustration.

Helen put her hand on Elisabeth's shoulder. "Don't worry about it. You wanted to do this because you knew you had something to prove. Now you have a chance to prove it. You know if you're going to win you have to beat the generals and guardians."

"Of course, but... I guess I hoped I could get through the first few rounds without having to fight anyone above my rank."

"Real battles don't let you work up, so here you have an even better chance to prove yourself."

Elisabeth smiled, and felt a little better. "Yeah, you're right. I better go get my company ready."

"Me too. Good luck." Helen ran off to where her company was gathering to wait for the announcement of the order.

Elisabeth's match was scheduled near the end of the day, so she had lots of time to be nervous and to watch as the teams went up two at a time. Each team had ten warriors besides the commander, armed with the bladed weapons used in Eldir and Efrim, and fought until the judge declared the commander or more than half the warriors out. Tatyana won easily, and, while the Efrim captain gave Helen a hard fight, she pulled it off too.

* * * ⭐ * * *

Sebastian and Joseph's match went on longer than most. Helen sat with Tatyana, Elisabeth, Aranin, Analisia, a friend named Clarissa, and Joseph's fiancée, Jane, to watch. They were interested, of course, but they couldn't help laughing.

"Oh, did you see that?" Tatyana had her hand to her mouth, and her gray eyes were dancing.

"Sure." Jane pretended to be serious. "I'm afraid your brother has forgotten how to aim."

They all smiled, and Analisia, Tatyana, and Jane giggled. Tatyana was

43

clearly in a very good mood since doing so well in the first competition. Helen was sure she was relieved. Besides, it was funny. Sebastian had gotten very close to Joseph and made a swing that went so deliberately wide Helen felt it was a wonder the whole audience wasn't laughing. The dear boy just couldn't bear to strike against his friend. It was a touch silly, perhaps, and she hoped people didn't think less of him for it, but she thought it sweet.

"Ah, yes. I don't know how he ever became guardian," Tatyana said, still giggling. "But look, Joseph's worse. You should tell that man to practice."

They all watched as Joseph made a sword hit so slow and wide that a ten-year-old could have blocked it. The rest of the warriors on their teams were fighting as well as they could, but their leaders seemed to have forgotten to command them.

"Evelina really should have intervened and made Sebastian draw again," Helen said. "I think if they didn't feel responsibility for their companies they wouldn't be fighting at all." She shook her head. "I just hope I don't get put in that position." She looked at Elisabeth and at Tatyana. She wasn't sure what she would do if she were paired with any of her friends, but especially them. This meant so much to them.

Someone in the crowd called something about a prince paying attention to his company or fighting better than that. There was a change in Sebastian then; a hard, bitter resolve came into his face, and he began to fight better. Joseph followed his lead, and for about ten minutes it was a battle as battles should be fought. Sebastian and Joseph were really quite well matched. They were of one height, although Joseph had a somewhat broader, more muscular build than Sebastian, and they had been practicing together since they were children. Sebastian, however, was the better commander, and in five minutes one of Sebastian's warriors disarmed Joseph and it was over. Helen and her friends cheered as the opponents walked off the field, talking, with their arms around each other's shoulders.

✶ ✶✶✶✶ ✶

44

Elisabeth stood in the courtyard half an hour later with her company. She took one more look at each of them. Several of them smiled, and some looked determined and gave a quick nod to show they were ready. They all wore mail vests and sword belts embroidered with their house emblems, and each warrior carried a long, graceful one-handed sword. The blade was double edged and two to three inches wide, although it was kept covered with a fine, light casing of reinforced leather that slipped easily into the scabbard. They also carried a dagger of similar make. The hilts of both were decorated with jewels and filigree. It made a very imposing sight.

Elisabeth looked across to the Efrim company. They were big, broad-shouldered warriors, mostly men. Not taller than her, but older. As she watched, the last rays of the sun sparkled on their mail, the painted falcon pins that designated their team, and the large white jeweled flower of their general. Then the sun set, and all was in shadow. She smiled a little. She liked dusk, and perhaps the general didn't. She raised her eyes to the royal porch where Princess Analisia was standing to start the match. The crowd fell silent as Analisia raised her hand. Then she let it fall and the two companies moved in.

After that, all Elisabeth could think of was the next move. She listened for the general's commands and watched what he was doing. Then she gave orders for her people to counter. All the while she was fighting, and she had to be watching the blade of the warrior before her. She did not register the passing of time until she heard Analisia's voice call out.

"First out for Elisabeth. Georgina, step aside."

Elisabeth glanced towards Georgina, who sheathed her sword and walked off the field. That was no good. In such battle games with covered blades no one really got hurt beyond a bruise or two, but a hit that would have been serious was an out. She took a deep breath and called, "Come around close together. Fill up her spot." She charged forward and two minutes later touched her sword on one of the Efrim's neck. That man had to sit out, and a minute later another of her warriors touched out one of the opposition's best.

Light was growing quite dim when Elisabeth found herself facing the general in the middle of the field. She ducked under his swing, then, spinning on her heel, jabbed. He blocked, and she dodged the other way. Then, midway through his swing, she whipped back from the side and laid her sword on his shoulder.

"A hit," Analisia cried. "Tinukal is out."

Elisabeth stopped speechless for a moment. She had actually done it!

The general took her hand and pressed it. "Very well fought, lady," he said with a slight bow of his head. "May you have a great career before you."

"Thank you." She looked into his face and knew that he meant it. She smiled.

He turned back to his company, and the next thing Elisabeth knew her company was around her.

"We did it!" several people shouted.

Everyone was cheering and embracing. Two men picked Elisabeth up so that her head was above the others. Everyone in the stands was cheering too. The whole world seemed to be watching.

A moment later, Helen was beside her. "I knew you could do it!" She was smiling with her eyes full of pride, and she hugged Elisabeth tight for a long moment, before Tatyana, Joseph, and Sebastian broke in to give their congratulations. Elisabeth didn't think she had ever felt this happy in her life. Not even the day she got her captain's star.

* * * ★ * * *

Great tables had been set up on trestles in the central square, and Clara had led a veritable army of cooks to fill them with roast meats, summer vegetables, and pastries for the opening night feast. Lanterns glowed in the trees around the square, turning the red and gold leaves of late September to luminescent jewels, and lamps with colored shades burned on the tables also. People everywhere, thousands of them, were talking and laughing. Forks and glasses clinked, and the lamplight shimmered on silk and satin and jewels.

Sebastian sat between Joseph and Tatyana at one of the long tables and said little. He was fairly happy. It had been a good day. He was relieved Tatyana had won her match and hoped he hadn't made too much of a fool of himself. It was just too hard fighting against his friends. A small part of him rather wished he would be out of the tournament before he risked being put up against Tatyana or Helen, but he didn't want to disgrace his new title either.

He sighed a little and scraped up the last crumbs of chocolate cake with the edge of his fork. The next pairings had been announced at the end of the day's competition and Tatyana couldn't seem to stop talking about her relative strengths and weaknesses compared to the Eldir captain she would fight tomorrow. Joseph was balancing his spoon on one finger, which was much more entertaining. Helen was sitting on the other side of Tatyana, listening with a patient expression Sebastian suspected was not entirely genuine.

He swallowed and looked back at his empty plate, tracing the lines of the apple blossoms painted on it. He hadn't really spoken to Helen all day. He knew he should be brave and not let his grief mess things up for them. She had made it clear she still wanted to be close, and he should be content with that. He wasn't mad at her for refusing. Not in the least. He was just sad. He knew it was a Sight thing, and she was worried. He was a little concerned too. All the same, he couldn't help feeling that it was something wrong with him that she didn't want to marry him after all these years he had been sure they were a couple. Could he have said something? Was he just not good enough? How could he ever be good enough for a smart, strong, skillful, kind person like Helen?

He felt a hand on his shoulder and looked up into Analisia's smiling face.

"Sebastian, would you walk with me a minute?" she asked.

"Sure." He rose from the table, rather glad to get away from Tatyana's strategic planning. They walked together away from the tables and around towards the garden. "What did you want to ask me?" he said when they had reached a quiet grassy space along the side of the royal house.

Analisia blushed and smiled. "Was it that obvious?"

He smiled too. He had known Analisia since she was born, and her mother used to bring her and Aranin when she came to have tea with his mother. He had realized years ago that he was the one she brought questions to, like a big brother, or maybe even a sort of father, even if he was only four years older. It wasn't that hard to tell when she had one. All he said was, "Probably only to me, but why else would you want to walk with me when there is a party going on? I'm sure I'm not the most festive companion you could find."

"Oh, I don't mind too much about that."

He could see her face in the starlight. She looked anxious and she was still blushing. "All right then, what is it?" he said in a gentle voice. "You don't need to be embarrassed."

"Well, you see, there is this boy... he's a year younger than me, but, well, I've sort of known him a long time. He was friends with Aranin in school, and he plays bat ball with us sometimes. I've talked to him some. He is very nice, friendly and cheerful, he has a nice laugh. He has started getting more and more handsome lately. Anyway, the last few months I've had a crush on him, and I want to ask him to the last dance, but I don't know how."

Sebastian swallowed and looked down a minute. How was he the qualified person to take love troubles to when it had gone so badly for him? He made himself look up and smile. He put a hand on her shoulder. "You don't need to be afraid," he said. "Do you know what he likes? Perhaps you could give him a little present, or talk about books or something, or is he one of those Efrim boys who doesn't do school or read much?"

"No. He stayed to the end like Aranin. He and Aranin were the only boys in either of their grades the last few years."

"Well, maybe there's something there you could talk about. I'm glad you chose an intelligent boy who is not afraid of customs. Make sure you treat him like an equal, but, you know, being the princess won't hurt your chances."

She looked downcast. "I suppose, but I don't think he's the kind who would marry just to live in the palace and sit next to me at banquets. I wouldn't want that kind of person. I want someone to like me for me. Don't you think that's possible?"

"Of course I do. That's not what I meant." His voice was still patient, but he felt tired and exasperated. She was so sensitive, and this whole subject just made him want to crawl into a hole somewhere and hide. He took a deep breath. "Look here, Analisia." He took both her shoulders gently and turned her towards him so he could look down into her face. "I don't have any magic words to give you." His voice was soft, low, and grave. "I understand how scary it can be. You never know what the other person will say..." he dropped his voice to a whisper, "even when you think you do."

"Helen said no? Is that what you're saying?" she asked in an incredulous whisper.

"Sort of." He closed his eyes for a moment. "I don't want to talk about it right now."

"I'm sorry. I can't believe she would—"

"Thank you, but back to your boy. There is no reason he can't like you for who you are. You just have to get to know him better. Do nice things for him and show interest in what he likes to do. You could ask him to the theatre if he likes that. Asking him to the ball is a great idea. I'm afraid all I can really tell you is to believe in yourself. You're just going to have to ask." He smiled down at her. She seemed so young to be asking boys to dances; but then he realized she was a year older than he was when he first started feeling differently about Helen. It was hard to believe little Analisia was so grown up, but then, he couldn't believe he was an adult now.

"I suppose so," she said.

"Is he competing?"

"No. He's an apprentice leather worker, not a warrior."

"Then maybe you could sit together during the competitions some time?"

"Maybe."

"For what it's worth, I believe in you. You have to trust your instincts. Get to know him better and see if he is really the person you can love. You have to choose wisely, but don't be afraid."

"Thank you."

They stood in silence a few moments. She ran her fingers over a climbing flower on the side of the house beside them. He looked at the flowers, too, thinking about the day in the tower with Helen.

"I suppose I'll go back. Mother's going to be gathering the people to go home pretty soon. You coming back to the party?"

"Not right now."

"All right. Goodnight then. I hope Helen changes her mind."

"Thank you."

Analisia walked back towards the noisy crowd and Sebastian wandered deeper into the garden. He felt sad and wanted to be alone. He sat on a favorite bench beneath a loaded apple tree and watched the slight breeze move the starlit leaves above him.

"Sebastian." Helen's soft voice startled him. "Do you mind if... if I sit with you?"

He looked at her. Her height would have been more common among the Efrim, but she looked entirely Eldir, with an even smaller-boned build than Sebastian himself, which made her an unusually small woman for either country. She was not a conventionally beautiful woman. Her form was straight and wiry, and her face angular and strong; but in Sebastian's eyes, everything about her was perfect. He didn't think there was any more beautiful sight in the world than her standing there with the starlight shining on her black hair and the dark blue silk of her dress. He realized she had asked him a question. "I never mind," he said.

She sat down beside him in a soft swirl of silken skirts. They were both silent for several minutes. Sebastian tried desperately to think of something light to talk about. Surely a few months ago they would have had a million things to say sitting together like this... or would they? He had always loved sitting quietly with her too. The silence used to be comfortable and intimate, but now it felt painful and strained.

"Pretty good first day," he said at last with little energy.

"Yes." Her tone was equally uninterested. She took a deep breath and started unwrapping something she had in a bundle beside her. "I wanted to give this to you," she said very low.

She pulled out a picture about fourteen inches square that he knew well. Aranin had done it last year of Helen and Sebastian posing together on a beautiful castle set Joseph had built for his graduation to journeyman set builder. It was a lovely picture. He and Helen looked so happy with their arms around each other, and the likenesses were perfect.

"Thank you," he said with hesitation. He wondered why she was giving it to him. Did she not want it?

"I'll miss having it on my desk," she said. "But I have a smaller one of you in the garden, and I... I thought you might like to have this at Westtower."

He relaxed a little. She meant it as a gift. Perhaps if he could just get his emotions under control they could go on as before. "I will treasure it," he said.

"I am really sorry about everything, Sebastian, I don't know how to say this, but I want you to know how hard this is for me. I have had so many dreams lately. I'm afraid something awful is going to happen, or at least it has the potential to happen if I don't do the right thing. You know what I mean?"

"Yes."

"When you asked me, I had yes on my tongue. I was so happy... and then I saw this vision, through a terrible shadow, and I was afraid if I said yes it might mean I would lose you." Her voice dropped very low. "I am afraid, and very confused, and I... I want to get married when I can be happy, you understand?"

"I understand," he whispered. He moved his hand ever so softly over hers on the bench and she didn't move away. "I had a dream, too, a couple years ago, about a horrible darkness; it was everywhere, suffocating, and there was a wall... It wasn't even clear as Sight dreams go, but it bothers me."

"I don't know when it will be, but I feel like it's coming. A few years at most, perhaps, or maybe there is something I can do sooner. A new breakthrough in herbs or something, or maybe the new storehouse your father is building—you should probably do that at Westtower, too."

"I will work on it. It can't hurt."

"Maybe one of these things we do will prevent the bad stuff, turn the branching of future fates, you know, and then... then I would be ever so happy to accept. Maybe next summer..."

He didn't think she really believed it, but he could tell she hoped for it, and that was almost as good at the moment. "When the roses are in bloom," he said wistfully.

They were silent for a few minutes. Then Sebastian got up his courage to ask again. "Helen, I understand you are not ready to be married yet, and I will wait as long as I must, but will you accept a betrothal?"

She looked up with soft, shining eyes in the starlight. "Yes, dearest. With all my heart."

With tears in his eyes, he unpinned the small diamond brooch in the shape of a seven-pointed star, the emblem of his house, that he wore on his tunic, and she let him pin it to her dress.

"I will be proud to wear it always," she whispered. Then she reached up and kissed him.

They sat with their arms around each other after that, and there were happy tears on both their cheeks.

★★★★★★★

The archery contests were to take place the second morning. Joseph was looking forward to them. For all he had said in jest to Sebastian, he really had no thoughts of winning them. He had sharp eyes and was a decent shot but nothing exceptional. He looked forward to them because they would be fun. He planned to wear the silly hat and jacket he had worn in the last play as the eccentric archer sidekick of the hero, and he looked forward to cheering for his friends.

In all, the contests lived up to his greatest hopes. They did standing archery first, at which he made a quite respectable performance, and better yet got a laugh for his costume on both appearances.

He caught Elisabeth kicking at a stone after being eliminated in the second round, which struck him as rather babyish, but he had never been able to understand her insatiable desire to be best at everything. It annoyed him a little. All the same, they were pretty good friends. She had always laughed at his jokes, and she was fun to go boating or climbing with because nothing scared her. It was unlike her to get discouraged, so he did his best to encourage her. Friends stood by each other, after all.

"It's not like you don't have good company," he said in a mild chiding tone. "I know it doesn't matter much that I'm out, but Commander Louranin is too."

Elisabeth's cheeks flushed a little. "I could have done better," she muttered.

"Perhaps you could. Contests are like that. Lots of luck. Nobody's perfect. You're not a goddess, last I checked. Unless you think your hair might be turning into starlight?" He pretended to be serious and picked up one of her golden-brown curls as if inspecting it.

She laughed a little.

He took her arm. "Come on. Don't you want to watch the finals?"

She followed him. Helen was out by the time they were in the front row, but Sebastian and Tatyana were still in. Sebastian came in third. Joseph was glowing with pride. Almost no one had the keen eyes or steady hands of his friend.

Tatyana was the last to go. She stood up there with complete calm and hit the target dead on. She never took her eyes from the target, and Joseph held his breath with the rest of the audience while she proceeded to split her arrow with both of the next ones. The crowd erupted in cheers. Joseph was perfectly happy as he joined his friends in swarming around her to give congratulations.

Next was the horseback archery contest. He did decently, Sebastian came in fourth, and Helen had a spectacular victory. Joseph rode with several other competitors who were still on horseback along near the track to have a good view. There was something special about the way she worked with animals, her power over her horse. They flew along the track together. Helen sat up straight with her bow in her hand and never once touched the reins or slowed her beautiful gray steed. She fitted each arrow with precise calm, aimed, and as near as he could tell hit the center every time. It was beautiful to witness, and Joseph was proud to be her friend.

In the afternoon there was another round of the team battle competition. Elisabeth won, but had a bad time of it, and her dark mood clearly had not improved. Joseph didn't have time to bother about it. He was supposed to play Helen next. He didn't like it, but at least they'd both made it to day two. He didn't really mind if he lost again. It was all for the entertainment of the thing, after all.

"I don't like fighting you," Helen said as they stood together waiting for the match to start.

"I wish we didn't have to," he said. "Battle games are fun, but I like having all my friends on my team. Still, don't worry about it. Bruise me as much as you need to. I don't mind. I think they deserve a good show, don't you?" It helped that he was pretty sure Helen didn't care any more than he did about the result.

"Yes, they do. I guess we had better give them one." She smiled. "And since neither of us cares about winning, let it come what may."

He grinned. "Here's to a good game."

They did have a good game too. The fans enjoyed it, he was sure, and when an hour later he felt the bruise on his leg from one of her warriors and heard Lady Josephine's announcement that he had lost, he didn't mind too much. He was a little sorry that two outs meant he wouldn't get to be part of the show tomorrow, but it was all right. There were other contests, and it was fun to watch.

The third day they had short distance races and then more of the team event. Elisabeth won easily against an Efrim captain, and so did Sebastian. Tatyana played Helen, which Joseph knew had been worrying both of them all day, but they made a very good show of it. They must have made a pact not to be easy on each other. Tatyana probably made Helen promise, but at any rate it appeared to be a real fight to Joseph. Helen lost after more than an hour. Helen seemed unusually light-hearted, perhaps relieved when she rejoined them, and Tatyana was grave but in a pretty good mood. Elisabeth seemed to be laboring under the impression for the rest of the day that Helen was hiding disappointment and was unusually nice to her, but Joseph was quite sure Helen was not unhappy. Helen was good at hiding grief, but not at feigning joy.

By the end of day four, Helen was out and Sebastian down to the second tier, but Elisabeth and Tatyana were still undefeated.

★★★★★★

It was the fourth evening of the tournament. There was an informal dance going on in the square beneath the colored lanterns. Tatyana had no shortage of partners and was enjoying herself. She went to get a drink of water between dances, and she saw her father looking very grave. Edward walked over to where two burly Efrim men were standing. They were broad and muscular and dressed in fancy blousy tunics. They made a striking contrast to the slim, dark-haired king in his fitted blue silk tunic, who was several inches taller. Tatyana walked closer to hear what was going on.

"Did you get my letter?" Edward asked.

"Yes, Your Highness," one man said.

"What do you think of my offer? Will you be able to fill it soon?"

"Sure can, Your Highness. We could do it easily within the year if the snow isn't too heavy this winter."

"Thank you," Edward said. "You will be provided with food and medical for all your team of course, and each of you will be paid in trade coin."

The men looked at each other and smiled. Trade coin was unusual for trades between Efrim and Eldir. Barter was far more common, but trade coin could buy anything even from foreign markets.

After a minute, one man's broad face slowly flushed brick red. "It is a handsome offer, but, Highness, I showed it to my wife for the totaling up, and the quantity of stone you have ordered is many times what you'll need for the new storehouse and a four-foot decorative wall. Is it possible you forgot to get a lady to calculate for you?"

Tatyana winced at the classic Efrim assumption that men couldn't do math. She hated the disrespect many of the more traditional Efrim showed to her father even after a thousand years of living side by side with Eldir ways.

Edward's lips pressed very thin. "I assure you I know how much it is. It is going to be a broad wall, so people can walk on it for the view, or put potted plants on it, and the extra beyond that I just want to have cut for now."

"It shall be done, Highness," the mason said quickly. He looked embarrassed. "It is a good offer. We don't mean to complain."

"Thank you, sirs," Edward said.

The men walked away, and Tatyana joined her father. "That seemed to go pretty well," she said softly.

"Yes."

"But why so much stone?"

"You know how, a few weeks ago, we were talking about how to make a wall the people would approve of?"

She nodded.

"I decided I couldn't persuade the people to like anything more than a four-foot wall. It won't obstruct anybody's view, and people can grow flowers on it. I can hope people will think of it as a decorative feature. I talked to your grandmother a lot about it, and your mother. You have been so busy preparing for the tournament lately it isn't easy to talk to you about anything else." He gave a faint lopsided smile.

She flushed. "I suppose I have been kind of obsessive. It sounds like a great idea, though. And then... the extra stone... Oh, I see! That is for finishing the wall if we ever need to, isn't it?"

"Exactly."

Chapter 4

Facing Hopes
26-27 September, YA 1121

Eldirad

BY LATE LUNCHTIME on the fifth day of the tournament, the best eight out of the fifty-four teams that had started the team competition had been selected for the final round. Sebastian had lost again, but Elisabeth went on, along with King Edward, Commander Louranin, Guardian Margaret, two Efrim generals, and one Efrim captain. Tatyana also just squeaked through.

Tatyana's friends were all waiting for her after her fight. Sebastian had laid his sword on the picnic bench to save her a place.

"It was quite a competition this morning." Helen smiled and passed the basket of bread. "It's nice just getting to watch without having to be nervous for my turn."

"Yeah. I guess I get to sit with you tomorrow," Sebastian said. "It will be nice. I was a little worried that I would disgrace my title, but I think I did well enough."

"You did great. That was a really good battle, and making it to second-to-last day isn't bad at all," Helen said.

He smiled and put his hand over hers on the table. "Thank you,

Helen. I didn't expect to beat Louranin. I'm just glad he didn't trounce me."

"Ham, please," said Tatyana, who had just slipped into the place beside her brother. Her eyes were on her plate.

Analisia passed the platter. "You did really well today, Tatyana."

"Well?" Tatyana checked the unexpected harshness in her voice and said quietly. "I lost five of my warriors."

"That's true, but you should've seen the fire in your eyes." Sebastian put his hand on her shoulder for a moment, his eyes soft and full of pride. "You were amazing. You never gave up, and in the end you won, and that Efrim general who's probably been commanding in competitions like this for as long as we've been alive is out instead of you."

She smiled just a little and took a bite of her lunch. "I'm sorry. I don't mean to complain." She looked from Sebastian to Helen, "I know you're out too, but..."

"I understand," Helen said. She and Tatyana had been best friends and confidantes since they were little. She knew there was nothing in the world Tatyana wanted more than the chance to serve her people as crown princess, and that she looked on the tournament as the best opportunity to make that dream a reality. Helen would have done anything in her power to help her.

"Me too. I'll be cheering for you tomorrow," Sebastian said.

After a minute, Tatyana asked softly, "I know you said you wouldn't, but I can't help knowing you wanted to... You didn't let me win day before yesterday, did you?"

"Why should you worry about that?" Helen kept her voice soft and even. "Yesterday we played other people and I lost again, and you won well."

"I just... I almost lost today, and I don't feel like I have done well enough. Tell me you didn't let me win." Tatyana raised her eyes to Helen's face, half defiant, half anxious and pleading.

Helen swallowed. She wanted to deny it outright, but Tatyana would detect even the smallest white lie and be more hurt if she felt Helen was shielding her. Helen had learned as all kids do growing up that the way of politeness is often through small lies, but she had also learned that in a world where some people had the Sight you had to be careful. Even a person with a Sight gift so faint they hardly noticed it, like Elisabeth, could still feel the slightest lie. "No, I didn't let you win on purpose," Helen said slowly and carefully. "I would have liked to, it is true, but I know you would not want to win that way. So, I did my best. If it comes to a difference in passion, I can't help that I didn't want to win as much as you did."

Tatyana held her eyes the whole time she was speaking. Then she looked down and nodded. "I understand. Thank you, Helen."

"How about the long forest race this afternoon?" Elisabeth said. "Are you all looking forward to it?"

"Yeah. It should be great." Sebastian's face brightened.

"Yes." Tatyana looked grim and determined. "I know the individual events don't count like the group one, but I think I have a chance this afternoon."

"You'll probably win," Elisabeth said cheerfully.

"I'm going to do my best." The look in Tatyana's eyes was so hard it could have cut steel.

* * * * * *

Analisia stood at the finish line of the thirty-mile forest run. Each time a new runner approached she went on tiptoe and strained her eyes to see who it was. This wasn't right. Elisabeth had come in, and then Sebastian and Joseph. A few minutes later Aranin showed up, panting, to drop to his knees at her feet.

Helen jogged up and looked around. "Where's Tatyana?"

"She hasn't come in yet. We're getting worried." Joseph handed Helen a cup of water.

"But I'm twenty-seventh," she said. Worry wrinkled her brow.

"I know. I'm afraid something happened." Sebastian was peering across the bridge into the forest.

They stood there and said little to each other until everyone had come back except Tatyana and one young Efrim man. Edward had gotten his horse to set back out in search of them, when she came into view. She was walking slowly with the young man on her back. Everyone who was still there cheered for her, but Tatyana wouldn't meet anyone's eyes as she walked in. Sebastian ran forward and tried to help her, but she hardly seemed to see him at first. He said her name and put his hand on her arm, and at last she allowed him to help her lay the young man on the grass. Then she knelt and rolled up his pant leg while Sebastian took off his boot.

At that point, Edward returned from the palace with first aid supplies and knelt beside her. Tatyana's hands were on the man's bare leg, moving softly over the broken bones. In a few deft movements the bones were straight. The young man gasped in pain and clung to Edward's hand, but Tatyana's hands running and stroking over the break soothed it. She was skilled at healing, and she also had the Healing gift. Through the magic and the touch of her fingers, her whispered words could actually lessen the pain and smooth and straighten a simple break. She could even begin the healing a little to stabilize the bones. It was a gift only possessed by a few among the Eldir, and Analisia always found it breath-taking. The linked abilities of the Sight and the Healing gift, both exclusively Eldir magic, ran by a blessing with especial constancy in the royal line of Eldir, and you couldn't be ruler without it. Analisia often wished there was something special she had to do to be queen, but she supposed the only thing she needed to be to become ruler of Efrim was a female royal child. It wasn't nearly as noble or romantic.

Tatyana rubbed an herbal salve on the leg and whispered words of healing. Then she bound it up in a splint, swift and sure.

When that was done, Edward and Sebastian helped the man up and carried him to a cart some of his friends had brought over.

Tatyana rose silently with a closed-off expression and tried to slip away. Analisia couldn't see why Tatyana was unhappy. In her eyes, what Tatyana had just done was the beautiful, noble, epitome of what the Eldir royalty meant. That was what Tatyana wanted, wasn't it?

Before Tatyana could slip away completely, the middle-aged Efrim soldier who had won the race called, "Please come stand with me for the honor, Lady Tatyana."

She stopped and turned. "You won, sir." Her voice was respectful and subdued but loud enough to hear.

"Yes, lady, but you were ahead of me the last time I saw you, and you gave up your chance when you saw Kalilin injured." He reached out his hand to her and she went with him up onto the porch to be cheered. As she stood there, a smile slowly returned to her face.

Analisia was so glad he had done that, and so proud of Tatyana. She couldn't help jumping up and down a little as she cheered, although somewhere she was sure her grandmother was glaring at her for being undignified.

"She deserved that so much," Analisia said to Sebastian who stood close by.

"She sure did." Sebastian was beaming up at his sister. "She's so special, and she doesn't even see it."

As the party dispersed in the golden afternoon light, Analisia kept her eyes out for Yeven. She didn't want to try to talk to him when there were other people around, and he always seemed to be with his mother and grandmother when she saw him outside the crowd. She was running out of time to ask him to the dance tomorrow night. She had spent more time than she was willing to admit thinking about what to say and trying to think of a present to give him. Then she caught a glimpse of him at a distance, and her stomach did a little flip.

He wasn't thin, but still athletically built, broad and big boned. Standing as he was now, with three young Eldir men, he looked short, but she guessed he was about six feet, almost as tall as Aranin. His wavy hair shimmered bright gold to just below his shoulders and contrasted beautifully with his dark green tunic. She felt herself blushing already, but she walked towards him. She had to act now or someone else would ask him. Her stomach tightened at the thought that someone else might have already. She took a deep breath, smoothed her unruly caramel curls and the long, flowing skirt of her sky-blue silk dress, and pulled the sash a little tighter.

As she approached, she heard the young men talking about the last play the Eldirad theatre had put on. She had loved the play, but she couldn't think about it now. Her mind seemed a little fuzzy. The Eldir men paid her a friendly smile, but little more, and Yeven bowed his head. That only made her blush more. Sebastian said to treat him like an equal, but that wasn't so easy when you were an Efrim princess and young men of your nation all felt they needed to bow to you. She felt her cheeks growing uncomfortably hot. Someone asked Yeven a question and he didn't hear them and had to apologize. Her heart made a skip at that. She made him nervous? Or distracted? Was that a good sign or was it because she was the princess? She had talked to Yeven a little around bat ball games over the last few years, and he had always been nice to her, but perhaps a little deferential.

"Yeven?" she asked, flushing more. She was usually comfortable with people, but the eyes of the four men on her made her forget everything. "Yeven, I want to show you something." She swallowed. She didn't dare look up into his face.

"Of course, my lady." His voice was low and warm.

She offered him her arm and he put a hesitant hand on it. They walked in silence around the side of the royal house to the back garden and stopped in her favorite place where asters and a few late roses were still in bloom.

"It's very... pretty." He sounded a little awkward, stiff.

She wondered if he meant it, but she knew he liked flowers. "I thought... the last purse you made with a rose on it was so nice... so I thought you must like roses."

"Yes. Thank you. I mean, it is very nice."

She looked up and saw that his cheeks were flushing too. "I'm sorry. I don't mean to be awkward," she said.

"You're never awkward." He blushed almost as deep as the red rose he was absently tracing with a gentle finger. "I mean, you're great at... at sports and dancing, and speaking to people and... and all that."

She swallowed hard. "I... I was hoping you would want to come to the ball tomorrow night, with me."

He was so silent she looked up. He had paled a little and his eyes were wide, then the flush came flooding back.

"Me?" he barely managed to whisper.

She smiled. "Yes, if you will. I'm not talking to the roses."

A smile slowly spread across his face, delighted and disbelieving. "I would be honored, my lady."

She could hardly think when she looked up into his sky-blue eyes and the expression on his face, but she made herself speak. "Please...

please call me Analisia. I... I don't want you to say yes just because I'm the princess. Please don't do that."

"No, I wouldn't. I swear. But you *are* the princess, and... and I never dared think you might like me."

She was so embarrassed and so delighted that she just stood there dumbly for a moment, and so did he. They smiled at each other, looked at their shoes, and then looked back at each other.

After a minute, she said, "Tomorrow night, then?"

"I will look forward to it." He hesitated. "What color are you going to wear?"

"Green, I think."

"I'll try to wear something to go with it."

✦ ✦ ✦ ✦ ✦ ✦

The next day was the sixth and last day of the festival. It was devoted to the last matches of the eight remaining teams to decide their final places, and the excitement was very high. After winning and losing a match in the morning, Tatyana was set to play the second match of the afternoon for fifth and sixth, against the only remaining Efrim captain.

Helen, Elisabeth, Sebastian, and Joseph sat together to watch Tatyana's match. The early afternoon sun was shining hot overhead, and she had lost four people in her company, but her opponent had lost three also. Elisabeth fidgeted with her fingers and shuffled her feet. Helen and Sebastian sat still and tense. Helen's face was intent, with her bright gray eyes fixed on Tatyana's blade, and Sebastian was biting his lip and gripping the bench until his knuckles turned white.

"She's doing really well," Sebastian murmured. "But he's awfully good."

"I know. He should be a general... but she can do it." Helen tried to believe it, but she knew Sebastian could tell she didn't.

"That was a good move," Joseph said, watching with fixed attention as Tatyana got her company to come into a V with her at the head to split the other group.

63

There were another few minutes of breathless silence among the watchers while Tatyana made progress, then Alerian's company closed around her and one of his warriors touched Tatyana's neck.

Helen sighed, Sebastian gasped, and Elisabeth cursed under her breath. They sat still for a moment. Sebastian dropped his head and looked at his soft leather shoes, and Joseph put a hand on his shoulder.

"I hope she won't be too unhappy," Helen whispered. "I know how much she wanted to win, but sixth really isn't bad."

"No, it's not. But I wouldn't tell her that right now if I were you," Sebastian said. He ran a hand over his face. "There's nothing we could say now. She is amazingly brave, but this meant the world to her."

"I know." Helen swallowed hard and searched for her friend in the crowd, but Tatyana was gone. The poor dear tried so hard, and she was never satisfied. "I wish there was something we could do."

"All we can do is let her be for now, I think," Sebastian said. "But I'll go find her in a little while and see if she's ready to talk."

✦✦✦✦✦✦

Tatyana felt the sword on her back. She sheathed her blade and stood still. Tears were pricking her eyes, but she was too proud to let them fall. She swallowed hard and walked forward to shake hands with the Efrim captain. He was smiling and his blue eyes sparkled in the afternoon light.

"Good game," she managed to say in a flat voice.

"You too," he said and shook her hand with far more energy than seemed necessary.

Then she was free. She couldn't face any of the people in her company. She slipped off the field as quickly and quietly as she could. As she passed the next companies entering the field, she felt a hand on her arm.

"You did really well."

She blinked. It was Aranin's voice, and he stood beside her. He was smiling, but although his words felt sincere there was sympathy in his eyes, and she could not bear that.

"Thanks." Her voice was so tight now it didn't quite sound like hers. "Good luck." She hurried off without waiting for him to answer, and going around the royal house through the hedge, went in the back door.

Once inside she ran through the kitchen to the living room and up the stairs. Tears were already running down her cheeks as she went down the hall and locked the door of her room. She threw herself onto her bed and buried her face in her brightly colored quilt. She had known this might happen. She had sworn she would be content only to test herself and see if she was good enough, but it was too much. She couldn't bear it. Her throat was painfully tight, and tears streamed down her cheeks. She shouldn't cry. She had done her best. She thought she had swallowed her pride the night before when she had given up her dreams of winning the race to take care of the poor injured man, but now she knew she hadn't really given up hope. Even after losing against Margaret and getting put in the fifth and sixth competition. Somehow, she had still hoped she could pull something off—she wasn't sure what.

She took an unsteady breath and tried to swallow the lump in her throat. As long as she could remember, there had been nothing she wanted more than to serve her people and to make her family proud of her. All these years of training to be fit to fill that role. She wanted to be a true princess, and to dedicate her life to her people, her country; but a true princess would want her people to have the best, even if it wasn't herself. She would be content to serve in any capacity she was good for. The pain was very sharp, her eyes stung, and tears rolled down her cheeks again. She wasn't good enough to be queen, and she didn't even have the dignity to accept that.

After several minutes, she sat up and looked around from the desk to the bookshelves and the picture of herself swinging from a tree that Aranin had done several years ago. She thought about her fears and Sight dreams. No, she couldn't make herself adequate, but she could have the dignity to accept it. There were many things she could do with her life. She wiped her eyes, splashed water from her washbasin onto her face, and was starting to wonder if she should go down when there was a soft knock on the door.

"Come in," she said. Then she remembered she had locked it and went over to open the door.

"Are you all right?" Sebastian asked. He stood in the doorway with a steaming cup.

"Yes." Tatyana ushered him into the room.

Sebastian felt that her answer was only half true, and noticed her puffy eyes, but he didn't comment. "I brought you some tea."

"Thank you, I was just thinking I should come down." She took the cup, smelling the bright peppermint and ginger of her favorite tea, and sat down at her desk.

Sebastian stood awkwardly fussing with his hands. He sat on the edge of the bed. "I know this tournament meant a lot to you, Tatyana, but you really did very well—"

"You don't have to baby me." Tatyana's voice was a little sharp. "I tested myself, and I can abide by the results. Don't worry, I will serve you faithfully."

He looked up with an expression of honest bewilderment. "What? What do you mean?"

"I mean," her voice was low, grave, and steady, "that I will be proud to serve King Sebastian, if he will have me."

"But, Tatyana..." He looked confused for a moment. Then his face softened. His voice was low. "I'm not king. I'm not crown prince. I'm prince of Westtower because a few dozen fools thought they might steal some cattle or some such from Obrin."

"You're a guardian."

Sebastian thumped his clenched fist down on the bed, and a touch of impatience came into his voice. "Sure, I'm a guardian, but in case you didn't notice, I got thirteenth place and you got sixth!"

Tatyana felt a perverse desire to contradict him, to insist on some stubborn sort of fake nobility, but she couldn't think of anything that didn't sound babyish. After a minute, she stood up and went to sit beside him. "I'm sorry I've been such a fool," she whispered. "And... thank you, Sebastian. I just want to serve my people so badly. I know with all the premonitions, and whatever dangers are coming, something like who is ruler shouldn't matter. It's just, I feel like our people need me. Maybe that's self-important, but I want to help them, to do my duty to them."

Sebastian patted her shoulder. "I know what you mean," he said gently. "And I think—" he paused, choosing his words carefully. "I think that is why you will make such a good queen, and be the one to bring our people through whatever this is. I know you were disappointed about the race yesterday, but what you did was just what a queen should do. It isn't winning that's important—you know that."

She smiled and squeezed his hand. She had gotten so caught up in the idea of proving herself in the competition that she hadn't thought of it that way. She felt a little better.

* * * * * *

Aranin was a little worried about Tatyana as he took the field, but he couldn't think about it now. He knew she was strong and hoped she would feel better soon.

Aranin looked across the field and straightened his shoulders. He was going to do well this time. He just had to. He wanted to make his father proud, and he finally had a company he didn't feel embarrassed fighting. He sort of knew some of them, but none of them were close friends, and he had no ties with Margaret. He had never had much trouble fighting in training, but it was hard with so many people watching, and he was always thinking about how much various people cared or didn't care about their results. He had gotten distracted and made a couple stupid mistakes in the match with Sebastian, and even though they had still won, his father had been angry and given him a long lecture about it.

The fight began, and he tried to imagine that Margaret and her company were some sort of horrible, vicious raiders out of a story, but it wasn't easy to turn Margaret, with her wavy dark hair and round face, into anything frightening. So instead, he focused on the thought of living up to Father's expectations. He fought hard, listening carefully for his father's every word and trying not to hear the crowd. When he was told to charge center left, he did so without realizing who he was going against until, twenty seconds later, he found himself standing in the middle of the field with his blade to Margaret's neck. He stood still, too surprised to move, while she stepped away from under the blade with a faint expression of frustration.

"Margaret is out," Analisia's voice was a little louder and more joyous than usual, and Aranin could hear faintly the voice of Elder Queen Josephine lecturing her on the neutrality of judges.

Aranin felt his father's hand on his shoulder and turned.

Louranin was smiling. His honey-gold hair had mostly come free of the leather tie, and his blue eyes shone with pride. "You did well, my son."

Aranin blushed and felt as though his heart would burst with joy. "Thank you, Father."

★★★★★★

Elisabeth clapped for a minute, then turned to her company and called them all around her. Her match was next. The last match, for first and second place.

"All right, everyone, this is it. We have made it this far, and I have faith in all of you." She glanced across the field to where Edward and his company stood talking. "I know your allegiance, like mine, is to him before me, but we have to put that aside. We are all equal in the games, and we must stand together and show everyone in this city that, win or lose, we will always do our best and make an honorable fight. Take a deep breath and focus, everyone, keep close together, and listen for my orders."

"We're behind you, Lady Elisabeth, never fear," Florence said. She put her hand on the hilt of her sword and looked out to the field.

There was a chorus of agreement, and Elisabeth smiled. Her company believed in her, even in this position, facing the king, and that was deeply gratifying. She couldn't quite imagine they would win this match, and yet she knew she would try and that she would be content so long as she made it a close thing. "Come, everyone. Five on each side. We'll go out to present ourselves."

They filed into the places they had taken before every other match and walked out to stand at their end of the field.

Across the field, Edward and his team were arranged likewise, facing them. The golden light of the setting sun sparkled on the bright silver mail vests of both sides. Elisabeth saw a single star sparkling on Edward's breast to match her own. His seven guardian stars, including the large Royal Star, were put away, a symbol that all was equal in this field. The sun turned the curly wisps of Elisabeth's hair to gold around her head and sparkled on the silver threads in Edward's ebony hair.

Both sides looked up to where Queen Evelina stood on the porch. The flower crown sparkled in her hair, which, like Elisabeth's, was turned to gold. She raised her hand.

"Begin."

The two companies ran towards each other in formation, and Elisabeth and Edward gave their first orders.

It was a close fight, and both companies had a couple people who had to sit out "injured." Elisabeth was full of the exhilaration of the moment. Her mind flitted from one move to the next, thinking of nothing else. Counter and attack, arrange her company to meet the way Edward moved his. Then, after tapping out four of his warriors, she found herself standing with her sword on Edward's breast. He stopped then.

"Enough," he said quietly, and all his people stopped as well even before Evelina could announce that Elisabeth had won.

All around them there was cheering and talking, but just for a moment Elisabeth hardly heard it. She couldn't quite believe what she had just done. She looked up slowly into Edward's face. He was smiling, even in his eyes. She sheathed her sword and stood a moment, and he took her hands—not one, as the others had to shake in courtesy for a good game, but both.

"Elisabeth," he said. "There is great power in you, and you are very skilled." He looked into her face and for a moment an odd look came into his eyes, one she had seen on Helen, of seeing past or through her. Then his eyes focused on her again and he squeezed both her hands. "Your name will be remembered, lady." His voice was earnest and grave.

"Thank you, Sir. I shall always do my best."

* ★ ★ ★ ★ ★ *

"Has your husband been talking to you about his strange decisions lately?" Evelina asked, standing at the kitchen door with one hand demurely on the sill.

Clara took a moment to make sure her face was diplomatic before she looked up. She had always had a decent working relationship with Queen Evelina. They called often, and it had been natural and appropriate to invite her into the royal house to freshen up before the ball. All the same, at this moment Clara was regretting it. "There is nothing strange about any of Edward's decisions," she said in a measured voice.

"But, my dear," Evelina protested in a very dignified tone, "between women of good judgement, what does your city need with another storehouse? You have gone a thousand years without another storehouse."

"There are more people than there were a thousand years ago."

"Yes, but not more than six or seven hundred years ago."

Clara couldn't contest that. After the first few hundred years in the new settlement, Eldirad hadn't grown much. In complete honesty, she wasn't sure herself what she thought about Edward's worries and his new precautions. She supposed he was right but rather hoped he was taking things for worse than they were. Sight dreams were so fussy. She would never betray a doubt to Evelina, though. "Not many, but we like to be prepared; besides, it will be a nice civic project. There hasn't been one in so long."

Evelina's face relaxed a little at that, and the look in her ice-blue eyes softened. "Yes, civic projects can be a good thing. A great opportunity for artists."

"Exactly." Clara picked up a towel and started drying the heap of plates she had just washed. She glanced with scorn at the perfectly clean, manicured fingernails on Evelina's soft, plump hands. Evelina had been a beauty when they were young, and she was still a handsome woman, curvy and elegant, if a little plump. But she had never done much of anything by Clara's lights besides be elegant. Clara had been quite a beauty herself, and she, too, was no longer quite slim, but she was strong with muscles in her arms and calloused hands from doing housework and working in her beloved garden. Evelina was a good queen to be sure, diplomatic, kind; Clara respected the way Evelina would listen to her people and try to make them happy, but she didn't think she could ever understand a woman who did no work with her hands and had once tried to get Clara to bring a royal escort when she came to visit, even though it was just four miles away.

"The wall, though," Evelina persisted. "Are you sure he was well advised? I sometimes worry about his health... is *his* majesty well?"

Clara's blood boiled, and she had to spend a long time in the cupboard putting away the dishes before she could turn back to Evelina. It was slight, but the way Evelina said 'his majesty' seemed calculated to remind her that in the Efrian language they spoke the two words could not go together. Most people ignored that, but traditional Efrim remembered. This whole conversation dripped with the unsaid prejudice that made Evelina perpetually bring matters of state to Clara rather than to Edward, and Clara deeply resented that. "He is quite well, I assure you," she said in a brisk tone as she picked up another plate. "Lady Josephine and he have decided they would like to build a wall. It will be pretty. A good place to grow flowers."

"You are quite sure he hasn't gotten paranoid these last few years?"

If only Clara was sure. She worried about him sometimes, but everyone she knew with the Sight seemed to agree. Besides, she trusted him. "There is no reason to accuse him of that," she said stiffly.

"But, my dear, I thought I saw some farmers out starting new fields. Why ever do you need that? The storehouse is a nice civic project for the people, but you can't actually need to fill it up, can you? Certainly not any time soon. And if your wall is just for flowers, you would do better to build a trellis. It is preposterous to think an enemy could ever threaten in the heart of the country."

"No one ever said that's what we thought."

"But the wall?"

"I told you. It will be nice to grow roses on, and people can walk on it and look at the view... As for the farmers in the fields, we decided they deserved a little contest, too, so they're working on it."

"Well, that's a very good idea. Did you think of it, my dear? Or Josephine?"

"No," Clara's voice was hard and cold. "It was Edward's idea."

★★★★★

When Tatyana walked into the Eldir royal ballroom that evening, she felt strangely calm. A little subdued, but no longer unhappy. Sebastian was right; she hadn't done badly. And she was right; she could serve her people and devote her life to helping them and protecting them from whatever was coming whether she became queen or not. She looked very much like a princess that night in a long burgundy silk gown with a full skirt, fitted bodice, and soft fabric around the shoulders. Her dark hair was done up simply but pinned with diamond stars. She had no shortage of dance partners and danced most of the night.

Helen and Sebastian danced together all night, as did Joseph and Jane, and Tatyana saw Analisia with a handsome young Efrim man she didn't know. Analisia was beautiful in dark green silk, and he wore a dark gray silk tunic embroidered in the same shade of green. They seemed to be having a good time and were always talking and laughing when Tatyana passed them. Tatyana herself danced with half the room. She danced with Aranin several times, and with her father and mother, and with Elisabeth, and Clarissa.

Tatyana was dancing with Elisabeth near midnight when Evelina and Edward stepped up onto the musician's platform and called everyone's attention.

Queen Evelina nodded to him, and Edward began to speak. "We want to congratulate all our warriors on their performances in this contest. We are both very proud. However, we are proudest of all to announce that there has been a vote this evening, and I have the honor to bestow two guardianships, while Queen Evelina and High Commander Louranin are tonight to make a new general." He looked at her and smiled.

She nodded and turned to the crowd. "Will Sir Alerian of the house of the Yellow Rose come up, please?"

The young Efrim captain who had come in fifth in the tournament made his way forward to loud applause to stand beside the queen.

Then Edward went on, and his eyes were shining. "Now may I ask Lady Elisabeth of the house of the Golden Deer, and Lady Tatyana, Crown Princess of Eldirad, to come to me please?"

Tatyana gasped and half choked as her throat tightened and her eyes got damp. She had done it! For the first time in her life, she had been addressed as 'Crown Princess.' Tatyana walked forward in a daze of joy. She could hear her people cheering as she stepped up onto the platform beside her father.

Louranin, who had waited respectfully at the foot of the platform with Evelina went up, joined her so that Alerian could kneel to each of them for the ceremony, and then Elisabeth knelt before Edward. At last, it was Tatyana's turn. She knelt before her father. She felt his soft touch on each of her shoulders and her head and knew he had drawn a star in the air above her. Then he took her hand and brought her to her feet. He pinned the seven stars to the neck of her gown, and the center one was a special star surrounded by little sapphires and emeralds. The star of the heir.

"I am so proud of you," he whispered. They smiled into each other's eyes and, for a moment, there was nothing but pride and joy. Then he turned her to face the crowded ballroom and presented her to the assembled peoples of both nations.

Chapter 5

Call to Duty

12 October, YA 1121 (about two weeks later) to 9 October, YA 1123

Eldirad

IN SPITE of the continued uneasiness of those with the Sight, prosperity reigned. Joseph's wedding in October was a delightful affair with several entertainments put on by his and Jane's many acting friends, and Helen and Sebastian both managed to enjoy themselves even though there were wistful feelings. Analisia came and brought Yeven as her guest, and they saw each other more often after that. They found they liked all the same books and plays, and they would talk for hours.

Winter came and went with the usual skiing, sledding, skating, and sleigh riding, and the next summer the new storehouse was finished. It was a simple, stately building of white stone, and a dozen Eldir smiths and jewelers were hired to decorate it to the standards of the city. In a place where new buildings were rare it was the opportunity of a lifetime for the local artists, and they threw themselves into the project with skill and enthusiasm.

It was a beautiful summer. The farmers of Eldirad had cultivated more fields and the weather was good. Crops grew well, and there were ball games and boating and swimming in the Silver River. The wall was finished in late summer, and people started to like it. Potted plants were put on it, and roses and wisteria planted by it. The pile of extra cut stones had flowers put on it, too, and was mostly forgotten about by the people. They liked their wall, and the decoration of the new storehouse was interesting and exciting.

Some people shook their heads when cart loads of grain, lard, and salted meats were taken to the new storehouse Edward had decided to build in Aldor. "Really," people said. "It's only twenty miles, a day's journey. What do they need with their own storehouse?" And when more cart loads went to Obrin for the new cellar being built onto Westtower, those who even noticed gossiped that preparedness seemed almost as unnecessary there, only two days' journey away.

Still, for the most part, people forgot to think Edward was being paranoid. They liked their wall and their new storehouse, even if they didn't see any practical use for them, and the land was prosperous and happy.

Efrim prospered as well. Louranin listened when Edward talked to him about matters of defense, even if he didn't always take his advice. He did not allow himself to have an opinion on Edward's role as civic leader since he didn't think it right or within a man's power, and in fact had a subconscious tendency to think of Clara as queen rather than consort, but he had great respect for Edward as a warrior and military leader.

Louranin was too proud to concede the idea that an enemy might make it in any numbers anywhere close to the cities, but in time he agreed that protections could do with renovation. He strengthened his garrisons at his guard posts, and in the early fall of the year after the tournament convinced Evelina, with the help of Lady Josephine, who Evelina still respected as a queen, to build a low wall atop the hills that surrounded the valley of Efrimiel proper. It was accordingly built and was finished in early spring. It was about five feet high and solid. At the top of the hills, it was far enough from the houses that it didn't attract as much attention as the Eldirad wall, or get as many flowers growing on it, but a few sharp-eyed young soldiers were assigned to walk along it to keep a lookout on the forest.

That same spring of 1123, Helen made a small discovery. She added a touch of another herb, and slightly altered the magic of the potion making process for their current disinfectant, and succeeded in improving its effectiveness. She briefly allowed herself to hope that between that and the filling storehouses the danger was averted. She even started writing to Sebastian about it, and then she had another dream of shadow and fear and knew whatever it was still threatened.

In early summer, rumors spread of a strange sickness among the trees to the north, and of strange moving shadows seen in the forest there.

✶✶✶✹✶✶✶

It was the ninth of October 1123, a bit more than two years after the tournament, and Helen was sitting in the comfortable living room of her family's house. She sighed and buried her face in her hands. She was so worried, and so confused. Her fear had only increased. She was afraid for her country, her people, her family... and sometimes she felt as though she were going mad.

She looked at the book before her again. It was the oldest volume of Eldir history. Very nearly the oldest book in the ancient section of the Eldir library, dating from the first ten years or so of the city. This was the only work with a detailed account of an important Sight dream the Eldir king of the time had on his first night staying with the Efrim. It was part of what made him decide he wanted to make the alliance and it was mentioned in several other places. This was King Steven's personal account and described it, but it wasn't written well.

According to Efrim records of the time, he was an intelligent, dignified, and articulate man, even though for him Efrian was a second language. Indeed, he must have been impressively so for the old Efrim, even before their traditions were somewhat weakened by years of association with Eldir, to accept and respect a male ruler in the way they had. Still, his written language showed none of that. He was middle-aged before he learned to read or write at all, since the Eldir had no writing, and he was never comfortable with it. The account before her was written in a stiff, awkward hand that was hard to read, and the language was a little confusing, being old-fashioned, but she was sure it was somehow important.

She ran one calloused finger along under the lines trying to find what was important, what it was that kept drawing her back to this passage.

> MY SECOND NIGHT IN THE FANCY ROOM OF QUEEN LAURIANNA I HAD A DREAM. I SAW TWO WOMEN. MIXED WOMEN. THEY WERE WARRIORS LIKE MY PEOPLE, BUT SHOWED THEIR MAIL LIKE EFRIM, AND CARRIED SWORDS. ONE LOOKED EFRIM, BUT HER EYES WERE LIKE MY SISTER CLARA. TOGETHER THEY MARCHED THROUGH DARK OF SOME FUTURE TROUBLE. THE TWO NATIONS SEEM TO STAND TOGETHER. I THINK WE NEED TO SHARE, OUR CULTURE, OUR SKILL, WITH THESE STRANGE PEOPLE IN THEIR FANCY PALACE, EVEN WHEN THEY WILL NOT RECOGNIZE MY PEOPLE MEN AND WOMEN AS EQUAL.

What was it supposed to mean? She felt like it was tickling the back of her mind. This had to be important, or why would he have dreamed it so long ago and nothing like that had happened yet? Unless it was something that had been avoided somehow, that no version of it had come to pass. If it had been soon after it could have actually meant something very small. Was it possible the incident he had seen had happened, but just turned out so small people didn't take notice? Sure, it was possible, but it didn't feel right... she rubbed her eyes and looked at it again. She had an uneasy nagging feeling about the line describing an Efrim woman with the eyes of his sister. She remembered dreams she had of Elisabeth in the last few years. They were often together facing something, and sometimes Elisabeth was alone and being sucked up in mist and Helen was trying to find her.

Helen sat staring across the room, but she didn't really see the comfortable chairs and beautiful wall hangings. Her fingers worried her cloth bookmark. How mad was it to start imagining your sister might be the person meant in a thousand-year-old prophecy?

Three fast, heavy raps on the front door made Helen jump. "Come in," she called. She smoothed out the embroidered bookmark, marked her place, and carefully shut the book. She rose and went towards the door just as it opened. It was Edward. He was slightly out of breath. His dark hair frosted with gray was windblown, and he smoothed wet strands off his forehead as he came into the house. His face was pale, and grimmer than Helen had ever seen it. He was dressed in warrior attire, dirty and travel stained, and she remembered suddenly that he was supposed to be out on border patrol in Aldor Forest to the east.

"Good morning, Helen," he said. "I'm sorry if I disturbed your work."

"Never mind that. What's the matter?"

He managed a faint smile. "Yes, we must get to the point. You have, of course, heard the stories of moving shadows in the north forest by the Efrim guard posts?"

"I heard something shadowy had been seen, and that a strange fear hovers around them. I also heard a rumor the trees in that area are sickening."

"Yes, and now they are in Aldor Forest as well. We encountered several; strange, almost man-like shapes." His face grew even paler and he shivered slightly. "There is something unnerving about them. They are utterly silent and respond to no language at our command. We didn't see a large number, but a patrol like our usual eastern forest guard is useless with creatures this silent and difficult to see. We would have to stand no more than a couple feet apart the whole length of the forest to keep them from getting past us. So, we came back. We met Commander Louranin on the road. Evelina has called back the guards from the eastern fort. Then, when I was almost home I got a bird from Margaret... Where is Elisabeth?"

"In the shop, I think. Would you like me to get her?"

"Please."

"Have a seat. I'll be right back." Helen turned and slipped out of the living room. She ran through the kitchen and out the back door. The sound of hammering rang from the blacksmith's shop. Helen stopped at the door, her gray skirt bunched up in one hand, her other hand on the doorsill. "Elisabeth!" she shouted over the din.

All three hammers stopped, and her father, his full-time journeyman, Steven, and Elisabeth looked at her.

"What's the matter, Helen? I'm trying to finish this." Elisabeth held up a red-hot ax blade with the tongs.

"King Edward wants to talk to you right away. He's waiting in the house. I think he just came in from the front and he must have run over immediately. It is something about the Shadows like the ones in the north. He looks more worried than I have ever seen him."

Elisabeth's eyes lit up and she almost dropped the ax blade on the table. "I'm coming. Will you finish that, Papa?"

"Of course, dear, in a minute. I hope it's nothing too bad." Their father, Clarence, locked eyes with Helen. His bright silver-gray eyes were troubled and anxious.

Helen pursed her lips and nodded. "I hope not, too," she whispered. But neither of them believed it. She turned and followed Elisabeth, who was already running towards the house, untying her leather apron as she went.

Helen arrived back in the living room on Elisabeth's heels. Edward had not sat down but was pacing back and forth. He stopped when he saw them enter and greeted Elisabeth.

"What is it you wanted me to help with, Sir?" Elisabeth asked breathlessly. Her face was serious, and yet it glowed with something like pride or joy.

Edward met her eyes and held her gaze with a searching look. "I have a commission for you, Lady Elisabeth. I know that you only just returned home, but I'm afraid we need you."

"I'm always ready when I'm needed, Sir." Elisabeth smiled and made a futile attempt to clean the soot off her face with the back of a dirty arm.

A trace of a smile came to Edward's face, and he relaxed a little. "Thank you very much, lady. I fear times are very serious right now. I saw Shadows in the east, as I told Helen, and the border guard has come in. Louranin's eastern force has also been called back. Then, I don't know if you heard, but there have been Shadows showing themselves in Aldor for the past few days."

"Tatyana told Helen that Margaret had come in from the southern guard station to make a closer defense of the town itself."

"Yes. These beings slip through scouting defenses, and the way station in the south was peaceful while the village was in trouble. I just got a bird from Margaret at Aldor and she is desperate. I need to send reinforcements to add to her guard company, and I want to send you to lead the forces of Aldor and be responsible for the protection of the town until this is over. It is a great responsibility. Will you do that, Elisabeth?"

"Of course. When should I leave? How many troops can I take?"

"I think I can send you with three hundred at daybreak tomorrow."

"I will be ready."

"Thank you. A test is before us, and it seems to be very different from anything we have faced before, but I believe I can rely on you."

Elisabeth blushed rose red under the soot. "Thank you, Sir. I'll start packing at once." She started to leave the room.

Just then, there was another rapid knock on the door. They all started, and Helen opened the door. "Come in."

It was Aranin. He was out of breath and his hands were shaking as he tried to tie his horse to the porch railing. Helen came to his aid and tied the knot.

He looked up at her. "Thank you, Helen," he panted. "Is Edward here? Lady Clara said he would be."

"Yes, he's here." She glanced from his sweating horse to his flushed face and disheveled hair. "Come in, and I'll get you some water."

"Thank you."

They went in the door together. Edward and Elisabeth had heard the conversation and were ready to meet them.

"What's happened, Aranin?" Elisabeth asked while Helen filled him a glass of water. "You look like something was chasing you."

"No. Nothing chasing me." He took the glass of water in trembling fingers and drank some. "But I rode all the way down from the north fort to Efrimiel, and Mother wanted to send word to you immediately, so I said I would just come on." He was looking at Edward now. His lake-blue eyes were unusually large and his expression deadly serious. "The attack has grown heavier by the day in the north, and this morning the shadow things claimed their first life. A young woman, a captain of our company.

She was only a few yards from me when she fell. It seemed to be an arrow, but we could find no sign of it afterwards. General Kalsian had me searching. It was an awful wound though. It was only in her arm, and yet she died in half an hour." There was a tremor in his voice. He put his hands over his face.

Helen put a hand on his shoulder. He suddenly seemed very young and vulnerable, and she wanted to comfort him. Or perhaps it was just a feeling besides that of the ice solidifying in her chest.

"Thank you for letting me know," Edward said gently. He looked about twenty years older than he had a week before. "We will try to be prepared." He patted Aranin's shoulder in a fatherly manner. "It must have been really hard. I'm sorry. Rest a minute. You're a strong young man. I know you can face this, but none of us feel ready just now." He straightened up, taking a few steps away, and gestured for Helen to follow him. "Do you know if Joseph is at home?"

"This time of day he's most likely at the theatre. He's working on sets for the next play."

"Oh, yes of course... I think I will send him with reinforcements to Sebastian at Obrin. We never know when it will strike there also." He looked at Helen as if he wanted her approval that it was the right thing to do.

"Whatever happens, they will be better off together," she said softly.

"I was thinking that," he said. "Every leader should have someone beside them in times of trouble. Someone close to them."

It occurred to her that he was asking if she would rather be the one assigned to the mission. After all, she and Joseph were both captains. Her throat got tight, and she swallowed hard. For a moment she wavered. She wanted to be with Sebastian. Then she thought of what Edward had just said, and of the dreams, and she knew what she must do. She took one of his hands. "No, I... I don't want..." She struggled to keep her voice steady, but she could barely get the words out. "I mean I do want to go to him, but no, I'm afraid I can't. I request that I be sent with Elisabeth." She looked up into Edward's face.

His sea-gray eyes were soft, shadowed, anxious. He seemed to be waiting to hear what she would say next.

"I have had dreams," she said, very low. "With me and Elisabeth together... and, well, it's like you just said. A commander needs someone close to them. Someone they can talk to and who can tell them the truth even if they don't want to hear it. You understand?" Her eyes were on Elisabeth now where she stood looking at them from across the room.

Edward followed her gaze for a moment. Then he looked back at her and nodded. "Yes. She needs you, and you are the only one who can do that for her. She is young and I worry sometimes she is a little rash. She will need your prudence and wisdom."

"I'm not sure about wisdom, and I'm only a little older than she is, but I'll do my best. I am the only person who can tell her those inconvenient facts, that is certain, but I fear this is something... something even worse than we can imagine."

Edward nodded. "I fear it, too, but we must hope that we can pass through the trial."

"Have you seen things too?"

"Little with the Sight, mine is not strong, but when I saw those creatures in the forest, I felt a terrible foreboding." His voice was hardly more than a whisper now, so that only she could hear.

Aranin was sitting near the window in one of the overstuffed chairs holding his glass of water with both hands. Elisabeth stood near him, but her eyes were far away.

"I would have liked to have you here with us. The rumors of the terrible illness, and the story of the wound Aranin just told worry me. You are our most skilled healer, but I trust you. If you think it best that you go to Aldor, go with my blessing, and may the Stars protect you." He paused and glanced at Elisabeth. "I am worried by the tone of Margaret's message and the fact that she doesn't want to hold the post herself. But I have faith in Elisabeth, that she has some great destiny... You know the day she beat me in the tournament—so long ago it seems now—I had a Sight vision then. I saw her older, a guardian, hardened, but there was a power about her, and somehow I felt that... that she would be great, famous, that she would be someone remembered in history with respect." He looked down. "You know the way the Sight is, but it gives me hope."

Helen felt that he might be leaving things out, and she thought of the vision of Sebastian she had seen, and a dream a few days ago in which everything had been laid waste. There were no people, crops, or even buildings left. "Not all visions come true, but we can hope that one may." She tried to keep her voice neutral, but she could tell by the fear in his eyes that he guessed there were dreams she desperately hoped would not come true.

He nodded gravely, "We must not ignore them, but neither must we believe them." He straightened his shoulders, raised his head, and said in a stronger voice addressing the whole room, "I must go talk to Joseph and gather the warriors I have promised you. I put my faith in you, Elisabeth." He met Elisabeth's eyes. "I expect you to take full responsibility for the people of Aldor as well as all the warriors for as long as this threat lasts. Helen will go with you as captain and healer. I may not see you again before you leave, so, Stars bless you until we meet again."

"You can trust me, Sir. I will not fail you." Elisabeth's eyes burned bright, and her chin was held high.

Edward looked at Aranin. "Please tell your mother that we are on full alert, and we will send word of anything that happens."

"Yes, Sir." Aranin looked up with a tense, pale face. He seemed to have gotten control of his emotions along with his breath.

Edward bid Aranin and Helen a grave, tender farewell, and left. Elisabeth hurried off to wash the soot from her face and start packing, and Helen walked over to Aranin.

"You can stay if you like. You have had a long ride, and surely your horse is tired if you aren't."

He sat looking at his boots in silence for a minute. "I suppose she is, but we'll go slow on the way back. I'm not really tired... I'm afraid it just shook me up a little. I'm a fool, perhaps, or a baby, but seeing her die like that... so close to me. I never saw someone die before." His voice began to tremble again. A few tears escaped his eyes and ran down his cheeks.

"I saw my grandparents die, but that was kind of different. He was a hundred and sixteen, and she was a hundred and nineteen. I understand. Even as a healer I have never seen a young person die." They were both silent for a few minutes. He looked at his boots and she stood with a hand on his chair, watching him. Then she asked, "The wound, what did it look like?"

"Terrible. I didn't touch it or anything. There are medics in our company for that, but I heard them saying that a sort of cold spread through her even before she died, and the wound was bloody and smelled bad."

Helen pursed her lips, thinking of what herbs might be useful to take.

"Helen," he whispered after a minute. He looked up into her face, and he looked frightened and troubled.

"What is it? Is there something else?"

"Yes. It was General Kalsian. I mean, he's been a general for forty years, and a respected one. I have been in his company since I apprenticed, and I have always respected him. He always seemed capable and strong but... but today... when the shadow things came out of the forest to attack... he just stood there and stared at them. And then he tried to give orders, but they weren't much good. His voice was higher, his eyes wide... he looked completely terrified, panicked, like he forgot all his years as a soldier. I think that frightened me as much as the Shadows."

Helen thought for a minute. Then she said grimly, "I suppose now is when we see who really passes the test of battle. For all his forty years, Kalsian had probably never fought a foe or been taken by surprise by anything more serious than a practical joke." She thought about Margaret. "Our commanders are mostly champions of the organized play fight." She took Aranin's hand. "Don't worry. You'll get someone new if he can't handle it. I'm sure most of our leaders will pass the test, and likely many new ones will rise to the challenge.

He nodded and stood up. "I hope so. I should go and let you pack."

He made for the door, but she took his hand. She felt suddenly afraid she would never see him again, and she couldn't tell if it was a premonition or a simple fear. "Stars protect you, Aranin," she said softly. "I'm afraid we are facing a great trial, and we see now that we may not all make it through... take care of yourself."

He smiled just a little. "I won't have time to go find Tatyana, but tell her Analisia and I are thinking about her if you have a chance."

"I will."

"May the winds of fate protect you, Helen." He hugged her briefly, then waved and left the house.

Helen turned and walked towards her and Elisabeth's bedroom.

Elisabeth looked up when she came in. Her eyes were shining, and she was smiling. "Did you hear what Edward said? He has faith in me, and trusts me, and he is giving me full responsibility for Aldor—not just a turn at duty, but full responsibility!"

"I was there; I heard him." Helen's voice was low, and she tried to smile at Elisabeth. "You don't mind that I'm coming, do you?"

Elisabeth smiled and patted Helen on the back with a pair of socks in her hand. "Of course I don't. I'm happy to have you as my captain."

Helen smiled faintly and pulled out her travel sack. Elisabeth would never mind having her along, so long as she was of a lesser rank and Elisabeth got to be the heroine. Not that Helen really minded. Elisabeth had always been the ambitious one, the one who reveled in the soldier's life. Helen couldn't see soldiering as the point of a life. It wasn't about fighting. A noble culture came from people believing other things were more important. She had joined the guard because she wanted to serve her country, and she had heard so many people talk about how having a well-trained border guard was the only way the country was kept peaceful. Now, all she wanted was for that to continue to be true. "Thank you," was all she said. She threw clothes, both summer and winter, into her duffel, hardly looking at them.

Elisabeth continued to chatter away about her new commission and the new prestige, and how it was almost like being princess of Aldor, and Helen nodded and tried to play along without hearing half of what her sister was saying. 'Princess of Aldor' reminded her of Sebastian and how she had been offered the opportunity to be the captain at his side. She thought she had done right, and she knew that Joseph was a loyal and devoted friend, but the pain in her heart was very intense as she wondered when she would see Sebastian again. She kept her head down so Elisabeth wouldn't see the tears in her eyes. When her clothes were packed, she spent a long time choosing the best books of healing and collecting her medicines. Elisabeth finished packing and volunteered to tell their parents.

"Please," Helen said softly. She didn't want to be the one to tell her mother they were leaving again so soon and for an indefinite amount of time. "You can tell them all about your honor."

"I will!" Elisabeth threw her duffel on her bed and ran out of the room, leaving Helen to sort books, herbs, and tools of healing in peace.

When at last in the evening after supper she was finished packing, she sat down to write a letter to Sebastian. She scratched out several drafts before she finished with this written in her neat precise hand:

> *Dear Sebastian,*
>
> *The Sight troubles me, and the stories I hear of the Shadows trouble me even more. You remember when I told you that I thought the thing I had to do had something to do with being with Elisabeth? Well, I am going with her now to Aldor, where she has a new commission for the indefinite duration of this threat. I will be her captain, and try to be of use as a healer against this terrible new enemy.*
>
> *I wish I could come to you, you don't know how much, but I know you will be happy to have Joseph, and he will do everything he can for you. You have to take care of each other for me. I love you so much, and will think of you every day. I will visit you with the Sight if duties permit.*
>
> *This is a dark time I fear, but surely it will pass soon now that it has come. I fear it won't be a battle of a week like the last serious battle a hundred and fifty years ago, but perhaps by next summer . . . I will imagine you and I getting married next summer in peace among the roses. Until then, may the Stars protect you.*
>
> *Forever yours,*
> *Helen*

She folded the letter, sealed it, and sat still at her desk. She let her head rest in her hands. She remembered a Sight dream she'd had where everyone was vanishing, going away from her and leaving her alone. She felt a little bit like that now. She was leaving everyone she loved except Elisabeth. The thought of leaving her parents and Tatyana, Edward, Clara, and Joseph was almost as painful as the thought of not going to Sebastian, and then there were Aranin and Analisia in Efrim. All her friends, and she felt sure, somehow, that these places that had once seemed so close no longer were.

Her only consolation was the hope that there would be spare minutes in whatever lay ahead in which to use the Sight. She had a stronger gift of the Sight than anyone she knew and most people she had read about, and she hoped that would finally be useful.

The part of the Sight that could be controlled was like a web of connections. Some threads were stronger than others, depending on the intimacy of the relationship. Helen was exceptional in that her gift was so strong she could trust even her weaker connections to let her know if a friend was in serious danger, and she could speak almost freely to her strongest connections when she went to them in spirit with the Sending. Further, she could use the Sending even on the weaker connections. That was almost unheard of. The gift was also the reason her dreams were more powerful and frequent than other people's, and that was painful; but now, as she prepared to leave almost everyone she loved, she felt a certain amount of reassurance in knowing she had that connection.

Chapter 6

Shadows

9 October, YA 1123

Eldirad

TATYANA WAS in the kitchen with her mother kneading bread. It was a beautiful October afternoon, cool and crisp with a scent of autumn coming on the breeze through the open kitchen window. They were singing.

The kitchen door flew open, and they both stopped short and turned. Tatyana felt her heart skip a beat. Her father stood in the doorway, breathless and pale. She met his eyes and ice spread through her chest.

"What happened?" she whispered.

Clara ran forward and put her floury hands on his arm. "Are you all right, my dear?"

"I'm fine," he said hastily. "But we are in danger. We saw Shadows, like those reported around Aldor and the north watches of Efrim, in Aldor Forest the last two days, and there is no way a spread-out guard can stop them. They are too silent and too sneaky."

"But are they really dangerous?" Clara wrung her hands together, worrying her apron. "I mean, I heard they made trees sick, but—"

"Yes." In a grim voice he told them Aranin's news and the urgency of

Margaret's message. "We need to see all the warriors at once. I am sending three hundred each with Joseph to Westtower and with Elisabeth and Helen to Aldor. The rest I will need to be ready to defend the city."

"I can call them." Clara was already fumbling with her apron strings. "But why put Joseph in charge of the company for Obrin? He's a dear boy, but I've never thought he should be a captain. Are you sure he'll be all right? Isn't there someone more competent you could send to help Sebastian?"

Edward shook his head. "I really don't think so. There aren't all that many captains, and very few guardians. Tatyana and I are needed here. Margaret doesn't wish to command, which worries me, but I must trust her judgement, so Elisabeth will be in charge there. Helen requested to be the captain to go with her, and she is right. It is a Sight thing; she feels she must. And she is the only one who really knows Elisabeth well enough to stand by her. Sebastian already has Captain Sarah at Westtower, and while there are others I could send, I believe having a close friend like Joseph with him is the most important thing. Joseph is a good and loyal man, and I have always felt there was something more to him. A strength he just has to find."

"All right, if you're sure." Clara hung up her apron and ran for the door.

"Mama, wait," Tatyana called when Clara was half out the door.

"What?"

"I think we had better call everyone. A general assembly."

Clara looked at Edward, who nodded agreement. "All right. I'll have them here in an hour." She shut the door and ran down the street.

"You're right," Edward said grimly, dusting the flour off his arm. "The people will be worried if we mobilize the entire army, and they will need to know what is happening. I would like to put defenses all along the river before the afternoon is out too. Maybe the civilians could help."

"They can. And what about the wall? Should we put it up now?" Tatyana looked anxiously into her father's eyes. They were a little wide in his pale face, and she knew he was frightened. That made her scared too.

He shut his eyes and took a deep breath. "I hope we don't need it," he whispered. "But the sooner it's up the better."

He hurried upstairs to get the plans for the top section of the wall that had been drawn up when the stone was being cut, and to tell Josephine and his father Thomas.

Tatyana was left standing in the kitchen. She looked down at her floury apron and the lump of bread in her hands. It seemed strange she was holding something so normal. Then she set it on the table and went upstairs too. Someone in Efrim had died that morning. It wasn't anyone she knew, but just the idea... She quickly changed from her dress to her trousers and long-sleeve shirt. She pulled on the soft, fitted, calf-high boots of a warrior, and slipped the fine light mail that was a specialty of the Eldir over her head. Her mail still had her stars pinned to it. Now she was a guardian rather than a princess off duty playing around with bread.

It wasn't playing, of course. They were making dinner for the family, but it felt that way at the moment. She put on her leather belt embroidered with seven pointed stars, and hung her blade in its fancy scabbard at her side. Then she ran down the street to the armory. There were swords and bows, knives and daggers, and a few vests of fine mail made by the smiths and stored there ready for use. Such things were often handed down, though, or made personally for a new warrior. What there were the most of were arrows. She took down arrows and began to fill quivers. Not just one for herself, but hundreds. Archers would be the best defense along a riverbank. Her mind was racing. An attack on the city... Father thought there might be an attack on the city as soon as tonight. And Margaret didn't want to command anymore. Tatyana couldn't believe that. She wished Joseph didn't have to go, but she agreed with her father. She liked to think of him and Sebastian having each other. She didn't even want to think about Helen going.

A bit less than an hour later a child she didn't know poked his head into the room and said King Edward wanted her at the palace. She took just her own quiver and followed the boy. She found her father in the living room talking to three of the best Eldir stonemasons.

He smiled and nodded to her when she entered. "The people are assembled. It is time to talk to them, and I think you had better be there with me."

She didn't know what to say, so she nodded and followed him out the big oak doors onto the front porch. It was raised a few steps and looked out over the large central square, which was thronged with people. The high porch was used for weddings and speeches and the like. The crowd was talking and shouting and asking questions, but they went silent when Edward waved his hands in the air.

He took a deep breath and began in a clear, ringing voice. "My dear people. I regret to inform you that a serious threat is upon us. A strange shadow enemy is coming through our borders. The creatures have shown themselves to be violent, and there has been a death at the north guard station of Efrim. Please don't be frightened, but it must be taken seriously. I hope every man, woman, and child will do their best to help our city be prepared for this threat. As for my warriors..." Here he listed off the groups of warriors and the individuals he was assigning to Joseph and Elisabeth, and told them to pack their bags and be ready to leave at daybreak. "The rest of the army: Please report to the riverbank, where we will set up our defense, as soon as you can collect your weapons, some shovels, and proper warrior attire. Civilians are also encouraged to help with the defenses but, please, no children, and don't come unless you're willing to work hard. The rest of the civilians, please clear the top of the wall and offer your assistance to the masons who will be bringing the wall up to the full height of defenses.

"There is no evidence yet that it will come to that, but the creatures are good at slipping through a scattered defense, and I consider it only prudent to have a solid defense around the city itself. We will be prepared for the invaders, and you need not fear. Princess Tatyana and I are dedicated to the protection of this city, and we will do all in our power to see this threat repulsed. Our nation has been tested before and never been found wanting."

The people cheered. Edward bowed his head, and he and Tatyana left the platform. People were talking up a storm now, but Tatyana didn't listen. She chose a couple warriors who had been in Edward's company that had just come in and were still dressed as soldiers, and she got them to go to the armory with her to help carry hundreds of full quivers in carts to the river. Her father's words had sounded so confident, especially in closing. The people were roused, excited, but for the most part they didn't seem too scared. She wondered if she would ever be good at making speeches like that.

Off the porch, though, she could tell he was still afraid, and the warriors from his company who helped her were all grim and silent. They didn't chatter like everyone else, but worked with an almost frantic energy. On some of the faces she could see the obvious signs of fear, or even desperation. They had seen the creatures, whatever they were, and their reaction was not heartening.

* * ★ ★ * *

It was almost nine o'clock in the evening and had been dark for close to three hours. Tatyana had always liked the dark, but tonight it felt spooky and oppressive, and she wished the October night wasn't so long. The wide stone bridge on the eastern road had been blocked off with heavy barrels filled with water and with traps that would drop stones on the heads of anyone coming from the forest. Lots of them. There was also a company of a hundred of the best swordfighters in the army stationed around the near end. It didn't look likely that anything could get across the bridge.

The soldiers remaining in Eldirad had been divided into two watches, and Edward and the other half had gone back to the city to rest about an hour ago when defenses were nearly finished. They would take over at midnight. For the time being, Tatyana was in charge. An older captain she trusted had been chosen to lead the swordsman at the bridge, and another commanded half the archers spread out north of it. Tatyana had taken personal command of the archers on the south stretch, but she remained close to the bridge so as to be near the center of things.

A berm of dirt had been piled up, making a sort of ditch behind it in the grassy riverbank. The archers sat in the hole. It was muddy and not especially comfortable. Tatyana looked over the riverbank in the starlight. The bustle had stopped. All was ready, and the warriors sat talking or looking across the sparkling water. A couple of archers close by were playing a game of pick up sticks. Another group not far away was playing a guessing game.

She could hear the noise of voices, footsteps, carts, and horses, as the civilians swarmed over the city wall. The nearest part was only a dozen yards behind where she sat, and the progress they had made in the last five hours was quite impressive. She would have liked to go and help, and she was sure most of her warriors felt the same. But there were more than enough people helping the masons, and the warriors must not leave their post. She turned her eyes away from the slow rising of the white wall, and the bobbing lanterns, toward the dark forest across the river.

"I suppose we might not get to go to the cross-quarter day ball," Clarissa said wistfully. "I had planned to wear my new blue dress, and I was making Jeremy a matching vest."

"I suppose not," Tatyana replied absently. She had known Clarissa since she could remember. She was the daughter of her mother's best friend and had always been a little like a big sister to her. She was a kind, gentle, good-natured sort of person, athletic and adventurous enough to be fun and to have joined the guard.

"Surely by Midwinter's Eve, though..."

Tatyana nodded vaguely. It didn't seem likely, but she wasn't going to say that.

Another archer close by rested some knitting on his knees and smiled. "We'll see. By Midwinter for sure. My wife and I are planning a new rose trellis around the back yard. I do hope I'll have time to build it before it snows. She's a potter, so she doesn't do much wood, and I promised."

"I just got home from duty at the south fort last week," a third grumbled. "My husband is not going to be happy if I have to do too much of this. It was supposed to be my turn to take care of the kids and do the laundry while he got some orders done in his furniture shop."

Tatyana listened in silence. They were all so relaxed—or if they were pretending, they were doing a really good job. How could they talk so happily of the fall and winter? Could they be right? She wanted so much to believe they were. Why shouldn't they be? The Eldir had never fought a war that lasted more than a month. The longest had been twenty-four days, and that was five hundred years ago. The most recent had been a quarrel with Ikkik a hundred years ago when her grandparents were little children. It had lasted a week. Thirty people had died. She didn't want to think of that many people dying again, so why was it she couldn't think beyond the threat? She didn't feel as though she could even imagine the normal life that was surely on the other side.

She tried to join the conversation. She suggested they put on a play for the Midwinter Solstice celebration. Clarissa liked that idea, and they talked for a while, but the words felt hollow to Tatyana. She knew if Clarissa had had the Sight, she would have been able to tell they were lies. Tatyana thought of the plays and parades of Midwinter, and of the great ball and concerts they were supposed to have for the Harvest Festival at the end of October. Three weeks was a long time. Logically, it seemed they might celebrate it... She had planned on dancing all night. She imagined the tables of food and the music and the people in beautiful clothes spilling out of the ballroom into the starlit courtyard hung with lanterns. Somehow, it all felt very far away.

Tatyana was tired. Time seemed to pass slowly. She kept peering at her necklace watch in the light of the torches along the riverbank. At about ten, a familiar voice behind her called her name and she looked up. Helen was standing a few feet away. She wore a dark gray dress, and only her hands and face showed up well in the dark. Tatyana rose to meet her.

"How is it going?" Helen asked softly.

"Quiet so far. We are as prepared as we can be. Everyone else is just planning the fall and playing games and doing hand work and such while we wait. They seem happy, but I'm uneasy. There is something in the air tonight..."

"Yes. I feel it too. I don't like it." Helen looked down and her bright gray eyes were shadowed. "I'm afraid I have come to say goodbye."

Tatyana didn't say anything for a minute. Her face was pale and grim. "I will miss you," she whispered.

"I will miss you too." Helen took her hand. "I will worry about you. But there's nothing I can do but my duty." There was a touch of bitterness in her voice. "I am sure I must go with Elisabeth. She needs me, even if she will never admit it. I would rather be with you or with Sebastian, but you have your father and mother and Clarissa, and Sebastian has Joseph. Besides, I think it is what the Sight is telling me."

Tatyana blinked back her tears and gripped her friend's hand. "I understand. I wish you every blessing. May the Stars protect you, Helen, and bring you back to me someday." She forced herself to smile.

Helen's face was like a mask, tense and expressionless, with her eyes down. Tatyana knew her well enough to know it was either grief or fear, and her own heart was heavy. She wondered against her will if she would ever see Helen again.

"Is... is there something you haven't told me?" she asked after a moment. "Do you think we won't see each other again?"

"I don't know." Helen's voice was low and tense. "Most of what I have seen is very vague. I think I have told you all of it. There was the one of the city broken and abandoned, but it had something else, a failure to reach something... like it was more of a threat... No, I have no reason to believe I won't see you again." She dropped her eyes, swallowing hard.

"Helen." They were a few paces from the others and there was no way anyone else could hear their low voices, but Tatyana lowered her voice even more all the same. "I'm afraid."

Helen looked up and squeezed her hand. "We all are, but we just have to do our best."

"I know."

"Aranin wanted me to tell you he and Analisia will be thinking of you."

"Thanks. I will think of them too. Though neither of us are likely to be able to tell them that soon."

After another silence, Helen said, "I should go try to sleep. It doesn't seem likely on a night like this, but I'm leaving at daybreak, and I still want to look over my books one more time.

"I should go back to the lookout." Tatyana hugged her friend close for a minute, and Helen squeezed back.

"May all the Stars bless you, Tatyana," Helen whispered. Then she pulled away and turned to go.

Tatyana stood watching her until she had passed behind the wall.

Then she returned to the archers' ditch and looked out into the dark forest. She did have her parents and grandparents, her home... but she felt abandoned without Helen. She understood why Helen had to go, and yet on some level she felt betrayed, perhaps not so much by Helen as by life.

The minutes seemed to go even slower after that, and Tatyana felt more uneasy. She pulled out her sword. She unhooked the strings that held the thin leather cover over the blade and pulled it off. The silver metal shimmered in the starlight. A battle blade. In order to be ready for attack, every man and woman of the guard had a battle blade that was their own. They trained with it from first apprenticeship and learned to feel it was a part of them, but it was possible, in fact, common, to go a whole career without uncovering it. She ran a finger over the sleek steel. Hers was a very fine blade made by a great Eldir smith of two centuries ago and etched with a touch of moonsilver. Moonsilver was a magical metal made only by the most skilled and powerful Efrim smiths, and it had power for purity and good. Although it was an Efrim invention, it had been found to be an aid to the Eldir power of Sight as well. It could give one strength, and it was said to have great power against evil. It also shone faintly whenever the moon was in the sky, even if the moon was hidden by clouds. She hadn't seen her blade uncovered since the ceremony when she became a captain four years ago. Usually, even in small skirmishes like the one Sebastian had faced at Obrin when he became guardian, no one uncovered their blades. She believed the last time they had been uncovered was the battle when her grandmother was little.

Quietly, she passed the word for all her people to uncover their blades. People did, and she watched as they all looked at the bright, deadly blades with awe and respect. People ran their fingers over them or turned them in the torchlight. Then they sheathed them and put the covers in their pocket. They were ready. It was the same in Efrim. Commander Louranin had told her father that they had uncovered their battle blades for the first time in centuries. Tatyana sighed and sheathed her own.

She drew an arrow from her quiver and fitted it in her bow. Then she sat silently, looking into the forest. Her unease was growing, and she thought the others were feeling it too. They grew quieter, put away hand work, and fiddled with their bows. The people behind them were still working in torchlight, but they seemed far away now. The river splashed and gurgled over stones, sparkling and catching flecks of gold in the torchlight. The air was cool, and the stars were thick and bright. Still, the silence seemed to grow. It took Tatyana a little while to realize that there were no insects singing in the night, no rustle of little animals. The air was still, and nothing moved in the forest. Only the river was unconcerned.

There were many dozen eyes peering anxiously at the forest, and yet they saw nothing. It was about a quarter of eleven. Suddenly there was movement. Faint shapes flew across the river, but Tatyana could see no sign in the dark trees of a being that could be shooting arrows. To her left she heard shouts, and shrieks of panic. A couple yards away someone gasped in pain. Tatyana felt desperation mounting in her throat, but that wasn't the way to command.

Where were the cursed creatures? There were some at the bridge to be sure, but there were also some in the trees across the river, and if she wasn't mistaken, they had shot at least one of her archers. After years of premonitions and vague fears the onslaught had come, and somehow, she must save her people from this threat.

"Keep your heads down as much as you can," she called to the others in the ditch.

The sounds from the bridge worried her. She still couldn't hear enemies or the clash of what she thought of as battle, but people were running and shouting. It sounded like chaos. What was the matter with the captain? Why wasn't he giving orders? Before her, the arrows kept flying. Strange black cords flew across the river and the arrows that held them stuck in the bank. If only she could see the assailants. She almost rose to go to the aid of the bridge. Then she saw them.

Tatyana squinted into the darkness. Keen night vision was normal among the Eldir, and she was no exception, and yet she couldn't really make out the forms on the opposite bank. She had heard the rumors from Efrim, and her father's report of shadowy beings, but she had never really understood. This was no sneaky creature that kept to the shadows; these things *were* shadows. She wasn't sure how that could be, but they didn't look solid, not really. They were just blackness, with no visible shape and contour save the outline.

"Shoot," she called to her warriors, and two hundred arrows flew just as, to her horror and amazement, the creatures started to charge across the light web of cords that had lodged across the river.

Her archers were good, and the line of foes very thick, so nearly every shaft found its mark. Those who were hit seemed to explode into a puff of strange mist, but Tatyana didn't have time to give that much thought. She reloaded and shot again and again. She was not only the best shot in the country, but she could load her bow in two seconds without looking, and yet it hardly seemed to help. Her warriors, or at least most of them, seemed still to be firing fast, but the enemy advanced. These beings, whatever they were, seemed to know no fear. It wasn't just that they did not seem upset by the death of their fellows, but rather that they didn't even seem to notice in the slightest way. As more and more of the strange beings were killed in quick succession, the black mist that came from them rose in an unpleasant cloud over the river.

She heard a breaking crash and a rush of water to her left. One of the barrels on the bridge must have broken. She had to see what was happening there. She glanced around at her group of archers. Some looked panicked, others were shooting hard and intently. A dozen yards away she saw an older, grim-looking man who seemed to be organizing those beside him. "Benjamin," she called. "Take charge of this stretch. I've got to check on the bridge." He wasn't a captain, but he nodded and went on without question. She figured tonight was the real testing ground, and he seemed to be taking it very well. "You may need to bring out swords soon."

"Yes, lady."

She crawled below the low dirt wall as much as she could until she reached the bridge. It was indeed chaos. The strange Shadows, shaped like rather short men in hooded cloaks, without a trace of features of any kind, were everywhere. Two of the water barrels had broken, and shadow beings were standing on them, and on the bridge railing. Many people were down on the stones, some stumbled as if blind, and others were fighting madly. A black cord flew from one of the creatures on the railing and caught around her right arm. In an instant she drew her dagger from her belt with her left hand and cut the cord, but even in that moment her arm began to tingle a little. She saw another man being dragged off by a similar cord; it was attached around one ankle, and he was screaming and trying to stop himself. The Shadow was dragging him past the broken water barrel towards the opposite side of the bridge. She took a few steps towards them and realized that the traps on the other side hadn't been sprung. Whatever these Shadows were, they were apparently too lightweight to activate the traps, but when the poor soldier was dragged across...

Without time to think, she sheathed her sword, ran, put her hands on the barrel like a vault in gymnastics and rolled to a sitting position on top. Then, drawing her sword and leaping to her feet, she slashed the trigger ropes so the traps could not be sprung. Unfortunately two already had been, and the poor warriors lay on the stone below. She leapt down and stabbed the Shadow thing as it pulled the young man past the water barrel. He scrambled up but couldn't stand.

"Crawl, no, hop if you can, it's faster. Get out of here!" she shouted. "And if you can, tell a couple others to come get these poor people." She indicated with a nod the figures on the ground. At least one of them was still alive.

Without a word, the man clawed his way to his good foot and hopped away into the battle behind. She was fighting furiously. The shadow creatures appeared to be everywhere, but after a minute, two men came and hoisted the fallen warriors on their shoulders. Then she retreated to the other side of the bridge with the others. She didn't see the captain. She had thought well of him, but perhaps he hadn't been up to it after all, or perhaps he was wounded.

"All right, everyone." She pointed to two men and a woman. "You three collect everyone who can't stand. Don't bother to see what's wrong now. Just get them behind the lines and call some of the civilians to take them back to the city. The rest of you form close ranks." She scanned the group and designated a few people she knew to be especially athletic and agile. "You, up on the barrels. We want the high ground, not them. And you, on the north bridge rail." She put one hand on the right rail and in a swift movement mounted it. "Now, keep close together. We must hold out."

The fight was hard, but the first panic began to subside. Seemingly thousands of shadowy beings poured across the river, and from her perch, when she could glance away from her immediate opponents, she saw that the archers on both sides were mainly fighting with swords now. Some Shadows were getting around the lower end of the defense, and Benjamin had sent some of his men to make a defense slanting back from the water to protect the city and the civilians who were still working on the wall. There wasn't as much action back at the rising wall as there had been half an hour ago. Arrows were flying and the people were mostly staying on the inside, but it was well over six feet high on the side closest to the river the one time Tatyana dared glance back at it.

A black cord caught her ankle and she almost fell into the river below. She forgot to breathe until she had cut the cord. The bridge wasn't all that high. A fall to the water wouldn't be deadly, but it could hurt, and that was not counting the mesh of strange shadow cords and the hundreds of demons that covered the river just now.

She lost all track of time, but it seemed like a great deal more than an hour and a quarter before the tramp of many feet came behind her and one of her warriors tapped her shoulder.

"Princess, it's the changing of the watch. The king wants a report."

She looked around, gave a few last orders, then leapt from the rail and ran to where her father was standing with the other watch.

"It looks pretty grim," he said when she was beside him. "Is there anything particular I should know?"

She told him very briefly everything that had happened, ending with, "We are holding a little better now, but, Father... people have died. One woman died from our own traps." Her strong, even voice broke slightly.

Edward's face, which had grown paler and grimmer as she talked, softened a little, and he took her hand. "Dearest," he whispered. "It is hard, but you have done as well as could be done." He straightened his shoulders and looked at the melee before them in the dark. "Now it's my turn to see if I can face it." He was determined, but there was also more than a touch of fear. He had never faced a real battle in his more than forty years as a soldier, and the Shadows had scared him in the forest. He lifted his chin. "Thank you, Tatyana. I will keep an eye on my captains, and make sure I find some of the better gymnasts to hold the high spots. Tell your people to rest and be ready to take over at six."

"I will."

They parted, and he talked to his people for a minute and then got them in place behind hers. She gave the order to retreat, and her people stepped back while his stepped forward. Then her troops crowded together as they all walked back into the city. A few people started to ask questions, but no one finished. They walked in silence. Tatyana felt a hand in hers and saw Clarissa had come beside her. They didn't say anything. What was there to say? Inside the wall, Clarissa squeezed her hand and she squeezed back, then Clarissa departed for home. Tatyana had told them all to be ready at six. Once they were home, ate something perhaps, or took a bath, that wouldn't leave much more than four hours before they would have to get up and start preparing for the next watch; five, perhaps, if they ate breakfast very fast. Everyone was in a hurry to get home.

Tatyana was alone by the time she passed the hospital. Most of the houses were dark, since it was midnight, but lamplight streamed from the hospital windows. She wondered if she should go in, find out how many were dead, and see if she could help with the wounded. She hesitated, put out a hand to the door, but she couldn't make herself turn the knob. She realized that, now that she was not in the fray, her hands were shaking. She felt bewildered, frightened, and on the point of tears. There were other healers, and she was tired. She had to lead another watch in a little less than six hours. That would be a whole six hours of fighting, not just the last hour and a quarter. She didn't want to imagine that. She turned away. She didn't want to know how many had died anyway. She knew at least two or three. She feared more. Dead. She couldn't quite think about it. Good men and women who had been under her command... who wouldn't go home to their mothers and fathers, husbands and wives, children and friends. It was too terrible to bear. She couldn't swallow, and her eyes were bleary with unshed tears by the time she let herself in the door of her own house.

There were lights in the kitchen. Tatyana half wanted to go right up to bed by herself, but her mother heard the door and rushed in to greet her.

"Are you all right? What happened? I heard they are crossing the river without the bridge. How can they?"

"Ropes of some kind. They are very light." Tatyana told her mother everything as simply as she could. She didn't feel like talking about it. It had been hard enough to say it once to Father. She left out the part about the traps, but it turned out Clara had been in and out of the hospital, where Josephine had been called to lead the healers, and knew already. Before she finished the story Tatyana's tears had overflowed. She turned away and covered her face, and Clara put an arm around her shoulders and held her for a minute.

"Come on. I have dinner for you," Clara said gently. "You must eat and get to bed."

The dinner was hearty and good and did make her feel a little better. It was after one before she went to bed, and the knowledge that it would be only a few hours before the little gold bird on her clock would sing to tell her it was five and she needed to get up and dress and get some breakfast before her six-hour watch made it hard to settle down.

She couldn't lie still, even though she was very tired. She wondered again who was dead, and whether she knew them at all. She thought about the lighthearted planning of the people near her before the attack. Some of them would never do those things... how many had died tonight? And how many were dying now? Or would on her next watch? How long would this go on? When would the wall be finished? She kept seeing the one woman whose head had been crushed by a trap she might have set herself. Tears streamed down Tatyana's cheeks, and it was nearly three before she fell into a troubled sleep.

Chapter 7

Setting Out

10 October, YA 1123

Eldirad: Aldor

IT WAS STILL DARK, and Helen felt tired and nervous when her alarm woke her from a fitful sleep at 5:20. She leapt out of bed and lit the lamp on her side dresser. She dreaded leaving, but it was a little bit of a relief to get out of bed. The best that could be done was to get the parting over and find out what lay ahead. She shook Elisabeth awake, and a few minutes later they went into the kitchen with their packs over their shoulders. Their parents were waiting for them. Mama was setting the table for an early breakfast with nuts, yogurt, and some doughnuts she had made the day before. A single candle burned in the middle of the table and sent shadows flickering across her face as she laid their plates and poured hot peppermint tea. Father stood at the window looking out, hardly more than a thin, straight silhouette in the dim light, with his black hair hiding his face. He still wore his boots and his leather apron. Helen walked to his side while Elisabeth sat down at the table.

Only the faintest gray was paling the sky to the east, and while her father, like Sebastian and Helen herself, had unusually good eyesight, even for an Eldir, he couldn't have seen much. Besides, there really wasn't anything to see from the kitchen window apart from the rows of the kitchen garden. Their house was near the city center, in the royal district, not near the wall. Still, she stood beside him looking out for a moment.

He put an arm around her shoulders. He was thin and small-boned like her, although of a more average Eldir height, but he had the strong arms of a smith. "It is bad out there," he whispered.

"It has come then?"

"Yes. It hit a little before eleven. It was horrible. Many of the civilians on the wall fled. There were arrows coming our way, and chaos at the river. I couldn't make out the enemy from the wall, especially keeping my head down, but I could see the warriors fighting. Tatyana got it more or less under control pretty fast, but some of the warriors panicked and ran, and some were stumbling around in a strange way. Things quietened down after a while. Edward took over at midnight, and he has things pretty under control now, although even with Tatyana's warnings, the first few minutes his people faced the strange threat were almost as chaotic and frightening as the initial attack." Clarence sighed and followed Helen back to the table. He didn't need to voice his fear and foreboding. Helen understood.

They sat, and Helen and Elisabeth's mother, Yevenia, fluttered about trying to make sure everyone had everything they needed. Clarence ate quickly and in silence. Helen forced herself to eat, although she hardly tasted it. Elisabeth ate heartily but didn't say much. Her excitement of the night before had faded. She wasn't all that worried. She still felt a sort of thrill at the drama of events, but she was tired, and she felt grimmer.

The gray light of dawn had strengthened and the eastern sky was turning red as Helen, Elisabeth, and Yevenia stood on the front steps saying goodbye. Yevenia stood on the doorstep, a sturdily built woman in a soft lavender bathrobe. Her golden hair fell loose around her round face, which was much paler than usual. Her strong hands were fidgeting with each other.

"Oh, my dear girls," she said softly. She looked at Elisabeth, who stood tall and proud looking off towards the unseen battle in the east. She put a hand on Elisabeth's shoulder. "I hope you are not gone too long, and... and that this is what you wished for."

Elisabeth smiled and looked down into her mother's face. "Thank you. This is my chance."

Helen watched them. Their mother had never understood Elisabeth's brash, ambitious ways, or her lack of interest in fine art, gardening, and books. Mama had never understood the national guard, for that matter, but Helen knew Mama and Elisabeth loved each other. Elisabeth was different from the rest of them, with her need for praise and people, but Yevenia was the open, affectionate, motherly kind of person who enjoyed bringing her daughters and all their friends into her house and under her wing even when they were different. Their parents, unlike Joseph's, were not the kind to judge or look down on someone who was different.

Helen's heart felt like lead. She loved her mother deeply, but she wasn't sure she could ever make her understand how she felt, or if she wanted to. Mama was so kind and gentle, but she liked her quiet life and had never looked much further. Helen took her mother's hand.

"I'm so sorry we have to leave like this," she whispered. "I hope... do... do you understand why I must do this now?"

Yevenia looked down for a moment. "I am not sure I really understand, dear," she whispered. "Strange things are happening tonight, and I see fears must be coming true, but I don't understand any of it. I trust you, though, and believe in you, whatever you think you must do. I will miss you, but on the whole I'm glad you will be there to take care of your sister. I just hope she'll take care of you too."

Helen hugged her mother close for a long minute. Then she glanced at Elisabeth, whose face was alight, and who couldn't seem to keep her eyes off the direction of the distant action. "I think she will," she said after a minute. "Either way, I'll be all right. Don't worry about me, Mama."

"As if." Yevenia gave a weak laugh. "Write to me, please."

"Of course I will."

"Do you think you'll be home by Midwinter?"

Helen didn't want to answer that question and was grateful when they were interrupted at that moment by Clarence coming out of the house with water bottles to put in their packs. They wouldn't take horses to Aldor. If every warrior was mounted, that would be three hundred horses more than Aldor already had to stall and feed, and it wouldn't make sense for only some to ride.

Elisabeth patted Yevenia's shoulder, squeezed Clarence's hand, and took her water bottle. "I'd guess we'll be home long before Midwinter," she said with an easy smile. Elisabeth felt she would be sorry when it was over, but she couldn't imagine it lasting more than a month or so. "I mean to make the best of it."

"Take care, Elisabeth. I'm proud of you," Clarence said.

"You take care, too. I'll see you soon." Elisabeth waved and trotted off towards the crowd that could be seen gathering a few blocks away in the square.

Helen wondered how Elisabeth could believe it would be that easy. She felt they would be terribly lucky if they were home by spring, let alone Midwinter, but she didn't say that. She took her father's hand. When she looked up into his face there was deep pain in his silver-gray eyes. She knew he understood. Papa always understood how she felt. She hugged him and lay her head on his leather apron.

"I pray I will see you again," she whispered so softly only he could hear her.

He stroked her hair with one strong, calloused hand. "I..." he took a deep breath. "I think we will," he whispered. "I pray so. May the Stars bless you, Helen, and protect us all."

"Yes." She felt a little better. She gave his hand a last squeeze and kissed her mother's cheek. "I love you. I will write often." She waved and then turned away, leaving them behind in the rising day.

Helen's throat was very tight for a while, but she pulled herself together as she approached the square. In some ways, that had been the hardest part. Now her duty lay ahead. The square was teeming with warriors and family and friends seeing them off. Carts of stones passed by, and people were shouting and even singing over their work way off by the wall. The sun broke the haze over the eastern forest and shone on the mail of the assembled warriors. It was about six fifteen, but the city was already buzzing. That night it had never stopped or even slowed down much. Helen scanned the crowd looking for Joseph. He was the last person she needed to say goodbye to.

After several minutes of searching, she found him; a tall, strong, slender figure under a tree at the side of the square. His long brown cloak was thrown about his shoulders in the chill of the early morning, and a large pack was strapped over it. The first rays of sun shone on his wavy chocolate-brown hair. He was talking to a handful of warriors near him, laughing about something, but he left them when he saw her approaching. They stood together for a moment. She didn't know what to say.

"Nice morning, isn't it?" he said with a bright smile.

She smiled faintly and looked around. The sky overhead was blue and bright, and birds were singing in the trees of the city. "I suppose it is." She pulled her letter out of her pocket. "Would you take this to Sebastian?"

"Of course" He took the letter and put it in an inside pocket. "Do you know if Edward or Tatyana is going to see us off? Or are we just supposed to go?"

"I don't know. I think Tatyana is probably back on watch by now." Helen glanced towards the royal house. It was so strange. There had never before in the history of Eldirad been two companies, exceptionally large companies at that, leaving with less than twenty-four hours' notice, or without a scheduled date of return. There had never even been one small one that she knew of.

"That's too bad. I had hoped she'd hang out the window and wave to us or something." He laughed, but it sounded a little strained.

Helen tried to smile. That wasn't something Tatyana would ever do. She couldn't really imagine it. She looked lovingly around the square, wondering when she would see it again—and when Elisabeth would call her and these goodbyes would be over.

Joseph went on talking about how much fun the long run would be, and how it was sort of a joke to fight shadows. "I heard they're just shadows. I've never tried to fight mine, but it doesn't seem to fight back." He pretended to stab at the long shadow cast by the rising sun and laughed.

Helen felt her stomach contract slightly. It was not so much what he was saying that felt like a lie. That was just silliness. No, it was his laughter that was the worst; nothing like his usual free and genuine good humor. It was a lie not so much to her as to himself. Her slight anger at his making light of something that had already killed drained away, and she pitied him. Somewhere, deep down, he was frightened. He just didn't want to face it, or maybe couldn't. She took his hand and tried hard to make her voice light too. "You had better keep an eye out, and..." her feeble attempt at lightness melted and her voice was a touch husky. "Take care of Sebastian for me, will you?" She looked up into his silver-gray eyes.

He paled a little. "I promise." Then he smiled. "Of course I will, but he's usually the one to remind me what I did with my shoes, or where I put my head." He laughed, and it sounded even more forced than before.

Helen swallowed hard. Then she squeezed his hand. "Well, take care of yourself, too. Don't lose your head; I think you'll need it. And remember, whatever you may think, he needs you."

Joseph smiled. "I'll do my best. Stars protect you, Helen. Save me a dance at the Midwinter ball, will you?"

"Sure," she found herself saying, although her heart felt heavy. She knew she wouldn't see him at Midwinter.

He waved and then was off gathering his warriors.

Edward climbed the steps to the royal porch and everyone went quiet. He was dressed for battle in boots and mail, with the royal star glinting at the center of his seven stars of a guardian. His clothes were stained with mud and some kind of black substance, and Helen knew him well enough to see that he was pale, tired, and strained, but he stood erect and strong as he faced them. "My dear people. The threat we feared did indeed come in the night, but we were mustered to face it. We have many sick and wounded, but Elder Queen Josephine has been in the hospital all night while Princess Tatyana and I have lead the fight at the river and I will join her there now for a time. The line is holding, and the wall will soon be finished. The city is strong. You must not fear for us here. You are still needed where you have been assigned, and I hope you will all go forth with hope and determination. May the Stars protect you and the fates blow fair and bring us all together again before too long. For now: Go, and be quick. My blessing goes with you."

Every warrior bowed his or her head a little. Then Joseph and Elisabeth gave the word to go. They walked together out of the square but then parted to go out the north and south gates respectively. It was better not to go by the fighting on the east side.

Helen lingered near the back and watched as Joseph led his company off. She hoped he would be all right. He was a good man, loyal, brave, and good-natured, but his captainship had always seemed a little like a joke. He had passed the tests, his company liked him, and he had never been mean to anyone or done anything wrong, so he couldn't have his star removed. His company liked him because he was lax about order and funny and organized fun things, but the other captains didn't respect him. He was good at acting and orchestrating people, and soldiery had always been a lot like acting—but could he handle it in the real world? Was he strong enough for what was to come? Would he ever learn to take things seriously? She prayed he would for Sebastian's sake, and his own.

She turned to follow Elisabeth south. At the gate, the whole company broke into a trot. She looked over her shoulder after a while and she could see people fighting hard all along the riverbank near the city, but the battleground was still in the shade of the eastern forest, and from this distance she couldn't make out the enemy other than a dark movement. She was worried about her home, her family, and Tatyana, Edward, Clara, and all the people she was leaving. But she turned her head to the south and didn't look back again.

After about two hours of trotting along, they came to the ten-mile rest station, a simple rain shelter building where travelers could rest, or even spend the night if they wished to. There, they took a half hour break. Then they went on. When the sun was about an hour from noon, they came in sight of Aldor.

Aldor, being a trade town and closer to the border, had always had a wall. It was not a high one but rose about six feet around the town with all its houses and gardens. There were a few small fields inside the wall, but, unlike at Obrin, where the ancient village wall as well as the tower wall enclosed fields, most of the fields were outside. Now those fields were empty save for a few squash and late vegetables that looked strangely sickly on the side near the river. That worried Helen. Aldor was a mixed town, and there should have been more than enough Efrim farmers with the magic gift for plants to prevent anything like that, or to heal it, and yet no one was out tending the fields or harvesting the crops.

The warriors slowed as they approached the town. Everything was eerily silent. No birds sang in the forest across the river, or in the bushes, or the meadow to the west. No insects chirped. There were no sounds from the town either. Even Elisabeth began to notice this and felt a little uneasy. She lagged behind her people as they neared the town, keeping to the river side and keeping her eyes out. She thought she saw something move.

"Pick up your pace. Run to the town!" she shouted to the others. "I'm going to be rear guard. I think I've sighted the enemy."

Elisabeth stopped. She was a little tired, and it took a minute to quiet her breath. Even then she could hear nothing, but she could see something moving in the bushes. Then it stepped out. There were several of them. They were perhaps five feet tall, and even in bright daylight she could discern no features. The things didn't seem to have eyes or, well, anything. They were shaped like men wearing long hooded cloaks that blended with their bodies. They were as black as anything could be, and yet the sun shining from behind them made them a little translucent. Elisabeth could just make out the bush behind the nearest one.

She noticed all this in a moment as she drew her sword. A dark arrow flew from the bush, and she ducked and ran towards them. Another dark arrow hit her boot, and she ducked a third before she was close enough. Then they sent cords at her. One seemed about to shoot another arrow when there was a faint sound from behind Elisabeth and a pale wooden arrow with a white feather pierced right through the being and stuck in a tree. The being went up in a puff of black smoke, and with a swing of her sword Elisabeth sliced the others. They went up in smoke, too, leaving only a small amount of a slippery residue on her blade. She turned to see Helen holding her bow.

"I didn't need help," Elisabeth said as she joined her.

"Suit yourself, but it was our first encounter. Anyway, I think we had better report and get the news before we begin fighting."

"Naturally, but I'm not waiting when they're coming up behind us."

"Fine. Let's go." Helen started at a good pace for the gate.

A young woman of mostly Efrim appearance, with very anxious blue eyes, was guarding the gate. She seemed very pleased to see them. "Lady Elisabeth. We're so glad you're here. We're all quite worried and, well, the soldiers from the south fort have been here the last two days, but still... the awful things are getting in. They have killed animals and trees, even in town, and we hardly dare let children outdoors—"

"Don't worry, lady," Elisabeth said with a smile. "We'll get things under control soon."

"Thank you so much. The warriors are taking over the hotel. We've been moving beds around and converting it into a barracks for the last couple days. That's where you will find most of the southern guard."

Elisabeth nodded, thanked the woman, and headed for the hotel. She knew the place well. It was an elegant white stone building near the central square of the town. It had large bunk rooms that the southern guard used when they stopped for the night on the way to the guard station. Sometimes the eastern forest guard would stop a night there too. The rest of the time, those rooms and the private rooms on the third and fourth floors were just for travelers. That meant ambassadors going both ways from Ikkik in the south, and mostly merchants and craftspeople coming to sell their wares at the large markets of Aldor.

As Elisabeth walked towards the inn with Helen beside her, she looked around the town. She had passed through it many times and had come a few times to stay a couple days with her father when he brought smith work to trade for foreign goods such as silk, chocolate, sugar, salt, and spices. It had always been a bustling town, full of noise and color. By this time of the day the markets should be crowded. There should be music in the streets, and people. She watched as a lone woman of middle age walked down the lane with a basket over her arm. No children laughed. It made her feel more uneasy, but, she told herself, here was a town that really needed saving.

The Efrim way was that everything should be beautiful, and in nearly all cases that idea had replaced the spare simplicity of the old Eldir way. The common room they entered was lined with shining wooden tables and chairs; there were paintings on the walls and crystal chandeliers hung from the ceiling. The tables were laden, and the room was crowded with men and women from Margaret's border guard troop as well as those who had come with Elisabeth. The dozen men and women in blue aprons who were serving had clearly expected the newcomers for lunch, and Elisabeth was glad. The food looked very good, and it had been a long run and a long time since breakfast.

She and Helen were only just in the door when a woman came up to them. This time, however, she only glanced at Elisabeth's stars before fixing on Helen's single silver captain's star and the little pink flower that designated a healer.

"Are you Lady Helen?" The woman's voice was anxious and eager.

"Yes. What do you wish?" Helen said gravely.

"Thank the Stars. I heard a rumor you were coming with the troop. We have all heard of your skill. Please, my daughter is very ill. Something happened three days ago. It was the middle of the day, but she was outside near the river. There was a bit of an odd mist, her friends said, but there is no wound or anything; still, she is so ill she doesn't know me, and so cold... Oh, please come, lady."

Helen's face was pale and grim. "I will come, but I can't promise anything. I have heard a little about this strange new sickness, but very little, and I haven't seen a patient." She wondered if this was like the sickness Aranin had described from the soldier's wound. It sounded related, but perhaps it was only an illness since it came without an injury. She kicked herself for not going to the hospital to talk to Josephine before they left, but it wasn't until she woke up that she knew the attack had hit, and when Edward had said there were wounded in the hospital there had been no time to go talk to her about it. She turned and followed the woman out of the room, thinking hard about what medicine might be best to try.

Elisabeth felt slightly annoyed that people were happier to see Helen, but she turned for the stairs without saying anything. She would put her pack away and then she would get some of that lunch.

She had only climbed two steps before a girl's voice called, "Lady Elisabeth?"

She turned. The girl was only about thirteen years old, slender, with large dark gray eyes. It was Margaret's second daughter who sometimes went to the fort with her as the older children of warriors often did. She must have been there when the warriors were called back.

"What is it?" Elisabeth asked, coming down a step.

"My mother, Lady Margaret, would like to see you as soon as possible, lady." She gave a little bow.

"I'll come right now." Elisabeth smiled and nodded to the girl. The sooner she got the information the better.

"Follow me please, then," the girl said with another dignified little bow. "They have made a guardian's room, a sort of office, out of the old hotel office. Just over here." She led the way to a polished dark wood door at the far end of the room. She knocked twice, then opened the door and ushered Elisabeth into a small, cozy room. There were two large windows with curtains looking out into a barren garden, a crackling fire with two comfortable chairs, a desk, and a single cot. Margaret sat at the desk but turned and looked up when they entered. Her face was strangely pale and there were dark circles under her eyes. She smiled at the girl. "Please leave us, Mary."

Mary nodded and left the room and Elisabeth stood by the door looking at Margaret. Margaret didn't look at all like the strong, confident guardian Elisabeth had always known.

"Sit down, Elisabeth," Margaret said in a tired voice. "I really am grateful you came so fast."

Elisabeth let herself drop into one of the easy chairs. She was tired after the long run and really would have liked some lunch. "Edward asked me yesterday, and of course we came as soon as we could. What can you tell me about how things stand?"

Margaret stood slowly with one hand on the back of her chair and moved over to sit in the easy chair opposite Elisabeth, near the hearth. Her face seemed even more tired, and when she spoke, her usually strong voice was faint and trembled slightly. "I don't know what to say." Her voice broke and she paused, looking into the fire. Then she took a deep breath and went on: "Day before yesterday dawned like any other day at the southern fort this time of year, fine, clear, colored leaves on the trees," her voice seemed a little lost or dazed. "Then we got a bird from Aldor that something had been killing animals the night before. Some were taken, with great sign of the animals having run frightened as from some large beast, but not a single track of anything that shouldn't have been there. The farmer showed it to me when we got here. The bird itself was in quite a state, talking about terrible blackness that crept up on bird and beast so that the birds were fleeing the forest. It also said that only an hour before, several strange, shadowy shapes had been seen by some youths by the river and one of them had fallen ill.

"I admit I was pretty disturbed, but I called all the south guard and we rode for Aldor at once." Her voice dropped to hardly more than a whisper, and her hands were clasped tight on her knees. "A huge troop of the things attacked us on the road in the afternoon. They are... they are... have you seen them?"

"I saw a couple on the road near the city, and I heard stories about them from some of the warriors of Eldirad this morning. They attacked the city last night."

"Is everything all right there?" Margaret looked up, her eyes large and scared.

"Seemed like Edward and Tatyana have it under control, but some of the warriors I talked to coming in from Edward's watch were pretty frightened."

"There is something about them," Margaret quavered. "A fear and dread that hangs about them, and when someone kills them, the black mist can make people's vision go dark or make them see their worst nightmares—images of friends and family being destroyed or burning, and whatever creatures they fear most. It's horrible." Margaret shuddered and looked down at her hands.

Elisabeth hadn't noticed anything of the kind when she killed the Shadows on the way, but she felt she must trust Margaret. Margaret looked like she had seen a ghost. "So, what happened next?" Elisabeth asked after a minute.

"The horses we had with us spooked badly. More than half our mounted warriors were thrown before they could dismount, and most of the horses ran off. I'm afraid I panicked. We ran towards the town, and fought with the things, and three of my people... fell. Many more were injured, and there are these cords the beings wield that are strong and cold and wrap around you. When cut they turn to smoke, but they cannot be broken in any other way, and they are strong enough to drag a warrior off their feet. Worst of all, in most cases, for most people, and if they remain more than a second, they leave the limb numb and useless, and so cold..." She rubbed her leg. "We got to the town late in the day, and yesterday morning I was at my wits' end. So, I sent the message to

Edward. We have tried to defend the city. They are coming mostly out of the forest across the river, but they had come into the town, over the wall, and were poisoning trees and killing animals. The people hardly dare leave their houses, and one house near the river had the windows broken and everyone was killed." Her voice broke and she put her face in her hands. "Some of my people are trying to keep them off in turns, but it only half works during the day and not at all at night. I don't know what to do, Elisabeth. I can't do this. I've been a guardian twenty-three years, but I never had to do anything. I fought a little skirmish once. I thought that was something to be proud of. I won competitions... none of that matters. This is totally different. These things aren't like our neighbors. They don't have human emotions or needs. They don't even seem to want anything... They just destroy. Perhaps that is what they want, but they frighten me, and people have d—died." She sat silent for a moment and her shoulders shook; her breath was ragged and uneven.

Elisabeth sat watching her. She didn't know what to do. Margaret had been a guardian since she was a little girl; she had been skilled and respected as long as Elisabeth could remember. Elisabeth had spent much of her apprenticeship under her, as well as her time as a captain. Margaret had always been so strong and confident, good-natured and always in command. Seeing her like this frightened Elisabeth far more than the strange Shadows on the road. For the first time, she felt her confidence shaken. Sure, she had beaten Margaret in the tournament, but, as she said, that meant nothing. Not really. It was only play; there were rules, and people faced each other to attack at a word. They were all about equal, understood each other's commands, and knew each other's styles. Her stomach tightened and her face hardened. What if she couldn't do this either? What if it would break her like it had Margaret?

No! She couldn't even think that! She felt her cheeks flush with anger. She had innate power. She had felt none of the fear Margaret spoke of when she saw the Shadows. She knew she had been a difficult child not only because she was different from her family, outgoing and ambitious in a way none of them were, more active and energetic and less inclined to fine arts. She was very powerful; that had been difficult for her parents, and far more so for her teachers. That innate power had better come in useful now.

"Where are your warriors holding the defense?" Elisabeth asked briskly.

"Some are at the river's edge, some at the wall," Margaret said weakly, struggling to steady her breath.

Elisabeth thought fast. At the river's edge there was no protection. The trees had all dropped their leaves early, perhaps due to the Shadows, so there wasn't even much cover. The wall was best, but it was not a wall meant to be used for battle. It was sturdy enough, but there were no battlements, no walkway with a parapet on which warriors could stand, and it was only six feet tall. Most Eldir men could look over it, at least on their tiptoes. "What sort of defenses do you have at the wall?"

"We patrol it. I had some walk on top with bows, but many were knocked off and one was killed, so we mostly stand in front of it." Margaret sniffed. "The defenses are a mess, I know it. I can't do this, Elisabeth." She began fumbling with the stars on her mail vest with trembling fingers.

"Edward assigned me in charge, sort of like princess of Aldor, in top command until the end of the threat, so you don't have to worry about it anymore." Then Elisabeth noticed what Margaret was doing. "You don't have to take off your stars; you can still be my guardian."

"No," Margaret's voice was still weak, but firm. "I can't. I know my limit. I won't give up. I'm not a coward." Her face hardened and she looked up, although tears still streaked her cheeks and glistened in her eyes. "But I can't lead against these things." She unpinned the last star and set in on the mantelpiece. Then she rose and knelt awkwardly. "I will serve you as well as I am able, Lady Elisabeth."

Elisabeth stood and took Margaret's hand, helping her to her feet. She felt very strange. "I thank you for your service," she said a touch uncertainly. "If you ever wish to advise me, I will listen."

"It is unlikely." Margaret moved away from the fire with a heavy limping step and picked up a few small things, which she put in a pack and slung over her shoulder. "This room is yours now," she said with a faint smile.

"Do you need help? You look injured."

"I'm all right, lady. I hurt my knee a little when my horse threw me, but I'm mostly bruised. I got one of those cold lashes on my leg, and it still feels a little tingly, but it is better." She gave a slight nod and limped out of the room.

Elisabeth stood still in the middle of the room for a minute. She no longer had any desire for lunch. Her heartbeat had quickened, and she couldn't stand still. She went to the desk and wrote a quick note to the stonecutters of Efrim, ordering several large carts of stone and promising bodyguards for the cart drivers to Aldor and back. She wrote another note to Edward, telling him she had arrived and was taking things in hand and that she was commissioning the modifying of the wall into a proper defensive battlement. Then she went to the window and whistled. She had to do so for quite some time before a mockingbird flew down. It landed on the open sill but seemed nervous and agitated.

"Will you take these letters?" she whistled to the bird. *"The first is for Silver-badger and the second for the group of men in the hills north of the valley who cut stone into pieces."* Since birds could not translate names, when a child who studied the bird tongue came to apprentice age he or she was given a name by the birds, usually something insightful and related to the natural world, since that was what the birds had words for.

"I'll take it. Fire-falcon, but I don't think I'll be coming back. We are all getting as far from the forest as we can. It is not a place for any honest bird to live anymore."

"I will see what I can do to help that." Elisabeth tied the two letters carefully to the bird's back like little backpacks.

"I do hope so," it twittered. *"May the wind carry you far."* With that, it flew away.

It worried Elisabeth that the birds were going. Even more than the serious problem of not having them to take messages, they were an indication of how dangerous the forest actually was. Elisabeth turned and went into the main room to divide her people into watches. She would go out with the first watch to set up an organized defense outside the wall.

✶ ✶ ✶ ✶ ✶ ✶

Three days later she sent twenty warriors back, and in the afternoon they returned, guarding the Efrim stonecutters' carts. Donkeys were pulling them, with blinders on, but there had still been one scare when a cart started to run away. There had been fighting on the road. There were only two stonecutters, and they were in a hurry to get home. So a new company of guards was sent with them the very next morning. Apparently, wall building was in fever pitch at Efrim, too, and they were needed. Luckily, there were a couple masons in Aldor, and many strong and willing hands. It took a lot of hard fighting to hold the land beyond the wall, and many warriors fell ill, or were wounded or killed, over the next month, but at last, with the civilians working on it day and night, the wall was finished. After that, the warriors settled down to defend their new wall. The two watches on six-hour shifts, much like in Eldirad, had been established from the beginning, and Elisabeth led one while Helen came to be in charge of the other, although she was not the only captain.

Chapter 8

Midwinter at Westtower

22-23 December (Efrian New Year's Eve), YA 1123/24

Westtower

THE WIND WAS bitter from the north, and it stung Sebastian's nose and whipped his hair into his face as he leaned on the parapet of the outer wall and peered into the dusk. He thought he saw something move. He put his hand to his bow. Then he stopped. It was just a fox hunting in the scrubland beyond the western borders of Obrin. In the two months since his father had sent reinforcements to triple the size of the garrison at Westtower, and commanded everyone to be on alert, nothing much had happened. The letters Tatyana wrote him weekly were mostly filled with news of the war. The Eldirad wall had been finished in two weeks, and the warriors had given up the trenches by the river and retreated to the wall. The outer fields were already empty anyway, but small companies of warriors were assigned to protect flocks of sheep and herds of cattle that were taken to graze outside the wall.

Tatyana sounded tired, and her writing looked tired. She had spoken less lately about the actual fighting, but it had been more evident reading between the lines. She was discouraged, and worn out with long watches in the hospital along with her time on the wall. He wished he could help her. From all accounts, his parents were doing all right. His father wrote little, and his grandmother not at all. Tatyana said they were too busy and tired. Josephine spent all her time in the hospital. Clara mostly wrote asking how he was doing and about things in Obrin. That seemed pretty unimportant to Sebastian. His family was fighting what was clearly the battle of their lives, or his father and sister were anyway, and his mother appeared to be working almost as hard as his grandmother in the hospital, and he was stuck here doing nothing. He worried about them, and looked at them sometimes in the magic mirror in the lookout room at the top of the tower.

The Prince's Mirror of Westtower was a one-of-a-kind magical treasure made by a great craftsman four hundred years ago for his son who was prince of Westtower then. It only enabled you to look at a person, not touch or talk to them as you could if you sent your spirit out with the Sight, but you didn't need to have the Sight gift to use it, and you could look at people to whom you only had a weak connection. Sebastian did have the Sight, but it wasn't as strong as his sister's. He had Receiving level, meaning he could feel when someone was in danger and he could hear another person speak with the Sight, but he could not send out his spirit. The mirror took power, too, and shouldn't be used constantly, but at least he could see them. Things seemed very bad in Eldirad. They looked more tired, and the prospect looked grimmer even than what he read between the lines of Tatyana's letters.

He knew it was his duty to stay at Westtower. As prince of Westtower he must keep guard over the people of Obrin, but he had begged his father to let him send the reinforcements back. All these warriors were just sitting here doing nothing but worrying about their families back in Eldirad, eating the tower's provisions that were meant for far fewer, crowding the dorms, and being of no use to anyone. But Edward had flatly refused. He said the attack could come there any time, and, if it struck as it had at Eldirad, bringing troops the fifty miles from the capital would take too long.

So, they stayed. Sebastian had been staring out like this night after night for two months; no wonder he thought he saw things when he didn't.

Behind him he could hear the sound of laughter and of flutes and violins. The Midwinter festivities were in full swing down behind the wall. Sometimes he wished he hadn't been born a prince. Here he was in Obrin, alone on a wall. His family was all in Eldirad, and his friends, besides Joseph, were in Aldor or Efrim. He was really glad Joseph had come with the reinforcements. He had never liked being parted from his best friend, and it would have been terribly lonely without him during the period of tension with no traveling back and forth. He still wished Helen had come with him. He could see her point. There wasn't another person he could think of who was little enough daunted by Elisabeth to be her right hand in a serious emergency, and that's what she thought her dreams had told her... Still, there was a part of him that couldn't help feeling hurt and a little abandoned. He only had one captain besides Joseph. There was no reason a reinforcement troop of three hundred warriors, if it really had to come at all, couldn't have come with two captains.

He had looked in the mirror for Helen a couple times. He had seen her fighting on the Aldor wall, asleep in a small dim room with a desk, and once tending a wounded warrior. He hadn't been able to tell what was wrong with the person, but Helen had looked very worried. He remembered last Midwinter when she had ridden in with the snow the night before and they had spent a week together. That had been heaven. Last year, there had been no danger to worry about. No one had kept guard. The nomadic raiders from the neighboring lands that the guard tower had been built to keep out would never come out on a cold winter night, but the Shadows apparently would. He had heard as much from Tatyana anyway.

He wondered what Midwinter was like for Helen tonight, but he couldn't look in the mirror until he was off watch.

He wondered if there were still Midwinter festivals in Efrim. The last time he had looked at Aranin in the mirror he had been dragging big, heavy water buckets to a bleak camp. It didn't look like there was going to be much cheer there, but Analisia might have a party. He missed them both, especially Aranin, and hoped he would get a letter from him soon.

Sebastian sighed. Of course, most of the warriors with him were far from their families, too. They had been stuck here longer than they expected. It was custom for a new guard to come to Westtower every two weeks so the men and women could go home to their families, but no replacement had come, and Father had written saying that he couldn't spare troops even long enough to rotate, but at least Sebastian's warriors were down behind the wall, out of the wind, celebrating, and many of them had family with them who were also in the force. Technically there were supposed to be twenty on guard at once these days, but since nothing had happened Sebastian hadn't had the heart to make his warriors miss the festivities. He had decided no more than one guard was needed on this night, and of course, as the prince, that unpleasant job was his. He sighed and tried to tuck the flying wisps of his raven hair into his hood.

"Sebastian!"

It was Joseph's voice. Sebastian looked and saw Joseph coming towards him wrapped in his heavy wool cloak. A lantern of shimmering crystal lit with a candle flame cast a dancing many-colored light across the dark parapet and showed that he carried a large silver tray in his other hand.

"What do you have there?"

"A bit of cheer for a lonely friend." Joseph came close and set the tray on the wide edge of the parapet. "I brought our suppers up, and some hot spiced cider. Careful, don't bump it, the mugs are full."

"Thank you. It smells wonderful. Almost like home."

"I can't leave my friend up here all alone while everyone down there is feasting and dancing. You deserve your share too."

"Thank you, I am glad you're here this year, though I suppose that's selfish. You should have been home with Jane by now."

"I miss her, and the Midwinter play festival... She keeps telling me I should come home, but she isn't making fun of guard duty anymore. Anyway, I couldn't leave you out here all alone, could I?" He smiled and jumped up to sit on the low spot in the parapet. He held up his mug of cider. "Toast to a new year where even princes have time to go home and visit their families."

"Sounds too good to be true, but I'll drink to it." Sebastian lifted his mug and tapped his friend's, then took a sip of the warm, spicy liquid. If he closed his eyes, he could almost imagine that he was in the town square at home with all his friends and family, dancing under glittering lanterns, or in the great ballroom smelling of pine and cider and glowing with lamps.

"I have mail for you. A letter from your family in Eldirad came in this evening. It's got all five of their names on it, so I'm guessing it's a Midwinter's day letter, and there's one from Aranin too."

"Thank you again." Sebastian eagerly took the fat envelope. He looked at the spidery writing, the hands of his family each adding their own name. He tucked it safely away in his tunic beneath his mail vest. He took the thin letter from Aranin and glanced at it in the dim light. Even the address didn't seem quite as elegant and perfect as Aranin's usual script. The loops and curls were a little sloppier. Things must be rough, but he was so glad to have a letter. He would open them later in his room where the light was better. "Nothing from Helen, I suppose?"

"No. Jane wrote that things have been pretty bad along the Silver River. There is no mail passing between Aldor and Eldirad, no news at all. The birds are too scared to be seen."

Sebastian bit his lip. He hated to think of not knowing what was happening. Glimpses in the magic mirror were not the same. Nothing like a good letter. Besides, he wanted her to get the ones he had sent.

* * * ✱ * * *

Half an hour later, the plates of ham, beets, onions, and potatoes were empty, and the last drops of cider were cold. They were both sitting on the battlements, looking out over the scrubby land, and talking about a Midwinter when they were still in their teens and they had staged a short comedy on the palace porch with Helen, Tatyana, Jane, Elisabeth, and Clarissa.

"Prince Sebastian!" It was a woman's voice, high and clear.

Sebastian swung his legs hastily over the stonework and jumped down to the walkway. He knew he really shouldn't sit up there. Somehow it didn't seem to matter when it was just him and Joseph, but he hated to be caught by anyone else. "What is it?"

The lady stood at the top of the stairs shimmering in a blue silk dress and a velvet cloak embroidered with jewels. "An old woman has come over from the village asking if the prince will be so kind as to come and do some sort of ceremony. Something about grain and fire and good crops next year. She stopped me just as I was clearing away the last of the feast, and I told her I would run and ask you. I know you are busy up here, and it is ever so kind of you to stay up here in the cold while the rest of us have fun." She looked suddenly less gay and a little ashamed.

Sebastian smiled a little. It was nice to be appreciated. He looked for a moment at the tedious scrub brush, with a few trees scattered at the edge of the forest. He and his people had watched these same tiresome bushes day and night for two months. He had spent the better part of every night peering into the shadows, trying to see something he had never seen in real life and had been told looked like just another shadow. A couple glimpses in the mirror and one dream did little to make the concept clearer. In all those long nights, nothing had happened. Surely he could leave the post for twenty minutes, just get a little taste of the celebrations. How could he let down the Obrin people? He was their prince, and they wanted him... but he had promised his father he would never leave the wall unguarded.

"Go ahead. Whatever this ritual is it must be important to them that you come. Anyway, you deserve to get a little fun tonight. You can't hog all the drudgery just because you're the prince. I'll watch for a while, and you can enjoy yourself." Joseph smiled and put a hand on Sebastian's shoulder.

"I mean, if you're sure you don't mind... Hogging the drudgery, you certainly have a different way of putting things. You're sure you'll be all right? You haven't been drinking or anything..."

"Nah, not tonight, a little hot cider doesn't count. I'd rather dance. But I don't mind a bit holding the wall for you for a little while. I'll keep as sober and sharp an eye on those plotting bushes as anyone could want." He jumped down from the wall and stood very straight looking out. "None of those stones are going to get away with anything."

Sebastian laughed. "Thank you. You can tell her I'm coming if you would be so kind, Karen."

"Certainly." She smiled, bright and gay again. Then she turned and ran down the stairs with her skirts trailing after her.

"It's a ritual to their harvest god. They throw grain on the bonfire that they have burning over there, and they believe it will help ensure a good harvest next year. They like to have the prince do it. I have done it the last two years." Sebastian looked at Joseph. "You aren't dressed for fighting. Do you even have your mail on?"

"No. Nor does anyone. Mail and party clothes don't go well together." He opened his cloak and looked down at the embroidered light blue top beneath. "I'll change if you think I should."

Sebastian thought for a minute. It seemed silly to ask him to change out of his party clothes into the woolen tunic and mail vest of a sentry when he would only be on duty for half an hour at the most. He opened his mouth to say no. Then he felt an uncomfortable twinge deep down. He could not do this. It was wrong to leave a man on duty in just a flimsy silken tunic. "I know it seems foolish, but I think you had better do it. I just can't leave you without it."

"All right, I won't be half no time. Though goodness knows I was in as much danger sitting here with you as I will be alone." He didn't wait for a response but ran down the stairs.

Sebastian turned his eyes reluctantly back to the dark scrub. He knew Joseph was right, and they shouldn't have been sitting on the wall in full view, but it was so hard to be good all the time. He couldn't make himself fully believe in a threat that had shown no signs of coming in two months. He couldn't wait to get away from this pointless post. Only a few moments later, he heard feet running up the stairs and heavy breathing. He looked up and saw that Joseph had returned. He still wore his gray silk trousers and low shoes, but the fancy tunic had been replaced by an old brown wool one, with his mail vest over it, and a leather belt and sword. Over his arm he carried a folded burgundy cloak embroidered with crystal lilies and a slender silver circlet.

"I don't suppose you will want to take the time to change yourself, but I figure you should at least wear your crown and your good cloak if you are going to officiate as the prince at their festival."

"You're right. I won't keep her waiting long enough to change, but this will do. If I keep the cloak around me most of the time, they won't see I'm wearing a plain wool tunic."

"Don't worry about it. You're a prince whatever you wear, I just thought you might like to dress up a bit."

"Thank you. I do want to." Sebastian unclasped the wooden pin at the throat of his dark gray cloak and lay it aside, pinning the fancy one with his Golden Lily pin, the sign of the prince. He put the circlet in his dark hair. "Is it straight?"

"You look great. Now have fun."

"I will. Thank you." Sebastian turned and ran down the stairs with a new energy in his step. Down behind the wall, lanterns glittered in the bare apple trees and something like fifty couples were dancing to a rollicking tune played by a flute and two fiddlers sitting on the porch of the little house that Sebastian was currently sharing with ten others. A pot of cider bubbled over a small fire and several more people were standing around it. Some of them waved at him as he passed. He spotted the Obrin woman waiting at the edge of the circle of light. Easily a head shorter than any of his people, she was watching the dancing with a pleasant expression on her wrinkled face. A thick white woolen shawl was wrapped around her shoulders over a soft brown dress. Sebastian stopped before her and bowed his head a little. *I am at your service, madam,"* he said in Obrinish.

"Thank you so much, Your Highness. I'm sorry to take you away from this gay party, but we really appreciate your coming to join in our little celebration."

"I'm always glad to come." He paused and glanced back at the festivities and the wall beyond, and decided not to tell her that he had been stuck up on the wall watching for dangers that were rumored to be coming. He had already told the people to keep an eye out, especially when traveling or working in the forest, but he didn't want to make them worry, especially on a night like this.

She turned toward the village. A short farm road paved with gray cobbles led past the snowy fields and into the center of the village beyond. Singing could be heard, and the strains of a silver flute. He followed the woman into the village square where a great fire blazed. The air close to it was hot and the snow was melting and dripping off the slate of the nearby roofs. The warmth felt good, and he held out his stiff, cold fingers eagerly to the blaze. His cheeks and nose tingled in the heat.

All the people stopped what they were doing and turned toward him when he appeared. They all bowed or curtsied, and many voices called, *"Welcome to our fire, Your Highness."*

Sebastian smiled and gave a little bow. These people had a very different idea of royalty than his own. It was mildly amusing, but it was also rather fun to be made much of, especially after so many hours alone on the wall. *"Thank you, all. I will gladly use any power I have to bless your harvest and your coming year, as well as to protect it."* A very pretty young woman with brown eyes and brown curls brought him a jeweled silver bowl filled with grain. He took it with a smile. He remembered how confused he had been the first time he did this two years ago. They had to explain everything, and he had been quite embarrassed. Now he knew just what to say. He dipped his right hand into the bowl and scattered a handful of grain on the fire. *"With this grain from our harvest I give thanks for the bounty we have reaped from our land and the health and prosperity we have enjoyed in the past year, and I give my solemn prayer with all my people that next year will continue in prosperity and fertility."* As he spoke, he had strewn the rest of the grain onto the fire, and a smell a little like bread wafted up on the smoke.

He handed the bowl back to the young woman. A middle-aged man came up beside him and invited him to stay a little while and have a mug of ale with them, and a woman offered him a slice of some kind of warm spice bread that smelled very good. He was just about to take a piece of the bread when he heard something. It was faint, and no one else seemed to hear it. It may have been inside his head, but it felt—or sounded, he was not sure which—like a call for help. A sudden cold chill ran down his back, and his heart choked him. He hardly believed it, didn't want to believe it, but the feeling was undeniable. He set the bread back down on the plate. *"I sorry, madam. I have to go. I think hear something. Feel something. Danger."*

She looked at him with wide, startled eyes. His voice was now tight, his Obrinish grammar failing, and his Efrian accent thicker. His face had set hard in his effort not to show fear. *"What ever is the matter, Highness?"*

"I am sorry. I can no tell now you. No time. I do not know, not exactly... I to tell you all it tomorrow. Thank you for inviting me. Enjoy your evening." He tried to keep his voice calm and struggled to think of the right words,

which usually came easily. He couldn't help talking very fast as he made his way through the crowd towards the street out of the square. When he came to the edge, he gave a little bow and then walked off. As soon as he was out of sight he ran as fast as he could. His crown fell off, but he hardly noticed. As he approached the tower he heard shouts from the wall, urgent, commanding, and some shrieks that sounded frightened or like someone in pain. The music was gone. The dancing area was deserted and the door to the tower hung open. He didn't pause a moment but dashed up the stone steps.

The top of the wall, so quiet for so long, was a whirl of activity. Black coils of rope were flying up and catching the wall in huge numbers and people were hacking at them frantically. Some had swords while others, apparently caught up in haste, wielded spoons, knives, or sticks. A black arrow whizzed out of the night, and he ducked out of the way only just in time.

"Keep low, everyone! Keep low, you hear me? Don't make yourself a target! Doesn't anyone have a bow? Anyone?" The voice was commanding, but there was an edge of desperation in it. Sebastian looked towards it and saw Sarah, a fine captain five years older than him. She was wearing a dreadfully conspicuous dress of pale turquoise silk that was torn in the front. In one hand she held her sword, with which she was fighting with a creature that seemed to be creeping over the edge of the wall. As he watched, she stabbed it and it vanished in a puff of black smoke that set several people nearby rubbing their eyes and stumbling as if unsteady. For a moment his blood ran cold. The attack had come, and after all those nights of watching it had come on the one night they were not prepared! He hesitated for a moment; what was best to be done? Then he turned and ran back downstairs and in through the open door at the base of the tower. On the kitchen wall by the door hung all the swords and bows that people had neglected to collect. Moving so fast that his fingers tumbled over each other, he put twenty-five quivers over his shoulders and filled his arms with as many swords and bows as he could carry. Then he rushed back out into the night and up the stairs.

"Listen up, everyone!" he shouted, "I'm coming down the wall with weapons. I'm going to give them out and I'm going to organize you. Please go where I put you." With that he rushed forward into the mass of people on the northern section of the wall. Many looked dazed, staggered, or rubbed their eyes, and these he pushed down against the back wall of the rampart where they would be out of arrow shot. He didn't know whether it was the effect of sudden fear, over-celebration, or some poison of the Shadows that made so many seem incapable, and he didn't have time to care. All those who seemed fit he handed weapons and pushed into a line so that nowhere were two people trying to fight in the same place. When he ran out of weapons he went to get more, and when he came to where the fighting stopped, he did the same thing to the south.

Once a young man caught him by the shoulder and begged, "Give me a sword, please, Sebastian."

Just by the frantic voice and the way the man clutched his shoulder as if it held him up, he knew there was something wrong with him and he was in no state to fight. "No, not now," Sebastian said and pushed him down roughly. There wasn't a second to lose.

When he had distributed the weapons, he took a place on the wall and set to work cutting the twisting black ropes that seemed to vanish in a puff of foul smoke when they were cut.

"Sebastian."

He glanced over to see that Sarah had left her place and was standing beside him. The stitching where her skirt met the bodice had come out, making it drag in the dirt, and it was torn in two places, showing the thick woolen leggings beneath. There was a spatter of blood on one sleeve. She looked a mess, but her face contradicted the rest of her appearance. It was controlled and grim, the face of a captain.

"What is it?" Sebastian looked quickly back to the enemy and cut a cord just before it wrapped around his left arm.

"Please let me take your place. There are many sick and wounded, and they need you. I promise I am in my right mind. I was taken by surprise, and there was such a crush of people trying to get swords that I was one of the last up here. Then it was chaos, as you saw, and I panicked a little. I can lead them now." He thought there was a touch of shame in her voice.

"I don't doubt it. I shouldn't have left, and I shouldn't have allowed everyone to dress up and party tonight. I am grateful to you for stepping up. But what happened to Joseph?" Sebastian nodded to the person next to him to move in a little to cover his place for a minute while he stepped back beside Sarah. "I left him in charge of my watch."

"He cried out, a terrible cry for help, and that was what set us running. As I said, by the time I had negotiated the flood of frantic people, and tripped on my confounded dress on the stairs, everything was much as you found it, only more chaotic, if that were possible. I have not seen him."

Sebastian pursed his lips as pain stabbed his heart like a knife. It was surely Joseph's cry for help that he had heard, whether with his ears or through the Sight. "I will gladly put you in charge, but not in that. You can't lead when you are tripping over your torn skirts. Run down and change as fast as you can, and I will give you my post as soon as you return."

"Yes, sir." She turned and, laying her sword against the wall, ran for the stairs with the torn skirt bundled in her arms.

Sebastian stepped back into his place only just in time to see a creature with more or less the form of a hooded man lift its head over the wall. While the man beside him was busy cutting the ropes of others, the creature lifted a hand and straight from it came something like a coil of shadow that seemed intent on wrapping itself around the poor man's neck. Sebastian cut it just in time, then swiped at the creature, which dodged and continually threw coils at him until he stabbed it full in the chest. It was the strangest feeling he had ever known, for the blade entered as easily as it would enter a fog and then, instead of falling dead, the creature vanished with a small puff of smoke, leaving only a touch of some shimmery liquid upon his blade.

Five minutes later, Sebastian heard Sarah again at his side. A quick glance showed that she was a warrior now, dressed in boots and trousers, a loose gray wool tunic, and her mail vest with the star of a captain. He let her slip into his place and turned to look at the people strewn all along the back wall of the rampart. Some still stood leaning against the wall, others sat against it, and some were sprawled upon the floor. He grabbed the shoulder of the nearest man who leaned against the wall with his head down on his hands.

"Sir?" The man raised his head a little so Sebastian could see his face. "James? What has happened to you? Are you wounded? Can you walk?"

"I think so." His voice was faint, and it wasn't clear which question he was answering. He tried to step away from the wall but kept one hand on it. He looked past Sebastian in a very disturbing way, and his free hand groped in the air.

"Can you see?"

"No."

Sebastian took the free arm firmly. "Let me help you down the stairs. There are a lot of people down and not a moment to lose. Come with me."

James said nothing, but he followed, leaning heavily on Sebastian's arm. Sebastian led him down the stairs and as far as the door to the tower. "Just stay here. You are in the kitchen. Sit tight while I get everyone else."

"I will." James groped for a chair.

Sebastian didn't wait, but turned and ran back up. The next person he found was an older man slumped against the wall and barely conscious. He wouldn't do more than grunt when Sebastian called his name, so Sebastian picked him up in his arms and staggered down the stairs. He deposited him on the floor of the kitchen and then went back to the wall at a run. And thus it went for the rest of the southern stretch of the wall. He grew steadily more frantic. There were so many, and whatever was wrong with them there was no time to lose. He called one other warrior to help him, and they worked feverishly. Many of those who could still stand seemed dazed and didn't have the sense to keep out of arrow shot, and those sprawled on the ground were in danger of being stepped on. He didn't take time to look for wounds, or even to look at their faces.

About the time they finished the southern stretch he almost ran into a woman standing in the door holding her arm. "Lilian, are you all right?" he panted. "Can you watch these people while I go look for the rest?"

"I'll keep an eye on them. I think I can even put on water for doctoring. I feel a little sick, and my right arm is as cold as ice, but otherwise I'm okay."

"Thanks." He turned and ran out of the room. The situation around to the north on the wall was much the same, and he kept moving faster. He carried two warriors down at a time; that many of them weighed more than he did didn't seem to matter tonight, although he sometimes staggered under their weight.

It was not more than half an hour later, though it felt much longer, when Sebastian stumbled into the crowded kitchen with the last unconscious victim. He was panting, his lungs ached, and his arms were shaking as he fell to his knees with the last person in his arms. "How... is it... going?" he panted as he set the man before the fire and looked around for Lilian. The man helping him had stayed on the wall.

"Not too bad," Lilian said. "The ones who were conscious I put over at the table there. I have heated water, but I can't pour it with one hand." Her face was deadly pale, and her good hand rested on the kitchen counter where she had arranged some eighty mugs for the people at the table. Her other hand hung at her side like a rag doll's.

"Make yourself a cup, too, and I will pour it. Then rest with the others and bathe your arm with a warm cloth. Thank you for helping."

He took up the large tea kettle and poured the herbal drinks. Then he looked with fear at the pile of people they had lain before the fire. He started counting them with a finger that still shook, and then he froze. There was Joseph, lying face down on the carpet in front of the hearth. His long brown hair tangled over his shoulders, his shining mail vest standing out so starkly from the others. For a moment Sebastian could neither swallow nor breathe. Of course he had known Joseph must be among the wounded, since he hadn't seen him. Perhaps that was the main reason he had been reluctant to look, but he couldn't believe it... couldn't bear it.

Chapter 9

Vigil

23 December (Efrian New Year's Eve) to 13 January, YA 1124

Westtower

IN A MOMENT, Sebastian was on his knees beside Joseph. He blinked back tears as he rolled Joseph over and smoothed the thick, dark brown hair from his white face. There were bits of the shimmering black substance on his breast, and red blood soaked through his tunic at the shoulder. Sebastian stripped off the mail vest, woolen tunic, and linen undershirt. The wound was in the front of Joseph's left shoulder just outside the mail. The puncture was over an inch deep, and half again as wide, and it was almost black with foul-smelling green slime oozing out of it, festering as if it had been left a week. The wound should not have been that serious, although he had lost blood, but his breath was shallow and his pulse scarcely detectable.

Why did they have to strike on the one night he had let the guard down? After so many long nights, why tonight? Why during just the twenty minutes he was away? The wretched creatures must have been watching them. Why had he left? Why under all the Stars had he left? He was the prince, the guardian. How could he? His best friend looked as though he was dying, and others might be too. He knew it might not have gone any better if he had been there, but at the very least it would

133

be him who was wounded and not Joseph. He couldn't bear it; he couldn't live without Joseph. He bit his lip so hard it bled, and two tears fell on his friend's unconscious face. Help me, help me! he thought. I can't do this. I can't let this happen!

* * * ★ * * *

Far away on the wall in Aldor, Helen was fitting an arrow into her bow. It was a bitter cold night, and there was very little in the whole town that would pass for a celebration of the holiday. She pulled back the string. Then a chill ran down her spine and she felt the urgent call of some great grief or misery. Her arrow went wild, and she stood stock still for a moment. In her mind she could hear the echo of Sebastian's voice calling for help. "I must go," she said in haste to the man beside her.

He didn't look at her, but nodded slightly, keeping his eyes fixed on the Shadow he was aiming for. She turned and ran, bow in hand, toward the nearest stairs. She ran down them and, laying her bow on the ground, she went to the wall. She leaned her forearms against it and put her head on her hands. Then she closed her eyes and concentrated.

* * ★ * * *

In the midst of his despair, Sebastian felt a hand on his shoulder. It was soft as a light breeze and as gentle as springtime, but it was firm. He closed his eyes and took a shaky breath. Then he wiped away the tears and stood up. He got the kettle of hot water and the healers' chest and began to clean the wound.

"Clean out the wounds, flush them no matter how small. They are poisoned. Use the normal antibiotics and disinfectants just in case of other infection in a bad one like this, but I'm afraid they do nothing to help the festering caused by the poison." He did not hear the words with his ears, but they came into his mind in Helen's voice and he knew that he was not alone.

The hands, which he could feel but not quite see, steadied his and guided him. He was a skilled healer; that was his business as a son of the royal house. He had the Healing gift, and he had trained many years with the great school in Eldirad. He was good at fixing minor wounds from the border skirmishes, and he had set bones and sewn up cuts from mining and farming accidents, but this was different. He had no experience with this kind of wound. Poison—a wound to the shoulder that could kill a man; this frightened him, and it helped to feel Helen's hands on his. Where he was a qualified healer, and quite good, she was exceptional. Besides, he was still trembling a little from the shock, and she was steady.

He washed out the wound several times and sterilized it, then bandaged it and moved on to the next victim. This person appeared untouched but was icy all over. He moved to the next. A woman with a cut on the outside of her shoulder. The cut was shallow and only a little blood came through her silken sleeve, but her arm and hand were cold as death—colder, for even if it were dead it would warm up so near the fire.

"Wash the wound, but for the cold there is nothing I know of. I have been trying everything. It seems to be directly linked to innate power, especially in those cases where there is no wound—although a person's innate power has everything to do with chance of recovery after a wound, too. I have found I can predict by looking into a person's eyes whether or not they are likely to fall to the blindness."

"What is it?" he whispered. "Many of my people are stumbling blind, besides those here unconscious."

"It is in the mist that comes from the Shadows when you kill them. There is poison in that, too. People who just get the blindness almost always recover in a day or two, and with mental preparation they may be able to face it the next time. It seems people can build up a resistance. The more powerful will never be troubled by it. The weakest, or least prepared, pass out and get the cold sickness. It is often deadly."

He found eight more people who were taken by the strange sickness without a wound, and two more with minor wounds. "Is there anything I can do that might help them? Besides try to get them warm?"

"A warming salve helps a little, and I'm using Elsinti and Farishti infusions for fever reducing. A fever often follows. Immune boosters don't seem to help much, but spells to address symptoms help a tiny bit. A general stimulant is probably the best. I vary between Seltan and Bernes, but it only helps a little."

Sebastian dug through his chest looking for the herbs Helen mentioned and gave some to those he had already passed over. Then he turned to the next patient. It was a young woman in a pink silk gown, and the whole front of the dress was soaked in blood. The wound was very deep. He took her hand, but there was no pulse; there was not the faintest of breath. He sat a minute looking at her with a lump in his throat. This was his fault.

"What happened?"

He heard Helen's voice, but this time wished he hadn't. He was ashamed. He knew she must be wondering why they were all in silly party clothes with no mail. "It's my fault," he whispered, hoping only Helen could hear him. He told her in a few words how he had let his people keep the festival, and about the ceremony at Obrin, and Joseph, and coming back to chaos. As he finished, his shame choked him again and he had to steady himself before pouring a spoon of medicine. What a fool Helen must think him. Why on earth had he been idiot enough to let the people dress up?

He felt her hands on his shoulders again and a kiss like the lightest touch of dew upon his cheek. "Don't be so hard on yourself. I didn't imagine you had peace all this fall. You were lucky."

He couldn't say anything. He thought of her so far away where there had been fighting like this for two months and all contact even with Eldirad had been cut off.

"Keep them warm, rub their limbs, and give them broth and tea if you can. I'm afraid only some will make it. Make sure everyone wears heavy tunics on the wall, two wouldn't hurt. The thick cloth isn't a guarantee, but it can stop all but the most direct hit. Look at the difference between the depth of Joseph's wound and that other woman's."

"I will never be this foolish again, but..." he looked at Joseph again. "I want to take it back."

"I know." Helen's voice was getting fainter. "I must go. If I talk more I'll get a headache, and I can't afford that. I'm on watch. I'll come again."

With that, she was gone. He was once again alone to do his duty, as he should have been in the first place. He was very grateful to her for coming, and he knew she would never tell about his foolishness or his weakness. He was glad to have her advice about the strange illness, although it didn't sound very hopeful.

✦ ✦ ✦ ✦ ✦ ✦ ✦

Helen came back to her body still leaning on the wall with the sound of fighting above her. Her hands were cold and there was a touch of a headache. She didn't move or look up.

Poor Joseph. She remembered his last words to her when they parted. "Save a dance for me at Midwinter." She had hardly thought about the holiday today, but this *was* Midwinter, and he... he would almost surely never dance again, or even wake to smile his sweet innocent smile. She tried to swallow, and two slow tears rolled down her cheeks. Her heart felt squeezed like metal in her father's forge. Joseph had never shown any innate power that she knew of, and it was a bad wound. None of her patients had survived a wound like that. Even a scratch was deadly, in spite of everything she tried to do, unless the person had a good deal of innate power. She knew Sebastian would do his best, and perhaps in a quiet moment she could use the Sight to help him, but she didn't want to think about the chances. Or how completely devastated Sebastian would be. It was many minutes before she could control the pain and steady her breathing enough to go back to her watch.

✦ ✦ ✦ ✦ ✦ ✦ ✦

137

Sebastian stood and looked at the group around the table. "Lilian, how are all of you doing over there?"

"A little better, I think. I don't feel so sick anymore, but I still can't move my fingers."

"I can see a little." The husky voice was Aron's. "What happened? The last thing I remember clearly, we were being attacked by something I could hardly see. Joseph was shouting to stop them before they scaled the wall. I was close beside him, and he was wounded and bleeding, but he was still fighting one of the creatures. I tried to come to his aid, but a thing like a cord came towards me. When I cut it, this black smoke came in my eyes and I couldn't see. There was this sense of terror in the mist as if death itself were chasing me." He shivered, then smiled very slowly. "I guess I got away."

"Thank the Stars, it seems you did." Sebastian stood up and crossed the room to the table. "Do you think you can get yourself upstairs to bed?"

"Yes, sir. I can see now, but tell me. What happened to Joseph?"

"His wound was poisoned," he said in a very low and slightly husky voice. "I don't know if he will live."

Aron nodded with tight lips. Then he stood unsteadily and made his way out of the room. Many from the table also stood and followed him. Sebastian helped the others upstairs and saw them all tucked into bed. Then he went back to the wounded and unconscious. He applied hot cloths to their faces and limbs and rubbed salve on them, and he gave them a little of the mild stimulants Helen had suggested.

When there seemed nothing more he could do, he went out and got the people on the wall to come down two or three at a time to have hot tea and biscuits and change their clothes while he took their place. Over the course of an hour, the force transitioned back into a properly attired army, and thus they fought on until dawn. Even though it had been after midnight when the attack began, that night seemed very long. The longest night of the year, to those on the wall around Obrin and Westtower, was the longest night of their lives.

When at last after eight o'clock in the morning the sky in the east at their backs finally began to pale and the sun kindled the clouds with gold and rose, Sebastian and his people welcomed daybreak with a gratitude they had never felt before. In the rising light hope began to rekindle in many hearts. The attack became less fierce, and the enemies were much easier to see and pick off with arrows before they came up under the warriors' noses. As the new year's sun broke the hazy eastern horizon, Sarah came close beside Sebastian.

"So, with this opens the new year," she said.

He followed her gaze for a moment to the east where the sun was turning the haze near the horizon to a fiery crimson. "Yes, the year begins with death and ill omen. May it not end so."

"May it not."

There was a pause. Then Sebastian looked at the warriors up and down the wall. "You take half... that would be about 175 I think, currently. Go get breakfast and a few hours' rest."

"Thank you. I will come to relieve you in three hours?"

"That sounds good. We may make the watches longer in time, but that will do for now."

Sarah and her warriors departed. Two more had suffered the blindness, and one more was wounded after the panic was over, but things had generally settled down. Sebastian did his best to give them the advice about mentally preparing to be strong against the dark, and it seemed to help. But he felt broken.

* ★ ★ ★ ★ ★ *

The next several weeks were the most wretched Sebastian had ever imagined, in fact, far worse than he ever could have imagined. Extensive precautions not to be visible above the battlements more than necessary, and to wear two layers of heavy clothing as well as mail, kept the number of wounded very low. However, people fell to the blindness caused by the black mist every night. Most of these cases were mild, and as Helen said, they were back on the wall in a day or two. The cases were much fewer than the first night, and most people did seem to get more or less used to it in time. It was an exercise of power to push the black fog and strange flickering images from their minds, and it could become second nature if one had the innate power. A few weaker individuals got it again and again and, in time, were assigned to cooking and laundry duty. A messenger was sent to Eldirad to tell the families of the wounded, but she never returned. Nor did any envoys come to Westtower.

That first day, Sebastian set up six-hour watches and assigned a new captain to take his day watch so he only had to fight the worst six hours in the middle of the night. All that day, he worked over the sick and wounded. He got his watch to make beds for them in the prince's house, and the thirteen sick and four wounded were taken there in the afternoon. Sebastian's house would now be the hospital. At sunset, they had a burial ceremony for the young woman who had died and one man with a seemingly minor wound who had died during the day, and Sebastian had to speak, although he was almost too choked up to be heard. He returned to the hospital immediately and worked furiously over the patients. He did everything he could, and he left three nurses tending them while he was gone for his watch, but when he returned from watch at four the next morning, another of the wounded, although it was only a small cut to the leg, was dead.

Sebastian felt terrible. The man wasn't someone he knew well, but he had a wife at the tower who sat by the bedside in tears. It was almost more than Sebastian could do to walk into the firelit room and face that. He worked even harder that day, but his appointed captain was struggling, and he ended up taking both his watches. Hard and terrifying as the fighting was, it was almost a relief to be away from the fear in the sickroom and the suffocating sense of guilt that weighed on him when he thought about the events of Midwinter's night. It would have been a relief if it hadn't been for the terror he felt at being away from Joseph for even a moment.

On the third day, four of those with the sickness died without regaining consciousness. He felt like the only thing he did besides bend over sick beds and fight Shadows was officiate at funerals. That was his duty, but his guilt and grief at such times were almost too much for him to speak. In fact, he didn't speak to anyone other than in command on the wall and at such ceremonies.

On the fourth day, another person was dead, and Joseph had a raging fever while his arms and hands remained ice cold. Kneeling beside his bed for hours that afternoon, Sebastian felt more miserable and desperate than he ever would have thought possible. In the dim room, while the snow piled up against the windowsills, slow, painful tears came; then he sat a long time past tears in a black place of pain and despair.

He was roused only late in the afternoon by a hoarse call for water. He struggled up out of the blackness and went over to the bed. It was one of the eight remaining unwounded sick, and she looked up at him with eyes that saw.

"Sebastian," she whispered. "What has happened? There were such terrible things." She looked around. "Such horrible dreams."

A trace of a smile, something now strange and foreign, came to his lips, and his eyes filled. "You're all right now, lady," he said in a husky voice.

That first recovery was a relief, however small, and he managed to sleep a couple hours that afternoon on a blanket beside Joseph's bed before being called for watch. When he got off the wall, two more of the sick knew him for the first time, and by the next morning there was another. The first woman even got up and about a little. By the end of the day, however, two more were dead, and Joseph's fever was dangerously high. The last three sick came around by the end of the week, and so did the woman with the scratch on her arm, but there were a couple new sick and one more wounded by then, and none of it could lift Sebastian's spirits even a little.

Helen visited a few times through the Sight. She sat with a phantom hand on his shoulder when he was in black despair and told him gently that he was doing the best he could, that there was no reason to feel guilty about it, but she couldn't say anything especially encouraging. She had never told Sebastian how little chance she saw for Joseph, or how astonished she had been to find him alive when she returned the next morning, let alone days later. She did try to encourage Sebastian that Joseph was resisting better than most, and she could not help letting a ray of hope creep back into her heart. A couple times Sebastian felt Tatyana's presence, too, and he was grateful. He talked to her when he felt her in the room, answering the questions he knew she must want to ask, and sending news to his family, but she never said a word. Her gift didn't allow many words at the best of times.

Sebastian spent most of his time off watch sitting on the edge of Joseph's bed, holding his hand. His hard, strong hand was frail now, and as the second week wore on, he grew much thinner. Joseph's face was white, and he was icy cold and burning hot by turns. Sometimes he cried out in terror or babbled nonsense words.

Slow tears often came to Sebastian's eyes as he sat holding that thin hand and thinking of all the things he and Joseph had done together. They had been best friends since they were little. Sebastian could hardly remember a world without Joseph, and he couldn't bear to imagine one. He remembered when they were eleven and twelve and had to put on a play for a group project in Obrinish class. Sebastian was good at Obrinish, but he had been terrified by the idea. But he and Joseph had been partners, like they were in everything, and Joseph had written a funny play for them to perform. They had so much fun over that... And there had been the time when Sebastian was twenty-one and had sprained his ankle in his first month of guard training. Joseph had come every day and sat beside him on the couch and read him funny stories, told jokes, and played games. Joseph had always been there when Sebastian was sad to cheer him up, and in his best memories Joseph was always there to share in his joy. Joseph had spent the night at his house nearly half the time as kids, and he remembered hundreds of evenings playing games or doing homework together on the living room carpet.

Sebastian would whisper to Joseph, telling him about how much he had loved so many things they did together, until he was overcome with grief and could not even whisper anymore. Then he would just sit there, holding Joseph's hands almost fiercely, with his head bent. Sometimes a tear or two would fall, and sometimes he would just sit in agony.

Sebastian used the spells of his Healing gift to strengthen his friend as much as he could and to ease the fever. He gave him all the medicines to treat symptoms, and some stimulants, as Helen had suggested. He even tried the most powerful and dangerous magical healing art of the Eldir. Those with the Healing gift always had the Sight to some extent, and this method used the Sight to send yourself into the land of death, the realm of shades, to hang onto a soul or bring it back. The standard method taught in the school, and the only one Sebastian had ever learned because his Sight didn't go to Sending level, involved holding the person's hand, reaching out with your spirit, and calling their name in your mind. It was sort of the Sight equivalent of reaching out a helping hand to a drowning swimmer, but not jumping in yourself. The powerful could do that with nearly anyone, but it was always most effective if you already had a connection. Sitting in the dark, reaching out, groping for Joseph's spirit, he was vaguely aware of a terrible world of nightmare, or worse than nightmare, of horrors beyond description in which his friend walked.

Sometimes he felt so desperate that once when Helen came with the Sight, he asked her about the full immersion method of bringing someone back. It was more effective because you were in there and could really search for them, like jumping in to save a drowning person, but if you weren't a good enough swimmer, or strong enough to manage the current...

"Please don't. Promise me you won't do that, Sebastian," she said in his mind. "It isn't like other Sight Sendings. Even that would be dangerous for you with your degree of the gift, but this is going into the land on the edge of the river of death. You could never make it out. Besides, it only helps. It doesn't guarantee he won't slip away again. Doing that won't heal him. Promise me, and next time I can use the Sight I'll see what I can do for him."

"I promise," he said reluctantly. Right now he didn't much care how dangerous it was, but he had a duty, and in his heart, he knew he had to keep doing it. Besides, for Helen's sake... "Just be careful of yourself."

"I will. I promise."

She left him then, and he held Joseph's hands and reached for him, but despair crept back in. The hands were very thin now, and the pulse faint and erratic. Slow tears ran down Sebastian's face and made dark spots on the blanket.

Two days later, the third week was drawing to a close. It was nearly ten o'clock in the evening, and the house of the prince was dark and silent except for the crackle of the hearth fire. His watch would go on soon—he always took ten to four because those were the darkest, most hopeless hours of the night—but the rest of his watch was in the tower kitchen eating dinner. Sebastian didn't want to leave Joseph, but he wasn't sure who he could trust to lead his watch. The young captain he had appointed was getting better, but Sebastian wasn't sure she would ever be able to handle it alone.

He reached out as hard as he could for the thousandth time, and this time he felt something a little different. The frantic turmoil of darkness had settled a little, and somewhere, seemingly very far away, he felt Joseph, the boy he had known since they were little, climbing trees in the forest near the city, playing at the river, skating or swimming, playing games, doing art. They had been inseparable from almost the first day they met as children. The young man he had come to respect for his cheerful humility, quick mind, and talent at making people laugh. He reached for him with all his might and called his name, and he seemed to come closer, like a small white light in the darkness. Not strong, but steady.

A nurse from the next shift came in and lit the lamps, but Sebastian did not move or acknowledge him. He held both of Joseph's hands and watched his waxy face. He almost forgot to breathe. The thick dark lashes fluttered, and Joseph's light gray eyes opened, startlingly large in his thin face. His bony hands clung to Sebastian's.

"Sebastian," he whispered, almost breathless. His hands trembled slightly. "The... they... were they dreams? It was so terrible..."

"It was only dreams, don't worry, you're awake now," Sebastian said gently. His throat got tight, and tears flooded down his cheeks as they hadn't when he was most miserable.

Slowly, a faint smile spread over Joseph's lips. "I'm so glad you're here, Sebastian."

"I'm so sorry, Joseph. So sorry," Sebastian could barely choke out the words he had wanted to say for three weeks.

"Sorry?" Joseph looked confused. He shut his eyes a minute and shook his head a little before he looked up again. "I remember every-thing now. Up till I passed out on the wall... It was so terrible. I panicked. I was useless, and that arrow came out of nowhere, and then the fire and the cold..." He reached a feeble hand to touch his shoulder. "But it... it wasn't your fault. You don't have anything to be sorry for."

"I left you," Sebastian choked. "I shouldn't have left you."

"It's not your fault I couldn't handle it. No..." The ghost of his old bright smile came to his eyes. "You saved my life, Sebastian, twice."

"What?"

"Just now, and on the wall, making me wear my mail. The first arrow would have gone right in my heart."

Sebastian couldn't say anything to that. The relief in hearing Joseph speak was too intense to allow for much other thought. He was startled when a knock on the door told him it was time for his watch.

"I have to go. My watch is waiting. Will you be all right? Is there anything you want?"

"Don't worry, Sebastian. I'm not going anywhere. I'll be here when you get back." He tried to give his cheery wave, then squeezed Sebastian's hand.

Sebastian rose and left the room, and although he said nothing, everyone could tell a great weight had lifted from his shoulders.

Chapter 10

Despair

19 February (about one
month later), YA 1124

Eldirad

THE WALL in Eldirad had been finished in the first two weeks, and things had improved a little. All the country people came flocking into the city in those first weeks from their small farms and herders' cottages in the rich meadowland between the rivers, and the city was crowded and bustling. An actual circle around the city could be maintained, so stray Shadows no longer got in, and the people felt safe there. The fighting was also a little better up on the wall with proper ramparts, and the enemy mostly below. All the same, the Shadows had only increased in numbers, and with the aid of their strange ropes they climbed the wall in the thousands.

By the end of the first two weeks, Tatyana had begun to get used to the sight of the dead and the wounded. It still pained her, of course, but the shock and bewilderment were gone. For the most part, she felt a tired bitterness. The twelve hours a day of fighting was much more intense than even the most ambitious training program, and she was pretty sore for a couple weeks. Besides her twelve hours on the wall, she spent at least three or four in the hospital every day, and she was always tired.

No messages had come from Aldor after the last Efrim stone carrier had passed through on his way home from there in October, and there was no word from Westtower after Midwinter. Tatyana was on the wall when Westtower was attacked, where she repressed her Sight somewhat so as not to be distracted. Still, she felt a sudden fear for Joseph. As close friends as she and Joseph were, Tatyana's Sight connection with him wasn't quite strong enough to trust, and she hoped she was mistaken. She could not, however, be mistaken about Sebastian's clear call for help.

She had wanted to go to him with the Sight, but the press of Shadows was intense, and by the time she could, the call had subsided. She thought perhaps Helen had gone to him or someone actually at Westtower had helped him.

It had been difficult because she was so tired, but she had used the Sight that night after she was off duty. It had been after two by then, and she had seen Sebastian fighting Shadows on the wall of Obrin. So, they were fighting there too. That wasn't surprising, but she had to know more, and she wanted to see Joseph.

She couldn't go to Joseph himself with the Sight. The only person besides immediate blood relations to whom Tatyana had a strong enough connection to use the Sending was Helen. But she couldn't bear the fear of not knowing what had happened do him, so she went to Sebastian again when she woke up at five. This time she saw Sebastian in the sick room with Joseph and her worst fears were confirmed. Joseph was wounded. It didn't look large, but she saw no way it could not be deadly. No one in Eldirad had survived more than a small cut, and then only those with great innate power. She couldn't hold the Sight more than a moment. Back in her room in the royal house, she wept a long time before she could get herself to get up and dress for her watch. Still, she went again the next day, and Sebastian sensed her and talked to her. She learned all that had happened on Midwinter night, and she tried to comfort him.

When she came again after a week, she was shocked and encouraged to find Joseph still alive, if very ill, and began to hope he was a good deal stronger than she had thought him. She was too tired to say anything with the Sight, but she went every few days for a minute, and it was a great delight to her the day she went to find Joseph sitting up on pillows and watching Sebastian, who was telling him an old story while he ground herbs.

Now, as February wore away, the routine had come to be second nature to Tatyana: dragging herself out of bed, eating, going to the wall, then some time in the hospital, and trying to sleep before she had to repeat it. She missed Helen and Sebastian especially, and Analisia, Aranin, and Joseph very much as well.

It was a fairly clear, cold morning. The sun was rising above the trees before her. The hardest press was always on the forest side of the wall to the east, and so that was where the guardian must be. She was fighting hard with three Shadows who were scrambling onto the wall, but around them and behind and through them, she noticed a little of the beautiful pinks and dark crimsons of the clouds and mist about the trees. The sunrises had certainly been redder the last few months, but she had to admit they were beautiful.

With a slash of her sword she cut through two of the Shadows and held her breath for a moment against the black cloud that came from them. Out of the corner of her eye she saw the glint of metal coming at her. She blocked the blow with her sword while slicing her dagger through a rope catching the edge of the rampart. Then she turned. Shadows with stolen Eldir swords were growing more and more common, but there was a certain difference in the way light bounced off the enemy weapons. The red sunrise light stained the silver Eldir blades pink, but those carried by the Shadows reflected a color closer to blood. It was faint, but Tatyana found she was learning to recognize it by instinct without having to think.

This Shadow was unusually large, and it gave her a good fight. The blade just grazed her wrist, and she felt a burning, freezing pain, even though the scratch was barely visible. She clenched her teeth against the pain and disintegrated the demon with a last stab. She decided Grandmother must be right that the blades were heavily poisoned.

Two more Shadows climbed into the place where the large one had been, and she lunged to kick the sword out of their reach before they could grab it. She heard a horrible cry of pain, both in her ears and in her mind, as it were, and her heart felt squeezed suddenly between blocks of ice. No number of Shadows could prevent her eyes from turning to her side. Four people away to her right, a figure in a pink tunic and purple hood had fallen to the stone floor. Her heart grew even colder until it seemed like it would stop altogether. "Rachel!" she shouted, slashing at the Shadows near her in a desperate fury. "Take over for a minute."

She saw Rachel, the closest captain, look at her but didn't wait for an acknowledgment. She ran to where Clarissa lay and knelt beside her. Clarissa lay on her back, clutching her right shoulder and arm where there was a deep wound. Her rosy, kindly face had grown thinner and graver the last few months. Now it was white and contorted in pain.

"Oh, Clarissa," Tatyana gasped, scooping her up in her arms. Her throat was so tight she could hardly breathe, and her eyes filled with tears.

"Tatyana," Clarissa whispered faintly. One hand clung to Tatyana's shoulder as she carried her down off the wall.

Tatyana walked as fast as she could towards the hospital, but Clarissa was as tall as her and a little broader, so she couldn't run. The grip on her shoulder grew weaker, and Tatyana looked down into Clarissa's face. It was gray, almost as gray as her eyes that were only half open.

"I'll get you to the hospital," Tatyana said. "We'll be there in a minute." She whispered an Eldir healing word and moved her fingers a little so as to touch the shoulder as much as possible.

The pain in Clarissa's face eased slightly. "It's no use," she whispered. "No one can save me." She looked up now, eyes large and full of tears.

"Of course we can," Tatyana's voice was sharp, angry, and desperate. "Just hold on."

"Tell, tell, Jeremy I love him. And... and my parents."

"No, you can't die." Tatyana's angry voice broke and choked on tears.

"Just promise you'll tell them."

"I promise."

"I love you too, Tatyana. I... I always have, even when you were the little girl messing up my toys..." Clarissa's voice faded, and she smiled faintly. She lay her head against Tatyana's shoulder.

Tatyana whispered spells for strength, healing, and pain relief. She put all her power into it. She clung to Clarissa in body and spirit, but it was no use. A moment later, just as she crossed the court in front of the hospital, she felt an emptiness. A void inside her as though a candle that had been burning unnoticed in her heart was suddenly blown out, leaving that space in darkness. It was the first time she had experienced the feeling, but she had no doubts what it meant. It was the feeling of a Sight connection being broken. That little place within her that had gone dark, that was the place that had connected her to Clarissa, the kind older girl who had played with her when she was little and their mothers used to exchange visits, bringing their daughters along. The girl who had braided her hair with daisies and made dolls out of flowers. They had not been best friends as they grew older, but Clarissa had always been like a big sister. She loved her, and she wished she had spent more time talking to her. She should have appreciated her gentleness, her kindness, and her cheerful energy more.

Tatyana fell to her knees on the frosty stones of the street. The body in her arms was limp. She checked for a heartbeat, and for breath, even though she knew what she would find. She checked again and again as sobs shook her body and tears ran down her cheeks. This couldn't be happening. It was too terrible. She couldn't bear it. Of course, many other people had died, and they had all had loved ones who were devastated. She told herself that, but she didn't care in the moment, and she hated herself for not caring. She felt it was all her fault. She had failed, failed to keep her friend safe, failed to keep her people safe. There must have been something she could have done. She held Clarissa's limp form in her arms and cried.

Someone came out of the hospital, and she hardly noticed. They went back. Then someone else came out. He knelt on the stones beside her and put his arm around her shoulders. She didn't have to look up to know it was her father.

They sat in silence for several minutes, and Tatyana's tears slowly subsided. She still felt miserable, and the pain of her loss was sharp and physical to her, but she didn't feel quite so alone, and that made her stronger. She lifted her head, which had been bent over Clarissa, and leaned it against her father's chest. He still wore his mail, having gone straight to the hospital when he got off watch an hour ago, and it felt cool against her wet cheek.

After another long minute, he spoke. "Come, dear, let us get up. Do you want to help me take her to her family, or would you rather not?"

"If you don't mind. I don't want to see them cry," she whispered. "I don't think I can bear it."

"I understand. If you are on watch again by the time they have the funeral, don't hesitate to get someone to take your place so you can go." He squeezed her shoulder gently as he got to his feet. "This is a terrible blow, and a terrible time, but we just have to keep going, together."

She stood and let him take Clarissa's body from her arms. She looked into his face and saw that it was drawn and pained, and a tear sparkled on one cheek.

"Go home for a few minutes," he said softly. "Take your time to pull yourself together. It is nothing to be ashamed of. Get some water, wash your face, and when you feel like you can fight with a clear head, go join your company." His voice was tender, gentle, and broken, but all the same it was a firm demand from a king. Tatyana was grateful. He knew her well, and knew she would need that sort of permission that couldn't be argued against by sense of duty. She felt she should go up at once, but she wasn't ready. She was shaken, and the energy and anger she had felt with the fear had melted away in her tears. She felt empty now, and worn out, sort of like an old grain sack that had sprung a leak and all the grain came out, leaving her a useless scrap of cloth on the floor. Except perhaps even that was too peaceful, tranquil. It didn't account for the pain, and the tears that came again to her eyes as she walked towards the palace to get a drink of water. No one would be there. At this hour, Clara would be working in the garden. The quiet would suit Tatyana now, she felt, but she wasn't sure she could bear it for long.

6 April (almost two months later), YA 1124; Efrimiel

Analisia threw her book down on the grass with a sigh of frustration. She had read the same sentence at least ten times, and she had no idea what it said. She leaned her head back against the blossoming apple tree she was sitting under and shut her eyes. She was tired, nothing was worth doing, but she couldn't keep still either. She stood and went automatically to look up at the nearest path that led to the wall on the hill. She was always looking that way, everyone seemed to be this spring, but that did no good either. Watching would not change when the next dead or dying soldier would be carried down.

She dreaded seeing another stretcher coming down that path, dreaded it always with the deep terror that she might know them. She wasn't sure she could bear to see another, and yet she kept looking. Not everyone who was brought down was dead, but they might as well be. About half of the unwounded sick survived, perhaps, and the blindness seemed to pass, but of all the wounded brought down, no matter how minor it seemed, only one person had survived. She thought with a leaden heart about Tatyana's letter in the beginning of January that said Joseph had been wounded. She was sure he was dead months ago by now. She had grieved about it much at the time, and it was still painful to think of. They hadn't been close but were always good friends. He was so cheerful and fun to be with, such a good actor and always ready to make people laugh.

She kicked savagely at the beautiful blooming bush before her. It was all wrong; the glorious and peaceful beauty of springtime in the valley of Efrim was like the wrong stage set. The play they were in was a dark tragedy. The sky shouldn't be blue. There shouldn't be flowers or green grass. It was all just wrong. This kind of set would be for a romantic comedy. She sat down heavily on the grass again. It was all unbearable. Her people were dying, all the joy was gone from the valley, and there was nothing she could do.

Twenty minutes later, she was roused from her stupor by a girl's voice calling her name.

"Over here," she called back.

Nelia came around the bushes. She was a girl of eight years, small and pretty with flying golden hair, who lived in the palace. Analisia had always been fond of her.

"The mail just came in," Nelia panted as she ran up. "From Eldirad. There's a letter for you from Princess Tatyana, and I thought you would want it at once."

Analisia sat up straighter and reached for it eagerly. She hadn't had a letter from Tatyana in months. The last had come in January, and she had reread it so many times the paper had fallen apart. She thanked the girl and broke the royal seal. The paper told a story of its own that made her throat tighten uncomfortably. It was unlike all the other letters Tatyana had sent her over years of correspondence. The paper looked battered, and it was smudged in many places. There were drops of candle wax, a grease spot just the size of a finger and not far away another. It looked as if it had gotten wet, and there were a few drops of something that might have been food on it. It was clear even before she began to read that things had changed in Eldirad far more than they had in Efrim.

> *Dearest Analisia,*
>
> *I hope this finds you in good health, as it leaves me. First off I must tell you the good news. Since I told you in January that Joseph was wounded and terribly ill, I must now report that today, it is the twenty-sixth day of the new year, I went with the Sight to Sebastian and found them sitting together. He still looks sick, but he is clearly past the worst and that is a great relief. I must admit I despaired of his life, and I am so delighted today that I had to write to you at once.*

Analisia took a deep breath and looked up at the apple tree. A smile crept across her lips. She couldn't believe it. She was so glad he was alive, but January 16th had been a long time ago. Why had Tatyana never sent the letter? Any number of terrible things could have happened since then. She looked back at the letter.

> *I miss you and couldn't help remembering what a grand time we had with all the games we used to play in the snow when we were children. Do you remember playing that game where we made two teams and chased each other with snow-balls, and if anyone got hit they had to try to walk across the river on their hands? Or the snow forts we made when we had snowball wars between the girls and the boys? I remember one*

time we crowned you queen of our country and Jane made you a crown out of icicles, and then it froze to your hat so you had to melt it off when you went home. And then Joseph crowned Sebastian with snowballs. What good times we had. Sometimes I miss...

Here there was an uncharacteristic blot and the sentence resumed in a slightly different color of ink.

. . . being little children, when royalty didn't matter, and we were as free as anyone else to play sports and games, read, or go to the theatre. Are there still plays at the Efrim theatre? Have you been to any lately? If so please tell me all about it in your next letter. There is a comedy running at the Eldirad theatre, I believe Jane is in it, although I don't know what part. I don't have time to go, but would love to hear about anything you have seen or anything nice you're reading.

I only do my duty. I have seen many fine sunrises lately. That is the advantage of the morning watch at the wall which my father kindly gives me. After an hour or so of fighting Shadows in the dark, there is nothing more wonderful than the sun rising, red and gold and pink, above the trees to the east. Just this morning a few hours before I write this I saw the most beautiful sunrise. First the sky turned dove gray, then dusty rose, and then as the sun broke the horizon the edges of the clouds kindled as if aflame. The light sparked on the swords and mail of my companions and glittered in the snow on the trees by the river like a blanket of diamonds.

Here there was another clear break, for up to here the letter was written in Tatyana's strong neat hand in black ink. After this the ink was brown as if the mix used had been past its prime, the quill seemed blunt, and the handwriting was sloppy as if written by a tired hand.

I am sorry this letter is taking so long to be written. I meant to send it months ago, but couldn't find time to finish it until now. I don't have much to say about my life, and I'd rather not talk about it. What are you doing? Is the spring as beautiful in Efrim as it used to be? I would love to see the cherries of Efrim in bloom.

Being a princess is a difficult lot. Most other professions seem rather like vacation to me just now, for all I know they work hard. That is of little matter though, I am proud to serve my people and I only hope I will be able to do so adequately. It is a tremendous responsibility, but also an honor, to be born to be responsible for the lives and happiness of others as we are. Especially now, when everything we know and love is threatened. Yes, it's true. I don't want to sound defeated or pessimistic, but I'm sure you see it too by now. I am at the walls twelve hours of the day. We have four shifts of soldiers; father leads two and I the others. There is no longer any security, no one talks of a swift victory. When I am not on the wall I am at the bedsides of the sick, as I am now. It is about an hour after midnight as I write, and the room is very silent. Most of the people who are not on the wall are asleep. Grandmother will take my place soon so I can try to sleep before my watch at six. Ah well, there is no rest for princesses, but that is how it must be.

In February my friend Clarissa died in my arms. I miss her very much and think of her often. Remember how she used to make the dolls with acorn hats when we were little? I must not say more though or I shall smear my ink with tears. I find my best comfort in my father and mother, and in still being able to write letters to you. There has been no word from Elisabeth and Helen at Aldor since I told you mail stopped running in October, and there still has been no contact with Westtower since the new year. I can't use the Sight much. I am too tired. I do worry about them, as we all worry about those we love these days, but *that is all I can do.*

I send all my best wishes to you, and all my friends in the valley. Tell your brother I think about him, when you have a chance, and ask Lisiana if she would send me a little sketch of her baby. I wish I could meet her. I will not say see you soon, but I look forward to seeing you someday when times are happier, and talking with you about the book you loaned me if ever I have two minutes to rub together in which to read it.

If this should, for any reason, be the last letter you receive from me until after the war, or ever, please remember that I will always be your loving friend,
Tatyana

Analisia reread the letter twice. Her heart, which had lifted a little at the news about Joseph, felt very heavy again. Things were so bad in Eldirad. Of course, she had known that. People were dying. It wasn't like Tatyana was safe, but to see it written pained her deeply... She stared at an impertinent little goldfinch hopping about the bush. How could it be so happy? Clarissa was dead.

She reread it again. She had always known her friend was amazing and special, and felt she was good at everything and the noblest person she knew, but it all just felt deeper and more important now. Tatyana was giving everything for her people. The lighthearted words about sunrises were Tatyana's way of trying to be cheerful for her sake. Analisia was sure of that. Tatyana was so brave, and what was she? Analisia put her head in her hands.

Tatyana had used "we" when talking about the responsibility and honor of being born a princess. Analisia felt like shouting that she didn't deserve that. She was a princess, sure, an *Efrim* princess... She supposed she had been taught that the happiness of her people was her responsibility, and she wanted to help them, but there was nothing she could do for them. She was worthless. Tatyana worked hard and went without sleep, risking her life every day for her people. She could fight and heal. Analisia did nothing. She couldn't fight, she couldn't heal; it was undignified for a princess of Efrim to even help in the kitchen or sweep the floor. Where was the nobility in her kind of royalty? How could Tatyana draw any kind of comparison between them?

* * * * * *

Ten minutes later, Yeven slipped quietly into the royal garden. It had been a year or so since Analisia had said he could come in any time he liked, but he was always very careful to be discreet. He didn't want to meet the queen or the queen mother. This caution was not really necessary now, since neither of them showed their faces outdoors anymore, but it was a habit. He had a feeling that he might find Analisia out here this time of day, though, and so had gotten leave of his mother to come. He was worried about Analisia.

Coming around a corner he saw her sitting under the apple tree. A letter was in one hand resting on her knee, and she was staring straight ahead at the trunk of a tree with glazed eyes. There was a certain pain in the expression of her face, and a touch of flush in her cheeks that did little to relieve the pasty white color her face had taken on lately. The last few months, nothing was right. Yeven and his mother, working all day in their shop, tried to pretend it was normal. They sang together and did everything like they always did, but he jumped when anyone opened the door, and they were both short tempered. They would get along, though. It was Analisia he worried about. She never smiled anymore. He could never get her to play ball or even walk by the creek with him. She had gained weight and grown pale and sickly looking, little like the beautiful, athletic young woman he had first fallen in love with almost three years ago.

He knelt on the grass beside her and put a hand on her shoulder before she noticed him.

"Oh, hi, Yeven," she said vaguely.

"Can't you tell me what's eating you?" he pleaded.

"The war, what else?" she said a little shortly.

He liked the anger better than the listlessness. "I know that, but I mean what specifically. Was there bad news? Who is the letter from?" He leaned forward anxiously, wondering if it was Aranin's hand.

"It's from Tatyana." She pushed it towards him. She didn't know what to say. She couldn't bear it, and she didn't know what to do. "There is good news and bad. A friend I thought would surely die is better, but another is dead. I wasn't that close to her, but she was really nice." Analisia's eyes were down. Just the effort of breathing seemed too much right now.

"I'm very sorry," Yeven murmured. He read the letter since she had pushed it into his lap. "Do you want to tell me about her?" he asked after a while.

"No, not now."

There was another silence. Analisia's mind shifted from thoughts of the kind things Clarissa had done for her, back to Tatyana's suffering and the nobility of her words—and what her words seemed to imply. Yeven watched her, wondering what the root of the problem was, knowing it was something deeper than this grief that had begun long ago. Birds sang in the blossoming apple tree above their heads.

Analisia gave an exclamation of frustration and punched the soft dirt with her fist.

Yeven jumped almost to his feet with a gasp, startled out of his thoughts.

She let herself flop backwards onto the ground, looking up at the blossoms without really seeing them. "I can't stand it," she mumbled rolling over so she was face down on the grass.

Yeven let out his breath and sat down again, watching her. He said nothing, hoping she would go on. When she didn't, he ventured, "What?"

"I'm so restless, and yet I can't concentrate on anything." She pulled blades of grass one at a time out of the lawn. "I try to read, and I just see the same sentence over and over; I try to sew and end up staring out the window. There's nothing to do! And I'm so tired and so restless!"

"Surely there's something you could do that would make you feel better?" he said hesitantly.

"Yeah. Like what? There's nothing a worthless *Efrim princess* can do these days. The whole valley is like a suspended scene in someone's miniature display. No one even breathes in the palace anymore. It isn't worth doing." She dropped her head into the grass.

"The valley isn't wholly stopped," he said with a great effort at cheerfulness. "There is a great demand for army boots, the farmers are in the fields, kids are playing bat ball..."

"None of that has anything to do with me," Analisia said hopelessly. "I'm not a cobbler like you, I'm not a farmer, and I don't have the energy or concentration for bat ball. Grandmother doesn't like me playing it anyway. She thinks it's undignified. I might get dirty, and I should have stopped years ago. Besides, it seems so pointless when people are up there dying. There is nothing worthwhile I can do, and, well, you read the letter, right?"

"Yes."

"Look at Tatyana. She does everything for her people. She talks about the duty of a princess, makes it sound like it is worth something..."

Yeven looked again at the letter. He didn't know Tatyana that well. He had met her a few times the last couple years, and he had seen her pitch in bat ball games. He had heard a lot about her from Analisia. He certainly respected her, and he could see the nobility in what she was doing. It looked like a hard and painful life to him, though. He looked up at Analisia. She was on her back again now, frowning up into the tree, grass stains on her pink dress. She looked so unhappy, restless, unwell, and trapped in her own skin. He thought of Tatyana the last time he had seen her: a tall, strong, confident, grim woman, kind, serious, and self-contained. He knew Analisia idolized her, and, even making allowance for the six years' difference in their age, he had to admit to himself that the strength and self-sacrifice in Tatyana's words made a much better impression of princesshood than did the moody and disheveled figure before him.

"Perhaps," he said at last. "Perhaps, you don't have to follow tradition all the time if it doesn't feel right to you."

She sat up and looked at him with wide eyes. "What do you mean?"

"I mean," he began, choosing his words carefully. "That Efrim traditions are not always kind, or always right, just because they are our customs."

"No. They often don't feel that way," she said slowly. She sometimes hated Efrim traditions about what princesses were allowed to do and not do. Princesses were supposed to keep tidy; princesses shouldn't work with normal people, or go to school with them. Princesses couldn't be warriors, healers, or farmers, or even go out walking alone. And the traditions that made Aranin, even though he was her twin brother, into a nobody, had always seemed wrong. Most people wouldn't even treat him like he had a mind just because he was a boy—most people in Efrim, that was... She hadn't thought about it much, but Yeven must run into the same thing all the time. He and Aranin had been the only boys in either of their classes, or within five years of them, who stayed all the way through school.

"It is my country," he said, watching her face anxiously, hoping not to offend. After all, she was a princess of this country. "And I love it. I am loyal to your mother, of course. But if you will forgive my saying so, it is hard being a boy in this country. You and Aranin are my only real friends. Most girls don't want to have anything to do with me, and neither do the boys, because I stayed in school and apprenticed with my mother."

She looked at him. It was true being a cobbler was still pretty rebellious for an Efrim boy. "I know it is my tradition that I am supposed to uphold like Mother is always saying, but sometimes I think it is all wrong. It isn't right how you and Aranin are treated, and how... how can I feel good about myself as a princess sitting around waiting for ambassadors that never come and doing nothing to help my people in trouble when I have Tatyana's example to look at?" Her voice was strong and fierce now, but when she finished she looked back down at her knees. "I don't know what I am supposed to do about it, though."

"What do you think in your heart is the right thing? What is it that would make you feel like you were fulfilling what you should do?"

She thought for a long time, then she said, "I think I would have to be like Tatyana. Really serve my people. I have no gift and will never be a healer, but I would have to fight for them like she does to feel I was being a worthy princess." She sat up straighter and brushed off her skirt. That was it. She had to find a way to make her mother let her apprentice in the army. Yeven was right. Traditions were not unbreakable. Men could be artistic and intelligent and learn crafts, and princesses could be warriors. She was not yet a woman, and it would be twelve years before she took her title, but someday she would be queen. A queen made decisions about how best to serve her people, she had to follow her conscience—and if her conscience told her to break rules and traditions, well, so be it. Times were changing. "I'll do it," she said with decision. "I must fight. I will make Mother let me go."

He watched her with a touch of a smile. She looked so much stronger, so much more alive already than she had in weeks. There was light and life in her eyes. And yet, it broke his heart to think of her going up to the dangers of the wall. He wanted her to be safe. He knew she could do it; and yet, he had to admit she didn't look it. "Before you..." He hesitated. He partially wished he hadn't suggested this, and yet, it hadn't really been his idea. He had just wanted to cheer her up. He hadn't suggested the army, only the break with tradition. "Before you go trying to get people to let you join the warriors and go away and leave me to fight at the wall, you know you will have to prepare."

"Why? You don't think I can do it? It was your idea, why are you backing out now?"

Something snapped and he lost his temper. His face flushed. "It wasn't my idea to have you go charging up onto the wall to get shot at by Shadows. It was your idea. All I did was ask you what you thought was right!"

"Okay. It's my idea then. Maybe it was, but does that mean you think it's a bad idea? You think I'm just a foolish dreamer?"

"I don't. I didn't say that."

"That's what it sounded like."

He took a deep breath. He was afraid, but what was there really to be so angry at? "I'm sorry if it sounded like that. You have to understand, Analisia. I love you. It is painful to have you go up there in danger, but I will support you in any decision you make. Perhaps I'm just weak. Forgive me."

She looked at the grass for a minute, and her cheeks cooled. "I'm sorry too." She looked down at her plump, smooth, white hands, and noticed the snugness of her dress. "I suppose you are right. I'm not in very good training. I never exercised as much as I should after Aranin left, and with Mother and Grandmother always wanting me to be lady-

like and study endlessly, and since the Shadows came, I have done nothing. Not being allowed to do anything useful, I got so depressed I did
nothing at all." Her face turned rose red. "I feel like a fool."

"Don't say that. You were miserable. I worried about you, but I know
you're strong and anything but a fool." He stood and reached out a
calloused hand to help her up. "If you want to be ready to be a soldier all
you have to do is set your mind to it. I'd be happy to help you train. We
could do it together. I've been somewhat out of training lately too,
really."

"All right. We will start today. I think let's start by running around the
valley. There's likely time before we're missed at dinner, and if I am, I for
one don't care. I am tired of caring what they think about what I'm doing.
I won't be alone, anyway, if you come." She took his hand and got to her
feet, brushing off her skirt.

"I'll just tell my mother, and I'll be right back."

He ran off, and Analisia walked through the garden towards the
palace to change into pants for running. Somehow, the flowers suddenly
seemed prettier, and she almost laughed at the hopping and twittering of
a little bird on a branch. Spring was coming. Things were very grim. Yet
there was hope still.

Chapter 11

Rebellion

6 April to November, YA 1124

Efrimiel - In the valley and at the eastern wall

RUNNING, or rather trying to run, the seven miles around the valley floor was far from easy and proved to Analisia how badly she had neglected her training lately. Moving felt good, though, at least at first. It felt nice to have the wind in her hair and to breathe deeply. They stopped often and walked slowly, or rested beside the path to catch their breath, and they ran little after three miles or so, but they didn't give up. By mile six, Yeven would rather have liked to be done for the day and make a straight path home to dinner, but Analisia, even though much the more tired of the two, wouldn't even think of giving up, and he wouldn't leave her. They returned to the palace after dark, walking slowly, very hungry and tired.

"I'm going every afternoon," Analisia said as they parted in the garden where they had started. "I won't tell anyone. They can think we are walking by the stream or I fell asleep reading in the garden. I think I'll stick with that unless anyone notices I wasn't there."

"You can tell them, just don't blame me, please. I'm afraid your mother doesn't altogether approve of me as it is."

"Well, I suppose not entirely. She's a traditionalist. But that's her problem. Princess or not, the one Right—and yes that, too, was once an

Eldir Right—but anyway, the only Right no one denies me is that of picking who I wish to be with." She didn't say to marry, although she thought it, but that much of custom she would hold. They were young for such things.

"I'll meet you tomorrow."

They met in the garden every afternoon after that. Yeven told his parents and grandparents, of course, but Analisia told no one the truth yet. Everyone in the palace was so worried and distracted that no one noticed the change in her or minded her sometimes coming in a little late from the palace garden. The third day they were so sore they barely made it around the valley at all, but after that it got better. At the end of the week, they introduced some other exercises along the way. Push-ups and sit-ups on the spring grass, pull-ups from trees. When they started Yeven could only do two pull-ups and Analisia none at all, but they got better.

Yeven worked hard with his mother in the shop in the mornings and evenings, and Analisia roamed the libraries and forced herself to concentrate on all the texts of war Aranin had once studied in the early years of his apprenticeship. She was often so sore she winced when she moved, but nothing could blunt her determination.

Analisia wrote a letter to Tatyana telling her about her decision, but it was never sent. The mail had started only going once a week ever since the walls had been manned, because the mail cart needed a bodyguard, and when the next cart set off they encountered a sort of barrier of floating dark mist over the road a dozen yards beyond the Efrim wall. None of the mail carriers would face passing through it, and even donkeys could not be taken near it without panicking, so the mail cart stopped running in the second week of April. Evelina, loath to have communication cut off entirely, ordered some soldiers to attempt the crossing, but by then the misty barrier had grown even thicker. They were hardy men, able to face the Shadows and their mist with ease, but they only got twenty yards into the barrier before they started passing out. Those who made it out were ill and raving for weeks.

Although Analisia was sad not to be able to tell her friend of her decision, these strange reports only made her more impatient to follow it, and she trained harder than ever.

By the beginning of May, she could run around the valley in an hour and a half and do forty push-ups, properly on her feet, and six pull-ups. Her clothes were no longer tight, and she felt lighter and stronger. She felt she was ready. Yeven tried to persuade her to stick to it a couple more weeks at least, and maybe practice fencing and shooting some, but she wouldn't wait any longer. She had to face her mother and, besides, practice swords and such were only available in the training field that had been set up for the new recruits to be trained for a few months before going up to the wall. She would never get in there without facing her mother first. Her father was scheduled to come down from the wall to survey new recruits the next day, and Analisia decided it was now or never.

She smoothed her hair and her dress outside the royal chamber, took a deep breath, and went in. Her mother was sitting at her desk shuffling papers and writing numbers in her ledger. Her grandmother was writing a letter at the table, and her grandfather sat in an easy chair reading a book. He was 115 and starting to get frail. He glanced up when Analisia entered, and he looked worried at the expression on her face. She looked at him a moment. This was going to get ugly, very likely, especially since both Evelina and Tinianna were there. She mouthed the words, "You want to get out," to him and pointed to the door.

He took the hint and rose stiffly, taking his book and leaving the room. He was a gentle, kindly man and had no liking for conflict. Analisia herself would rather have found her mother alone, but either way Tinianna would have her say, so she supposed it was better to get it over with.

"Mother," Analisia said when he was gone. "I need to talk to you."

Evelina flinched, startled, and looked up from her papers. She was paler and a little thinner than a few months ago. She looked tired, worried, and a little annoyed. "Does it have to be now? I'm busy. Your father comes down to inspect the volunteers tomorrow, and I need to decide how many I should let him take and organize the fitting out of each with proper gear, let alone the provisions that have to be sent up."

"If it is actually so much work, why have I had nothing to do?"

A shade of a flush came to Evelina's cheeks. She lifted her chin. "Not more than one person can do, certainly, only today is a busy day. You wouldn't know. You've hardly been indoors lately."

"I have. You just didn't notice. I've been in the library a lot, and here where you didn't even notice me." Analisia tried to keep her voice even. "No, what I have to say is important. You raised me to feel that as a princess I should always be respected and have a right to my opinions and to make judgements for my people someday. I have made a big decision, and you must hear it."

"You are too young to make decisions for the nation. Not even womanhood will grant you that Right. Not while I'm still queen." Evelina's voice was hard and cold.

"That's why I'm going to the trouble to ask you," Analisia said through clenched teeth.

"What is it then?" Evelina sighed and looked resigned to hearing a bunch of foolishness.

The expression made Analisia flush with anger, but she kept her voice steady. "I have made up my mind. I want to apprentice in the army. My people need me, and I can't stay away."

Evelina's eyes went wide, and her cheeks flushed. Her hands fluttered and worried over the pen in her hand. "Why on earth would you think such a thing? You are a princess, remember your place!"

Analisia had expected that, and she was ready. "Times have changed. This crisis is different. I can't bear sitting around here any longer. I want to protect my people like Tatyana does."

"You are a shameful disgrace! Don't you have any honor? Don't you care about your people, our traditions?"

Analisia's eyes flashed. "Of course I care about my people. That's the point!"

"Be sensible. A princess can't go up there. Princesses don't fight. Besides, it is dangerous."

"Tatyana is a princess."

"The Eldir are different. I never should have let you spend so much time with their royal family as a child. We were here first. You must understand. We have our customs, and our pride!"

"I don't care if our people were here first! What difference does that make?"

"You selfish girl. You don't even care!"

Analisia stomped on the floor, her hands in fists at her sides. She forced herself to take a long shaky breath and steady her voice again. "I thought the whole point of the alliance was that we each took the best parts of the other culture. I believe that, at least in this situation, their tradition of queenship is right. I thought a princess was supposed to do what was right."

A chair creaked as Tinianna stood abruptly. "You always think what you want is more important than tradition! You are a shame to your family, your nation, and our proud history, Analisia."

Analisia felt a moment's pang of fear and hurt. Her throat got tight, but then she was angry again. Even more angry. All her life her grandmother had lorded it over her, nothing she ever did was good enough, her hair was never neat enough, as if that was what mattered in a real, serious world.

"No," Analisia said forcefully. She turned to Tinianna. "I'm not being selfish, you are. You just hide behind tradition. You don't have to think, don't have to do anything but sit here, and, if you believe the traditions, we aren't even supposed to feel guilty for it."

Evelina opened and shut her mouth. "How... how could you!"

"Our traditions are sacred. They have stood for three thousand years!" Tinianna snapped.

"And we have never had a threat like this one before," Analisia countered, forcing herself to keep most of the frustration out of her voice.

"That's beside the point," Evelina snapped.

Tinianna walked over to them, her blue eyes flashing. "You don't deserve to be crown princess, you wretched girl. There are things that are sacred. That shouldn't be defiled by willful children who don't understand."

"I may not be a grown-up yet, but I'm not a willful child."

"If you go on like this, I can disown you and take away your title." Evelina's face was hard and her eyes filled with rage.

"You wouldn't do that," Analisia snapped. "What? Find some new more docile girl and then force Aranin to marry her against his will?"

"The laws permit that," Tinianna said coldly.

Analisia was furious, but a cold fear stabbed at her heart. Would they really do that? Aranin had never disobeyed anyone, much less Mother. Would he be such a good child he would actually consent, even if he hated the woman and she wasn't nice to him? Analisia took a slow shaky breath and looked her mother in the eyes. "Please give me a chance, Mother. This is what I think right, no matter what. You are the queen. The people have you here. When it is time for me to take the crown, maybe then I will come and live in the palace and abide by the old rules as you do. But for now, I am young and of no use here. Young men and women are needed badly on the wall defending our nation. The threat may not last long, and the sooner over the better, but I want to help, and you must let me."

Tinianna was silent. Evelina shrank away from Analisia's stare.

She looked down at her papers, suddenly small and defeated. "I will write to your father. You may go if he will take you."

Analisia looked at her mother's bent head. She glanced at her grandmother, who had looked away. She noticed how worn she looked. The last seven months had changed her, too. She was very thin, and now with the fire gone, half turned away looking out the window, she looked frail and gaunt, older than her III years. Analisia felt a little guilty for causing them pain, and hoped it wouldn't be too hard on them, but she wasn't going to change her mind. She couldn't. "Thank you, Mother," she said softly. Then she left the room.

* * * * * * *

The next morning, she was eager for the meeting with her father. She wanted so badly to get up where the action was. She was the first one up, and she dressed carefully in the bedroom she used to share with Aranin, off the royal chamber. Analisia had been trained in diplomacy, which is half mild deceit, so she gave careful thought to how she looked for the interview with her father. She chose a dark brown tunic and plain, dark gray trousers. They were serious enough, she thought, and they also helped hide the fact she still wasn't really as fit as a warrior, although she could do more pull-ups now than she had since she was seventeen.

She slipped out of the house before her mother or grandmother could change their minds or, even worse, any of the court ladies— the ambassadors and advisors—could have their say on the matter. The diplomats of Efrim were as traditional a bunch of old ladies as you could find anywhere, and Analisia had no desire to meet them. She was allowed to go out to the palace garden alone, and once there she slipped through the hedge with her hood up and ran to the base of the path that came down from Father's station, which was the one just up the hill from the palace.

It wasn't long before she heard a firm, brisk tread and saw him coming down the path. Louranin was a broad, bulky man with muscular shoulders she could see even through his blue linen tunic. His hard, square-jawed face looked grim and tired, but when he saw her, he smiled a little.

"I didn't expect to find you waiting, Analisia," he said gravely.

"I wanted to see you first thing."

"So, you want to join the guard?"

"Yes, I do. I can't feel right doing anything else." Analisia raised her chin a little and looked into her father's face.

"Your mother sent me a message last night." His tone was grave and his keen sky-blue eyes seemed to see every inch of her. "She doesn't like the idea at all, but she is the only person who could outright forbid it, and she didn't. I don't like breaking tradition, but I don't feel it's my place to judge it either."

"Things are different now," Analisia said, trying to be perfectly grim, but she worried a bit of pleading or whining was creeping into the edge of her tone.

"You don't need to tell me that," Louranin said sharply. "This new threat is certainly serious, and quite unlike anything I was ever taught in warrior training or read in any war history."

"There's nothing remotely like it in any of our histories; believe me, I've read them all."

"I don't doubt you have, and I will take your word on such things. That point is not contested. Tell me, have you thought very seriously about your decision? Your mother says you have seemed very unlike yourself these last few months; are you sure this is what you want?"

"She would hardly know what I've been like. She has been too worried and fussy to notice me," Analisia said a touch sharply. "I will admit that I got very depressed for a while not having anything to do. Yes, I have thought about this a great deal, and I made up my mind quite firmly more than a month ago. Mother may think I fell asleep reading in the garden—that is admittedly what I told her—but I've been training the last month to be ready for this."

Louranin smiled just faintly, then grew deadly serious again. "If you are that certain I will not contradict you; however, there are two things I require. The first is your word. I am a soldier. I do not presume to know anything about the duties of queens and princesses, statesmanship or scholarship, but when it comes to running my army and my guard station, I modify my decisions only for specific orders from the queen. If you join the army, you must submit to being treated exactly the same as everyone else. There will be no allowances. I would take you to my post at once, rather than leaving you to train the first few months in the training field, even though you will need all the basic training, because I cannot trust anyone not under my eye to treat the crown princess without any mercy."

She started to protest, and he put up a hand to silence her. "No. It will do you no good to get angry. You cannot daunt me like you can your mother, and to let your temper get away is the worst thing you can do for your cause."

"Sorry, but what do you mean by no mercy?"

"No favoritism. You will get up when told, eat what you are given, do what you are asked, and train every day ten times harder than you can have been doing on your own. Following the Efrim tradition, as you have all your life, you remain the spoiled princess given everything she wishes and treated with deference, but if you take the Eldir model of royalty, then you take all of it. The rigor and strictness of the army is for a reason. It would be dangerous to you if it were relaxed in your case. Will you promise me to submit to that?"

Analisia took a long breath. 'Spoiled princess' ruffled her, but she supposed he was right. She raised her head and met his eyes. "I swear by sun and water, I will do anything I am asked, and I do not want to be treated differently."

Louranin bowed his head a moment. "So be it. There is only one other thing. I must test you, as I would any prospective warrior these days."

Analisia's throat tightened, and her heart rate sped up. She wasn't sure she was good enough to pass a test in sword fighting or exercises or anything. "How? What do I have to do?"

"Just look me in the eyes for a minute and hold it. Don't look away before I say, unless you have to."

That didn't sound so hard. Analisia raised her eyes to meet his and held his gaze. She could feel him pushing at her with his power, and her own rose instinctually to meet it. They stood thus for what seemed a long time. Then Louranin looked away. He looked both satisfied and a little sad.

"Did I pass?" she asked after a pause.

"Easily. It is only a test of power. Those with little innate power cannot face the Shadows at all and will sicken and often die in days, run in terror, or be afflicted with blindness every time they step on the wall."

"So," Analisia hesitated. "When can I come up?"

"I presume it would be intolerable to stay even a few days more in the palace now that you have defied your mother. I have to see the new recruits this morning who will start their training at the training field tomorrow, and I'll assign to companies those who are graduating from basic training. You may come with me if you wish. Then I will stop in at the palace and go up in the early afternoon. You will come with me then. We will find you a sword, mail, and a bow this afternoon, and you shall start learning to use them this evening."

"I beg your pardon, Father. I am very glad to do all that, but I do know how to use a sword and a bow. I need training, of course," she added hastily, thinking she might sound rebellious or spoiled. "But I don't think I should have to start quite at the beginning."

He had started to walk towards the fields where men and women were gathering, but he stopped and looked at her. There was surprise on his face, but a faint smile. "Where did you learn to use a sword? Surely your mother doesn't know about that."

"No, she doesn't. Tatyana taught me when I was sixteen and I begged her."

He shook his head and started walking again. "I suppose it proves all the better now." Then he stopped. "I should give you this." He fished a pin of silver and light pink mother-of-pearl shaped like a morning glory out of a pocket and pinned it to the neck of her dark tunic. "Now it's official."

"Thank you. I will do my very best to live up to it." She smiled and fingered the pin, the badge of an apprentice warrior. Then she trotted after her father. Life was going to be different; it would be hard, but nothing could be worse than sitting around the palace worrying. On the whole, she was excited.

* * * * * *

Aranin was surprised, and mostly pleased, when Louranin told him his sister wanted to join. He couldn't believe she had defied Evelina and Tinianna, and didn't even want to imagine the scene that must have occurred. He didn't really understand why she would want to come up to the wall. He so often wished he could get away from it and go down to the valley. He was frightened and tired, and the valley looked so beautiful and peaceful glowing with spring flowers in the May sunshine when he looked out from the shadowed hills, where many of the plants were sickly and the tree leaves were yellowed even in spring. That said, and the fact that he hated her coming into danger, he still yearned to have her with him.

The wall had been finished for some time now, although the stone barracks Louranin had commissioned were only just starting to go up at other posts. Aranin, as an apprentice in his sixth year, had been put on the wall only in daylight for the first six months or so, but now he was on at night too. That was the worst. His first night watch had been terrifying. He felt blind and helpless, and there were so many Shadows. The burning lanterns on the wall didn't seem to cast as much light as they should have when the Shadows were close. He was starting to get used to it after almost three weeks on full warrior shifts, but they seemed to make no progress whatsoever, and his spirits were very low.

The barrier growing in the trees beyond the wall terrified him too. No one at the post talked about it. They acted almost as if they didn't see it, but they all did. At the same time the mist stopped the mail carts to Eldir, the same sort of mist barrier grew in the trees beyond the wall all around the valley. The trees might be dense, and the mist from the Shadows thick, but this was different. It was almost like a wall of mist, and nothing lived in there. No sound came from it, and in daylight when you could see in just a little, Aranin could see that even the hardy grass that had begun to sprout with spring was dead within the barrier. The Shadows had not found a way to breach the Efrim wall, but they had built their own wall, cutting Efrim off from all the rest of the world. Aranin told himself it shouldn't bother him so much. Efrim was strong and self-sufficient, but he felt trapped, and that lifeless blackness haunted his dreams.

That day, however, he put aside his fears and felt a new energy to work hard, waiting, hoping that Analisia would come back with their father and bring a bright spot into the dreary, hopeless life of the wall fort.

He was off watch before they came up and was looking out over the path from a favorite tree when he saw the two familiar figures walking side by side. Father was walking uphill with a steady, easy pace, his face composed and unreadable as it so often was, and Analisia was almost running beside him. Her face was flushed, and she was clearly out of breath. Aranin felt a little twinge at his heart as he always did when reminded of how unequal, athletically, they had become.

He looked at her as she came up and saw that she was changed in many little ways. Flushed as she was from the climb, there was something lacking in her color, and a slight change about the eyes. There was a touch of shadow beneath them that hadn't been there before, and something else... Her cheeks were as round as ever, yet there was something sunken about her face, something missing. Perhaps it was more spirit than physical appearance, maybe the lack of light in her eyes.

He jumped from his tree and ran towards her, but not with the joy he had expected. There was a part of him that didn't want her up here, that wanted to keep her safe, but mostly it was the pain of the realization that she was not immune to the dark nightmares that had become their life.

"Welcome, Analisia, I'm so glad you came." He hoped she could not detect the flatness he felt in his words.

She smiled and ran into his arms. "I missed you so much," she whispered.

He held her tight. "I missed you too," he whispered back. He released her and looked at her again. "You look different. I don't know. Maybe it's the mail."

"You look different too, older, more like a man."

"I guess." He didn't know what to say. Sometimes he felt older, sometimes he just felt tired and frightened like a little boy. After an awkward silence he took her hand; so smooth and soft it felt. "Come on, let me show you the camp."

"I'll leave you. I should go right up and relieve Stelisian." Father nodded to them and left them alone.

Aranin showed her the well, the sleeping tent, and the mess tent, he introduced her to the warriors off watch who weren't asleep. What had once been natural required them both to make an effort, but they did and soon began to talk more freely. They went to dinner with Aranin's watch when they were called, and Analisia talked almost non-stop, answering everyone's questions about the valley. Aranin watched her, still trying to figure out what had changed. She seemed almost like herself now, telling stories. Then Aranin had to go up to the six o'clock watch on the wall, and Analisia and the eight other apprentices who were not yet doing the night watch had training. Aranin wondered how she would do, and worried about her a little, but once he was on the wall he didn't have time to think even about that. When he came down at midnight, she was asleep.

The next morning, in the faint light before dawn, Aranin went to his sister's side. She was still asleep, her round face pallid except for the faint darkness beneath her eyes. He told himself he should stop trying to figure out what made her feel different and strange. This great horror hung over them all. It changed everyone, and made everything feel uncomfortable. Perhaps it was just the dimming of their happiness. He put a hand on her shoulder. The arm beneath the linen nightgown actually felt stronger than he remembered.

"Analisia," he whispered. "It's morning."

She grunted, and groaned a little as she rolled over. "Already," she mumbled half asleep. "I don't want to get up."

"You don't have a choice anymore," Aranin said softly. "You're in the guard now, and we're apprentices. We have to draw water for the next watch's breakfast."

"Oh, yes." She sat up with a grimace.

He smiled faintly. "How did it go in training yesterday? Lady Lestina is really tough."

"She is. It hurts to move at all, but that's a good thing, I think." Analisia smiled as she dragged herself to her feet. Then she dropped her eyes. "The other apprentices were laughing at me, though, I know it."

Aranin gave her hand a quick squeeze. "Don't worry. They always do that, although I suspect, as princess, you may be spared some of the tricks they played on me my first year. They may have laughed, but they all know they were there once too."

She smiled at that, and the light in her eyes made her look, for just a moment, more like the sister he knew.

They were silent while they pulled on their boots. Then he made up his mind to ask the question that had been bothering him. "Why did you decide to come up here, Lisi?"

She looked up, surprised, and their eyes met. They looked at each other a moment and then her astonishment turned to sorrow. "I had to," she said. "It is my duty. I cannot feel like a princess of any worth sitting around doing nothing for my people when they are in trouble. Besides..." She dropped her voice even lower and kept her eyes on the ground. "I don't think I could have stood it any longer. It is awful sitting around doing nothing but waiting for bad news. Only children smile and play. It is a feeling like there is no energy to do anything active and yet there is no concentration to do anything like read. Everyone seems to be holding their breath, waiting to see the next warrior come to the hospital or hear of the next death." Her voice quavered and broke.

Tears filled Aranin's eyes and one spilled down his cheek. He hadn't thought what it must have been like at home. He had thought of it as a wonderful place, almost a vision, a dream of a place he wanted to be. That was why he hadn't understood the shadow on her. He had wanted life at home to be unchanged, happy, peaceful—but that couldn't be. He thought of her sitting in the palace with no dignitaries to entertain, no trade to organize, nothing to do but worry. "I'm sorry," he whispered. "I wanted so much to think you were happy down there. I suppose I was a fool."

After a while, he said, "At least we're together now."

"Yes, and... well, here is where it is happening and..." She hesitated, looking up into his face. "It isn't really easier here, is it? You still wait for the wounded to come down."

"Yes, we do."

"You are helping, though."

"Yes." He smiled slightly. "We have no shortage of work here. We keep busy and try not to think too much. Only to train and to fight. It is a hard life, Lisi, cruel and merciless. Sometimes I want to be home so badly, but thinking about it, I suppose you're right. I would rather be here than at home waiting for news in a false and suspended peace."

"I would." Her tone was strong and decided.

✶✶✶✶✶✶

After that, everything fell into a routine. Aranin still had his two six-hour watches every day. He got more used to standing both of them, but he also became sadder and more discouraged. He never really wanted to be a warrior, and sometimes he wondered if he was really cut out for this. The Shadows did not diminish, no matter how many they killed, and he was exhausted and depressed. He kept thinking there must be something more he could be doing, and yet just getting himself out of bed and going up for his watch was sometimes almost more than he could bear.

For her part, Analisia remained glad to be with the soldiers. She had some small conflicts with her father and sometimes almost lost her temper. She realized she had been spoiled, and as much as she didn't want to be anymore, it was sometimes hard to get used to. She didn't like getting up really early to help prepare breakfast when she wasn't yet allowed on the wall, but it was sort of interesting to learn some basic cooking from the other warriors assigned to the task.

She struggled for the first couple weeks of training, but then she started to be able to do everything, and she found that exciting. In the mornings, she trained by herself under the stern eye of one of the older warriors. Every so often, some new apprentices would join her for a day or two, but no one else came up to the camp until they were almost ready to go on the wall. This was a little frustrating, since she was impatient to get up on the wall herself, but it made her work even harder.

She had her chance for the first time during a day watch with her father in September, and she did well. It was her first real sight of the Shadows, and they sobered her enthusiasm but did not quench it. She was so proud to be helping that fear and worry were put aside. She was concerned for Aranin, who spoke little and never smiled, but she didn't know how to cheer him up.

When November brought more than a foot of snow on the hilltops, the guard barracks for their company was still unbuilt. There was a floor and foundation, covered with tarps, but the snow still filtered in onto their blankets and faces in the night. Everyone was cold most of the time, and Aranin's spirits sank still lower. To make matters worse, there was a slight but worrying change in his mother's letters. She wrote to him much more frequently than she ever had during his apprentice days, and to Analisia little. That in itself was strange. What worried him, however, was a change in her writing style. Her handwriting wasn't as clear as it used to be, and every once in a while, there was a tiny error of spelling or grammar that was unlike her. She never spoke of Analisia's defiance, but he felt it had shaken her, and that the war was pressing on her. He didn't speak of it, even to Analisia, not wanting to worry her, but he wondered if his mother, for all her command, for all he had been afraid of her most of his life, really had the strength to endure the atmosphere Analisia had described in the valley.

Sometimes he wondered if he himself would break; it seemed so often that it was too terrible to bear, and yet he kept getting up and going onto the wall, and sometimes there were moments when he remembered why life was worth living. Standing at the spring at sunrise with Analisia, looking up into the blue sky, waking to find Analisia had made him a pancake for breakfast in the shape of a flower. Her cheerful determination was often what he clung to.

Chapter 12

Who am I?

10 February to 27 May, YA 1124

Westtower

IT WAS early February before Joseph could get out of bed and move about without help, and another week before his fever was entirely gone. Standing made him dizzy at first, his legs shook, and he was always cold away from the fire. Sebastian took care of him when he could, and several of the other nurses were kind in a parental sort of way, but it was very hard for Joseph. He had never been unable to run and jump. He hated physical weakness and had always been a little disgusted by it, so to find himself too frail to walk across the living room without a hand on the tables and chairs was almost unbearable.

Still, he would rather walk. Slowly, wearily, he made his way around the house for hours until he was too tired to stand. But in bed the nightmares came, shadows of the horrible dreams of his illness haunted him, and he thought over and over of what a mess he had made of things on the wall.

He had been sitting there watching when something leapt out of a bush, leapt up faster than a jack-in-the-box. It was large and dark, like something he had seen in a childhood nightmare, and he jumped to his feet with a gasp of horror, but he didn't do anything. He didn't call the others or duck and fit an arrow into Sebastian's bow. The first arrow came in, whistling faintly, and hit him right over the heart before he moved. The mail had turned that one, but then the swarm had come. The Shadows charged up the wall. Joseph had started fighting then, but a second later the pain came in his shoulder. Only then did he have the sense to shout for the others, and he just fought madly—and likely quite badly—after that, until he fainted. He didn't remember much of the rest of it, but he went over it again and again, and every time it seemed more shameful and more frightening.

* * * * * * *

Sebastian was trying to sleep when he woke feeling Tatyana's wrenching grief the day Clarissa died. Unable to bear not knowing what had happened, he got up and went to the tower to look in the mirror. There he saw her as she knelt, weeping over Clarissa's body, and saw Edward come to comfort her. He had never been as close to Clarissa as Tatyana had, and yet he had always been fond of her, sort of like an older cousin. He let the image in the mirror fade and sat still on one of the benches with his head bent for a long while before he made his way down and back to the cottage. Joseph saw him come in as he made a slow pass around the room, and he asked what happened.

Sebastian told him in a low voice, and Joseph put a hand on his shoulder, trying to comfort him, but he couldn't think of anything to say that didn't seem terrible, callous, or out of place. He, too, was sad, but he didn't know what to do with that. They were silent. Then Sebastian went back to bed, but it was a long time before he slept, and everyone noticed he was even more silent than usual for the rest of the week.

* * * * * * *

By late February, Sebastian saw Joseph's desperation for something to do and taught him, with great patience, how to prepare some of the medicines he was using for the sick and to tend the potted herbs in the greenhouse attached to the back of the cottage that they all relied on. That was something to do, but Joseph felt shattered.

"Did you water the plants and give them the compost tea this morning?" a woman asked when Joseph hobbled into the main room of the cottage one morning in early March.

"Of course I did," he snapped with a flash of his eyes. No one besides Sebastian seemed to trust him even to water the plants. Then he was embarrassed for getting angry. "Don't worry, that is the one thing entrusted to me. I'll forget my head first." He tried to laugh, but it sounded strange and hollow to his ears.

The woman nodded and looked back at her mending. Perhaps the expression on her face was only a mix of exasperation and pity, but he saw scorn and distaste. He turned away and went slowly into his bedroom. He had a bedroom again now that he wasn't really a patient anymore. He shared it with two others, but they were both on the wall right now in Sebastian's watch. Inside, where no one would see him, he stood leaning his head against the wall.

No one had a trace of respect for him, and maybe they were right. He was a failure. He was just a weak, silly person; a joke. His family had never liked him. He was too flighty, too silly, too good at getting into trouble, and too curious about things far beyond him. His mother had always said they should leave the big matters of the world to the rulers. Her world consisted of little outside her neighborhood and her cobbler's business. It had always seemed so small to him, but perhaps he would have been better off if he had stayed. He wasn't up to the standard of the big world he had always liked so much. Of course, he hadn't been up to the standard of the little world either—not even close. A joke all through, that's what he was. People had liked him in times of peace, but now jokes were out of season, and they had no more use for him. He stood still there for a long time with a pain in his throat, and a few slow tears ran down his cheeks.

* ★ ★ ★ ★ ★ ★

It was early April. Sebastian sat at his desk grinding some leaves in his mortar and pestle. He was so tired his eyes went out of focus every once in a while, and he had to blink hard to bring them back. Rain dripped from the eaves of the cottage with a slow melancholy sound. He knew he had once liked rain. A perfect day to read or make miniature things for his village. He glanced at the six little houses on the table by the wall and felt a little pang at his heart. There was a coat of dust on the roofs, and most of the stuff had been knocked over by busy people in the dark. What a different life that had been, when there had been time for fun hobbies.

Spring was nice; sure, it was less cold, there were fresh greens to eat, and most importantly, the lengthening days made the terrible dark hours on the wall shorter. But there were still sick and wounded, and everything he did seemed so ineffectual. More men and women under his command had died. When he thought about that, and thought about their parents and children, husbands and wives at home, the weight of the horror seemed almost too much to lift. Then there were the Shadows on the wall. They frightened him, but he couldn't admit that to anyone. He didn't even dare say it out loud. They were so terrible, so silent, and no matter how many were destroyed they never seemed fewer. Those hours, especially the long night watch, haunted him even in daylight, and especially when he tried to sleep. There wasn't time for sleep anyway, there was so much to do making medicines and tending the wounded and organizing what should be planted this spring to feed the large garrison without hope of supplies from Eldirad.

His eyes unfocused again, and he rubbed them feverishly with one hand.

"Sebastian," Joseph's voice came from the floor nearby, soft and concerned. "Are you all right?"

Sebastian looked over. Joseph had been trying to do his exercises, and he lay propped up on his elbows, looking at him with a flushed face.

He was still terribly thin, but not as bad as he had been a month before. "Sure," Sebastian muttered. "Fine."

Joseph did a couple more sit-ups. He didn't think getting into warrior training had been anywhere near this hard the first time. He wasn't sure he was really brave enough to go back on the wall, or if others would want him there, or if he had the innate power to withstand the black mist so many had fallen sick from, but he hated being weak, and training was something to do that stopped him from thinking.

He certainly could never be a captain again. He really had no idea why he had become one in the first place. Sure, he had thought it would be fun and taken the test—that was his fault. The written test was easy; he studied for it with Sebastian, so it was no problem to pass, but why anyone had been foolish enough to vote him a good score on the competition when they knew how unqualified a person he really was had always been a mystery. That part wasn't his fault. He supposed they had thought it funny or something. None of them had ever dreamed it would really matter.

Soon, he was short of breath again and his muscles screamed; he was shivering a little too. He fell back with tears of frustration in his eyes and watched Sebastian again. Joseph was worried about him. He was so grim and silent these days, worked so hard, slept so little, and looked so tired. Long ago, perhaps it was really only a few months, but it seemed like another lifetime, Joseph had been the one who cheered people up. He had always been able to make Sebastian smile, at least a little, even when he was really sad. But not anymore. The black dread and terror that seemed to sit over the fort of Westtower was far beyond his power to lift.

Joseph wanted to be himself, the man he had been before, but every attempt he made fell worse than he had when he tried to climb a tree too fast to impress some boys and tumbled to the ground the day he met Sebastian. The cracked wrist that day had been more than worth making his first real friend when Sebastian took him to the healers, but that was another life, when things worked out and he was happy and lucky. It was a bad analogy after all. It was more like a play that was so bad everyone left before intermission. Maybe that's what his life was. Maybe he was supposed to have died.

He rolled over and tried to do a push-up, but he only got up three inches before his left arm gave out and he fell painfully on his nose. He stayed there for a few minutes without moving or making a sound. The room was silent except for the dripping of the rain and the labored breathing of a couple invalids near the fire. The sound of Sebastian's pestle was erratic, then it stopped.

Joseph sat up and looked at him. Sebastian's hand still held the pestle, but it wasn't moving. His head drooped forward. In another moment his forehead would knock over the bowl of medicine he was making. Joseph opened his mouth to call his name and then thought better of it. He stood as fast as he could and moved the dish out of the way. Then he put a hand very gently on Sebastian's arm. "Sebastian," he whispered.

It was well he had moved the dishes, for Sebastian woke up with a start, flinging out his left hand as his right reached to his hip where his sword would have been if he were on the wall. He opened his eyes, blinked, and gasped. Then he rubbed his eyes. "It was the night Ellen was killed again," he muttered in apology.

Joseph nodded. What did you say to that? Neither he nor Sebastian had known Ellen well, but she had been a good warrior, and Joseph knew every death haunted Sebastian. Joseph took a deep breath. He hadn't died, and so he had better try to be useful somehow. "Sebastian, you must rest. I know you don't want to, and the nightmares—"

"There's so much to do," Sebastian cut in.

"Please let me do the medicines for a little. You taught me how to make that one, please trust me, let me try?" Joseph went down on one knee as he might have long ago to be silly, but it was a stiff, heavy movement, which only made it feel pitiful.

Sebastian rubbed his forehead again. "I trust you, Joseph," he whispered. "I always have. It's just so much..." he had a headache, but he wasn't sure he could bear to rest. Looking down at his friend kneeling beside him, he felt a tender pity for how frail he was and the pleading in his eyes, which felt real even if intended to be a jest, but it made him smile faintly. "All right. Finish it if you like. I'll try to sleep. Call me at nine."

"I will. Never fear." Joseph smiled a little, too, as he watched Sebastian rise and go towards his bedroom. He wondered if Sebastian had meant that about having always trusted him, but at least he was going to let him do this. He would be useful.

★★★★★

The May morning was getting warm as the misty sun made its way up the sky. Joseph was hot and rather muddy but didn't feel too bad. Now, near the end of May, he was finally back to the physical strength he had possessed before the wound. His left shoulder was still a little stiff and sore, but otherwise his body felt pretty good. The last month or so he had spent many hours working in the fields, planting wheat, and then setting out vegetable starts from the little greenhouse. He had always liked gardening and was really quite acceptable at it, and that had made him feel better. He still didn't know who he was anymore, though. He wasn't the man he had been. Mostly his attempts at jokes still fell flat, although occasionally in the gardens he would get a smile, and when he wasn't trying to joke the fears and the hauntings of the nightmares still crept back.

The disrespect hadn't gotten any less, for the reason that it had never actually increased in the first place. People had liked him, but he had never been respected, and it was unlikely anyone had ever called him a title of respect except in jest. It had never bothered him. It felt different now, though, and Joseph couldn't convince himself it hadn't changed. He felt scorn or disgust in every word, almost accusing him of having failed and of not being worthy. It didn't get better, and he didn't expect it ever would, but it didn't sting quite so much as it had when the failure was fresh in his mind and the shame of his weakness ever present.

There were half a dozen other people who had gotten sick from the black mist more than once, or who got the blindness repeatedly, whom Sebastian had ordered off the wall entirely, and Joseph worked with them all day in the fields, joined at times by the off-watch. He had begun to think that maybe his place was with them, but he kept training. He wasn't sure why. Because that was what he did, he supposed. And this morning... he really couldn't say now why he did it. He wished he hadn't, but he had. He had told Sebastian that he was ready to try going up again.

His heart started racing at the thought, and he almost knocked over a little tomato plant he was placing in a cart to go to the fields. He let out his breath slowly. It was only natural. Warriors were needed. Unlike the others who didn't go up, he had not been judged unfit. He hadn't had the time. He had certainly frozen and made a complete fool of himself in his one chance, but he had not had long enough yet to find out whether he would get the blindness and such. He was back to his full strength, and it was high time he went up. That was why he had told Sebastian he was ready. It was his duty. He wasn't brave, but he just had to try to pretend he was. He finished filling the cart and pulled it out to the field. Then he knelt and started digging a hole.

A bell rang at the door of the tower. Joseph jumped, and most of those around him stood as well. Sebastian's watch had gotten up two hours early to work in the field, and now they were called to eat quickly and go up. This time, Joseph had to go with them. He tried to make a joke about abandoning their work as the group stood and left the field to only six people. But if anyone heard it, they made no sign. It wasn't funny, and he knew it. It was just all he could think of.

He ate his porridge without tasting it, buckled on his sword and dagger, and took his bow and quiver from their peg. His heart was thundering in his ears now, and his fingers fumbled over the buckle. What if he stalled, froze, panicked when he saw a Shadow again? What if he fell to the sickness at once? He didn't have innate power, and he wasn't even brave or sensible. How was he supposed to withstand it? He couldn't bear the idea of going into that world of the sickness again. It was too terrible, the dreams, he saw them in his mind just thinking about them, vaguely, and yet the feeling was there and a few terrible images. He tried to steady his breathing. They were only nightmares. Just ordinary nightmares; he had had nightmares as a child, terrible ones, and that hadn't ruined his life. But he just couldn't stand it again. Why did Sebastian not just admit he wasn't up to all this and relegate him to camp worker like the others?

Sebastian came out of the cottage to join them. He smiled at Joseph with tired eyes. "So, you think you're ready?"

"I don't know. How am I supposed to know?" He tried to sound light, to laugh it off. "I'm as strong as I ever was, whatever that means, and I'm ready so long as no one is too upset about bringing a rather silly little boy up with them." He tried once more to laugh, but it was brittle and strained. The problem was, deep down it wasn't a joke. He meant it, and that spoiled the jest.

Sebastian watched his face. He felt without thinking about it the lie in the laugh, and he could see the paleness and tension in Joseph's face. He was glad to see him strong enough to come back to help him on the wall and felt it would be nice to have him there, but it was hard to see him go back into danger. He wondered whether or not Joseph did have the strength to fight the Shadows. He had always felt there was some inner strength to Joseph, but he looked so frightened right now it disturbed him and made him wonder. "Of course we want you," Sebastian said, making himself smile. "I always feel better when you're there."

Joseph wondered if Sebastian was just saying that, but he wasn't sure he wanted to know. It made him feel better to think Sebastian wanted him there. That was enough reason to face it. As Sebastian called the group together and they began to file up onto the wall, Joseph took a couple deep breaths and tried to clear his mind. Sebastian was always going on to the warriors about how that could help you resist the sickness and the blindness. To clear and calm your mind, focus, even to think about flowers or something right when a flash of mist came into your face. Joseph wasn't sure if anyone could actually think of flowers when they had just killed a Shadow and were being attacked by another, but he supposed he would try. Clearing his mind didn't work, though. The turmoil just seemed to get worse, and the best he could muster was a sort of desperate determination not to let the blackness in. He knew it wasn't much of a defense, but it was all he had.

He flinched when he first saw the Shadows on the wall, and it was a moment before he could bring himself to take his place near Sebastian. No one seemed to notice he was there or question what he was doing there. Even the woman whose place he took only gave a general nod of recognition as she stepped back. The Shadows were easy to see in daylight anyway. He started fighting at once, because there was no other choice, and training kicked in. It wasn't long before he had killed several. He certainly didn't remember to think about flowers when the mist washed over his face, but he realized after half an hour or so that, although it sometimes made him cough, the mist had no effect whatsoever on his vision.

10 October, YA 1124; Aldor

Helen stabbed through the center of the Shadow fighting above her on the parapet, then slashed several cords coming up from below. The things seemed to be able to stand on anything, and once they got up, they had no problem standing on the narrow edge of the wall a few feet above the walkway where she and her warriors stood. Stepping back for a minute, she made a routine glance up and down the wall to see how her people were doing. Things were bad, but they were holding on.

Almost hidden around the curve of the city wall, she saw Elisabeth. Elisabeth could never hide from her; it didn't even matter that she knew the cloak and purple hood that had been so often strewn on the floor of her bedroom, just Elisabeth's silhouette out of the corner of her eye would be enough. What was that fool girl thinking? She wasn't supposed to be up here. It wasn't her watch. As if twelve hours a day wasn't enough for anyone. Did Elisabeth think Helen couldn't do this, that she needed to try harder? Perhaps Helen should try harder, but what else could she do? Elisabeth had to rest, as well as doing the million other chores that filled her time off the wall.

Helen slipped out of her place in line, indicating to those near her to fill in. She gave advice and quiet commands to those she passed as she went along the wall, inspecting the line as a good captain should every now and then, but her thoughts were mostly on Elisabeth. When she reached her sister, she put a hand on her shoulder and pulled her away from the front edge of the wall.

"What are you doing here?" she asked in a low, tight tone.

"What does it look like?" Elisabeth snapped. "Fighting Shadows!" She looked at Helen. Her jaw was set, and her heavy eyebrows were drawn together in an expression that Helen thought was more like a stubborn child than a commander.

"That's not the point." Helen's voice was icy. "You are supposed to be in bed."

"We need to fight harder. This isn't enough."

"I'm doing my best." Helen's voice trembled slightly, and her steel-gray eyes were hard and deadly cold. "You staying up here when it's not your watch won't help anything. You will just make yourself sick if you don't eat or sleep." Helen's whole body was stiff with the effort of controlling her rage. It was insulting to the other watch, it was foolish and useless, and Elisabeth was going to kill herself that way. She couldn't let her get away with this. "You must go down this minute and get something to eat and at least a little rest."

"I won't. I'm the guardian. I'm the princess. I'm always in charge. It doesn't matter if it's your watch, you can't make me do anything!" Elisabeth's voice rose and her eyes flashed like pale gray flame.

Helen held her gaze. "Perhaps not," Helen said very low and hard. "But you know better, Elisabeth, and what does it look like right now, you shouting at me in front of the warriors?" Helen wanted to shake her, or else break down in tears, but she could do neither in front of the warriors. She held Elisabeth's gaze. Her sister's eyes were fierce, but there were dark circles under them.

At last, the fire in Elisabeth's eyes went out. She looked away and left the wall without a word or another look at Helen. Helen turned and walked back down the line of warriors. There was an uncomfortable lump in her throat and her eyes stung, but there was work to do. She took a place on the wall and drew her sword.

✶✶✶✶✶✶

Elisabeth was still furious as she walked down the stairs and back to the old hotel. Helen was right. No matter how good she was, one more warrior on the wall wouldn't make the difference they needed. She was ashamed she had lost her temper in front of the warriors, and that only made her angrier. She just felt like she had to be there all the time. She had to make sure that everything possible was being done everywhere, by everyone. Still, none of it was enough. It was a year since she had been given this assignment, and things were only worse. She was supposed to have cleared this all up ages ago. That's what a heroine worth her salt would have done, like all those in the histories. Battles were supposed to be glorious and decisive, not long, tedious defenses.

Her place was left on the table in the mess hall when she arrived. The rest of her watch was already upstairs asleep or taking baths, fixing equipment, or doing one of the other things people sometimes allowed to cut into their sleeping hours between breakfast and lunch and going up for the next watch. Elisabeth ate quickly without tasting the plain bread and beans, but it wasn't easy to make herself take the time. On the other side of the room a woman was refilling quivers for the next watch and hanging them up. Elisabeth jumped up after a minute, leaving some of her beans forgotten, and rushed over to help her and make sure she was putting enough arrows in each.

"I can count, lady," the woman protested weakly as Elisabeth took the quiver from her hand and counted the arrows. "I know you gave orders for twenty in each last week."

"Let's make it thirty," Elisabeth said briskly. "It is better not to have to get more too often, and it seems much could be done if we shot more arrows." She started stuffing more arrows into the quiver.

The woman watched her, her hands fluttering a little. "B-but, lady..."

"What's the matter now?" Elisabeth's eyes flashed and the woman flinched.

"Nothing, lady." The woman turned away and went to clear the table.

Elisabeth kept stuffing the arrows with rather more force than was necessary until she realized what the woman must have been trying to tell her. The quivers weren't big enough for thirty arrows. At twenty-five it didn't push in well, and tugging on one she realized she had been pushing much too hard and the arrows would now not come out with any ease, or likely without taking many with them. Clenching her teeth, she wiggled the extras out. "In the future, twenty will do," she said in a hard voice, feeling the woman must be laughing at her, "but make extra for the next watch and have them in a cart right at the bottom of the stairs before seven, you understand?"

"Yes, lady." The woman nodded and ducked away with the dirty dishes.

Elisabeth went into her room and wrote a letter ordering more arrows from one of the local smiths and giving detailed specifications of how they should be made. Then she lay down and tried to sleep. She was exhausted, all her body ached, and her eyes were puffy. She had been exhausted for months, but she kept tossing and turning, worrying about what was happening on the wall and what on earth she was going to do to end this war. It wasn't at all as it should be. She wanted heroism, but far too many people had died, and, even worse, civilians had fallen. None of this was like the stories, or like her dreams of glory.

She wouldn't admit it, not to anyone, perhaps not fully to herself, but she just wanted all of this to be over. She was tired. She had to do something. She kicked the straw mattress viciously with one foot, rolled over, and stood up. She couldn't just lie there. Something had to be done. They had to make a decisive move and end this once and for all, and the sooner the better. She went to her desk and pulled out some maps, wondering what she could do for a plan of real attack.

* * * * * * *

Helen left another captain in charge for the last five minutes before midnight and headed down to give her report. Not that there was much to say. Everything was terrible, but not differently than it had been for a year. After the fight earlier she still felt a little angry and hurt, and she didn't much like the idea of facing Elisabeth just now, especially alone where Elisabeth wouldn't feel restrained by the gaze of her people.

Helen entered the guardian's room, shutting the door quietly behind her. Elisabeth was sitting at her desk scribbling on something. Helen came up silently and looked over her shoulder. It was a map of the forest.

"What are you doing?" Helen asked a touch suspiciously.

"We have got to do something dramatic. Just sitting on the wall isn't doing any good. I'm planning an offensive attack."

"What are you going to attack exactly? The whole forest?" Helen's voice was a little chilly and her chest tightened. This was desperate, ludicrous.

"The enemy, of course," Elisabeth snapped. "It is weak and dishonorable to sit around letting the enemy come on and on. I have to make an offensive move."

"It is never dishonorable to defend innocent people." Helen's voice grew harder. What more could they do? Perhaps she wasn't doing well enough, but she didn't know how to do better.

"Of course I want to defend them. But people are dying during this siege, even civilians are dying! That's why I have to end this now."

Helen swallowed hard, and for a moment, tears pricked her eyes. She knew better than Elisabeth of the deaths; wasn't it she who had sat by most of their bedsides, trying vainly to save them? Civilians dying was not Elisabeth's failure, it was hers. "You can't just end it. It isn't that simple."

"I must. The enemy must have a stronghold somewhere in the forest, there must be somewhere they come from. Eldir has never been defeated and it shan't start now!" Elisabeth was on her feet now and her eyes flashed fire.

"There is no indication the stronghold of the enemy is anywhere near us. You know perfectly well that the first attacks were up north of Efrim, and they are fighting Shadows at Eldirad, too, and Westtower. Dashing out blind into the forest against a foe like this is the best way to break that victory record you are so proud of, and to get yourself killed and abandon the rest of us to our fate." Helen's voice trembled and was so cold the temperature of the room seemed to drop several degrees.

"I'm not abandoning anyone," Elisabeth snapped. She was too furious to say anything else. She turned and stalked out of the room to start her next watch.

Helen stood for a minute after she was gone, shaken, angry, and desperate. She prayed that Elisabeth wouldn't really try to do anything so rash and foolhardy, and feared she couldn't stop her once she made up her mind. Such a venture was doomed before it was conceived, and yet what could they do?

Helen's anger passed, and she threw herself down on the bed she shared with Elisabeth and wept. When her tears were spent she tried to sleep, but with little success. She made herself a mild sleeping tea and left a cup on the desk for Elisabeth as a sort of peace offering. It helped a little, and Helen managed to rest for a couple of hours.

At about three, she rose and went upstairs to the hospital that had been set up in a few of the larger third story rooms. She was so tired, much more in spirit even than body, but she had to keep trying. She rubbed her aching forehead and tied her straight black hair back with a bit of leather. She mixed two different fever-reducing potions that she was thinking maybe worked the best at the moment and, shutting her eyes, whispered an Efrim plant-strengthening spell that she had found would improve the potency of plant-based medicines. She took the mixture and spooned it into a couple mouths.

She had made sure to let Tatyana and Sebastian know about the latest combination, but she wasn't sure it was really much improvement. She had tried so many different combinations of things over the last year, but she had made no breakthroughs and found nothing really new since she had told Sebastian all her recipes when he was first attacked. She had tried everything she could think of, and a lot of things that didn't even make much sense, but nothing seemed to help. She was desperate, and her heart felt like lead when she looked at all her patients. She would try more combinations if she could think of anything she hadn't already tried, but she had the distinct feeling that she was on the wrong path altogether. If only she could imagine another way to go at it.

The room was dark. No other nurses were there at present. She had only one candle and went from bed to bed. She rubbed some warming salve on frozen limbs and did a fever-reducing spell that seemed to have little effect on a poor young woman with a wound. The groans and the labored breathing were almost too much to bear sometimes.

It was after four. In another hour or so someone would come to relieve her and tell her to go to breakfast for her watch. She walked over to a bed in the corner. The man's face was white and still. As soon as she touched him she knew he was dead, even before she carefully checked for his pulse and his breath. He wasn't anyone she knew, but she had been caring for him for days. She couldn't even remember his name, although she knew he had a wife who had come in a few times. He was her patient, her responsibility. She had failed again. Somehow, in that moment, it was too much. She felt so terribly helpless, hopeless, and alone.

Letting herself drop to her knees, she lay her head on the edge of the dead man's bed and wept. She wept for a man she had never known, and for all the others who were dying around her; for the town, and for her failure to live up to the hope in people's eyes. She missed her parents. She wanted her father so badly in that minute, so kind and quiet, always understanding how she felt. She wanted someone she could really talk to, cling to.

"Oh, Papa," she whispered through her sobs. "Oh, Papa, why did I come here? I can't do this. I can't bear it all alone like this, and Elisabeth and I only yell at each other."

A gentle phantom hand touched her shoulder. "So sorry, my girl," Clarence's voice whispered in her mind. "This is a great trial, but you are strong. Can do it."

She was very glad not to feel alone, and she would have clung to him if her hands would not simply have gone through him. "Oh, Papa," she whispered again. She cried more than ever for a few minutes, and he held her gently. Then at last the tears died down and she started to get control of herself. She knew he couldn't speak very much with the Sight. Every word cost effort, but he could hear her speak aloud no problem. In a broken whisper, she told him about her fights with Elisabeth and her struggles to help the sick. "The people, somehow they still look at me with so much hope, the families and friends of the ill and wounded," she said with tears in her eyes. "I don't understand where they find hope anymore, but the sight of it is almost unbearable. I keep failing. I can't live up to that hope in their eyes, and that makes it even worse than failure. I feel so alone. I hardly even see Elisabeth, and we never could talk. Now we just fight, and I don't know anyone else here. Not really."

"You're never alone, Helen," her father whispered. "I will always come."

"Thank you, Papa." She felt a little better. She felt he understood her pain, and that was comforting. Not being alone. She stood slowly. "But, Papa, what can I do? I can't bear the hope and the failure, again and again. Why do people look at me with that hope?"

"People need hope. It is our duty."

She nodded. She knew that was true, and she supposed it would really be worse if no one had any hope at all. She wiped the tears from her face with her sleeve. "Yes, I suppose duty is all we can do. It helps to talk to you. Will you give Mama a hug and a kiss for me, please?"

"Yes. We love you. Remember that." He dropped a phantom kiss on her forehead and was gone.

Helen was alone in the hospital again. There was still a new casualty to be prepared for burial, but she felt a little stronger. Somehow, she could keep on.

Chapter 13

Broken Window

3 December (about two months later), YA 1124

Eldirad

TATYANA ONLY WANTED the watch to be over. Wanting anything beyond that seemed hopeless, and too much effort. Clarissa's familiar face, see-through in the morning sun, rose yet again over the wall. Tatyana's mouth and throat hurt with the repression of tears. Not again. She blinked, failed to swallow, and stabbed with her dagger. She was hesitant, and a poisoned blade swept by an inch from her cheek. She slashed. The likeness wasn't perfect, and she clung to that, but as her sword pierced the misty heart of the imposter, she felt that another little part of herself was dying. How many more times could she stand seeing that face on a Shadow? The Shadows must know she was attached to that person and hoped somehow to trick her by making an imitation.

For the first few months, she had thought she was just seeing it that way. The Shadows had the ability to trigger images of friends and family being destroyed in terrible ways, and of snakes or whatever animals put greatest fear in a person, details they couldn't possibly know. Tatyana hadn't experienced much of that, but she had heard stories from her warriors and the patients at the hospital. After a little more than a year of fighting, the theory was that the general terror magic the Shadows spread, whatever its precise function and composition, triggered deepest fears and worst nightmares. It made those fears visible. In its most powerful form, or on the weakest minds, it could be overpowering, preventing them from seeing the world around them at least for a short time. This, however, was different. Those near her had confirmed that these apparitions could be seen by everyone. Tatyana wasn't sure it was comforting or if it made her feel any less like she was going insane.

Twenty minutes later, sore and exhausted, she tramped down the stairs. Her father gave her a pat on the shoulder and an encouraging smile as they passed on the stairs, but his eyes were sad and red-rimmed. There was no report to give. Nothing substantial had changed in months. Tatyana was tired, her muscles ached, and her stomach hurt. She was so hungry. Even the midday sun that shone in a pale blue sky overhead wasn't very warm this close to Midwinter, and the north breeze was chilly and biting.

She went in the kitchen door. There was melting snow on the tile floor and dishes in the sink and on the table. A bowl of porridge and a few nuts sat out for Tatyana, who pulled up a chair and ate quickly and hungrily. Tasting wasn't the fun part anymore. Plain porridge with no sugar was much too common, and not special at the best of times. With more than a year since any contact had been made with the outside world and the trading ports, sugar and most spices had run out. Chocolate was gone, and salt was being carefully rationed. All the same, oat porridge still tasted good when she was this hungry, and she liked walnuts. She thought about sneaking a little of the precious maple syrup to put on it—they could still make it, though the access to good trees was limited—but she decided against it. Mother would notice if any of the provisions changed even a little.

She stood and piled her dishes in the overfull sink. She rinsed a glass to get some water. Nothing was the same since Grandpa passed away. He had been failing for a couple months, and then in September he had fallen sick and died. The place he had left in the house gaped. He had always been the quiet, unassuming one in the background. He never spoke in public, and seldom even gave opinions to the family on larger matters, but he was always there. Kind and gentle, washing dishes, helping her and Sebastian with homework when they were little, or teaching them games or funny songs. Tatyana had hardly noticed until he was gone how much he had done to make the house cozy and still like a home even through the crisis. The rest of the family was always too busy working on other things.

Something about the large, empty kitchen felt haunting. Normally her mother would have been there to greet her at watch changing time, but not since Grandmother had fallen ill. Tatyana hesitated. She really should go to the hospital at once and give her two hours before she went to sleep, but she wanted to go up and see them just for a minute. After a moment's hesitation, she gave in to the desire.

She climbed the dark oak stairs to the second story. She still wore her supple leather boots, but they made no sound on the thick carpet that lined the upper hall. The light, dim and dusty coming in through the window at the end of the hall, was just enough to illuminate the spider-webs on the chandeliers. She knocked softly on the door of her grand-parent's room and then went in. The room was bright with winter sun, but it didn't feel that way to Tatyana. She looked at the old oak desk with the birds and rabbits carved on it that she had always loved, and for a moment she was tripped up. The woman who sat at the desk with her back to her reminded her of Grandmother ten or fifteen years ago; a thin, straight figure with long gray hair. Tatyana swallowed hard. She hadn't thought about how much thinner her mother was now, and she wasn't sure when her hair had become completely gray. Clara was a couple inches shorter than Josephine, but the resemblance frightened Tatyana a little.

Tatyana turned her gaze to the bed. Josephine had opened her eyes at the sound of the door and was looking at her. Tatyana knew Josephine was starting to get old. She was 113, but she had been so strong until recently. From the beginning of the crisis, she had always been there, spending most of her time in the hospital, a strong pillar everyone could count on. She had been overworked like the rest of them, of course, and losing her husband had been hard on her, but she had never let it show. Then, two weeks ago, she had collapsed in the hospital. She was very ill now, feverish, and with a chill like that of the Shadows. Her face was almost as white as her pillowcase, waxy, and hollow. As Tatyana approached, Grandmother raised a thin, gnarled hand, and Tatyana took it.

"Don't fret, dear," Josephine whispered softly. "I know you are a strong woman. You have power, a well of courage that you haven't found yet."

Tatyana nodded mutely as she sat on the edge of the bed. She didn't feel as though there was much left inside her. She wasn't sure how she even got up in the morning anymore, but she didn't say that. The thin hand in hers was icy cold, colder even than the snow piled in the streets below, in spite of the crackling fire and warm blankets. "Do you feel better at all?" she asked. She wasn't sure what else to say. She wasn't sure she even wanted to know the answer.

"The ice spreads, and the fever is worse. I have seen something like this kill young warriors, something from the mist..." Her voice was weak. "Just promise me one thing, Tatyana."

"Anything." Tatyana could feel the tears starting to come again but blinked them back.

"Never give up on yourself, or our people. Even when you feel like you failed, don't be hard on yourself, because I know you are doing your best, and that is the best that can be done. I know you will find your strength to keep going... and to see this through."

"I'm not sure I can," Tatyana whispered. "I don't feel like I'm strong."

"Believe me, dear, and promise. Please?"

Tatyana took a deep breath. "I promise."

"Thank you." Josephine squeezed her hand weakly and shut her eyes.

Clara came over then and put a cool cloth on Josephine's forehead. Then she looked into Tatyana's face. "You should rest, my dear," she said.

"No, Mother, I haven't done my time in the hospital yet."

"Are you sure you should? You look terrible." She ran a finger over Tatyana's pale cheek.

"There are people dying," Tatyana whispered. She stood and went out. She knew she had to go. People needed her, and yet... how much good were even the most skilled healers just now? She wouldn't think about that. She had to keep thinking about a new medicine that might help a little more, but her mind felt dull and full of fog.

She went to the hospital where she cleaned and sewed up a wound. Then she mixed up a combination of the stimulant Helen had recommended last time she had come with the Sight and a certain fever reducer her father had discovered to work well. She gave some to the wounded man.

She went and sat at another bedside. Her stomach was still growling. This year's harvest had been very bad because they couldn't protect anything growing outside the wall, and very little of what they had planted out there survived. The big fields had all been outside the city, so while the kitchen gardens still produced well, the staple crops were in short supply. Animals were still taken to graze outside the wall, but they could no longer be left to roam and needed a lot of guards. Consequently, rations had been tight in Eldirad the last several months. Edward had decided the food in the storehouses would be released only very slowly in allotted amounts to each family based on number of people. It wasn't a popular decision. Tatyana knew the people were grumbling, and it worried her father, but no one questioned his authority or complained outright, and that was a blessing. She knew he had been sensible. Who knew how long this would last, and next year's harvest might be worse, but she was still hungry. She wanted a piece of apple pie or a big plate of sausage and biscuits.

Tatyana blinked. She was holding an open bottle of medicine in her hand. She should be paying attention. She poured some into a spoon and fed it to the woman on the cot before her. Then she just sat there for a second, looking at the pale, feverish face of her patient. Her vision blurred and she walked on the wall on a winter morning. Clarissa fell beside her. Then the imitation Clarissas all surrounded her yelling that she was a lazy good-for-nothing.

She woke with a gasp when she fell from her stool onto the polished wood floor of the royal ballroom that was now an extension of the hospital. She sat up, rubbing her hip and blinking back tears. She was so tired, but what good was going to sleep when she had perpetual nightmares?

She felt a hand on her shoulder.

"Lady Tatyana," said a gentle motherly voice.

She looked up into the face of one of the older healers she had known since she followed her father and grandmother to the healers' school as a little child. She blushed, wishing the woman had not found her on the floor, and got up quickly. "I'm fine."

"No, you're not," the healer said firmly looking into her face and meeting her eyes with a strong gray gaze. "You need to rest. You are going to overwork yourself, and you are unhappy."

"Who could not be unhappy right now?" Tatyana snapped, shaking free of the woman's hand.

"No one. But you are taking it very hard."

"Why shouldn't I? I should have stopped this. I've failed my people."

"No, you haven't." The woman was not daunted as many would be by the fire in Tatyana's eyes. The career healers tended to be people with innate power, and Linda was no exception. "You have done, so far, a noble, heroic job of protecting your people against a terrible enemy. You only fail if you give up—or overwork yourself to the point that you, too, fall ill."

"That's not—" Tatyana stopped and checked her sharp voice. She dropped her eyes. The steady, unbendable look in the kindly old woman's eyes reminded her a little of Helen, and there was an echo of what her grandmother had just been telling her. She thought about it. "You..." she began timidly. "You really think I've done a good job? You think my people think so?"

"Yes." There was perfect confidence, not even a trace of a lie in the woman's words or her eyes.

Tatyana felt a little release, a lightening of her burden. Just a little bit. Everything was still terrible, she had lost Grandpa, and Grandmother could go any day, and the fighting wasn't getting easier, or the trials of the hospital. But perhaps Linda was right. Perhaps Josephine was right. Only giving up would be failure... and maybe, just maybe, there *was* strength in her that she didn't know about. She looked up and met Linda's eyes again. "I will not give up," she said in a strong voice.

Linda smiled. "That's the girl I know. Remember back in your training when something was hard. You have always taken setbacks painfully, but you never gave up, and you always managed before most other people." She paused. "Now, will you go to bed?"

"Yes."

7-9 February (two months later), YA 1125; Westtower

In the nine months since Joseph had returned to the wall, things had fallen into a routine at Westtower to the point that no one thought about it much anymore. Seasons changed things only a little. All the warriors stood their two six-hour watches every day. Sebastian's company, of which Joseph was still a part, took the darkest hours of the night, which meant they also got midday. The midday watch was the best in winter, but in summer, with the high sun beating down on two layers of heavy woolen clothing under their mail, it was miserable. There was ice water, and ice to put inside their clothes, that was harvested in winter and kept in an insulated cellar. They threw water on themselves, too, but while it mostly kept people from collapsing from heat exhaustion or heat stroke, it was still dismal. All the same, few complained, and no one suggested taking off the heavy layers, since wearing them had greatly reduced the number of wounded. A double layer almost always turned the arrows. In fact, the number of sick and wounded the last year had been quite low, thanks in part to the heavy clothes and in part to evidence of people becoming more resistant to the mist, as Helen had suggested. Of course, there was also the grimmer fact that all those who were most susceptible had either died or been banned from the wall that first few months.

They had planted many extra fields that spring to feed the large garrison. It hadn't been easy, but with a great deal of work when people probably should have been sleeping, and some help from the villagers of Obrin, they had gotten off to a good start. However, in July a touch of mist in the air seemed to make everything a little sickly, and about the same time the village farmers started having too much trouble with their own crops to help. In the old days, when the warriors stationed at Westtower had little else to do, it had been easy to tend the fields, but now it was a struggle. Still, they kept working, and the crops survived until near harvest time, when a few Shadows managed to get across the wall. A portion of the wheat had a black blight on it before the creatures could be killed.

The rest of the crops were safely harvested, but between the light harvest and the inability to get supplies from Eldirad, provisions were pretty tight that winter. Sebastian refused to take more than the minimum from the emergency storehouse, and while some hungry warriors grumbled, no one complained outright.

Sebastian felt the death of his grandparents and was deeply grieved. He used the mirror to look at his family often during those hard times as they sat by first Thomas's and then Josephine's death bed, but it wasn't as if he could speak to any of them or touch them. Joseph grieved also, for he had loved Sebastian's grandparents, especially Thomas, who had always been very kind to him. Joseph tried to think of ways to lift Sebastian's spirits but with little success. He didn't know how to face the deeper emotions and was left shaken and at a loss.

February had come in cold and buried in snow. The hours on the wall were bitter and simply something to be gotten through. Joseph no longer thought much about being afraid of the Shadows, or about whether he belonged with the soldiers. There was no question about either. He did belong with the soldiers. Everyone was needed, and he could kill Shadows as well as anyone. No one didn't want him up there. They didn't much care it was him, perhaps, but one more pair of eyes, and one more bow and sword, were always welcome. As far as whether he was frightened: well, sure he was. Everyone was. But he could not think about that. He forcibly blocked it out most of the time. One could only be really frightened for so long.

Tonight, as he followed Sebastian down from the wall, all he was thinking about was whether there would be any canned fruit with his bread for breakfast, or dinner, or whatever the four AM meal ought to be called. In the kitchen, there was cold bread and two jars of raspberry preserve. He smiled as he warmed his cold, stiff fingers by the kitchen fire. Two warriors behind him ran into each other trying to hang their swords on the same peg, and one cursed and the other snapped at him. Everyone was tired and hungry.

Joseph wanted to make some kind of joke, or at least say something cheerful, but he had tried so many times and it never worked. He was tired and hungry, too, and a desperate feeling seemed to be waiting just beneath the surface if he dared let his guard down.

"You're going to count every raspberry, I hope, Silvia," one woman said near him, peering over the shoulder of the woman dividing the preserves onto the plates.

"Don't ask her to do that, especially in this light," Joseph said in a brittle, cheerful tone. "It will take hours, just let her shut her eyes and follow her instinct, so long as she doesn't take it all for herself."

"I shan't," said Silvia shortly.

"I know. I was just joking." Joseph felt his cheeks get hot and had to swallow hard.

Silvia went on as if he hadn't spoken. "You each get a spoonful, and if you want to fight over the size of the pile on the plate, go ahead and waste your own time."

Joseph had nothing to say to that. He grabbed the nearest plate and ate in silence sitting next to Sebastian, who was also quiet. Then they went over to the prince's house with the others who slept there and got ready for bed. There was only one patient at the moment, by the fire in the living room, and Sebastian went to check on him and give him some medicine before going to bed. Joseph went straight to bed in one of the little bedrooms of the house with the two other people who slept there. He was exhausted, and although he was still hungry, he fell asleep at once.

He woke suddenly not long after. It was still pitch dark, and the room was silent except for the soft snores of one of his roommates. Still, he felt uneasy, and there was a strange coldness in his shoulder where the old wound still sometimes hurt. He sat up in bed. At that same instant, there was a smash of shattering glass. He looked towards the bedroom window as the last fragments fell and Shadows poured into the room.

He leapt to his feet in an instant, just ducking clear of one of the black lashes. He was barefoot, unarmed, and in his pajamas, but there was no time to think about that or anything else. He ducked again, and punched one of them with his left hand. It was the strangest feeling. A little like plunging his hand into cold water, only with less physical resistance. The Shadow evaporated, but his arm and hand went numb and tingly. Across the room, the woman on the top bunk had woken at the breaking glass and was cowering against the wall holding her blanket up to her neck and trying to block the black lashes with her pillow. Below, the man was still asleep. In a half instant, Joseph saw the outline of a black knife in the hand of a Shadow bending over the sleeper. He snatched a heavy cloak pin off the table near his bed and flung it with all his might at the Shadow. It went through two others and then through the head of the one leaning over the bed. All three went up in smoke. The knife clattered to the floor with a muffled sound and then burst into a plume of especially nasty smoke.

A cord was around Joseph's left leg. He yanked and kicked at it, but it was as tough as rope and his foot was going to sleep. The rest of the house should be roused. What if this was happening in other rooms, or the Shadows got out the door into the house.

"Wake up!" He screamed as loud as he could. "Shadows in the house!"

The man in the opposite bunk stirred, looked up in terror, only half awake, and hid under his quilt. The woman on the top bunk was crawling around trying to reach something to throw. Joseph saw some of the Shadows near the door where his and his companions' swords were hung. Could Shadows lift human weapons? Would they take them? He stooped as a cord tried to twist around his neck and groped desperately in the faint starlight for a piece of glass. He grabbed the closest shard and cut at the cord on his ankle.

"Get the swords if you can," he gasped to the woman.

She reached from her bunk towards the wall, but it was too far. She started to climb down just as Joseph cut his numb foot free, and she was grabbed by a Shadow. She was wrestling with it as Joseph stumbled towards the swords himself. Three Shadows were ahead of him, and one took one of the blades, lifting it easily. However, the others did not. He couldn't see why. The blade swung and he rolled under it, jumped up, and reached for his sword. A cord caught his good leg and he fell, but he managed to get the sword down with him. He had it unsheathed in a moment and slashed up, blocking the blow of the armed Shadow while kicking at the cord on his leg. The woman screamed. The Shadow was choking her. He rolled to his knees and stabbed the thing in the back.

She struggled to her feet and grabbed her sword too. The cord on his leg pulled suddenly from behind. He fell forward fast, his still tingly left hand almost unable to catch him, but as he did so he slashed the Shadow holding the sword and its blade clattered to the floor with a ring of metal. The woman cut the cord on his leg and stabbed the last Shadow.

It had all happened in a few seconds. Now there was a moment of breathless silence. She put out a trembling hand and helped him up.

"Thank you, Joseph," she said. "I was taken by surprise, and it's different without a sword. You saved my life. And his, too." She nodded towards the man still hiding under his blanket.

Joseph smiled a little. He felt unsteady on his feet and realized now that both feet, his right hand, and one knee stung badly. "It was all I could do," he said. He looked down at his hand. It was bleeding. There was a dark stain on the knee of his blue flannel pajamas.

Just then the door burst open, and Sebastian stood there breathless with a dozen other men and women in night clothes and carrying swords. Several looked bleary eyed, but Sebastian's eyes were bright and wide. He looked from the broken window to the black slime and glints of glass on the floor and then to Joseph.

"I think we got them all for now," Joseph said, still a little out of breath. "They broke the window and tried to kill us in our sleep."

"Is everyone all right?" Sebastian asked. His eyes went to the blood on Joseph's hand and knee. "Are you wounded?" His tone became very tight, and he barely managed to get the words out.

Joseph looked at his hand and then picked up a foot and looked at that. "Nothing serious," he said after a minute. "It's just glass cuts. I'd be obliged if you'd take a look at them when you have time. There's probably still some in my feet. But I want to get away from the open window first."

Sebastian let out a breath as his chest slowly unclenched. So long as the blood was not from a wound of the enemy it wasn't serious. "Yes. We had better all get out at once. There is no knowing when more might come. That might have been all that have gotten past us on the wall—perhaps they even took several days to do it, staying hidden—but no one is going to sleep in here again." He turned to those around him, dim shapes clustered in the dark hall. "Go get your blankets and go over to the tower. Someone bring James's boots. He may as well avoid the glass getting out since he has so far."

The man who had hidden was sitting up in his bed now, and he looked a little ashamed. Mary, the woman from the room, was close enough to the door. She picked her way out and followed the others, clutching her sword to her breast and rubbing her neck with her left hand. Joseph stood where he was. James's boots were brought, and he left, too, taking his and Joseph's blankets with him.

Sebastian put out a hand to Joseph. "Why don't you come here and let me carry you as far as the kitchen fire in the tower? We'll be safe there, and I can look at your feet."

Joseph nodded and clung to Sebastian's shoulders as he lifted him in his arms. They walked slowly out of the house. Someone had taken the invalid, and someone else was putting out the fire.

The others soon went to bed again. Sebastian built up the fire and lit a lamp, and he and Joseph sat between them while Sebastian picked the glass out of his friend's feet and knee. Sebastian asked many questions, and between wincing, clenching his teeth in pain, and clutching the arms of his chair in an attempt not to move his foot, Joseph told him everything that had happened.

Sebastian's face grew a little paler and his lips were a thin line, but when the recitation was over he looked up with a small smile. "You did really well, Joseph," he said. "We all came when we heard your shout, but we would have been too late. You saved the lives of both your roommates, and very possibly the rest of us in the house, too. If you had cowered like the others, and hadn't shouted, we might have slept through it, and they could so easily have snuck out your door into the rest of the house without any noise at all."

Joseph shivered. "I don't want to think of that."

"I'm sorry. We needn't. No one will sleep there again, and there are no windows in the tower that don't have heavy stone shutters that shut smooth on the outside and lock inside. Those on the lower levels shall not be left open again. All I'm saying is that I'm proud of you, and grateful to you. You were a real hero tonight."

"It didn't feel like it."

"I don't suppose it generally does. At least, not until afterward. If you are actually being a hero, you wouldn't have time to waste feeling like one." Sebastian's tone was grim, but when he looked up from the bandage into Joseph's face, he smiled. The threat had scared him, and it saddened him that they would have to abandon the little house now, but he was also deeply relieved that everyone was safe, especially Joseph, and he was very proud of his friend.

Joseph smiled back and felt warmth inside. Perhaps that was true. He didn't really care. What he did care about was the look in Sebastian's eyes. Even Joseph couldn't doubt it this time. Sebastian wasn't just being nice. He meant what he said. He really was looking at him with pride and even, perhaps, respect... The first test, a bit over a year ago on the wall, he had failed, but there had been another tonight, and he had actually done quite respectably. Perhaps he was equal to this life after all.

That night, in one of the upper dorms when everyone else was asleep, Joseph let himself think, for the first time since the wound, of the silver star in his duffel. Maybe he wasn't a disgrace to wear it. Maybe he was brave enough to try again—or at least he could pretend to be brave enough, and that might do just as well. That was probably foolish. One night in the dark, even if he had done well, wouldn't make people willing to follow him again. It wouldn't make up for his years of never really being a captain, even though he had the star to claim. Still, perhaps... He sighed. The next watch would be all too soon. He rolled over and went to sleep.

* * ★ ★ * *

During the course of the next day, the off-watch gathered everything of use from the house. Sebastian's watch got up a little early to begin, and Sarah's watch was charged with a couple hours of work before they went to bed. Then, at four in the afternoon, as the light slanted lower over the western wall, Sebastian and Joseph and their companions came back off the wall to finish the job. Everything was taken out of the kitchen: pots and pans, dishes, a small amount of food Shad condiments.

Joseph and two others helped Sebastian wrestle his desk up the stairs into the lookout room. It was quite a task, but they managed in time. The lookout room at the top of the tower had always sort of been the prince's room, too, and Sebastian decided he would make it his quarters now. He

had to have more room and a place for his desk since he needed to organize things and prepare medicines, and that was the only place. A single
cot was brought up there, too, and a chair, and all the books from the
house. It was true only a few of them were reference books that would be
actually useful, but Sebastian couldn't bear to leave them, and most of
the others agreed, so people carried them willingly and piled them by
the walls of the lookout room. Of course, they also collected bedding and
blankets, and all the personal effects, toiletries, toothbrushes, etc., of
those who had been living in the house.

Sebastian walked through the house after it was all done, looking
around with a heavy heart. It was silent now, and the sun had set behind
the wall. Shadows inside the wall were still rare, and a part of him kept
protesting that the house didn't really need to be wholly abandoned. But
he knew no one could risk sleeping there again unless the windows were
covered, and there was really no reason to keep it in use. It was just more
space to be heated in the cold, and fuel was not plentiful. There was no
practical reason for the house except the greenhouse, but that could still
be used in spring, and protected with guards, perhaps. For winter, the
perennial plants could be kept in the windows of the lookout room.

He just felt sentimental; it was his house, after all, not the others'.
They had been here more than a year, it was true, but little of that time
had they been happy. None of them had settled into it like home. He had
lived there more than three years, and for the first two, the house had
just belonged to him and his guests. He had settled in and been happy
there. Had imagined he would live there, at least most of the time, for
forty years or so. And now he had to abandon it. He took the pictures off
the walls. One of his parents, one of Tatyana in a favorite spot in the
garden, and the one Helen had given him the night they were betrothed.
Even the shape of the windows and the worn spots on the furniture
seemed suddenly precious, although he had not noticed them in
months. He looked at the tables in the living room where his little village
was set up, six little houses with people and furnishings. They were
neglected now, from another life when there had been time for fun
hobbies. He turned away with a lump in his throat and left the house.

When Sebastian had gone, Joseph went in one more time. Inside it
was starting to get dark, but he, too, took one more look. He had spent

many pleasant hours in that house. He took from a shelf a deck of trivia cards he had often played with Sebastian and Helen in that room. Then he gathered up several of the little people from the houses that he knew to be especially dear to Sebastian, along with several of the miniature works of art; little items of furniture, paintings, dishes, and so on that were especially nice, or had been given to Sebastian on a special occasion. He hid them in his duffel. Someday he would bring them out when Sebastian was sad. It could never hurt to have a little something like that. Then he, too, quit the house. He went to the tower for a late, and all too small, dinner, and went to bed.

* * * * * * *

The next day was cold and bitter. A snowstorm started at about three in the morning. Now it was somewhere around noon, or so Joseph thought, and it had not let up. The watch seemed endless. There were no clocks on the wall and no time to look at them if there were, and the sun was so thickly covered in clouds it was hard to tell in which direction it lay. The tiny icy flecks of snow whipped in the wind and bit their faces. Joseph squinted into the gale, shielding his eyes with his long black lashes. His fingers were painfully cold, and so were his toes. Snow didn't seem to bother Shadows at all. He supposed they couldn't get cold. They had no warmth to start with, and the whipping wind didn't seem to disturb them much or even flap their shadowy robes. It was eerie, when he thought about it, but he realized he had started taking it for granted.

Joseph was fighting next to Sebastian, near the tower, when someone came running up the stairs behind them.

"Sebastian," she cried. "Sebastian!"

Joseph and the person on the other side moved into Sebastian's spot so he could turn away to talk to the woman. Joseph knew it wasn't really his problem, or his business, but he couldn't help keeping one ear on the conversation behind him. It wasn't like ears did any good in fighting Shadows anyway.

"Sebastian, it's a man from the village," the woman's voice was breathless. "He came knocking on the tower door until he woke me up on the second story. There's a child. He was out with his father in the barn and apparently made a cow angry. The beast stepped on him and broke his arm. The father is in tears and desperate."

Sebastian looked from her to the fight on the wall. The poor kid. Strange as it might seem, such a natural kind of emergency was something of a relief. This was the sort of healing Sebastian had actually been trained for, a wound he could heal, but how could he leave the wall? "Tell the father not to worry. The child should be seen to at once, but he'll be as good as ever in time. I can't leave the wall without a commander, though. I'm afraid I'll have to stay up here while you wake Sarah. I know she's tired, after six hours of this, and probably only just thawing out." He rubbed his hands together ruefully. "But it can't be helped."

Joseph took a deep breath and asked the man next to him to cover for a minute. He wasn't sure exactly what made him brave enough, perhaps it was the feeling that he had done something competent the other night, or the thought of the child's pain. "It can be helped," he said sturdily. "I can lead until you get back." He wasn't sure people would want him, or if they would really follow him, but he had to try. Sebastian needed to get to that poor kid as soon as possible. The child would be frightened and in pain.

Sebastian turned and looked him in the eyes. It was a searching look, and in spite of his doubts and fears, Joseph forced himself to meet the gaze with determination, if not bravery. After a moment, Sebastian nodded. "So be it. I knew you could take back command when you were ready." In the beating wind he quickly unpinned one of his stars and pinned it to the front of Joseph's mail.

"Thank you," Joseph said. "I'll do my best."

Then Sebastian turned and ran down the stairs after the woman, who was still in her bathrobe under her cloak.

Joseph turned to the others. He wasn't sure he was brave enough or strong enough, but he could pretend, and he was determined to try. He knew the principles of leadership. He had passed the theory test with flying colors, after all, and he now knew the ways of the Shadows. The only question was could he make others follow him? He went back to his place at the wall and called out an order saying he was in charge now and rearranging swordfighters and archers, since the trading of spots gave some relief from the weather. To his great surprise and relief, everyone obeyed. Perhaps he had managed the right tone of voice? Or were they too cold and tired to care who commanded, so long as someone did? It was no good thinking about that. Right now, he had a job to do, and, either way, he could do this.

Chapter 14

Growing Up

22 July (about five months later) YA 1125

Valley of Efrimiel at the palace and east rim wall

It had been only a little over a year since Analisia came up to the wall. It wasn't until late November that she had joined the watch with Aranin and begun to stand the night watch as well as the day. Even her energy and optimism had received a serious shock from her first night watch. The watch after dark was a different experience altogether from the day, but she rose to the challenge. At last, she was in the true heart of the threat, and she was still glad to be there. She worked very hard, fighting fiercely alongside the other warriors who had mostly trained much longer. Her people needed saving, and she wouldn't give up for anything. Aranin just kept going. Nothing got better, but having a roof on the barracks in February was nice. The daily routine, terrible, exhausting, and frightening as it was, became second nature to them both. It seemed as though they had always been there, waking at five to eat, sometimes bathe, and then go up to the wall. It didn't even matter much whether it was five in the morning or in the evening.

Today, however, was different. It was a little before three in the morning and they were walking together down the hill in the dark. They had gotten off watch early to sleep so they could leave a little after two, and they wouldn't have to go on watch again until six tomorrow morning. It seemed inconceivable. Analisia felt a little strange as she came down into the valley in the faint early light of dawn. They had looked down on it from the wall that ran around the ridge of the surrounding hills every day, but it had seemed impossibly remote. It might be only a walk of a bit over an hour, but warriors didn't go down. No one had three free hours for the round trip, let alone time to spend down there. A day off was very rare.

There were flowers, white and ghostly blue and yellow, in the grass. The trees were thick and lush, cherries, apples, pears, peaches; there was dark fruit among the shadowed leaves of the plums. Shading the path they came down on were great oaks, hazels, and maples. Aranin looked at all the beauty of the valley with tears in his eyes. He wanted to stop and examine every little flower, to sketch the trees or maybe climb up into them and hide amid the thick branches. It had been close to two years since he had seen the valley close up, and it felt like a fairyland, a place magical and half unreal. A place he didn't belong.

He might have lingered on the white stone path lined with flowers between a field of wheat lush and thick on their right and a wide, flowery meadow full of sheep on the left, but Analisia had his hand and she pulled him on. There was no time to tarry. They came into the courtyard of the palace in rising gray light. All was still. All looked as they knew it, as something seen somewhere in a dream. There was no one guarding the doors. There never had been, but now that seemed strange.

With hesitation, feeling almost as if she no longer had the right, Analisia opened the big oak doors. Aranin followed reluctantly. He felt shy and small, as if coming here made him a little boy again, or perhaps more like he was a stranger of a different race trespassing in the palace of a fair queen. They took off their boots in the wide reception room with its polished marble floor and comfortable chairs. Then they went up the stairs. It was almost dark indoors, with only the faint gray glow of the large windows on the landings, but they didn't need light to know where they were or where they were going. They reached the top floor. Aranin felt strange, almost afraid to step on the thick, soft rugs in the royal hallway. They came to their own room at last and entered through the hall door.

Their room adjoined the royal chamber on one side, and there was a door into it as well as the hall. It looked just as Analisia had left it, and not that different from when Aranin had last seen it. His closet and dresser didn't appear to have been touched. His desk was unusually tidy, and it appeared someone had used most of his pencils. A military strategy book lay on Analisia's desk amid a pile of notepaper.

"I suppose we should get dressed," she whispered.

"I suppose. Do you think anyone will wake up soon?"

"The ceremony's at daybreak, so they have to. Even if it is at a quarter after four this time of year."

"If they even remember." Aranin shook a cloud of dust from the curtain around his bed. "I'm not sure I ever wholly existed in this world, and perhaps now that you rebelled you don't either."

She considered that, but shook her head. "No, Mother asked me if I was coming down for my coming of age in her last letter, in an odd, humble way. I told her we'd be here. I'm sure there'll be something."

"All right. I think I might have heard someone in the kitchen when we passed the door."

"Me too."

Aranin went to his closet and found a pair of silver silk trousers and a silk top the color of cottonwood leaves in the sun. It was thickly decorated with green and white glass crystals, and he had always been fond of it. It was perhaps a shade or two darker than the proper light spring green traditionally worn by youths on this day, but it was the closest he had. The light green was meant to be like a spring shoot representing innocence and youth. He had to admit the darker shade seemed more appropriate. He didn't feel all that young and innocent. How could he after two years at war?

He took the clothes and passed behind the thick blue velvet curtains that surrounded his bed. There was a small window, a comfortable single bed with a dusty quilt depicting a great oak tree full of birds, and a small washstand with an empty china water bowl and a little hand pump for water. He pumped up some water, washed his face and hands, and poured it down the drainpipe. Then he dressed in the fancy clothes. The silk felt soft and light on his skin after the heavy woolen clothes of a soldier, but the buttons up the back of the top were difficult. Warriors' dress was loose and needed no buttons, and he was out of practice. He got most of them, then he paused to shake some of the dust off his quilt and run a finger along one of the little birds.

"Aranin, help!" Analisia called in frustration from beyond the curtain.

He went out just as she stepped from behind her own curtain. She was wearing a fluffy silk underskirt that hung loosely at her waist. A pale sage gown with white lace and pearls was draped over it. She had her forearms in the sleeves but had not pulled on the top and was wearing just her bra top.

"What's the matter?" he asked. "Are there buttons on the cuffs? Did you get your hands stuck?" She held her arms as if she were handcuffed.

"No, no buttons," she said with a crooked smile. "But my arms are stuck, and there is no way in all earth and sky that I'm going to get into this thing."

Looking at her he felt he should have thought of that. Physically, he had changed very little in the last two years and his clothes fit just fine, but she had changed a lot. She had always been somewhat athletic, and had the big-boned build common among their people, but she had become a serious athlete in the last year. She was much slimmer. Even her face was harder. Her round, rosy cheeks had given way to a strong, defined jawline that he thought looked commanding and dignified, but her arms and shoulders were much bulkier and more muscular. Having a body inclined to be broad about the shoulders already, it was even more pronounced now. He took hold of the edges of the sleeves and helped her free her arms.

When she was free, she made a face of slightly comic dismay and put her hands on her hips. "Whatever shall I do now?"

"I don't know. That dress couldn't even be taken out enough, I don't think, and anyway it would take too long. Perhaps you could borrow one."

"If we found a palace woman's dress with big enough arms and shoulders it would be huge on me, and there's not time to take it in."

"A working woman, certainly. Can you think of a woman who was in the army before the war who might have something?"

Analisia thought for a minute. "There was one lady in the palace.

She lives on the second floor, if I'm not mistaken. Room eight. Her name was... Mornita, dark hair for an Efrim, but I think she still had an Efrim build; but if she's alive she won't be home."

"No, of course not." He looked around the room, thinking. "What if you wore my light blue top with the skirt for your green dress? I think it would look nice together. The shades would complement."

"I trust you on color matching," she said with a little smile. "I'll try it. Do you have any scissors? We will have to cut the stitches to take the bodice off the skirt."

He found some scissors in his desk, and while she removed the too-small bodice he got the tunic. It was a man's tunic, of course, without the shaping for a woman's body. So it was quite loose about the waist, and a bit too long, and of course his shoulders were even bigger than hers, but it draped nicely. Analisia found a green scarf in her dresser, and he tied it in a sash for her. She tacked the skirt in a couple places while he brushed his tangled hair.

They were nearly dressed and the light outside the windows had grown greatly when there was a soft knock on the door. Analisia had her hairbrush stuck in a knot of curls, so Aranin went to the door.

Their mother stepped into the lamplight in a shimmering silk dress of midnight blue. The bodice hung in folds and ripples and had been tied, much like Analisia's, with a silver scarf at the waist. Aranin noticed more lines around her eyes, which were deeper set. Her once-round face and soft hands were thin, and her ice-blue eyes seemed larger. There was little golden brown left in her curly hair. He dropped his eyes, feeling both sad and shy as he stepped back and ushered her into the room. "Please, come in, Mother. We are almost ready."

"Oh, I'm so glad, so glad you could come down. It is a special day and all, very special... my children." She looked up at him and then at Analisia, who smiled. "Are you feeling well? Is everything all right? Is your father well?"

Everything all right? Aranin wondered why anyone would ask that. She seemed so different, the way she talked, the fidgety way she moved her hands.

"Father's quite well. He sends his love," Analisia said. "And as for us, we're all ready to become adults." She smiled as she set down the brush and pulled back some of the unruly curls with a fine jeweled clip.

There was an awkward silence. Then Evelina began fussing over Analisia's dress. She wasn't pleased with the unorthodox outfit, to be sure, but Analisia explained the situation in a matter-of-fact tone and Evelina satisfied herself with fussing over the sash and adding a brooch to Analisia's shoulder. Then she turned to Aranin. He felt shy and stiff as she looked over his clothes too. She had not done that since he was small, and there was something in her quick flow of words as she worked that bothered him. She used to be more reserved. He had a strange desire to hug her or pat her on the back. He didn't think she had held him since he was four or five years old, and he had always been a little afraid of her, but it was somehow different now. Her thin white hands seemed so fragile as they fussed and straightened the lace on his tunic.

After a minute, Aranin glanced at the pale gray light outside the window. "We should go, shouldn't we?" he asked timidly.

"Yes, we better hurry." Evelina led the way out the door and down the hall. She led them out onto the wide fourth-floor balcony through a door at the end of the wall. As she stepped out, she put the pearl and crystal flower crown on her silver hair. She straightened her shoulders a little, lifted her chin, and looked a bit more like the woman they knew.

The sun coming over the eastern hills had touched the tops of the tower roofs with a red light that made the slate look a strange sort of reddish eggplant color, and the silver on the spires blazed as if aflame. There were people in the courtyard below now. They had gathered in the time Aranin and Analisia had been changing, and the large green space before the palace gates was crowded with people in fine clothes. Silk and satin shimmered in the gray light of dawn, and all the faces were turned up to the porch.

Evelina turned to the crowd. "This morning we gather to celebrate with solemn rite the passage into adulthood of our Crown Princess Analisia and her brother Prince Aranin."

The people cheered loudly from below. Then Evelina went on to speak the ceremony, asking for the blessings of the elemental goddesses of the Efrim: Earth for long life, health, wisdom, and having enough to eat all their lives; Fire for energy, warmth, and power; Water for strength and persistence, and that they might always have clean water to drink. Air was the winds of fate that were believed to bring good or evil fortunes. The goddess of the moon was asked to give them strength in nobility and purity. Even Efrim religion had changed a little over the past thousand years, and here a few Eldir deities were also asked for their blessing. "May Arthala, the north star, goddess of truth, guide you in honesty, and her handmaidens, the guardian angels of the sky, protect you all your lives, and may Estemel, the evening star, bring you hope and everlasting love."

It was a long blessing, and by the time these last words were pronounced the red dawn light had found its way down onto the porch. As it touched their hair, making it glow warm gold, they were officially adults. Aranin reached out a hand to Analisia and she squeezed it. The people were cheering, and she scanned the crowd for Yeven, finding him at last jumping up and down and waving.

They went down then. A long table of breakfast things was laid out, and everyone ate and talked. It seemed almost like the old days. It felt strange to Aranin to have people come up to him, congratulate him, and wish him happy birthday, but Analisia was in her element. She had made up her mind to have a very good time today, and she talked with everyone. Of course, they wanted to know what it was like up on the wall, which wasn't what she wanted to talk about. It wasn't a happy subject. Many of them also wanted to know why on earth she had gone off to the wall when princesses were supposed to stay in the palace. She told them, very firmly, although as cheerfully as possible, why she had gone up; that it was for her people, and that so long as she wasn't queen and she was a strong young woman who could defend her people, she felt that was her duty. She got tired of saying it, but she remained earnest and didn't lose patience.

Analisia was glad when the music started and dancing began just after five in the morning. The dance lasted until people got too hot and began to disperse around ten, and she danced every dance, mostly with Aranin or Yeven. Aranin liked dancing, and it was a relief from answering questions. For a time, especially when dancing with his sister, he managed to forget his fear and grief. Still, he didn't have the heart for parties he once had, and he never was an outgoing person.

He wandered off among the trees when Analisia was dancing with Yeven, and no one noticed him. He came to the royal garden where roses bloomed in profusion, cascading down from the boughs of a huge walnut over grass carpeted with white daisies and little yellow Lissa flowers like flecks of gold fallen on the grass. He sat down and leaned his head against the trunk of the walnut. It was quiet back here, with the party on the other side of the palace; quiet with actual peace. Birds were singing, and in the distance, there was the gurgle of the river. It was nothing like the eery silence of the forest near the wall.

He wondered if Analisia would miss him, and if he ought to go back, but she had Yeven. He wondered if he would ever find the woman he could love the way Analisia loved Yeven. It seemed like a special thing. He had always felt much too young and hadn't had much interest in romance, but now he was sensible of something more precious. Whoever his true love was, he was sure it wasn't any of the women at his guard station, and he didn't see any likelihood he would meet anyone else any time soon, and how did you meet someone... He didn't know how to talk to people intimately like that. He wasn't sure exactly how he had made the friends he did have. Usually, they had just been brought together by other people or were friends from before he could remember, like Sebastian and Tatyana.

He supposed, whoever she was, he had probably seen her before, but he hadn't known it. He looked up into the swaying leaves of the walnut and imagined meeting her. He liked to think it would be magical, sort of like a fairy tale. In the moonlight, perhaps, among cherry blossoms by the river. If there ever was a moment of that kind of peace in his life again... He could paint a picture like that. It would be lovely, with the river sparkling and perhaps a touch of silver mist in the trees, but what would she look like? He closed his eyes, trying to envision the picture. She was hidden by the mist. He had a nagging feeling that he imagined her with dark hair, more like an Eldir woman. Perhaps that wasn't so surprising. He had never felt comfortable with women of his own country other than his sister. As a highly educated young Efrim man he was an outsider.

The woman of his dreams would be tall and dark-haired, quiet and grave, willing to treat him like an equal, with soft, kind gray eyes, perhaps not so intimidatingly beautiful as Tatyana, but fair, and with something like her strength and dignity... He laughed a little at himself. What a daydreaming young romantic he was being. It was all foolishness. At this rate, he was more likely to meet his true love on the shores of death than at some pretty, peaceful stream. All the same, a meadowlark was singing, the day was warm, and the soft breeze smelled like ripening strawberries. He couldn't feel too grim at that moment. He looked up into the tree, and before long, he fell into unusually pleasant dreams.

✶✶✶✶✶✶

Analisia noticed Aranin was nowhere to be seen as the dancers began to wander off, wishing her well as they went. She had not seen him for maybe an hour, perhaps longer, and she wondered where he had gone to, but it wasn't wholly unlike him. He had never felt as comfortable in the center of a party as she did. She thought with a twinge of worry about how depressed he had been lately, and she hoped he was not off somewhere being unhappy.

Yeven came back with a glass of water for her. "Do you want to go for a little walk?" he asked with a shy smile and flushed cheeks.

"Sure." She smiled back, putting cares aside for the moment. It seemed like forever since she had seen Yeven. They had written, of course. He had sent her a letter with the laundry people every week, and she had sent one back. They had talked about the war, and about books he had read and theatre productions that still went on in Efrim, but it was different being together. She reached out a hand and he took it shyly. It occurred to her that she was old enough to be engaged now, but it would be nine months before Yeven came of age. She would wait. For now, it was good just to feel his hand in hers.

"I have something to tell you," he said in a low voice as they walked away from the others.

"What?"

"I've apprenticed again—in the army this time."

She looked up in surprise into his grave sky-blue eyes. "You loved being a leatherworker so much..."

"Sure, and I'm not giving that up entirely," he said almost lightly. "Mother says I'm close enough. I'm going to do my own belt and scabbard as my journeyman piece, and then Mother and Grandmother will graduate me, so I can always be a leatherworker too."

She felt a little sad thinking of him giving up something he loved so much; she supposed it was a little like how Aranin had given up a career in painting, but Yeven had gone all the way through apprenticeship. She knew why he was doing it, though, even if he didn't say it. "You said once how much need there was for boots," she said.

"There is, too, but I'm not the only young artisan who feels there is a greater need for strong young feet in the boots." He smiled, trying to put aside the very grim reason he had decided to put down his beloved art. "You and I always liked the heroic stories and, well, I can't justify sitting in peace and reading them when we have fallen into a real one, if you know what I mean."

She nodded. "I suppose so, but it seems in the stories the heroes and heroines usually are better, greater, more noble somehow, and they make more progress against the enemy."

"I don't know," he mused, looking up at the cherries that hung thick over their heads. "I think often in the best stories they are pretty hard put to it, at least for a while. As for the heroes, I don't pretend to be one of them. I suppose I'll be one of the foot soldiers who're lucky to get their name mentioned—but I think you are a heroine every inch."

"Thanks." She blushed and dropped her eyes for a few minutes.

"It was pretty funny yesterday on the field where my group of apprentices were training. There were a bunch of sheep and they kept getting in the way. One of them started eating a jump rope, until someone picked up another jump rope to use, and then they all fled in a big wooly stampede." He laughed slightly, then grew sober. "It is an interesting apprentice group I'm in. The others are nearly all artisans, many my age or older, and more girls than boys—or women than men, perhaps I should say, since few are still in their apprentice years. We tend to get into conversations about our crafts after practice. Some of the ladies are willing to talk to me, and there are a couple young blacksmiths and a male bookmaker ten years older or so who talk about craft with me when we are resting."

"That must be nice, but you know... you know you won't be stationed together."

"No, of course not." His voice was just a touch sharp. "I'm not a fool. New apprentices have to be spread out."

"Sorry, I didn't mean that. Just... I will try to get Father to take you at our post. We only have four or five apprentices newer than me who still don't do the night shift. I think he will take you. It would be so nice to be together more."

Yeven smiled, feeling that there would be a bright side to doing what he saw as his duty in leaving the valley.

After a while they wandered around the palace and came back into the royal gardens. Yeven picked some blue flowers and put them in Analisia's hair. Then, as he went to get a rose, he saw Aranin. He put his finger to his lips and pointed. "He makes a picture he would like to paint, don't you think?" he whispered as she came to his side to look.

"Yes." Analisia looked on him a little anxiously. He lay on the flowery grass beneath the big walnut covered in roses. His green tunic was almost the same color as the grass. One arm reached out and his head rested on it, several locks of his thick caramel curls fallen forwards across his face. The soft rise and fall of his side was easy, but she felt she had to reach out and touch his hand with the tip of her finger. It was warm in the sun, not cold or uncomfortably hot, and she smiled. He wasn't sick; only weary. Life on the wall was hard. "Let him sleep," she whispered. "He's been awfully tired lately."

Yeven nodded, looking at his friend, and turned away. They found a spot at some distance and sat and talked until a little boy came looking for them, saying the queen hoped they would join her for lunch. Yeven jumped up and bid Analisia farewell, promising to be back later. Then Analisia went to find Aranin. She knelt, lay a gentle hand on his silken shoulder, and smoothed the hair out of his face.

"Aranin," she called softly. "Time to wake up."

He stirred and blinked. For a moment he almost imagined she was waking him for breakfast in the old days. Then he looked up at the strong, firm-jawed face among the hanging curls and the leaves swaying beyond and remembered where he was. "I'm sorry. I just wanted to be away from all the questions and such. Came here to dream a little... I guess I fell asleep."

"I'm glad. You needed rest, but it's time to go in. Mother's calling us for lunch."

* * * * * *

That afternoon, Aranin went to visit the bookmakers' shop. It looked the same, but there were fewer people, and many desks were empty. Only a few older ladies greeted him when he entered, but they knew him and were nice to him. He had never apprenticed to them officially, perhaps just because he wasn't brave enough, but he had worked with them often. They showed him a couple projects and let him help paint flowers in an illustration for a fine old story that was being refurbished.

Analisia spent the afternoon with her mother, who insisted on telling her all about the organizing of provisions and all the little things that were happening around the valley and going over the paperwork with her. In the evening there was another dance, but Aranin and Analisia couldn't stay long. They had promised to be up for their watch at six the next morning.

Mother said goodbye to them in the entrance hall of the palace. "Take care, my children, please," she said softly.

"We will." Analisia took her hand and smiled.

Evelina hesitated and then pulled out two small packages. "I know going up to the wall there aren't many presents I could give you for your birthday, but I have a little thing for each of you."

They took the small packages, which they opened to reveal moon-silver amulets. Analisia's was fashioned in the form of a cluster of the magnolia flowers that adorned the Efrim crown, although small, only about an inch and a half across. Aranin's was of similar size and depicted a thrush in a weaving of honeysuckle. They both smiled and thanked her earnestly. Analisia kissed her mother's cheek.

Aranin shyly pressed her hand. "Thank you, Mother, it is truly beautiful, as well as sacred."

"I hope they bring you strength. I had them made by our master smith just for you. I have heard rumors that the power of such sacred things helps one resist against our enemy."

"Yes," Analisia said gravely. "Moonsilver always gives power against evil, and they cannot stand the touch of it. It is a lovely gift, Mother, and I am very grateful."

It was dark again as Aranin and Analisia walked back up the wooded hillside to the wall.

"Do you suppose there's a chance Father will take my apprentice mark away now that I'm a woman, even though I've only been up a bit over a year?" Analisia asked presently.

"Likely. You've been on the wall full-time for months now, and the head captain doesn't seem to treat you differently anymore." Aranin wondered if he might be given the badge of captain. He had always planned on trying to be one, and told his father that, so he had no choice but to take the test. He wasn't really sure he wanted to be a captain anymore. It was so much more responsibility, and yet... He did want to help, and he wanted to make his father proud. He had taken the written test two days ago and only awaited his score and the decision of his father and the captain at their post on his performance in fighting.

It was half an hour before midnight when they reached the camp and their father's watch was sitting around the fire eating dinner. Louranin looked up and rose to greet them when they stepped out of the trees.

"Did you enjoy your day off?"

"Very much," Analisia said.

Aranin nodded. "Yes." There was no use asking how the day had been at the wall.

"Happy birthday, both of you," Louranin said with a smile, thumping each of them on the shoulder—the closest he got to tenderness. "I'm proud of you, and I'd like to make your adult status in the army official before my watch. Then you had better sleep and be ready to go up at six."

He led them closer to the firelight and took off Analisia's little morning glory pin. "You have done well, daughter. You are a full member of the fighting force now. That is something to be proud of, and if, after a few more months, you were to choose to take the captain's test, I don't think that would be amiss."

Analisia beamed. She felt like she was glowing. To be a captain would be an even better way to serve her people and gain true respect, and just to be a full member so soon was gratifying. "Thank you, Father."

"As for you, my son, strong and dutiful, you have trained long and done well." He removed the morning glory pin and pulled from his pocket the small golden bird of a captain. "You have passed easily the qualifications to become a captain. Congratulations, Aranin. You will start duty as second in command with Lestius at six tomorrow. Your watch needs a second captain since we lost Gorhinder a month ago."

Aranin nodded gravely. He was proud but also nervous. "I will do my best, Father."

"That is all that can be expected."

Looking at his father, Aranin could see pride in his eyes, something sweet to see when they looked on him, but there was also a touch of repressed anxiety. Father looked tired. The firelight flickering over the hard angles of his face showed lines that had not been there a year ago, and there were dark circles under his eyes. The light played in his hair, which was nearly all gray now even though he was only seventy. His father might never say as much, but Louranin knew well how hard the post of leader was these days. Aranin bowed his head, then he followed Analisia into the barracks. They got to go to bed a little earlier than the rest of their watch. That was one last birthday present. Aranin felt nervous and uncomfortable, but he was still tired, and holding his new moonsilver amulet in one hand, he was soon asleep.

20 September to 18 October YA 1125; East rim of Efrimiel

A couple months after the coming-of-age party, Aranin was starting to get used to commanding a stretch and was being given more freedom by the head captain in charge of the watch. Head captain was a new rank. When the hard fighting on the wall began and the guard posts were set up all around the valley, Louranin had realized they needed one. A watch ideally had two leaders, and even if there was a general to be in charge of one watch at a post, the other watch would need one captain with authority over another. Some posts only had captains. So, Louranin had invented the title. Someone in the valley had even made a leaf that could be added to the golden bird pin of a captain. Aranin was glad getting his captainship hadn't made him fully in charge. It seemed strange to give orders at all, but it was his duty, and, to his lasting wonder, people obeyed him without question.

One day, Analisia and Aranin came down from the wall tired and hungry as usual. It was a few moments before Aranin noticed Louranin hadn't gone up but was still sitting not far away, talking to the head captain of their watch. Something about taking men from other watches and posts to create a full attack force.

"Begging your pardon, Sir, but we are only just holding the wall as it is," the captain quavered. "New recruits come, but they're not so good. Farmers and artisans, mostly ladies and scholars who know a good deal more head learning but not so much of the sword, if you understand me. I don't see where we'll get the men for an attack."

"It may take time," Louranin said in a hard tone. "But it must be done. Scholars may learn to be soldiers as they learn anything else, now they see the need. Defense is not good enough. It will not bring us an end to this war."

"What is it that you expect of me, Sir," the captain said, "if you do not ask for my opinion?"

"I want your agreement, input, and help, Lestius."

"I will do my best, Sir, but we need to train more, better soldiers before we try something like that. It seems to me like a risky venture."

"We have to do something," Analisia spoke up. "I mean, just defending's a risky venture with no end in sight, unless we do something."

Louranin looked at Analisia and smiled grimly. "Exactly right. The defense is only a timekeeper, holding a siege, and it wears down our men while the enemy seems to have no shortage of strength or sign of weakening. They only grow stronger while we sit still."

"We can't go until we have a good plan and a target, though," Analisia said, sitting up straighter under his gaze.

"True, and it will take a long time. I grudge the time, but we must not be hasty. More men need to be trained, and we need a detailed plan of attack, which will require scouting and logistics. I must coordinate all the other guard stations. I think there might be something in attacking here and a bit north where the strange black barrier is farther from our wall—so many Shadows seem to come from that way. We need to know more about that barrier, though. For now, I just want the agreement of my close captains to work on the plan." He looked at Aranin. There was a heavy weight in that look.

Aranin knew something more should be done, yet not this. The plan as it was looked like suicide. He thought of that horrible black barrier out there, and the limitless Shadows that seemed never depleted, never even dismayed or given pause, no matter how many they killed. He imagined facing them beyond the wall... but what could he say? "Of course," he said. "I will do my best, Sir."

Aranin prayed it would take long enough to plan that his father would have time to come to his senses. An end to the war he might get—in fact, it seemed likely—but Aranin couldn't see any chance it would be a good end.

Aranin's dread only deepened.

A few days later when he and Analisia were sitting next to each other on a bench in the dark barracks taking off their boots after a long watch and dish duty, he decided to say something.

"Lisi?" he said softly. "This idea of Father's... it worries me so much."

"Why?" she said looking towards him. "It seems like hope to me."

"I know we need to do more, and I often hate myself for being too tired to work harder, you know that, but charging out... There is no way —I mean, the Shadows only increase and people act so strange among too many of them. They lose heart, go blind, or lose their senses altogether. How can we fight like that? And that black barrier..." He shivered. "Nothing lives there, no bird, not even insect sounds come from those trees, and I can't even see the toughest grass still alive, have you noticed?"

"We are strong warriors." There was a fierce glint in Analisia's eyes and sharpness in her voice. She hadn't noticed any of that, didn't want to notice it, but she didn't see why it should matter. "We have never been toyed with, and we won't be now. We cannot let the enemy call every move. In that way we can never win and will find only disgrace."

"Yes," Aranin said. His voice trembled slightly. "But can't you see what might happen... I mean, what do you expect to do to the Shadows?"

"Scare them, at least. No—destroy them."

Aranin didn't say that he didn't think the Shadows could feel fear, nor did he ask what she would do if they took refuge in the black barrier or if all her warriors fainted or went blind. There was no use trying to make her see the chance he saw of the whole valley being left to ruin with the warriors away, and perhaps it would be an unkindness to try. Either way, she would not listen to him. There was anger in her eyes and her voice, and a stiffness in her back, tension, tenacity. He had hoped she might listen, at least let him speak and give the comfort of listening with a little understanding and compassion, if not agreement. There was no one else left to talk to. She was hard now, and moving away from him. She would not or could not give up the idea they were invincible in spite of all the evidence to the contrary. He swallowed hard and dropped his head, but he couldn't keep the tears from coming. "I suppose you're right," he whispered.

She looked at him. It worried her how tired and sad he seemed these days, but she didn't know what to say, and it made her mad when he questioned the honor and strength of her nation. They could do it. They had to. It was insulting to suggest they couldn't. She went to clean her sword and sleep, and he remained sitting on the bench by the door in the dark.

He was exhausted, and felt horribly alone, abandoned by all his friends, and now even Analisia wouldn't talk to him. It was the most painful thing to be silent when he saw his father leading his people to destruction, and yet he could change nothing. He dared not contradict his father and he couldn't bear anything that would push Analisia further away. No one noticed him sitting there in the dark as the dorm settled into sleep, and he didn't move. Tears streamed down his cheeks, and he did his best to control his ragged breathing. He just couldn't stop crying. It was well after the others were deep in slumber before he got himself to move. At last, he dragged himself to bed, but it was still a long while before he could sleep.

It was a great effort of will to get up at the bell the next morning, but he did. He talked very little, but he had to keep going. It was the only thing to do. With or without hope, he had a stretch of wall to command and people who looked to him.

He wasn't sure how he dragged himself through that period. Yeven joined the troop two weeks later, and that should have been pleasant. Yeven had always been a pretty good friend, but it only seemed to draw Analisia further away from him. He felt jealous and resentful of Yeven because he and Analisia talked so much together. As a new apprentice, Yeven had many chores, and Analisia helped him in her unbelievable energy. They didn't seem to want Aranin.

In truth, they did want him, and were both worried about him, but he was silent and often on the point of tears when off watch, while Analisia could not bear to stop moving. It seemed to her there was always so much to do, and they needed to work harder. Yeven was mostly cheerful, even if a little short-tempered and jumpy at times, and some-times they managed to talk about pleasant things far away. So recently come from the valley, Yeven was full of news and stories, and Analisia took pride in showing him around. There were a thousand little stories around every object in the camp. Tedious, painful, or unpleasant most of them had seemed at the time, and trivial still, but she found it was fun to tell them to him. Somehow, over dirty dishes or arrow feathers, some of the little incidents even turned amusing, but so many included Aranin, and that was a pain because he was no longer at her side and, contrary to his thoughts, she had not forgotten.

One day in the middle of October, Analisia came off the wall with Yeven by her side. Yeven had gone on the wall in the day watch right away, as all apprentices did nowadays. It had scared him more than he would admit the first few times. It still seemed a marvel to him the way one could get used to something like that. How could anyone get used to going up on a wall to fight with all mind and body for six hours against creatures made of horror and shadow that made no noise and were bent on killing you? Yet it was just daily routine for the people at the wall. When he first went up, he had not been able to believe that, but now he found himself feeling that way too. Rather than trembling and going over what had happened in his mind, he was only tired and thinking about what he would be given for dinner and how many chores he might have before he could go to sleep. There were likely to be a lot since, at this time of year, when harvests were finishing up, few people in the valley would have the time to come up and help with things like dish washing.

"Do you think there is anything we could do?" Analisia asked in a low voice.

"About what?" Yeven asked, coming out of his thoughts and looking around.

She was handing him a spoon, but her eyes were on Aranin as he walked down the stairs, last off the wall. "Aranin, of course. I just worry about him. He still commands well, but I haven't heard him speak off the wall in a week. Do you think he's thinner?"

"A little, maybe. I did notice he didn't finish his breakfast yesterday, but he usually does, same as everyone else. I haven't heard him speak either, though."

"What can we do?" Analisia said again.

"How should I know?" Yeven snapped.

"You're his friend."

"You're his sister. You know him way better than I do."

Analisia stiffened and her face flushed. Then her shoulders sagged, and she dropped her eyes to the ground. "I'm not sure anymore. Sure, we used to be really close, but we have both changed so much. I'm not sure I understand him anymore."

"I don't know. You've changed, true, but not deep down. He's still your twin brother. He's just depressed. You can hardly blame him. I get pretty down sometimes, too, if I think too much about all those Shadows."

"I suppose. I suppose that's why I can't stop working. I don't want to think." Her voice was very low. "It's like when I was at home, when there was nothing to do. I was so depressed I wasn't sure I could bear it. Now that I'm here, though, it's different. There is work to be done. There is hope, and we can fight."

"How long has he been like this? He seemed subdued, maybe more than normal, but not this much at your coming of age."

She thought a minute. "He's been down for a long time. The war was hard on him from the beginning, I think, but it has been worse lately. I used to be able to cheer him up. Now he hasn't spoken to me since... since... I'm not sure."

"Do you remember the last thing you said to him? Did you fight?"

"We never fight," she snapped.

"Says the woman who just said she didn't understand him anymore. How do you know you didn't hurt him if you don't understand him anymore?" His voice rose a little.

There was a tense moment. Then Analisia let out her breath. "Perhaps I did. There was a time... he was worried about Father's plan, I think. He seemed to doubt our strength and it made me mad. I don't think I said anything I shouldn't, and he didn't protest, but I suppose I might have."

"I don't pretend to know him intimately like you do. I know he likes heroic storybooks and books about interesting people, and drawing and theatre, but I don't know what he might find offensive or what is in his heart. I am only sure that he loves you more than anything. That was always obvious when he talked about you, and I know he was close to Sebastian, Helen, and Tatyana, and he probably misses them too. It couldn't hurt to make a little gesture to make up, even if you don't think you did anything wrong."

"I suppose, but how? I don't know what to say."

"I'm sure you will think of something." Yeven squeezed her hand, feeling with a tiny thrill how strong and rugged it had become.

Analisia took a deep breath and stood up, setting aside her empty bowl of harvest stew. She walked over, but Aranin did not look up at her. She felt slight resentment at that but forced herself to go ahead. She put a hand on his shoulder and sat down on the rough wooden bench beside him. "I'm sorry if I ever said anything to offend you, Aranin," she said with an effort.

He looked up then. "No, Lisi," he said softly. "Don't be sorry. I'm sorry I can't be like you, or the strong, brave person I should be."

"But you are," she protested, trying not to lose her temper again. "You command so well on the wall, and the Shadows' fog never seems to bother you at all."

"No, not really, but I see what it does to others. That is what I cannot face. I'm sorry, Lisi."

"Isn't there something I can do?" she whispered. "You used to tell me everything, and it made you feel better. You have always worried too much about pleasing Father, I know that, but you shouldn't now. You have done everything he could hope of you."

"No, there is always more I could do."

"I suppose we could always do more somehow, but, I mean... You fight well. That is nothing to be ashamed of." She wasn't sure what to do. She always felt she needed to do more, but it made her work harder, it didn't make her depressed.

He was still looking at his unfinished stew in his lap. "Thank you," he whispered. After a moment he added, "I'm sorry, Lisi. I'm afraid I'm the one who said what I shouldn't have. I didn't mean to offend you. I was only tired and worried, and I misspoke. I... I miss you so much..." His voice broke and dropped so faint she could hardly hear it.

Her eyes softened and she reached out a hand and raised his chin. He looked at her. There were tears in his lake-blue eyes and one shimmered on his cheek.

"I'm not angry," she said gently. "I miss you, too, you know."

"Really?"

"Of course."

Aranin reached out a timid hand to her and she met it halfway. He held on tight. It didn't change the horrors around him. His father was still planning something he firmly believed would be a disaster, and he could never say anything about that to anyone. Yet, at least he wasn't completely alone in the world. The darkness lifted a little.

"Why don't you try a new illustration for a story? I have some nice paper in my satchel. I'd love to see it."

He smiled faintly. "You're sure?"

"Of course I'm sure." She smiled and patted his shoulder. "How about you finish your dinner while I search out the paper? I'm going to help Yeven with the washing for a little while; maybe you could sit with us and design the picture. I need to study for my exam, too, and perhaps you would like to help. You were always the best at helping with my homework."

He smiled more this time, and it even touched his eyes. "I'm always ready to help if I can." Perhaps he still had no hope for the future, but perhaps he didn't need hope. He had Analisia, and there were still fine things left in the world. His eyes rested on a lone hardy aster blooming in the trees beyond the camp. Life could go on.

Chapter 15

To Move a Wall

2 to 23 September, YA 1125

Aldor

EVEN THOUGH IT was only early September, the wind in Helen's face as she led her company out the door of the barracks was chill. It seemed ominous, threatening an early frost or even snow. The crops couldn't handle that. There would be so little already, even with the Efrim farmers doing their best. The big problem was that the fields were mostly outside the city. Only those on the west side of the town could still be worked at all, and that required the sacrifice of assigning many warriors to the protection of the farmers rather than the wall. Even so, at night, Shadows destroyed and poisoned crops so that it was often more than even the powerful Efrim could do to heal them. Sometimes Helen went out to try to help them, but when she wasn't on watch on the wall she was seldom out of the hospital, and hard as it was to spare the time she had to try to sleep sometime.

She paused as a farmer's cart came in at the town gate. The back was half full of mostly ripe corn and a heap of green squash. There was also the body of a dead warrior. She hailed the farmer who drove the cart. The woman wore the grim, tired expression that seemed to have replaced all other emotion in Aldor the last few months.

"What happened?" Helen asked.

"Usual," grunted the woman. "We need more guard or we will never bring in a crop on the outer fields. We need a guard at night too. All my corn and squash were cut up and killed last night, and half the corn had the black poison on it. That isn't fit for animals, unless we can find a way to purify it, and no one has. I went out to try to salvage it, but the Shadows attacked. The guards tried to protect me and my family while we rushed to gather what we could. This poor man died trying."

Helen bowed her head for a minute. She could never give more of her watch to the farmer's guard, and Elisabeth certainly wouldn't consent to more of hers. The wall barely held with the depletion as it was, and they could not spare them at night, not in large enough numbers. It would take a huge troop to do any good at night. Even during the day, the defense seemed to be growing futile and dangerous. "I'm sorry, lady. Enough warriors to make a real difference simply cannot be spared."

The farm woman looked down, her tangled golden hair falling about her face. "As you say, lady, but without them it will not be worth trying to plant outside the walls next spring."

"I fear that," Helen said gravely. "Extra power will have to be put into the kitchen gardens in the village. I think next year only stock will graze outside the wall. They can be watched with relative effectiveness in daylight and brought to safety at night."

"I will do what I can with my kitchen garden, then," the woman said. "I'll go to work over it as soon as I take this man to see if he has any family and where he will be buried."

"Thank you. We must all do our best with what we have." Helen turned away more worried than ever. There was still the storehouse, but last year's crops had been far from good and the emergency provisions were already beginning to be depleted. Perhaps Elisabeth was right, that they had to do something drastic. Helen just wasn't sure. She hardly saw Elisabeth anymore, but they wrote notes to each other and left them in the guardian's room. Ever since they came to Aldor, Elisabeth had let Helen share the guardian's room with her. As head healer, Helen needed her own desk to do her experiments with herbs; besides, they had always shared a room and it just felt right. Perhaps Elisabeth liked having Helen get fed up and pick up her dirty socks off the floor. Anyway, Elisabeth had treated Helen as second in command from day one, which had been gratifying as well as wearing.

They had never been on the same watch, and so there was no problem sharing one bed. Sometimes Helen wished she could see her sister more, but she liked that they still shared a room, and they could leave notes on Elisabeth's desk that no one else would see. Elisabeth was still advocating an offensive attack, although to Helen's relief she no longer seemed entirely bent on not listening to reason about the suicidal nature of her plans. Helen, for her part, continually tried to bring Elisabeth to reason about the consequences of her rash schemes, and to suggest doing something more modest if something must be done.

Helen led her watch up the stairs and waited while they spread out along the wall. Then she walked up beside Elisabeth. They made no reports anymore. Nothing was new. Helen considered telling her about the farmer she had met, but that wasn't really new either. In the end, all she said was, "We're here. You're off now."

Elisabeth nodded and sheathed her sword. "It's a day watch, Helen. Can you come talk to me in private for a minute?"

Helen glanced around and called to one of her more seasoned captains to take charge. There had never been many captains, and three had been killed, so Elisabeth had set up a written test for new captains to pass along with performance tests on the wall and leading alongside her to help ready them to take their places. Trust Elisabeth to remember everything on the captain's test she took years ago. In general, Elisabeth wasn't much good at school or studying, and it was usually Helen who came up with obscure facts, but when it came to soldiering it was different, and Helen was quite impressed.

Elisabeth turned for the stairs and Helen followed, subconsciously bracing herself. It had been months since they had really spoken. Four times a day they passed on the wall in an endless pattern that made no allowances for years or seasons. Very seldom did one come down during her watch so they could talk in private. The last time Helen could remember had been in April. They had argued about how much planting to try in the outer fields and how many soldiers could be spared to guard them. It had gotten pretty bitter. Helen thought they should plant and the guard was worth it, and Elisabeth wouldn't spare enough soldiers. Elisabeth had been right that more warriors couldn't be spared, and Helen was right that without them the crops could not be protected. They had gotten some food from the outer fields, and they would need every bit of it, but it had also cost lives. Helen felt a horrible responsibility for that. It couldn't be done again, but how would they grow enough without it? Mulling these things over and wondering what the argument was to be about today, Helen followed Elisabeth into the guardian's room.

Elisabeth went to her desk and shuffled through notes they had left there over the past summer, as well as heaps of other papers. Then she looked up with determination. "I'm tired of notes," she said in a hard voice. "We need to talk. Something just has to be done. Even you must see that by now. Caution only gets us so far."

"Perhaps, but caution is better than charging out and getting killed."

Elisabeth felt bitter, but almost too tired to be angry. She took a deep breath. "I don't like it, but I have conceded that I cannot make an attack without a fixed target. No good military leader would do that. In spite of the code of our people that the guardian must take the hardest and most dangerous job before they can assign it to others, I have conceded that at present I cannot be spared to go out scouting alone. I have sent out a couple volunteers, strong warriors with innate power, and they never came back. That means the enemy is strong out there, but nothing else, and I am not sending anyone else walking blindly into death alone even if they beg me. All the same, we have to do something. I am determined to make at least a small sortie before the fall is out. We must show them we aren't beaten."

"That is only pride," Helen said coldly. "It won't do any good, and people will die."

"You have seen the fields." A touch of fire rose to Elisabeth's tired eyes. "I have spent Stars only know how many hours on the paperwork and records of this town, and I know how much we need to grow in order to feed everyone. There is no way around it, Helen. Starvation will conquer us before force will." She raised her head and her voice grew louder. "And I will not be beaten like that. If I am going to die, I will die bravely by the sword making our enemies suffer. I will not stay here to be starved out like an animal in a hole."

"Elisabeth," Helen rose and put a firm hand on her sister's shoulder. Her voice was very hard. "We must not talk of dying."

"Even when death is our closest companion?"

"Accepting death, even be it a fighting death, is giving in. It is despair." Helen took a slow breath and pulled herself up as tall as she could be. She was still six inches shorter than Elisabeth, but she was grim and imposing. "There is more than enough despair in this town these days. What it needs is hope."

"And how do you expect to give them *that*?" Elisabeth snapped, pulling away and walking to the window.

"I don't know." Helen could feel her voice breaking a little and tried to steady it. "All I know is that we have to try. What we need are more fields that can be protected. If only the wall here was bigger, like the one in Obrin. We could hold a bigger wall. I think they are still managing it in Obrin, but trying to defend the outer fields with no barrier is futile. The outer fields will not be planted again."

"More fields," Elisabeth muttered. "You are always saying that, but where?" She paced back and forth, then went back to the window and stared out. "What if we moved the wall?"

"Moved it?"

"Yes, one side of it anyway. I could make a good-sized sortie into the forest across the river, make a dent in the enemy forces at least." The energy in her voice was mounting, and she stood up straighter. "I have been planning that for some time. You can talk me out of a campaign, maybe, but I will have at least a sortie. Then behind us you could hold a defense force and we could have the masons and civilians move the east side of the wall, perhaps even all the way across the river. It is only a few dozen yards east, but that would all be planting ground, easily watered. Those used to be the best fields—and people could fish in the river again!" When she turned away from the window to look at Helen there was life in her face again, and light in her eyes that had been long absent. While she could fight and make a difference there was hope. She hadn't felt a hope like this since the early months of the war nearly two years ago.

Helen didn't like it. It sounded terribly dangerous. The town would be exposed while the wall was down, and Elisabeth's foray could come to no end of grief in the darkness that pervaded the forest across the river. Still, what could she say? They had to do something, and every possible plan was desperate. She also knew she could only talk Elisabeth into so much caution, and it was good to see the despair lifted from her sister's face. "We will need more stone to extend the wall, but we could take down some houses where no one is living anymore," she said at last.

"We can, and we could shape river stones if we have to. They might not be as good as the white stone of Efrim, but it could work. We have good masons in Aldor."

"You had better talk to them. That is far too big a project for one day, and we must not have the wall down after dark. We would have to build the extensions with the new stone first, and have everything ready to fly into place, or there won't be a chance." Helen wondered if there was a chance anyway, but she didn't say that. She supposed, if they did it right, there was. It might not be a big one, but it was all they had.

"You agree, then? You will help me with this and lead the city defense force?"

"Yes, I will, if you promise to make the plans well and get as much done before the sortie as possible. We need to get started right away if there is to be a small chance of growing anything in the new ground before snow, but we have got to be prepared."

"I will go talk to the masons at once."

"I must return to my watch. Let me know how it goes."

They both left the room and the barracks. Helen hoped Elisabeth would remember to eat sometime before her next watch but figured Martha, the head cook, would probably track her down in time. The lady was good at her job not only because she could make pleasing food with their limited supplies, but also because she kept track of people when they missed meals and would usually see to it that even someone as distracted as Elisabeth got lunch eventually. Helen knew because she had often run off in the middle of a meal, to check on a patient, usually, and Martha or one of her helpers had come after her with her unfinished plate.

★★★★★★

Everything was ready, or at least as ready as it was going to be. The planning, dreaming, scheming, and desperate hoping of the last year had culminated in three weeks of flurried activity. Elisabeth had slept even less than usual, with the piles of things to organize, but when she did she had slept better than in more than a year.

The masons and civilians had taken the project to heart and worked very hard. Houses were dismantled and raw stone of lesser, but acceptable, quality was found and cut, and the building began only five days after the idea was decided on. The first new wall grew like a branch coming off the side of the town wall and reaching for the river. The masons were always busy around the growing tip of this branch in the daylight hours, with a strong guard of warriors around them, and people worked late within the village cutting stone, planning, and fixing carts. After a week, the first arm had reached the river and spanned it with a small arch over the water. Then the second arm was built, reaching out from the other side of the eastern stretch of the wall, parallel to the first and curving in slightly. That side was finished in six days, and then there were bridges to build and the ground to prepare where the wall would be moved to on the other side of the river. Elisabeth had trouble being patient, but the masons had finally given the go-ahead.

Now, at last, the day was here. Elisabeth had almost enjoyed her breakfast that morning when she came off watch early to prepare. Something was finally going to happen, and she felt her blood stirring like the sap in the trees after a long winter. She had always disliked the slow, enduring resistance, but she had never realized quite how much she hated it until today. The whole town was waking up. There were actually people in the streets. There was still no laughter or music, and little color, but there was life. She ran lightly up the steps of the platform in the central square that had once been used for the band when there where dances and festivals, and she looked out at her people. Helen and her watch were not there. They were still on the wall. That defense could not be let up for a moment no matter what else might come, but all her own warriors were there, and all the civilians of Aldor crowded into the large square of yellowish grass and sickly trees.

A chill wind flapped Elisabeth's purple cloak and made wisps of hair fly about her face as she looked out; a tall, strong figure outlined against the flush of dawn in the east. It thrilled her to see all those faces looking up at her, but not so much as it once might have done. There was a touch of pain behind the pride and excitement. These people were suffering, and they depended on her. That was a great responsibility. She raised her head and spoke in a clear, ringing voice.

"My people. Today will be a great day in our history. Some time, many years from now, our children's children will read and sing of the events of this day when, besieged and beaten down, a brave people put aside despair and took hope. Today we can make a difference to our lives and the lives of all that come after us. We will open up new land to be planted, regain access to the river, and if the winds of fate blow fair, we may do a deep and irreparable harm to our enemies. We are not so easily beaten back as these Shadows may think. We are strong, and together we can triumph."

Everyone in the square cheered. Men and women stood straighter, brandishing swords or tools to be used in the wall moving. There was a light in the faces of the crowd that Elisabeth hadn't seen in a single face in the last year or more. Children jumped up and down.

"Come, my warriors!" Elisabeth cried, and she leapt down the steps and made for the eastern gate in the wall.

All the warriors assigned to come with her followed, while a portion of her host waited to go out with Helen. Elisabeth had agreed, if reluctantly, that it made sense to leave over half the warriors to guard the city since it would be vulnerable without the wall. The civilians old enough to work all reported to their individually assigned posts along the wall to be ready when the word was given to begin the moving. Horses, donkeys, and cows hitched to carts fidgeted uneasily near them.

Elisabeth waited until all her company was gathered close around her. Then she pushed open the beautifully carved iron gate and led her people out. She commanded them to spread in a wide V with her at the point, and they pressed outward, filling the whole corridor between the new arms of the wall. Then they charged forward to the banks of the river, clearing all the Shadows from the land that would be within the new wall. At the river they had to pause because the front line was forced to break apart to cross the three wooden bridges. The back row held the river's edge with bows to keep back the Shadows, and in a few minutes the vanguard spread out again on the far side of the river. Elisabeth waited while the back row crossed the river to join them. Then she shouted the command to charge and led her warriors across the prepared ground, where the moved wall would go, and into the trees beyond.

The Shadows were very thick and, although the sky was mostly clear above, the morning light didn't seem to touch the forest floor. The ground was black. Nearly all the bushes and undergrowth were dead, and their brittle twigs stuck up in a haunted manner, as in a winter that never passed. At the moment, Elisabeth found that it was something of an advantage for warriors to have the underbrush be so dry and brittle. It caught in their clothes, but it usually broke off with little trouble. She plowed through the cracking twigs, calling always to her warriors to keep close and in formation.

They slew thousands of Shadows as the morning wore on. The ground they had passed over, beneath the dead bushes, shimmered with the black slime of slain Shadows, and the mist they gave off grew thick in the air. Elisabeth coughed a little, and realized that some of her warriors were starting to stumble or faint. The blasted mist was getting to them.

She hesitated for a moment, glancing back. They had been fighting for hours, and her people were getting tired. Helen would say she should stop and hold her ground, or even retreat. Elisabeth could almost hear her annoying lecture, and yet... And yet the foray so far had killed so many Shadows. Some people were falling, but they had done so well. They might find a source farther on in the dark forest, and at least more Shadows, thousands more Shadows, could be killed. Surely there was still a chance of victory. There had to be. She couldn't turn back short of victory.

She called to her people, rallying their spirits and bringing them tighter into formation, and pressed on. Her sword flashed and gleamed with power as she mowed down the Shadows in her path. Her heart was pounding. She laughed aloud at the grim thrill of it. The dark of the forest seemed to recede a little and some of the bright afternoon sun filtered in. They came to a small glade where the light was better. Elisabeth's hope surged. There must be some kind of base here somewhere. They must be getting close. She charged ahead with an energy that brought all her companions to follow.

Just then, a wave of Shadows poured out of the trees before them and on both sides. There were thousands, or perhaps millions. It was hard to tell where one ended and the next began. The warriors on either side of Elisabeth fell to the ground. Out of the corner of her eye she saw one of them being dragged away. He was screaming and clutching blindly at the grass.

Whirling her sword through several Shadows in the process, she swept sideways and sliced the cord on his leg.

"Drag the unconscious to the middle; if you can sit or kneel, hold the circle immediately around them. Everyone else, tight circle. We'll beat them yet."

The orders were obeyed. Elisabeth could feel people moving around her, but she could not look. Her eyes were occupied with the Shadows before her. Sword in one hand, dagger in the other, there was nothing to do but fight. It was a long, hard fight, but slowly the Shadows were depleted, leaving nothing but pools of slime and mist that thickened and clung to the blackened branches of the trees above. Good light was gone, and Elisabeth and her warriors could not have said what the hour was.

"Come, my people," she called. "It is time to make our way back. Everyone, come to me!"

The people followed, struggling, fighting, staggering, rallying to her call. Some stumbled through the mist, dragging the wounded and unconscious; some with numb feet or legs crawled over the forest floor. They made some progress, but it was slow and disheartening.

When they had made only half a mile fighting back through the forest, and the light was getting dim, a sudden company of Shadows crashed in on them from the north. They were huge, taller than grown men, and all carried stolen Eldir-style blades glinting with the sickly glow of poison. Mist was about them, too, and many warriors screamed and fled. Those crawling threw themselves to the ground and covered their heads with arms and cloaks.

"Come, come! There is no hope in flight. They are only Shadows like the others!" Elisabeth shouted. "Stand by me for the glory of the people of Aldor! We will not be beaten!"

Elisabeth's blade flashed and flamed beneath the mist of the enemies. She charged forward, and many of the large Shadows fell before her, but with their swords they were harder to fight. The blackness that went up when one of them was killed was thicker, and some of those who fought beside her seemed to go mad of it, striking blindly at who knew what horror they saw in the mist. Elisabeth felt a blade coming from the side. She ducked and moved sideways, but the blade cut her sleeve and grazed her arm . A moment later she felt a searing pain in her left leg. She neither looked nor cried out, but fear came then. Her people were falling around her, and she was wounded. They would never make it back to the village. There was no time to close her eyes or concentrate, but that hardly mattered since she didn't have the Sight. She let pride go and loosed all her fear into a mental scream. "Helen! Help! Carts! Warriors!"

✦✦✦✦✦✦

Helen had not greeted the dawn with the joy her sister had felt, and far away from the motivational speeches, many of her people felt likewise. They were grim and silent, fighting on and waiting for Helen's word of command. Helen had not been able to sleep the night before, tormented by bad dreams—the ordinary kind, not Sight dreams, but still unsettling. She was determined. She knew why this must be done, but she didn't like it. It was such a great risk. There was a shadow on her heart when she watched Elisabeth's company charge out from the wall. Still, she did her best to put such feelings aside, or at the least to hide them.

As soon as Elisabeth's company was a few yards from the wall, Helen called to her warriors to go down off the wall and follow them through the gates. For the moment, the advancing force had pushed all the Shadows back from this side of the wall and Helen could lead a portion of the warriors down the stairs and out of the gates without danger of having the wall overrun. They marched quickly to arrange themselves just behind Elisabeth's force.

They followed close in their wake as far as the prepared ground on the other side of the river. Helen had some of her soldiers carry back a few wounded warriors from Elisabeth's company who fell near the river to close-range arrows that still made their way through their heavy wool clothes. Then Helen and her warriors took up their station a dozen feet beyond the line of prepared ground connecting the ends of the two new walls. As well as the warriors she had left to man the rest of the old wall, she had also sent forces to man the new stretches for the first time, so the space within was completely surrounded. As soon as they were all in place, Helen blew a long clear note on a silver horn that hung at her belt. Behind them, the civilians set to work taking down the stones of the wall and loading them into carts. It would be an awful lot of work. Helen wondered if, even with the many hands that worked hard and fast over the project, there was any chance of finishing before nightfall.

She turned away from the work. There had to be a chance. For the first hour or so there were relatively few Shadows. Elisabeth's attack had pushed them far back. Helen weighed the dangers, and then allowed many of her warriors to help with the wall building as soon as the civilians started bringing stones out to the site close behind the defensive line. By noon, though, the Shadows were getting pretty bad, and her warriors were getting tired. Most of them had started watch with her at four that morning, two hours earlier than usual, after a shorter rest, while those in Elisabeth's watch had been on four hours before that. The day stretched long before them, so she started sending small groups back to the barracks to eat and rest. She made the civilian workers do the same. Those whose turns didn't come until late afternoon were getting pretty beat down, but they all held on. As the afternoon progressed, the last stones of the old wall were loaded into the carts and the new wall started growing faster. The people looked weary, but they didn't lag, and the building site behind the line of warriors was still swarming with people. Perhaps the immediate threat of a nightfall without a high solid wall spurred them on, or perhaps the determination of the warriors defending them inspired their work. The Shadows were getting thicker and thicker, and the warriors were struggling.

It was much harder to defend a line of ground than a wall, many, many times harder, and the trees of the forest that loomed so close over their heads didn't help. The Shadows could climb trees with no trouble at all and jump down on the warriors. Warriors were falling to the black mist and the numbing touch, as well as, of course, the deadly wounds of the enemy. Elisabeth's attack force had long been out of sight, and Helen wondered how far they had gone and if they were coming back. She hoped Elisabeth hadn't completely lost her head. Helen had never approved of Elisabeth's plan. She thought it rash and foolish and would have liked her to stay with the guard force by the wall, but there was no convincing her. Still, she had hoped her sister wouldn't go too far away from the project she was supposedly protecting.

The sun sank lower. Its last rays disappeared behind the rising wall at the back of Helen's company. The wall was over Helen's head now, and in some places it was as high as her tallest warriors. Another half an hour and they would be putting on the battlements. Another hour and a half, and she might be able to retreat with her remaining soldiers behind the blessed protection of stone. But it would be dark by then. The mist coming out of the forest was thick and seemed likely to make dusk settle even faster. She began another swift rotation of the troops, sending just a dozen at a time for a minute or two behind the wall, a glass of water, and some bread.

Helen heard Elisabeth's scream for help in her mind. It was clear and full of fear, desperation, and immediate danger. Elisabeth wanted carts. Helen cursed. It was only too easy to guess what the carts were for. She wondered how many. Helen hated to send more people into danger, but she had no choice. She glanced back at the wall. The masons were standing on the top, fitting and directing the first stones of the ramparts. She looked at her warriors. They were struggling to hold the line in front of the wall, and the sun had set. She turned to the trees, where dusk was getting deeper by the moment and thick mist floated.

Every choice was bad, but there was only one she could make. She looked up at the people on the wall. "I need four carts at the gate. Not with animals, just the carts."

"Yes, lady," someone on top cried.

Helen turned to her warriors. Quickly, and as randomly as she could, hating the choice of whose life to endanger, she assigned four pullers and ten guards to each cart. Taking animals into the forest with so many Shadows would only be more dangerous, so four big men would pull each cart. Then she found a fairly new captain who was still on her feet and put her in charge until she returned.

"Now, follow me!" she cried to the people with the carts. "We have a rescue mission."

They were weary and reluctant, but they rallied to the strength and purpose in her ringing voice, and they followed her into the forest.

Chapter 16

Standing Together

23 September to 15 October, YA 1125

Aldor

ELISABETH FOUGHT HARD, putting every fragment of innate power and concentration she had into the task. She would not think about the wounds yet, and she almost managed to block out the pain. She pushed back the tingling, burning pain that came into her fingers with sheer will. People were falling around her, falling fast. The mist was thick. Faint phantoms, and lurid colored shapes, danced in the corners of Elisabeth's eyes, but she forced them back. With a great stab she slew the last of the pack of large Shadows. Panting and choking, she looked around her. There were some two dozen men and women still on their feet, but the forest floor was covered in the wounded, numb, or unconscious. She had started with a hundred and fifty warriors, and where were they now? A horrible pain and shame came over her, but there were still Shadows around. The respite was only momentary. She started dragging all the wounded and unconscious that could be found into a heap at the center of the circle of standing warriors. Everyone who could helped, but before they were done, Shadows were on them again.

The sound of footsteps, creaking wheels, and crashing bushes was like a blessing from the Stars. Elisabeth glanced in the direction of the sound and saw the light of lanterns hanging on the carts and the flash and gleam of at least one fine moonsilver blade wielded by someone with considerable innate power. It was a great relief. She would never have admitted how great.

"Elisabeth?" Helen called.

"Here!" Elisabeth shouted back.

The carts rumbled up through the trees, casting their lantern light on the shimmering black slime of the forest floor and the heap of unconscious forms lying in it.

"By Earth and Stars, Elisabeth," Helen gasped. "Those that we found strewn among the trees on our way were bad enough." A vise closed around her heart at the number of fallen, and for a moment she was struck by a horror not even the recent terrible years had prepared her for.

"It was a good foray until a huge host with swords attacked us on our way back," Elisabeth panted. She was angry, but her voice just sounded tired. "The mist got really thick. I think that's mostly what got them." She glanced at the unconscious forms.

"We have to get out of here. My people are falling to it also." Helen left the defense to Elisabeth and her remaining company while she gave hasty orders to her warriors to begin collecting all those on the ground, as well as the swords both of their friends and of the enemy. Those the enemy had used were set apart and wrapped in sacking so they would touch no one. It might take a lot of careful cleaning before they could be used again by people, but they couldn't let the enemy get them back.

The warriors worked with grim speed, but the number unable to walk was so great that the four carts were heaped much higher than was remotely safe. When Helen called her cart-men to retreat, the number straining at the traces of the wagons had to be doubled, and the Shadows were now aware of them and were pouring in around them.

They made a hundred yards, then two hundred. Their progress slowed. Elisabeth now had fewer than two dozen standing, and with eight at each cart as well as those who had succumbed, Helen's guards were down to four or five per cart. They were still a mile from the new wall, and there was no way it was enough. Helen looked from the carts of wounded to Elisabeth and her people holding the rear guard. It was nearly pitch dark under the trees now.

Elisabeth was fighting furiously. Helen's arrival had given her new strength and hope. She didn't think yet, she just fought, giving way no faster than the carts moved forward. No Shadow would get past her.

Helen, too, was fighting hard. She squinted into the darkness ahead and looked at the sick in the carts. Many of them dripped with slime. She thought of Sight connections. Her father—he had likely heard Elisabeth's first desperation. Yet, would he? Elisabeth's distress would usually have come to him, certainly a general cry of fear would have, but Elisabeth had addressed her call specifically to Helen, so it would have been much stronger for her. Thinking of or crying out to a certain person in distress was the surest way for them, specifically, to hear. Helen got a couple people to step into her place and retreated a few steps to the carts. Then she shut her eyes and concentrated a second, reaching out a little, "Tatyana, Father, can you come to me?"

For a moment, she waited. She was too tired to risk really putting herself out towards them. Then she felt her father touch her shoulder. "I can't explain now," she whispered. "I need to do a light weaving. A really big one, or we'll never make it out of this. I am weary, and I need your help."

"I'll help while I can," he whispered.

Helen took a deep breath. She wasn't sure she could do this. It was a very big spell, but the Shadows were shooting at the unconscious, and there were thousands of Shadows again on every side. She walked slowly between the middle two carts and began to weave the light from the lanterns. It was a delicate task, and the result was scarcely visible: A pale gossamer web of light, woven from the golden lantern light, and also from the pure part of the air where light of the world yet remained. In a few moments it surrounded her, and the evil of the dark could no longer touch her. She felt her father giving her strength as she stretched the spell. It covered one of the carts near her, and then the other. She began to walk around the carts.

The Shadows had never seemed to have real eyes. Certainly, they had no pupils or irises or retinas. They couldn't see the same way people did. There was always a certain amount of mist in the air around the

Shadows, not to mention that pure air had an element of shadow even in daylight, and Helen's theory was that the Shadows saw or sensed people through that shadow, since they were made of shadow themselves. To hide from people, one would have to weave shadow, too, with and around the light, but she couldn't do that on this scale and she hoped the pure light barrier would have the power to render them invisible to the Shadows' senses. The faint shimmer, like a very fine silver mist to the keen eye, spread over the carts, and indeed the Shadows stopped shooting at them.

Helen felt another touch on her shoulder. Tatyana said nothing, and Helen didn't need to tell her what she was doing. Tatyana put both hands on Helen's shoulders, and Helen could feel her giving her new strength. Her father had gone now, he had done all he could, but she had Tatyana. Helen stretched the spell a little more, and it covered the whole party. The Shadows still fought them and tried to stop their progress forward. Arrows shot among them once again—the thin, tenuous spell could not hold them back even though they were made of dark—but they shot wild. It was still a hard fight, but they moved faster now. Helen fought no more herself, leaving Elisabeth to command the warriors. She walked slowly, just in front of the carts, clutching her sword in both hands and struggling not to drop the spell.

They could hear the river gurgling and splashing, the shouts of many voices, and the heavy noises of moving stone. They were very near the wall now. There were thousands of Shadows all around them like a sea. The people in the front line were struggling and falling in spite of the concealment. Was the charm wearing thin or were there just too many Shadows? Helen opened her eyes. Her vision had become blurry. Overexertion of a person's power through the Sight or otherwise had similar side effects. The headache was starting to grow, and her vision was going. She didn't dare do this longer. Except in the most extreme cases of overuse none of the effects were long lasting, but she had many long, hard hours still before she could rest.

Tatyana was gone now, too, and she could not do it alone. They were only 150 yards from the new wall, 120, 110... Warriors from the wall were running towards them. She let the spell fall and, stumbling, caught herself on the side of a wagon. The Shadows were everywhere now, pouring over them, but for a minute she could not go to fight them. Elisabeth was shouting, the warriors were pulling ahead as the line before the wall surged forward to meet them. Helen blinked hard, shook her head a little, and went to join Elisabeth in the rear guard. Her eyes were clearing, and with great effort, she forced the darkness back from her mind and managed to distinguish the Shadows again.

The two sisters held the back line until all the carts had gone in through the newly moved gates. Then Helen looked up to see the battlements nearly finished in the faint misty moonlight. She lifted the silver horn that still hung at her waist and blew the call to retreat. Her exhausted warriors made for the gate in orderly fashion as she had instructed them and appeared soon after atop the new wall.

Last of all, Helen and Elisabeth backed slowly to the gate and slipped in. Elisabeth looked around at the sparkling river, the meadow beyond, and then up at the new wall; for a moment, her heart was lifted. But then she thought of the warriors. Helen and her warriors had been on watch since four that morning. That had to be something close to fifteen hours by now, but Elisabeth had almost no watch to take up to replace them, and those she had were even worse off. After only two hours' rest, they had fought over twelve hours in terrible conditions, and even those who remained on their feet were likely at least a little sick. Some of them were stumbling with weariness. Elisabeth felt sick, too, if she let herself think about it, and the tingling in her arm made it take will power to keep her grip on her sword—and yet surely Helen must go with the wounded, and it was for her to try to rally the exhausted warriors on the wall.

Helen looked at Elisabeth, rubbing her temple with one hand. Then she looked at the wall and sighed. "We have no replacement watch," she said in a low, even voice. "But the warriors must rest. Those who held the remainder of the wall all day will have had it the easiest. Why don't we spread them to cover the new wall in the east? Do you think you could hold the wall an hour or two with a half watch of tired warriors? All your warriors, and those of mine who were outside the wall all day, must rest at once, and we have to let them rest more than a few minutes at a time or we won't hold the wall 'til morning."

Elisabeth nodded. She felt like a fool and a failure. All she had done was deplete the force so they might not survive even one more night. "I can," she said grimly. "I have no choice. You must see to the wounded." She turned without more words and ran up the stairs. If she stood still, she might realize how tired she was. She sent half the warriors down and kept a stronger force on the east wall than the rest, but they were more spaced out than was good, and it was a hard fight. Two hours seemed an eternity.

Helen went back to the inn. She was exhausted, but her work had hardly begun, and she knew it. She gave the cooks some herbs to put in the food of the soldiers who were off watch to help them recover, took a dose herself, and then dragged herself upstairs to where two of the second-floor dorms as well as several third-floor apartments were now full of sick and wounded. One whole room was just those with numb limbs, and she gave them what herbs she could, passed around salves, and left them to tend each other. Then she mixed and administered the best herbal concoction she had to the ill and unconscious before she mounted to the chambers of the wounded. When she entered there, her heart felt like lead and the air seemed unbreathable. Compared to the total number of fallen the wounded were blessedly few, but there were still too many, and what hope could she hold out for their lives? How many had been dead when brought in she did not know or wish to know.

With a heavy heart and great weariness, but as much haste as she could, she set to work cleaning the wounds. The two civilian healers came in to help her, and they worked in silence as the minutes dragged by. Helen felt more and more bitter towards Elisabeth. Why did she have to be fool enough to go charging out so far? What was the point of the offensive anyway? Elisabeth was always such a proud, arrogant fool. All these poor people... it wasn't fair.

"Your watch will be going back up in ten minutes, Lady Helen," a voice called from the door.

"I can't go now," Helen said a touch sharply. She was so tired, and her head ached, and her eyes ached, and mostly she was angry and grieved.

"Someone must, lady."

Helen kept her eyes down and took a deep breath. Then she stood. She couldn't leave the hospital for another watch, but it was her duty to organize her warriors before they went out. She followed the girl down the stairs in silence. She organized the tired warriors below, assigned two captains to work together, and they left. The chef asked about more herbs. Then someone wanted to know the state of some of the sick. The steps of the returning watch were on the porch by the time Helen started back up the stairs, but she didn't look back.

"Lady Helen!" It was a man's voice this time.

Helen turned reluctantly from the top of the second flight and looked back into the face of a middle-aged warrior, pale and soaked in the black slime of the Shadows. She supposed he must have a loved one from the sortie and want to know if they were alive. She didn't want to deal with it just now, but she braced herself. "What is it?"

"It's Lady Elisabeth," he panted as he came up beside her. "Won't you come down and see her, please?"

Her body tensed and she half turned back to the stairs. What did Elisabeth want now? "Why?" she said in a chilly voice. She had so many more important things to do.

"She's not well—I don't know, exactly—but there is blood on her trousers."

Helen cursed under her breath. She ran down the stairs past the man, all her anger replaced by fear. As she came down the first flight, she saw Elisabeth standing by the door. Or sort of standing. She was leaning against the wall and one hand clutched, white-knuckled, on a cloak rack. Her head rested on the wall with her hair over her face, and she seemed not even to notice the circle of people who had gathered and were looking at her anxiously. Helen ran up, shooing the other people away with a wave. She took Elisabeth's free hand. It was bloodless and icy and trembled slightly. With her other hand, Helen lifted the tangled golden-brown curls from Elisabeth's face. Her face was chalk white and her eyes were down.

"Elisabeth, are you all right? Can you walk as far as our room?"

Elisabeth stirred. She noticed the people staring and tried to straighten up. "Sorry," she mumbled. "I... I let myself think about it... about, I mean I was safe inside and... just tired, my leg hurts... Fine." She forcibly straightened up and took a step forward, but she was unsteady.

Helen got Elisabeth's arm around her shoulders and helped her into the guardian's room away from the staring crowd. She sat her on the cot and looked in her eyes. "Now tell me what happened. Are you sick?"

"Don't know," Elisabeth mumbled. She looked at her lap. "I think I'm just tired. My leg hurts. I think it needs bandaging up."

Helen felt the lie in "just," and knew it was more than that. Of course Elisabeth was tired. The others from her company had all been exhausted and a little ill. Helen hadn't let any of them go back up on the wall with the relief watch. They weren't up to it. And Elisabeth had fought an extra two hours on top of it. Still, it was more. The wound. Wounds were deadly. There was a good deal of blood on her pants, but with a wound like that from a Shadow, no amount of innate power or willpower should have kept Elisabeth on her feet this long. "Lie down and let me see your leg at once," Helen said.

Elisabeth obeyed without a word. Helen rolled up the torn pant leg and cleaned the wound. To her great relief, the wound, although deep and nasty, was not festering like the poisoned wounds from the Shadows did. There was none of the blackness or the nasty smell. It was disinfected, stitched, and bandaged before long. "It doesn't appear to be a Shadow wound," Helen said gently.

"I suppose it was one of my warriors," Elisabeth said weakly. "Some of them saw things in the mist, I think, and stabbed wild."

Helen pursed her lips. Elisabeth had lost a good deal of blood, but so long as the exhaustion and blood loss hadn't made her susceptible to the heavy exposure to the black mist, she should be fine in a few weeks. That was a blessing, but it would be no good telling Elisabeth that right now. "Is there anything else?"

"Only my arm," Elisabeth rubbed her right arm, which looked white beside the left. "It's all tingly. I got a scratch. Hardly broke the skin, but it hurt."

That sounded more serious than the leg wound. Helen found the slit in the fabric made by a sharp blade and below it the scratch. It was only that. A line no more than a hair's breadth and a couple inches long, but it was oozing dark gray slime and starting to smell.

"Could you just wash it up, or give me a salve or something?" Elisabeth murmured. "I want to sleep, and I'm taking my watch up again in less than four hours."

Helen turned her sister's face towards her where it lay on the pillow. "No, you aren't. The watch you were with must go up then, but you must rest. You are wounded. The stitches in your leg need to heal, and this scratch on your arm is something people have died of." There was a little fear in Elisabeth's eyes, and Helen hastened to go on. "Now, I think you'll be fine in a few days. You are strong. However, that doesn't mean you're invulnerable. I will clean the scratch as best I can, and I'll give you some medicine, but none of it is the cure. As for your leg, I can do a healing charm that will speed it up and start the knitting of the flesh back together, but only if you promise not to walk on it for at least eight hours."

"I promise," Elisabeth said very low.

Helen did the charm, which took almost more power than she had left. Then she went back to cleaning the wound. She saw a moonsilver pendant her mother had given her long ago that hung above her desk. She had hung it there for good luck and not thought about it much, but now she took it down and held it a minute close to her chest. Moonsilver could give strength to both Eldir and Efrim power, and she needed all the help she could get. Still holding it, she put both hands on Elisabeth's arm and whispered a purity charm. There was a strange boiling feeling. The pendant felt a little hot. Helen looked down. The moon was still up, and the pendant glowed faintly, and where it touched the black slime of the wound it made it bubble and sizzle. Whatever evil was in it couldn't stand the purity in the moonsilver. Some of it went up in smoke. Maybe the touch of moonsilver really helped! A thrill of excitement ran through her. Tired, grieved, and worried as she was, perhaps she had made a new discovery.

When she had finished with Elisabeth she went back upstairs and finished tending to the wounded. She used the application of the moonsilver along with the purity charm on all of them. It did seem to get the wounds cleaner.

By the time she lay down to sleep herself, in a cot in the upstairs dorm, she was so exhausted she could barely stand, but the wounded had all been seen to.

Helen was too busy in the hospital to go back on the wall for the rest of the week. She came down before each of her watches to talk to the other captains and organize things. She wasn't sure why, exactly. Really, she was just a captain, too, but she had been in command for so long that she felt she had a duty to her watch. It had become habit. She barely slept, and when she did it was usually in one of the hospital dorms to be on call. It was a very dark time. There were so many ill and wounded. However, by the third day all those who had the blindness or numb limbs were recovered, and that room could be converted back into a dorm. That evening they were divided and joined the two watches, making the work on the wall a little easier. Some of the milder cases of the sickness were also on the mend by the fourth day, but there was still not a minute to spare for Helen. She had assistants, to be sure, but there were only two other healers in Aldor and even they looked to her and were always asking her questions. She used the moonsilver charm every time she did purifying spells to clean the festering wounds, and had the one other healer with the gift do so also. It did seem to help. She tried laying it on the sick and using it in healing spells over them, but she couldn't decide if it made any difference. By the end of the week, many of the ill had died and most of the rest were at least on the path to recovery, but the percentages didn't seem any different from the average since the weaker people were gone from the ranks.

In the room of the wounded, however, the difference was measurable. It was no cure. She had still lost half her patients already, and many were still doubtful; but by the beginning of the second week, nearly a quarter of the wounded were mending.

After the first long watch in which six of the wounded knew her, sat up, and asked for food, she found a hidden spot and sat and wept for a long time. Even if those six were her only survivors from the room of wounded it was a blessing and an enormous improvement. It wasn't good, and yet after two years of working hard over patients with no hope in her heart, knowing that almost no one with more than a pin scratch would survive, it was an overwhelming relief. When her tears subsided, she took a deep breath and used the Sight for the first time since the big battle. She went briefly to Sebastian, finding him sitting at his desk in the lookout room at the tower making medicines.

She told him what she had found. She couldn't spare energy just now to say anything else, but she lingered a few moments, stroking his hair with a phantom hand while he thanked her and told her how things were going.

"There is nothing new lately. Everyone sleeps safe in the tower now. Joseph and Sarah hold one watch and I the other. I miss him, but it works better this way. We're getting along. Don't worry about us, Helen. I felt you were in danger last week. I have looked in the mirror a couple times and see you have a lot of wounded. I do wish you could tell me all about it. Is everything all right now?"

"Yes."

"I'll take that, but I worry about you, Helen, and I miss you so much," he whispered.

She didn't reply, but kissed his cheek and slipped away. Then, after a few minutes' rest, she went to Tatyana. She had to spread the word of her discovery. It was five in the morning and Tatyana was just getting up.

"Helen, I've been so worried," she said as soon as Helen touched her arm. "That was a terrible situation you were in there. So many wounded. What happened, can you tell me? Are you holding out all right there?"

"Foray, moved the wall, went bad. Fine now."

"I won't ask you to say more, although I want so much to know. I'm just glad it's all right now. I hope I was of help. Thank you for coming. I have been working so hard, but I went to you once last week when you were too busy to notice, and it looked so bad in the sickroom."

"Touching wound with moonsilver during purity charm actually helps."

"Really?" Tatyana jumped out of bed. "I don't know why I never thought to try that. I had better run down to the hospital before my watch. Take care, Helen. I miss you."

Helen grasped Tatyana's hand with her spirit fingers for a moment and then let herself relax, dropping the Sight. She was back in the dark corner of a storage closet where she had retreated. She sighed and wiped the tears from her eyes. Then she rose and found herself a bed to sleep in.

* * * * * *

The next day two more wounded were dead, but another recovered. The hospital was back to its usual size, and Helen had time to be concerned about Elisabeth. She had only taken the one watch off for her injuries, and she was doing her duties with clockwork regularity, but when Helen came down to get medicines or change Elisabeth's bandages, she noticed that Elisabeth never spoke. She had asked a couple other people and learned that Elisabeth hadn't said a word to anyone except in command since the foray.

Helen started standing her watches again that day, but she often came in a little early to work on medicines and tried to speak to Elisabeth. Simple greetings got no response, inquiries about her health might as well not have been heard, even asking her for advice on organizing troops on the wall brought no reaction. The foray had gone badly, and Helen had been very angry with Elisabeth herself, but her anger had gone now, and she felt bad for her.

One afternoon, Helen sent her watch up ahead of her. She told them she had to finish some medicines and promised to be up in half an hour. She didn't look up from the herbs she was grinding when one of the people from the kitchen came in to put Elisabeth's dinner on her desk. She did have a lot of medicines to make. When the woman was gone, however, she added a couple herbs that were good for stress and depression to Elisabeth's soup.

Helen had almost finished the new batch of fever reducer she was mixing up when the door opened again, shut heavily, and a faintly uneven step crossed the room. Elisabeth's leg must still be hurting her. It wasn't surprising. It had been a bad wound. The desk chair was pulled out and Elisabeth sat down heavily. Helen let her eat in silence while she finished the medicine and took it upstairs to the nurses on duty. When she returned, Elisabeth had stopped eating and was staring out the window. There was a pen in her hand and some paperwork on the desk.

"Lizzy," Helen said softly. "Have you seen the farmers out in the new fields?"

"No," Elisabeth grunted without looking up.

It wasn't much, but Helen was encouraged. It was the first time she had even been acknowledged. "They have prepared the land," she said in a soft voice as she came to stand beside Elisabeth. "Already they have planted peas, lettuce, kale, onions, rutabagas, and turnips. I think they are putting in some carrots, too. With Efrim farmers at work, they will grow before the snow easily."

Elisabeth looked up with the ghost of a smile. "You sound just like Mama, all excited over her garden."

Helen smiled too. She missed her mother. "Perhaps, but it is important. The wall move was a victory, Elisabeth. You have done well. This attack may have saved the village. That much more food will make this winter a good bit better, and next year it will be even more important, and we can grow way more food there. You should be proud. People are fishing in the river now. We won't starve anymore. That gives us time."

Elisabeth fiddled with her pen. Her eyes were fixed on the desk. "I didn't do well," she muttered. "I lost so many people. I wanted so much to make the enemy feel our strength, but the Shadows cannot be depleted. It made no difference. I came back with almost no one."

"Many of your company is back on the wall or mending now."

"Yes, most. Thanks to you. But not all." Elisabeth dropped her voice even lower. "You were right, Helen. I should have stayed close and helped you protect the wall."

It was hard to know what to say to that. Kind lies were no good with Elisabeth, and it would have been more prudent to keep all the warriors together. "You didn't know that before. Hindsight is perfect, foresight is mist, as they say. You made a brave job of it. It turned badly, but it wasn't for lack of effort, or skill on your part."

Elisabeth was silent for several minutes. Helen put on her mail and her boots.

"Perhaps you're right." Elisabeth sighed and stood up. She knew Helen had been angry with her, with good reason, she felt, but the gentle, sincere words now were very comforting. "You really think we had a worthwhile victory?" she asked, not because she thought Helen could have said something insincere without her feeling it, but because she wanted to hear it again.

"Yes, I do." Helen's voice was firm.

Elisabeth hesitated. Then she came over to where Helen stood buckling on her sword belt. "I have something I want to talk to you about."

"What is it?"

"The warriors, all of them, came to a consensus, and a couple came to talk to me a few days ago. They have voted you guardian, Helen. There is a fine smith in the village. His wife, I'm afraid, was one of the warriors I lost last week. All the same, he volunteered to make you a set of guardian stars. All that remains is your consent and the king's blessing. I don't know if you could contact Edward and get that?"

Helen was speechless for a minute. She was deeply honored and gratified. She had not thought of this. "I will, of course, consent. I could not refuse such an honor and duty to the people. As for Edward's blessing, I don't know. Perhaps I could try. I have a connection with him, certainly, not quite as strong as that with Tatyana or Sebastian, but I might be able to."

"I could take the responsibility myself, I think, as princess of Aldor, but I would really like to do it properly if we could. Anyway, I guess I mean to say that I am proud of you, Helen. I will go talk to the smith."

Helen smiled. "Thank you, but promise you'll finish your dinner first and get some rest."

"I will."

Helen left and went up on watch. Perhaps being a guardian didn't change much; she had been second in command for a long time now, and would remain so, but it felt different knowing the people had voted her the honor. She felt the weight of an extra responsibility as well as a certain gratitude that her hard work had been noticed by those she tried to help.

* * * * * *

Helen's hopeful words to Elisabeth had all been true, and yet she still felt worried and desperate herself. When she came down from her watch at midnight, she went back to her desk and started fussing with herbs. Yes, the extra planting ground would give them time, and the moonsilver trick was her first real breakthrough in healing, but none of it was enough. She had to find some way to help the ill, to really help them, or they could never stand for any length of time. When she finally put aside her work and made herself lie down, she thought again of Edward, and of her guardianship. She knew his watches were from twelve to six, like Elisabeth's. Helen made up her mind to go up a little late again to the next watch so she could try to contact him.

A little before six she saw her watch off, talking to her captains and promising to come out soon. Then she went back to the guardian's room and waited until she heard Elisabeth's watch come in from the wall. She sat down at her desk. She was very fond of Edward, who had always treated her like a daughter, but could she do it? It would be nice to see him, and she would be happier with her stars if he gave his blessing. She took her moonsilver amulet in one hand and the handle of a medical knife that had moonsilver on it in the other. Then she bent her head and concentrated. The blackness lasted longer than was common, but then most people with the Sight could never go to anything less than a very best friend or close family. She almost gave up, but just then the darkness opened out into the familiar kitchen of the royal house. The room was lit by the gray light of the coming dawn, and she saw Edward sitting at the table eating bread and beans. He was alone. There were dark circles beneath his eyes and his cheekbones showed more than they used to. His hair was nearly all gray now, and he looked tired. He started in surprise when she touched his arm.

"Helen?" he whispered.

"Yes."

"I am glad you came, not least because it proves you are still strong, but there must be some reason you have tried. Has something happened?"

"No bad." She tried to think of the shortest way to say it. Once she was there, it was no harder to speak to him than to any of her connections, and his Sight enabled him to hear her easily, but it had taken extra power to get there and she couldn't spare any. "People vote me guardian. Elisabeth want to give it. We hope for blessing."

His grim face softened into a smile that made him look several years younger. "My dear girl. You didn't need to ask, when you are so far away, but I'm touched that you did. I am very proud of you. I heard a little about that last mission of yours from Tatyana. I wish we could know more, but I'm sure you did well. The concealment charm was a very good idea for a retreat. Regardless, if all that is left to make you a guardian is my blessing, I give it very gladly. You are a great woman, Helen, and I'm glad the people of Aldor see it."

"Thank you," she whispered. She squeezed his hand and dropped the Sight. There were tears in her eyes and a warm feeling in her heart. Her head ached a little, and she had to blink a few minutes before her vision cleared, but it was worth it. More than worth it.

She told Elisabeth what he had said before running up to join her watch.

✷✷✷✷✷✷✷

When she slept during her next rest period, she had a Sight dream for the first time in many months. The sun was low in a hazy sky. A haze so thick and black that the light was almost choked. Then there were words:

From death and from pain
When courage finds fear
Blood of the slain
And fallen near
Red mixed with black
Life breath brings back

With the words the haze dissipated, and she woke up. She sat up in bed. What could it mean? Somehow, it must be the answer. The missing link to a way to cure the wounded, but it was so hard to know what precisely was meant. Death and pain they had in plenty, and the courage of her people had certainly found fear. Perhaps that meant the time had come. Blood of the slain and fallen? It seemed an odd line. The fields certainly ran with it. The last two lines seemed the most important. The substance that was to bring life after the tragedies of the first four lines was something red mixed with black. There were herbs that were red and black, or at least had it in their names. She must try them all. She jumped up and went back to her desk.

Chapter 17

Taking Command

27 February (six months later) to March 5, YA 1126

Guard Station east rim of Efrimiel

THE SUN WAS SETTING across the valley, spreading an orange light over the branches of the bare trees overhead. Aranin sat at the campfire in the center of the little camp. His fingers were cold and stiff, and he ate his porridge and milk mechanically. He looked around at his people. A hundred and fifty men and women gathered around eating porridge out of earthenware bowls. Their faces were all tired and worn. There was dread and resignation in them. Nothing unusual. He knew the looks well, the unbrushed hair, those men and women who were apt to have red eyes and those who got smudges of dirt on their faces. It was another cold morning in February. No, that was foolish, not morning. Just getting-up time. It was sunset, not sunrise, but what difference did that make to them anymore? That question had a ready answer that he didn't like. Sunset meant the beginning of the horrible night watch.

"It's a clear night, anyway, my friends," Lestius, the head captain, was saying to someone.

Aranin started slightly and looked at him. That was an odd observation for him to make.

The person beside him nodded. "Better'n clouds."

265

Aranin felt something was off. It wasn't what Lestius had said. It was the words he chose. He might have said, 'At least we have a clear night,' but the 'anyway' and 'my friends' sounded strange on his lips. Aranin watched him a moment. There was something just a little different about him. Not something anyone else seemed to notice. It was so small, perhaps he was imagining it, and yet... Lestius hadn't brushed his hair, which, although not unusual with many, was odd for him. He was always neat and dignified, but there was a faint shadow of dirt on his left cheek. Aranin wasn't sure why it mattered, or why he couldn't help noticing tiny things like that. So what if the head captain didn't brush his hair; the despair that pervaded the camp might be catching up with him. Yet, it made Aranin uneasy. There was something ever so slightly off about the way he held his spoon, too, the angle between the fingers was tighter.

When he followed Lestius up onto the wall he was still uneasy. He came up beside Analisia. She was fighting a large Shadow and he stabbed it as he stepped into her place.

"Hope it's not too bad a watch," she said. The sun had gone, and her face showed up pale in the thick dusk that was falling.

"Thank you." He thought about saying something about Lestius, but it was such silly little things. It seemed foolish to say and would take too long to explain. "Get some rest," he said instead.

She nodded and turned away. Those minutes on the wall had to be short. The Shadows were leaping up out of the shade east of the high wall where dark fell long before it did in other places. The Shadows didn't allow a moment of inattention, yet this was all the time the siblings had together these days. Analisia had taken her captain's test just before the new year and passed with flying colors. He was proud of her, especially because it had made her so happy, but now they couldn't be on the same watch. Father had sent the much more experienced captain who had been the second on his watch to be a head captain at another post that was in need and had taken Analisia as his second. At least that meant she was still in the same camp, but being on different watches they seldom saw one another. Of course Yeven had chosen to change watches with Analisia.

Aranin put those thoughts aside and faced the menace of the trees. He had always loved trees. He liked to draw them and could spend hours studying the curves and textures that made each tree unique, but the forest that faced him daily on the other side of the wall had ceased to seem beautiful. Rows of bare trees. Many, especially a bit farther away where they neared the black barrier, were losing their bark, standing stark and naked like bones in the faint moonlight. Every tree made a shadow on the snow, and every shadow was a hiding place for the living Shadows that assailed them.

Tonight he tried to keep closer than usual to Lestius. Perhaps it was a foolish precaution, but there was something not himself about the man, and Aranin didn't like it. Lestius was fighting normally enough—or was he? Perhaps there was less snap in the turn of his sword... but he kept ordering Aranin away. Aranin had no choice but to obey, but he didn't go all that far, and he kept glancing towards his commander when he had half a moment free from the constant fight. Things went quite normally for the first two hours. The noises of talk and work behind the wall died away into the silence of a sleeping camp. The dark of the night settled. The moon was only a misty crescent, and the stars could hardly be seen. The torches kept lit on the wall were a dim, flickering light on the hazy shapes the warriors endeavored to fight.

The tone in Lestius's voice changed; harder, cold. He began to order his warriors closer to him, bunching people on the southern half of their stretch of wall. Aranin didn't like it at all, and he saw worried looks and hesitation on the faces of those about him.

"No, don't use your bows, draw daggers instead. Drop the bows now!" The captain's voice was almost shrill.

Some people dropped their bows and drew daggers. Others stared in amazement and uncertainty. Aranin drew his dagger but didn't drop his bow, only slung it on his back, and he forced his way through the crowd towards his commander. He couldn't disobey his superior officer, and yet, as second in command, a captain in his own right, surely he had the right to just have a word with him. He needed to find out what was going on and if the man was all right. Aranin was only three or four yards from the head captain when screams broke out on both sides of him. From away to the left where the wall was all but unmanned came cries of panic and shouts for aid, and from directly in front of him there were screams of terror and pain. Frozen for an instant, torn between the urgency of the two calls, he looked at Lestius. His blood ran cold with horror.

The man's eyes were wild, and he had turned on the men crowded close to him with a swing of his shimmering sword. Taken completely at unawares, several had fallen to the stones. Others were screaming and holding up swords and daggers in defense. As Aranin leapt forward he saw Lestius stab one of his own men. Red blood spilled from his blade. Aranin's heart stood still as he stepped forward and met the madman's blade with his own. This was no longer his commander. Whatever had happened, Lestius was not himself. All the same, it went against everything in Aranin's heart to fight another man to the death.

There was no time to think; battle instinct and years of training only just kept him alive. Lestius was a master swordsman and by far his elder. Around them was utter turmoil. Shadows were coming over the wall in force, and many of his people had run down to the farther end in answer to the desperate cries for help that came from there.

Block and stab. Aranin ducked and got inside Lestius's guard. He could have killed him. One stab upwards under the mail... but he couldn't do it. He couldn't kill a man, a man he had known so long, not even after what he had just done. He dove sideways instead and cut deep into the flesh of the sword arm. Lestius was bleeding and yet he didn't seem to feel the pain. He kept fighting until two others came to Aranin's aid and they knocked him down. By this time the cries on the wall had roused the off-watch, and people were running and shouting behind the wall too.

"Ropes! Someone bring ropes to this spot," Aranin shouted into the darkness behind the wall. "Hold him," he added in a lower voice to the men beside him. "Whatever you do."

Then Aranin jumped to his feet and ran the length of the wall, calling his people together, rallying them, and spreading them out into an ordered line. "We must fight on. Lestius has fallen to the enemy, we know not how, but the Shadows will not enjoy the benefit of their trick. They mean to breach our walls, and we must stop them now."

"There are Shadows already beyond the wall, sir," one of the men from the far end called.

"We cannot go down. We must stop the rest before they get over.

Hold your places, everyone." Then he turned and called behind the wall. "All is stable up here, but there are Shadows beyond the wall mostly in the north stretch that must be stopped."

"We will have them," Louranin's voice came from the darkness. "Just hold the wall."

For an hour or so the fighting was intense, and Aranin could hear the rumor of war behind the wall as well. Then the noise of swords, shouts, and running feet in the forest behind them diminished and ceased. The press on the wall itself became less intense, and the warriors could breathe again. Louranin came up, and he and some of his men took Lestius away. Aranin had the whole stretch to command now, and that kept him busy until at last he felt his father's hand on his shoulder. He looked up.

"It's midnight," Louranin said quietly. "You have done very well. Go and rest now."

"Thank you, Father," Aranin said softly. He turned and walked down, making sure all his men were safe off the wall before him.

It was only then that it hit him. Sitting on the bench, cleaning his blade while his dinner was served, he found he was shaking. There was red blood on his blade. It showed up sinister in the flickering light of the flames. Red blood. Stabbing Shadows was different. They didn't really even have blood. Or bodies, for that matter. He remembered his fight with Lestius and the mad look in the man's eyes and tears came to his cheeks. He kept his head down, but his hands shook as he took the plate of meat and potatoes that was handed to him.

"What..." His voice seemed small and quavery. He cleared his throat and tried again in a stronger tone. "What happened to Lestius and the men he struck?"

"He killed three," said the man serving the food, with a grim look. "There are five wounded. All have been sent down to the palace, of course. Lestius, though. The commander would not send him because of his madness. We kept him tied and tried to get words from him. He was weakening with the bleeding, but he did not stop fighting the bonds. We were searching him and trying to force some information out of him when there was a horrible explosion. Something small and black was deep in the skin on the side of his head behind his ear, and it exploded, killing him instantly." The man shuddered. "He will hurt no one else, but we will never know what happened to him."

Aranin nodded, feeling sick. "We will have to keep a closer eye on each other."

When he was in bed that night he wept again. He was still shaken and didn't know exactly why. He thought of his friends far away—Sebastian, Helen, Tatyana—where were they now? Were they even still alive? Sometimes he had nightmares in which he was going over to play ball or some such silly thing, but no one was there. All of Eldirad was empty and bare. Nothing left but the stone houses. He had no Sight, no one in Efrim did, and he knew it meant nothing. Still, it was hard to get the image out of his head.

He wished he could warn them about this terrible new trick, even if he didn't understand what had happened very well, but there was no way. Helen was the only person he knew who had the Sight strong enough to go to good friends as well as absolute best friends. They *were* good friends. There was some chance, if she was alive, and not too tired, that she could come to him if he called her by name with enough desperation in his voice. He thought he could manage the desperation pretty well just now, but he would never know if she came, or when she came, or when to start talking. Those without the Sight couldn't hear people speak with it, however close the connection, and even feeling their presence was sketchy. The chances she would have felt his danger on the wall seemed very low. His personal danger hadn't been much more than usual, and he hadn't really freaked out until it was all over. No, she wouldn't know, and there was no reliable way to tell her. There was no way for anyone in Efrim even to know whether Eldirad, Aldor, or Obrin still existed. There was no mail and no Sight, and the few mockingbirds that remained in the valley positively refused to even try flying over the black barrier.

He sighed and got up, too anxious to sleep. He took his little bag of stuff out to the table, lit a candle, and drew until he felt a little calmer. He didn't draw the drama of the night but found himself sketching a scene from long ago. Tatyana sitting on a swing in the royal garden, with Helen on the grass at her feet. They had been quite young, so he must have been only a little child, but it came back, comforting, far away. Peaceful.

After a while he went to bed and slept until the bells on the clock woke him in the dark.

It didn't occur to him until he was almost finished with his eggs and buttered toast that he was the sole commander on his watch now. For all practical purposes, he was a head captain. That was a little unnerving, yet it was better than watching his commander go mad. He would be in control; there was something a little steadying about that. Then a chill went through him. What if it happens to me? What if it is catching? Something behind his ear that exploded in his head they said... but where did it come from? Were these things in the camp like parasites? Did they fly in on the mist?

He turned to the man beside him. "Aaron," he said quietly. "Will you check in my hair for anything dark and unusual? I think we should all be checked after what happened to Lestius."

Aaron nodded, looking reluctant, uncomfortable, and a little scared. "Yes, sir."

Aranin gave the order that all his people must do the same. It was a strange sight. Grown men and women picking through each other's hair as though they were children who had been rolling in leaves. Still, it made Aranin feel safer when everyone came up clean. His watch was uneventful that day, and he was grateful. It was still hard, of course, and taking on the responsibility for the whole stretch of wall was even more to think about, but he managed.

The days passed. Louranin institutionalized the checking of every man and woman before and after their watch for the black things and sent the command through the army. Aranin remained sole leader on his watch, since another captain wasn't readily available.

When Aranin came down from the wall at midnight five days after the scare, he found his father waiting for him. He looked at him in surprise. It had been Analisia who had come to his side to relieve him, but he had assumed Father was there also.

"What is it?" he asked, instinctively searching for something he might have done wrong.

"I wish to talk to you, my son."

Louranin's voice lacked some of its usual hardness, and Aranin looked into his face with surprise. Louranin was actually smiling a little, and there was a shine, a softness in his eyes. Aranin cautiously smiled back. "Of course, Father. What is it?"

Louranin led the way to a bench a little apart from the others. "You have done very well," he said in a low voice as he sat on the bench. "You had a sore trial with Lestius, and you proved worthy."

"Thank you," Aranin said hesitantly. He couldn't imagine what his father was getting at. Surely there must be something he wanted him to do better, and yet his eyes and tone remained kind.

"It took a few days to spread the story and contact the other captains and generals to request approval, but no one was slow in response. I am going to make you a general, Aranin."

"Me?" Aranin gasped. There were very few generals in the army. Only three living, last he heard. How was it he could be one of them? He had only been a captain for seven months.

"Yes. Don't question your worth. It is not manly." A touch of the more familiar sternness came to his father's voice.

"I will not, Father. I am honored."

"Generals are needed, and you have the strength and the presence of mind. It is your duty to your people to use them."

"Yes, Sir. I will always do my duty to my people."

"The ceremony will be tomorrow morning. I have already sent for a new flower for you, and I have sent for another captain from one of the south posts to take your place. He is ready for the promotion to head captain, and there cannot be more than one general at a single post."

"Where will I go?" Aranin asked, forcing his voice to be even and not betray the way the bottom of his stomach seemed to fall out at the thought of leaving everyone he knew and going to command strangers in another place.

"Over to the next stretch north of here. Things have been bad there, and they need a strong commander. There are only two captains there at present, and they lost their head captain two weeks ago."

"I will be ready, Sir."

Louranin nodded farewell and went up to the wall, and Aranin sat still, staring at a single dead leaf moving across the snow in the light breeze. Ready? He said he would be ready, but could he ever be? Those two captains, would they want him? For two weeks they had been leading themselves. The chances were good they were both older than he was. Would they not be unhappy about him coming and taking command over them? And was he really up to it? Was he strong enough to face that sort of full command? There was nothing special about him. He was just the boy who was never quite good enough, the disappointment, the crybaby. He had only done what he had to do, nothing special. But there was no choice. He would never contradict his father.

"Everything all right, sir?" a woman's voice asked as a bowl of warm stew was pushed into his hands.

"Yes," he said hastily, looking up at the woman. "Everything's fine."

He didn't know what else to say. It wasn't easy to swallow his dinner because his throat kept getting tight with tears at the thought of going off alone. He had felt alone here sometimes. He was more shy with Analisia than of old, and that grieved him, and now of course he seldom saw her. He had often wished for someone he could talk to freely, and yet... Analisia had been there at least, and Father. Hard and demanding as Father could be, it was nice to be near him. Now Aranin would be on his own. He had to draw for a little while before he could go to sleep, and he slept fitfully and woke weary.

He did not go up on watch at six the next morning. The new captain had arrived and Aranin spoke to him, telling him about the tricks of this stretch. The places where the crenelations were just a little narrower, or where a height in the hillside gave special vantage. He told him of the warriors, too, their strengths and weaknesses. He felt compelled to tell him. And then he watched the other man lead his warriors up onto the wall. Aranin waited, restless, while Louranin's watch ate their breakfast. The light grew, until at about six-thirty the sun came up red and gold over the next ridge to the east and its light crowned the tops of the trees within the wall with fire that made them glow for a moment and forget that it was a long time since their bare branches had been fully clothed even in summer.

It would be near noon before the light actually came into the shadow of the wall, but day was come and now was time for the ceremony. It was very simple.

Aranin knelt before his father in the center of the clearing and laid his sword at Louranin's feet. "I pledge to you once again, Louranin, high commander of Efrim, my service, accepting the high honor you have granted me."

"Stand, my son, General of the Efrim, to serve your people and your queen, body and soul so long as you live."

"With body and soul I shall serve them," Aranin said, standing.

Then Louranin removed the captain's badge from Aranin's mail and replaced it with a large white flower. It was shaped something like a dogwood, only thicker and with more petals, the image of the blossoms that hung thick and sweet-smelling on the great trees by the door of the palace of Efrim. He stood a moment looking at his father, and he could see pride in Louranin's eyes. There was a time that pride was all Aranin wanted in the world. Now he was shaken and nervous, but it was still sweet.

When the ceremony was over, Louranin and his watch went to bed. Aranin followed them into the barracks to get ready to leave. It wasn't as though he had much to take with him, nor was there much opportunity to have it anywhere besides his satchel, but there was a little packing to do. Mostly it was saying goodbye. Even the rough stones by the head of his cot seemed friendly, and he felt he would miss them. He stuffed two pairs of clean, almost-dry socks into his bag, and carefully wrapped his folder of pictures and old letters in a cloth before putting it in as well. He knelt on his bed to unfasten the picture of the garden at home that he had hung there.

He heard a bumping across the room and looked to see Analisia gathering up the two necklaces she had hung over her bunk.

"What are you doing?" he whispered.

She looked at him with a half smile. "Packing, what does it look like?"

"Packing?" Aranin repeated, incredulous, as a flame of hope started to force its way up in spite of him.

Her eyes sparkled a little, dancing in the faint dawn light that came in though the curtained windows. "Of course. You don't think I would let you go off and leave me, do you?"

He felt a wave of relief sweep over him. "Oh, thank you, thank you, Lisi," he whispered. "But how did you get Father to let you?"

"It wasn't easy, I'll admit. Begging doesn't do much good with him, and of course he's not one for sentiment, but I pointed out that there were only two captains where you were going, while a stretch could really use four leaders. He could just as easily get two new ones here, where he could keep an eye on them and all, and let me go to fill that hole. It took a while, but he consented. I wasn't going to take no for an answer anyway. I would go even if he didn't give permission. We are not supposed to be separated. We agreed on that, remember?"

Aranin smiled. "I remember, but, well, I wasn't sure that was still how you felt."

"Of course it is." Analisia came over and took both his hands. "Things have changed a lot, I know," she said very low. "I am different, and sometimes I worry I don't know you anymore, but I don't want that. Of course, I fell in love, so I don't suppose I can say you are my other half anymore." She glanced towards the far end of the room where Yeven was working over his bag too. "Maybe someday you'll find your love. But that doesn't change how much I love you. I'm still not whole without you, you know that. We stick together." She looked up into his face and a touch of anxiety came into her voice. "That's still how you feel, too, isn't it?"

"Forever, Lisi," he whispered. Tears were running down his cheeks.

She smiled and hugged him tight. When she let go, she reached up and dried his tears with her sleeve. "It's all right. We have a new adventure to start on, and remember, you can still tell me anything like you used to."

"Thank you." He didn't feel as if that were true. The offensive action was still being planned, and he would never try again to share his fears about that, but perhaps in other things he could open up without risking her anger. "I'm so worried the captains won't want me, or that I'm not up to being in full command. Do you really think I can do it?"

"Of course I do. I don't think the captains will be a problem. As I see it, most people are relieved to find someone above them to take the responsibility, and you'll make a general they'll be proud to serve. And, well, if you ever do have any trouble or need help, I'll be there. Together we can do anything."

"Maybe we can." He smiled and pressed her hand. "I will feel so much better having you there. And maybe... if *you* don't mind acting under me... we could have the same watch again so we could see each other more."

"I will insist upon it," she said with a smile.

19 June (4 Months later), YA 1126; Eldirad

Tatyana woke to the alarm like every other morning, but it wasn't just any other morning. Perhaps birthdays didn't mean much, were not even important or worth thinking of in a time of hardship like this, and yet, somehow it still felt like it ought to be special. She turned thirty-seven today. She was nearing traditional childbearing age, and she couldn't help wondering if there would ever be a time when such things would be possible for her. She wondered if she would ever even have a husband. She had been thirty-four when the war started, but she hadn't fallen in love and hadn't been in a hurry. Now, all courtship was out of season. No one spoke of such things, and there had been no weddings and no children born in three years. No one wanted to bring a child into times like these.

If her soulmate was out there, had she met him and not known? Had he been too young back when such thoughts were free? What were the chances he still lived? Oh, well, Sebastian's children could inherit her crown if there was anything left to inherit... and, of course, if Sebastian and Helen lived to have any children. It was no use thinking of it now. She wondered sometimes if she herself would ever inherit the crown, not that she had any great desire to anymore. When the second-hardest job in the city seemed every day on the point of breaking her, why should she want the hardest?

By tradition, an heir could inherit any time after thirty-three, but a ruler didn't retire until they were seventy-five. Her father had been unusually young when she was born, and he was only seventy-one. Not that any of that mattered right now. There was no use even considering that he would retire while his people needed him. The retirement of the ruler, and of warriors in general, at that age was only a courtesy, for their pleasure and freedom to stay in the city and pursue other crafts and passions, and to allow the heirs to take their place. It would be something like thirty years before there was much chance age would actually render him unfit to lead in battle and force him to surrender the crown. By that time, if not by the time he turned seventy-five, the war would be long over one way or another. If something didn't happen to stop it in the next few years, the city would crumble or starve, and it would end that way. Father would never give her the crown unless they were victorious, or, of course, if he were wounded. She couldn't bear to think of that—or of the worse thought that hovered behind it.

She got up with a sigh and went to get dressed. She missed her friends so much, especially Sebastian and Helen. She worried about them every day. She hadn't been to Sebastian with the Sight since shortly after the scare when the prince's house was abandoned. She had felt no more especial fear from him. It was hard to be sure when one had multiple people one was connected to and most of them were in peril for their lives on the walls twelve hours a day, but she was too tired to go to him without some very good reason. It seemed only foolishness. She hadn't heard from Helen since that time shortly after she had gone to her aid last fall.

The moonsilver trick with the purity charm really did help, but it still wasn't enough. Nothing was enough. Tatyana wondered about Aranin and Analisia. Who knew if Efrim was even still there after all this time? Sebastian might know, she supposed. Certainly, he could find out with the mirror, but she wasn't sure she could muster enough words in the Sight to ask him. Besides, what good would it do her to know? Did she even want to know? She missed Analisia's bright laugh and Aranin's gentle patience, and she prayed they were alive.

She took out a fine necklace of silver with leaves of jewels and little trumpet flowers of silver from a box on her dresser. Analisia had given it to her for her thirtieth birthday, and somehow today, seven years later and in a whole different world, she was drawn to it. She slipped it on. It was a foolish thing, but she could hide it beneath the neck of her tunic, and no one would know. She reached for a new hair pin to keep the stray locks out of her face and noticed a miniature Aranin had painted of her right after she became crown princess. It had been on her dresser ever since, but she had not noticed it much. The picture, only about six inches high, showed her sitting beside a white rose bush in her blue silk dress with the heir star pinned over her bosom. A beautiful young woman with rosy cheeks, sparkling eyes, and jewels in her ample black hair. Could that only have been five years ago? Was she even the same person now?

She didn't feel like the same person, nor was the woman who looked back from the mirror that hung on the wall much like her. She looked at her reflection critically for a moment, as she fastened the hair pins. She looked a lot older than thirty-seven. The reflection in the mirror lacked most of the curves of the womanly figure visible beneath the silk dress of the portrait. She had been slim, but now she was thin, hard, and a little gaunt. Her cheeks had lost their softness and their color, and there were shadows around her eyes. She still had plenty of black hair, but it was less shiny, less clean, and there were a few threads of early gray in it. She thought she could easily pass for fifty. She sighed and turned to go down for breakfast. She felt older than that. Tired, dispirited, and hopeless.

Halfway down the stairs she noticed a heavenly smell and stopped in her tracks to sniff. By the Stars! Her mother was making sausage and fresh baked bread, or she was imagining things. She wondered where she'd found a delicacy like sausage these days, and bread took so much time.

The sun had already been up more than an hour, but the breeze that blew in through the open kitchen window was still cool and sweet. There were flowers in a long-neglected vase on the table and the three plates fairly glowed with bright strawberries. Tatyana smiled and took a deep breath. It smelled so wonderful, and the smell took her back to happy times.

"Happy birthday, darling," Clara said coming forward with a smile.

"Thank you, Mother," Tatyana whispered as she hugged her close. "I didn't dream you would do anything like this."

"You deserve a special treat." Clara kept hold of one of Tatyana's hands and led her to the table. Then she put two sausages and a slice of crusty fresh bread on her plate beside the strawberries.

"Where did you get it?" Tatyana asked.

"The sausage is the end of the pork from last year. I've been saving our share for a special occasion." She smiled as she served herself and sat down beside Tatyana. They had become used to having a family of three, and the large table was no longer sad. In fact, the extra end was now piled with partially finished projects.

They enjoyed their breakfast. It was the most delicious thing Tatyana could imagine, even if they did use sausage dripping on the bread because they were out of butter. They reminisced about the fun parties they used to have for her birthday when she was little and her friends would come over and play hide-and-seek on the lawn, do crafts, and play board games, and when Clara at last noticed the clock, it was five forty-five and Tatyana had to run to brush her teeth and get her boots on.

"Your father and I have arranged for you to get your evening watch off today," Clara said as Tatyana sat on the floor pulling on her boots.

"Why? Birthdays aren't that important. How can I leave the wall?" Tatyana looked up surprised and a little indignant.

"I'm worried about you," Clara said softly. "You work too hard. You need a break, and a birthday is as good an excuse as any. They're putting on a comedy at the theatre. They don't have as many actors as they used to, it's true, and the sets are all being reused, but Jane is in it. I believe she's still playing the lead even though she's joined the apprentice training camp. Anyway, I want to take you to the theatre tonight... please let me."

Tatyana hesitated for a moment. It sounded awfully nice, and yet, "But, Mother, I'm crown princess. I have to fight. I don't work any harder than Father."

"No. I'm worried about him, too. Twelve hours on the wall, and four or five in the hospital every day, and then I find him asleep over a desk full of paperwork. However, he is as stubborn as a goat about that sort of stuff. He has let me take most of the paperwork, but so long as he is king I can't actually make him take a break. Still, for your sake, I got him to promise to come off his afternoon watch two hours early so you two can play a game, and we can eat dinner together. It will do you both good, and then..." A sparkle of a smile came into her eyes. "I figure if we have dinner before six and you and I go up to get ready for the play, we may trick him into getting an extra hour of sleep tonight."

"All right." Tatyana found herself smiling. "I'll look forward to it." She jumped to her feet and gave her mother one more tight hug before she ran out the door to meet her watch. She would not be late to go up, and make Father and his people stay up past their time, but she would have to hurry.

The prospect of the evening made her watch easier to endure, as did the good breakfast. She woke up an hour early that afternoon and, going down, found her father taking off his boots in the hall. He had come in at four as he promised, and she ran to greet him. It was a little strange at first. They had forgotten what they had done when they used to relax, but after a minute Edward pulled out a trivia game they had once loved to play and started setting it up. Tatyana joined him, and in half an hour they were enjoying themselves. It was like old times, and the cards gave them something to talk to each other about besides the real world. They even laughed a little over some of the silliest ones. After a while, Clara called them for supper, just as she had in the old days. It was just the three of them now, but having all three at the table at once felt cozy and almost like a party.

"Now," Clara said a little after six when she rose to clear the table. "For tonight, I'm in charge. I'll be queen. Tatyana, you have time to take a nice bath before we go, and Edward, I have told the ladies at the hospital that you aren't coming this evening, so you may as well go get some sleep."

"I will, dear." Edward rose and kissed his wife's cheek with a twinkle in his eyes. "Thank you for this evening. It reminds me what is important. What we are really fighting for. And thank you for tricking me for my own good sometimes." He bid them both goodnight and went upstairs.

Tatyana took her bath and put on a nice dress for the first time in years. It was a good play. Most of the actors were older or very young, and the sets and costumes were not what they once had been, but it was still funny. The audience was mostly warriors taking this time out of their rest, or those on sick leave, and everyone went out with smiles on their faces. Jane did very well, and Tatyana congratulated her afterwards.

"Thank you," Jane said, flushed and beaming. "It has been really fun. I hope I get to do something like this again. I suppose I won't have time now, though, if I'm going up on the wall." She grew grave, but a twinkle remained in her eyes. "Joseph will tease me no end when he finds out I've joined the guard, and after the way I used to tease him about being in it I suppose I will deserve it."

"Perhaps. I won't tease you, though," Tatyana said. "Although I still think you're doing a service right here as an actress."

She smiled and they said farewell, for Jane had many admirers after her performance.

Tatyana walked hand in hand with her mother back to the house, and as they parted at the head of the stairs to go to bed she said, "Thank you so much, Mother. It was a really good day. And... I think I realized that, so long as I have you and Father, well, everything will be all right."

"We will always stick together," Clara whispered as she kissed her daughter goodnight.

Chapter 18

A Scare in the Night

19-20 October (4 Months later), YA 1126

Westtower

THE HARVESTS of 1125 had not been very good, and those of 1126 looked like they would be worse. The spring had been late and cold, and things were only now mostly ready to harvest. Meanwhile, it was harder than ever to get the hands out in the field to bring it in while keeping enough force on the wall to keep back the Shadows. People had to sleep sometime, although at Westtower that fall many avoided that inconvenient fact.

After retaking his captain's star, more than a year and a half ago, Joseph had been transferred to help Sarah as second in command on her watch. It made more sense to have the two captains help each other and the guardian have to do it alone. Neither Sebastian nor Joseph liked this arrangement, but both accepted that it made sense. In spite of his fears, Joseph did well as a captain.

In fact, back in the spring, Sarah had been sick for a couple weeks and Joseph had taken over full command of their watch. On the first day she came back up on the wall with him he had found himself leading the way up the stairs with her beside him.

"I assume you will wish to take command again," he said as they neared the top.

She had stopped and looked up at him. "I'd rather not, if you don't mind, sir." She looked down and her cheeks flushed slightly as if this was difficult to say. "I don't wish to face that full responsibility again and, besides, I think you are the better captain."

Joseph stood still, speechless. In the old days he might have made an expression of shock with his eyes wide and his mouth open, but that would have been half feigned. This was much more genuine, and he only froze for a moment. He had been called 'sir' by another captain, and she had said he was better than her. That wasn't right. It didn't seem possible. He had only been trying to do his job. There was nothing he could say. The whirlwind of doubts and questions was welling up, and he had to stop that. He gave a curt nod. "As you wish, lady. Take the east half." Then he ran up the stairs to where Sebastian and his warriors were waiting to be relieved.

To Joseph's continued bewilderment, when he had time to think about it, the arrangement had remained so all summer and into the fall, and everyone seemed satisfied with it.

Sebastian would have liked a captain to help his watch too. It was a long wall to watch, but he didn't have the time or energy to try to train or test people to become captains. All he could do was keep fighting, his thoughts every minute on the Shadows, seeing them in the dark, or shooting them farther away in the daylight. Not that they didn't make it to the wall in daylight too. There were so many of them they could not all be shot. But Sebastian himself, being one of the best archers with the sharpest eyes, usually stuck mostly to the bow during the day. And when he wasn't fighting there was so much other work to do.

Now, it was noon. The sun was high, and even though it was mid-October, Sebastian was drenched in sweat in his two layers of wool clothing. His clothes felt sticky and smelled. They didn't have enough time to wash clothes nearly as often as they needed. His hair stuck wet and lank to his forehead, and he brushed it away with the back of his arm. That morning he had gotten up at seven, after only two hours' sleep, to spend the rest of the time before his ten o'clock watch scything wheat. His body was beyond tired already. So much beyond tired that there was no point thinking about it anymore. There was no time for weariness.

Behind him, Sebastian could hear singing. It was a comical marching song from a play. It had a good beat and a light melody and talked of being home again soon. Not appropriate, perhaps, but pleasant. Joseph's strong tenor voice led the singing—and was the only one at times. Sebastian could tell it was a little hoarse and out of breath, and there was a strain in it. He was fighting to keep up the cheerful words, but he wouldn't stop. Sebastian smiled a little to himself as he swiftly fitted his next arrow. Joseph really was brave. He should be resting, of course, but he had talked more than half of his company into following him out to finish the grain fields before they went to rest. Sebastian was proud of him. He had enough trouble getting himself to get up and work sometimes, although he had managed to get quite a few others out there with him this morning.

There was an unusual disturbance away to the right up the north stretch, and Sebastian hurried to help. A sortie of Shadows so thick you could hardly see one from another had inundated the wall, and it was chaos.

"Hold your ground. Swordfighters in front," Sebastian shouted, seeing several archers beating at the Shadows with their bows while they struggled to get at their blades, even though they were girt at their waists. He called several men and women by name and organized them, quickly surrounding the affected area of the wall. Hundreds of Shadows went up in huge puffs of black smoke, or mist, or whatever it was. Sebastian had to blink several times, and strange shapes danced in the corners of his eyes. It was hard not to try to turn and look at those phantom shapes and movements, but turning did no good when they were in your own eyes. He blinked again harder and pushed with his power, and the phantom shapes in his eyes cleared even as someone near him killed the last of the influx of Shadows.

"Did any get past?" he asked, breathless.

"I don't know." The man was gasping and rubbing his eyes as he looked back over the wall. "I don't see any, but my eyes went a bit funny in that cloud."

Sebastian looked too. His eyes were quite clear again and he saw nothing but the few bare trees, the grain fields with the men and women toiling in them, the broken windows of the abandoned house, and the boarded-up stable and greenhouse. They might have succeeded, but there were a lot of places a Shadow could hide. He assigned two people to go down and search. They went gladly. Most anything was preferable to fighting on the wall as they would be doing for the next nearly four hours. Sebastian turned back to his duty. An hour later, the warriors came back to report that they had looked everywhere and found nothing. One more crisis averted. Shadows getting through at harvest time was the worst. They were so good at destroying, and poisoning, crops in the field.

When Sebastian came down at four, he was too tired even to think about going back out into the wheat fields, but when he looked the grain was all shocked at last. It had taken days, but at least it was that far. It still needed to be threshed and sacked for storage, and there was lots of canning to do. Two dozen men and women who had been let off duty for the harvest were busy putting up tomatoes in the kitchen, and there was little room for the incoming watch to eat. They didn't stay long. Each ate the little corn bread and tomato bean soup that was their lot and went up to bed.

When Sebastian came into his room at the top of the tower, he found Joseph sitting at his desk chopping herbs.

"What are you doing?" Sebastian asked.

"Making medicine. What does it look like?" Joseph said shortly.

"I'm sorry." Sebastian swallowed and looked down. Joseph always seemed tense these days. He supposed he was, too, but mostly he was tired. "I was just surprised not to see you when your watch came up."

Joseph stopped chopping and took a slow breath. He looked up. "Don't mind me. I'm not mad. Just a fool, I suppose." He tried to laugh. "It was just that during the short scare you had at twelve-thirty, two people were brought in sick, and I was making that medicine you taught me to give to them before I went back up. You can finish it if you would rather, but I don't mind. Sarah can handle it by herself just fine for a few more minutes. It's daylight, after all."

"Go ahead and finish." Sebastian pulled off his boots. "I'm so tired.

And tomorrow I must go over to Obrin. There are several sick there, and somehow we must get the onions in."

"Go to sleep. We'll manage."

"Did you sleep at all since three this morning?"

"No. I'll sleep after my watch tonight, I promise, but the wheat has to be gotten in. I think it's going to rain. Maybe tomorrow. It's in the wind."

"I suppose so. I'll get my men up early tomorrow morning again and we'll get the wheat heads cut off and stuffed in the storeroom at least." Sebastian rolled over and went to sleep without bothering to take off his mail.

✶ ✶ ✶ ✶ ✶ ✶

When he woke at nine-thirty that night he felt a little better. He hurried down to eat hastily, telling himself that after the crops were in he could get up early and have a bath like a civilized person. The watch that night was chill. The north wind had picked up, and Sebastian began to fear the rain Joseph had talked about might be snow. It was early for snow, but not impossible. Was anything with weather ever impossible? Perhaps not, but snow in October wouldn't even be very surprising.

The press of Shadows was unusually light that night, however. There was still something of a press close to the tower and to the south, but the northern and eastern sections had it quite easy. Sebastian stayed fighting near the tower and was grateful for the slight relief of the pressure on his exhausted warriors. The weather was his main worry tonight, and around midnight he called thirty people and sent them down off the wall to dig onions by lantern light and carry them into the tower where they would be safe.

Somewhat lighter watch or not, Sebastian was very tired when he came down after six hours of fighting Shadows in the chill, starless dark. He lay down on his bed, but it was no good. Tired as he was, he couldn't sleep. He got up and worked on medicines until the sky began to lighten, about six. Then he went down and coaxed about three quarters of his people out of bed. Together they went and started cutting the heads off the wheat and carting it into the storehouse. After three and a half hours' hard labor, working at a fever pitch as the threat in the cold wind became moister, they were called to drink some hot peppermint tea and eat biscuits and beans a couple of their number had prepared in the busy kitchen. The canners were at work again, and the watch stood about and ate their warm food as near the fire as they could. Then Sebastian called them, and they followed him grimly up for another watch on the wall.

Joseph's warriors barely stopped to eat but went straight to the fields. Sebastian could hear the work songs on the wind again. The pace seemed faster today, and the tone a touch more desperate. The fighting was hard that afternoon, and Sebastian could spare no warriors to help those in the fields. At about three, it started to rain. It was a cold, hard, windblown rain that stung when it hit face and hands and drenched even woolen clothing in a short time. There was water coming through Sebastian's woolen hood and running down the back of his neck by the time he heard Joseph and his warriors coming up the stairs to relieve his watch at four.

"We got everything that could be saved," Joseph said as he came up next to Sebastian. "The wheat's all in. It only started raining when we were bringing in the last vegetables, and that doesn't matter much. The frost a couple days ago got some stuff, but we brought in every last wilted green pepper and underripe squash. I left a dozen of my people in the kitchen to get a start on it."

"Thank the Stars," Sebastian whispered, stepping out of the fray and looking at his friend. "And you and your people."

"And you and yours." Joseph tried to smile. He looked really tired. His nose and cheeks were red from the cold, but there were dark circles under his eyes. His clothes were wet, and wet strands of dark hair stuck to his face.

"Are you sure you're all right for a whole six hours?" Sebastian asked, glancing from Joseph to the likewise tired faces of the warriors coming up behind him. "You look exhausted."

"I'm fine," Joseph said just a little shortly. "You're the one who looks worn out. When was the last time you slept?"

"Yesterday after this watch. You?"

"Your night watch last night. But that doesn't matter too much." Joseph smiled. "I mean 'tired,' what's that? If you don't remind me there's anything else, I shan't know what I'm missing." He laughed a little. It was strained, but when he looked up his eyes held Sebastian's firmly. "No, get some sleep. It's your turn."

Sebastian nodded and called to his warriors to leave the wall. Halfway down the stairs he realized he still had to go to Obrin. He had promised. He grabbed a couple biscuits and ran for the village. It wasn't easy. There were a few cases of the black sickness among the villagers, and there was still little he could do. He did his best to help them with medicines, and he used the Healing gift. That required power, and so was very difficult, weary as he was, but he wouldn't show weakness before the people of Obrin. He made sure every little thing was right for the poor patients. Then he walked back to the tower in the stormy dark. By the time he reached the tower itself he was shivering, and he was so tired he could hardly walk straight. He ate his plate of cold beans, climbed the stairs with one hand on the railing, and sat down on his bed. By now it was almost six-thirty in the evening. Three hours seemed a terribly short time to sleep. He lay down, without even bothering to take off his boots this time, and with the most immediate worries abated was asleep almost instantly.

★★★★★★★

Sebastian woke suddenly in pitch dark, but not to his alarm. He had been having one of his recurring nightmares about terrible moments on the wall, and for a moment, as he lay perfectly still, breathless, heart pounding, staring into the darkness, he thought that was all that had woken him. He was cold, his clothes still damp and his blankets now also damp. He had been a fool not to change before going to sleep. Perhaps that was what had woken him. But he felt uneasy. Something was wrong. The clouds were thick and there was no moon, so the fact that no light came in the windows whatsoever was not surprising. The room was silent. He heard no noise downstairs. Perhaps it was too silent? But no, that was foolish. His warriors were all exhausted. They would be sound asleep.

He lay quite still. Surely he could hear someone breathing nearby. How could that be? He held his own breath and could still hear it. Was that a stealthy footstep? Another? He sat up slowly, listening hard. There was something wrong with the air. He began to see strange shapes, shapes of darkness, darker even than darkness could be, and of strange vivid colors. There was fear in the air, and then images in his mind. He saw Helen crying out without sound as she slowly smoked and disintegrated into black flame. Then his mother, her face turning to a skull and then to a dragon. For a moment, terror took him. Then the thought managed to get through. Nightmares, not Sight visions. Nightmares. Black mist. It was hard to think. There was black mist in the tower.

He leapt to his feet and reached for the window nearest his bed. His hand only just touched the clasp as something hard like a sword or knife blade struck him forcefully in the upper back. It was a good thing after all that he had been too tired to take off his mail before he went to sleep. He cried out in fear and surprise as he was thrown down against the window, just managing to pull the latch. It swung open a little. He felt the cold air, but he could see nothing. The form attacking him was heavy. He spun around as he fell, putting his arms up to shield his face and neck, and felt a cut on his forearm. Something that felt alarmingly like a human hand clutched at his arm.

"Who's that?" he shouted, half choking in the mist. "What are you doing?"

No answer. Sebastian groped in the darkness for the other being. He clutched and felt the sharp edge of a blade cut his hand. His other hand flew to where the hilt must be and gripped over a human-feeling hand that clutched a solid sword hilt. Horrible and frightening visions flitted through Sebastian's mind. His eyes didn't see, whether there was anything to see or not. He tried to push back the visions, but he couldn't do it. He felt another blade whistle by his head. At least the other being didn't seem to be able to see either. He grabbed for the sound and clutched a muscular forearm covered in damp woolen cloth. It felt too terribly human. What was happening?

Human or not, the thing was fighting him, and fighting hard.

Sebastian didn't have a sword in the tower room. He kept his with everyone else's downstairs by the door, and besides, he couldn't let go of the man's arms lest one of the blades kill him. His fingers on the sword hilt dug into those of the other and tried to pry his grip loose. The other man knocked him to the floor, and they rolled over several times kicking and struggling while Sebastian clung to the man's hand and arm and the other tried to get away or to bring the weapons closer. Sebastian couldn't tell if the slightly open window was doing any good. The visions were getting worse, and it felt as if the darkness was pressing in on him, suffocating him and sapping his will and strength. The terror of the unreal that he saw, and felt with his emotions, seemed almost more real than what he actually heard and felt with his body. He was coughing and short of breath.

The other was heavier than he was and about the same height. They rolled up against the desk. Sebastian felt a corner of it dig painfully into his shoulder. The pain helped him hang on to the real world. He used all his strength to wrench them over so that the hand holding the dagger knocked full on the carved edge of the wood. There was a clatter as the dagger fell onto the stone floor, and Sebastian let go the forearm and grabbed. He was the faster, and he gripped the dagger in his right hand. The grip felt solid, soft and familiar, much like his own. It didn't feel evil.

His heart felt like lead. This was no Shadow, even with stolen Eldir weapons. The thing had a body that felt like a man's and, further, a man dressed in the wet wool that Sebastian himself wore. He could hear the being's labored breathing. Yet it was trying to murder him. There was no question of that. He tried to stab at it, but he couldn't make himself go for a kill. Some part of him beyond all the visions and terrors was afraid this was one of his men. He felt the sword graze his neck and swung his leg up, kicking the extended sword arm of the man with all his might while still holding the hand on the hilt. He felt a bone break and the man made a very human, but strangely groggy, groan of pain, like someone under not quite enough sleeping medicine during surgery. Or at least that's what Sebastian's struggling mind thought it sounded like. The man didn't let go of the sword, but Sebastian was able to pry his fingers from the hilt. The sword clattered to the floor, and Sebastian kicked it away, but the man still fought him.

"Sebastian?" a faint voice, seemingly distant, spoke somewhere to his left.

"Who is it?" he managed. He was having more and more trouble thinking.

"Lilian. What's happening?"

"Black," Sebastian panted. "Something bad. Windows. Can you open?" That was what they needed. He was still almost sure of that.

"Yes. Windows..." Her voice sounded vague. A moment later, he heard the window latches clicking.

Broken arm and all, the man was still fighting him. He threw Sebastian against the stone wall with a force that knocked the breath out of him, but Sebastian couldn't let go. He wouldn't let go. As he clung to the form he was fighting, he felt the air was cooler, more breathable. He gasped and gulped at it.

There were pounding feet on the stairs, and the hatch to the prince's chamber slammed open. "By the Stars," Joseph gasped as he entered.

The crescent moon was in the sky and the moonsilver on Joseph's blade shone faintly. The power of his will and urgency made it shine brighter as he raised it. In the faint light, he glanced around the room. Lilian stood at one of the open windows, hanging her head out, panting. Sebastian was on the floor fighting, wrestling, with a big, burly warrior named Connor. Sebastian had a dagger, while Connor was unarmed, yet Connor still seemed to be getting the better of the fight.

Joseph ran forward and dragged Connor off Sebastian by the back of his tunic. "What's happening, Sebastian? By the North Star, what on earth is going on?" He was too frightened and confused to know what to do. He wasn't even sure who needed restraining, but he couldn't believe it was Sebastian who had gone mad, so it must be Connor.

Sebastian lay on the floor, panting and gasping. "He... it... he attacked me in my bed. All the mist. I don't... I don't know. Can't see or think..."

Joseph felt panic rising. It must be the Shadows' mist. That's what people said when it was really bad. That is, before they passed out. Connor was fighting him. Fighting like a mad man, but blind. One of his arms didn't look right, but he was still using even that one as though he couldn't feel pain. After a moment's struggle Joseph knocked Connor over the head with the hilt of his sword. Connor crumpled to the floor, and Joseph ran to Sebastian. Kneeling, he helped him to his feet.

"Come on, Sebastian. Come to the window. Get some fresh air."

Sebastian groped for Joseph's hands and clutched them. Something solid. He was starting to be able to breathe better now, but he still couldn't think. He only held onto Joseph. Then he felt the cold night air against his face. He took deep breaths and coughed. He fought to retake possession of his mind, and the shrieking phantoms began to recede a little. He blinked hard and gasped. His mind began to clear. Still catching his breath, he told Joseph briefly everything that had happened.

"I heard you scream through the open window," Joseph said. "And I came running as soon as I had shouted to Sarah that I was going. There's mist in the tower, but mostly in the floor below this. It's so thick there I could hardly breathe."

"Did you see the phantoms?" Sebastian asked with a shiver. "When you went in there, or in here?"

"No, I was too busy coming to find you."

Sebastian smiled. There really was more to Joseph than even he had guessed. Whatever errand one might be on, to walk into mist this thick and not see something seemed remarkable. "You can see now, then?"

"Sure."

"Did you kill it?"

"It?"

"Whatever it was that attacked me?"

"No. It was Connor. I knocked him out."

"Connor," Sebastian whispered, shaken. "Could you find some rope downstairs and tie him up?"

"Of course." Joseph lit a candle that stood on Sebastian's desk and hurried off downstairs.

Sebastian waited with his head out the window. The air smelled like rain, and that now seemed blessed. Every now and then, an eddy of wind blew some in his face, and it felt fresh and woke him up a little more. By the time Joseph returned with the rope and tied the unconscious man securely, Sebastian could once again make out the points of light in the village away to the east.

"I'm sorry I wasn't more help," Lilian said after a few minutes. "I'm afraid I was only barely conscious by the time I got up here. I woke. I think I heard something. I imagined, or dreamed, or perhaps really heard, something break. I thought someone had just dropped something. I was too tired to help them clean up, so I was going back to sleep when I began to feel terror, and danger, and to see visions. Sometime in there I heard steps on the stairs. Then I thought I heard something up here. I started to come up, thinking more of escaping the horrible suffocating than anything else."

"We need to get the windows open down there too," Sebastian said. He made a move to go, but he felt dizzy and unsteady. He was sure if he stepped into a mist that thick he wouldn't be able to think or see again at once.

"I'll get them," Joseph said, picking up the candle again. "I'll only be half a sec." He ran down out of sight. They heard windows banging open in rapid succession. Then Joseph came back up, holding the candle in one hand and something else in the other. He came to stand in the window beside Sebastian. "Look what I found. It is like a broken egg or a ball made of something I never saw before. It is silky and cold on the outside, but there is some kind of power in it. It sends tingly shivers all up my arm when I touch the inside."

The two halves of the broken sphere were of a dark crystal. It seemed black, but in certain flickers of the candlelight it shone an eery red. It was beautiful, and also a little creepy.

Sebastian touched it with the tip of a finger and shrank away. For a moment, the black phantoms that lingered in the corners of his eyes increased and his sight dimmed. "That's bad," he whispered. "I wish I knew how it got in, but I'm sure it had something to do with what happened tonight. Take it outside, will you?"

"Of course. I think we had better do something about all the people asleep in the room below, too. The whole fourth story was subjected to black mist worse than this room. Lilian's tough or she wouldn't have gotten out. No one down there's conscious. Most are still in their beds. A couple others tried to get out but fell down halfway across the floor."

"Is the mist cleared out down there?" Sebastian rubbed his forehead and turned from the window. He thought he had been tired before, but now he felt as if he might drop. Still, he could see again, and there was work to be done.

"Yeah. There's a north wind. They'll be getting cold, I reckon, but most of the mist's likely gone." Joseph went back to the stairs and started down with the broken sphere held gingerly in one hand. "No, it's not bad down here," he called up. "At least, I don't think," he added as an afterthought. He remembered with some confusion that he had been able to see just fine in the lookout room and Sebastian and Lilian couldn't, but of course he hadn't been in there as long. Still, he couldn't restrain the thought that he never had experienced the effects of the black mist. He had seen the horrible dreams during his illness, and still saw echoes of them when he slept, but he had never felt the effects of the black mist in waking. For some reason, that thought made a surge of fear and discomfort rise in his chest so strong that in desperation he pressed four fingers against the inside of the mysterious sphere so that the tingling jolt of black magic brought him back to the moment. He ran for the stairs to take the thing outside as he had been asked.

Sebastian began to descend after him into the second chamber. Then he remembered he might need medicines and would certainly need a lantern or candle. He climbed back up and lit a small jeweled candle lantern that sat on his desk. Then he gathered some medicines. "Lilian, do you feel up to helping me?"

"I think so." Her voice sounded weak, but no longer vague. "I'm afraid I won't be up to going on the wall at ten, though."

Sebastian bit his lip. He didn't want to know what time it was now. He wasn't sure he could fight more anytime soon, but he remembered how exhausted Joseph and his warriors had looked at four. He couldn't make them stay up past their time. He took a dose from a bottle of the stimulant herb; a concoction that just gave a little more strength and could help a person wake up. Then he went down the ladder with Lilian following. They hung the lantern on the wall and started by getting those sprawled on the floor into their beds. Some mist still lingered in the room, and Sebastian saw more fluttering shadows than the candle flame cast, but it was dissipating fast. They started airing and shaking the blankets out the windows, and by then Joseph returned to help them. In ten minutes, the last traces of the mist were gone, but still no amount of herbs, shaking, and calling their names would wake any of the sleepers.

They heard groans and thumping from above through the open hatch and Joseph and Sebastian went up and dragged Connor down to his own bed. He was fighting the ropes now, and crying out in a strange, strangled voice, as if in his sleep. When Sebastian touched his brow, it was feverish.

"We've got to find out what's wrong with him," Sebastian muttered. "We simply must. We can't have the risk of this happening again, or we will have to tie every last one of us up when we go to sleep."

"His eyes are still quite mad," Joseph said holding up the lantern. He shivered. "I've never seen a look like that."

"Are his cords good and tight?"

"Yes. He won't get away."

"I'll have to examine him. What time is it, Joseph?"

Joseph looked at the clock on the wall. Then he looked at Sebastian. Joseph was dead tired, but he wished lying was an option. Sebastian's face was gray in the lantern light. That fight in the black mist had to have been a terrible ordeal. Still, lies to Sebastian were useless, no matter how well meaning. Besides, Joseph had convinced the warriors he had left on the wall under Sarah to miss their rest entirely that afternoon to get the crops in. Now they were wet and freezing and would never agree to staying past ten. "Nine-thirty," he said reluctantly. He took a deep breath, thinking fast. "See here. You can't leave these people just now. They are in a serious way, and you have to figure out what happened to Connor before he hurts someone else; besides, what if it spreads? Anyway, here's my idea. I know my ideas are often foolish, but please listen. You have to stay here. So I'll go down right now and rouse up the rest of your watch that was sleeping on the other floors, and I'll tell them what happened and that you're busy and take them out to relieve Sarah's warriors at ten."

Sebastian didn't like it. He had to go out there. Joseph couldn't stand two watches in a row, especially when he had spent the rest period before working hard in the fields. On the other hand, Joseph had a point about Connor, and as much as he hated to admit it, Sebastian wasn't sure he could stay on his feet long enough to fight just yet. He sighed and hated his own weakness. "All right. Just for a little while. I'll come out to take your place by midnight."

"Fine." Joseph turned and went downstairs to wake the next watch. Weariness is an illusion, he told himself over and over. It was something the old captain who taught the first-year warriors' training camp used to say. In very different situations it was true, but all the same Joseph liked it. Somehow, it helped to think it was all in his head, like a fantasy story or a play, or at least to pretend that, even if he knew it wasn't true. He was cold and his eyes felt puffy and uncomfortable, but at least he got to eat something with the watch before he took them up on the wall.

Sebastian kept working over the beds. Lilian brought him some water and some of the apple juice, beef jerky, and bread from the hasty meal being eaten downstairs. The assigned cook for the watch swore he had set his alarm for nine and someone had disabled it. After eating and drinking, Sebastian felt a little better. He had Lilian hang four lighted lanterns over Connor's bed. Then he began examining him. Connor was fighting hard again, and while the ropes held, Sebastian was afraid he would hurt himself and so gave him a dose of sleeping medicine to put him out for a short time. He could find no outward sign of illness. The man's only wounds were bruises, the broken arm, and the skinned knuckles that Sebastian knew all too well he had given him during their fight. It was some time before he came on something strange. There was a lump about the size of a big beetle behind his left ear in the edge of the dark, rather dirty hair, and there was an unpleasant cold, prickling feeling about it.

"Lilian, hold a lamp close, please," he cried.

She came and held one of the jeweled lamps close to Connor's head. There was indeed something behind his ear. It was a dark lump, and it was worked well into the skin, although it didn't seem to be entirely under it. Whatever it was seemed to have made its way into the skin slowly over many hours, and might still be doing so.

"Get my surgery kit, quick."

"That dark spot, you think that's what drove him mad?" she asked as she returned from the top room with a wicker basket.

"It's possible. Whatever it is, it is very foul. I'm sure it will kill him if left much longer."

They said nothing after that. Sebastian disinfected his knife and touched the healing runes on its handle. Then he began to cut away the skin and used long tweezers to pull at the thing. It put up a fight almost as though it were alive, although when he finally got it out it seemed no more than a black, crumbly lump. He smashed it with a metal instrument without touching it and sealed it in an old medicine jar to be disposed of safely, whatever it was. Then he flushed the wound and the area with water and disinfectant and scraped out any trace of blackness. He also used Helen's trick of the purity charm with a piece of moonsilver tracery he had taken off a book for that purpose when Helen had told him. When that was done, he set Connor's arm.

By the time he finished it was eleven-thirty. Sebastian was still exhausted, but he didn't feel wobbly anymore. He thought about going out to take Joseph's place, but he was still nervous about Connor. He wanted to see what happened when he woke up. The medicine should be wearing off. He shook Connor's good shoulder gently and remembered that there was a wide cut on his right palm and an only somewhat smaller one on his left forearm.

He asked Lilian to sew and bandage them for him, and when that was done Connor was stirring. Sebastian knelt beside the bed.

"Connor, can you hear me?"

"Yes. What... what happened to me? The dreams were horrible, and my arm hurts something awful. Was I wounded?" He looked at Sebastian and blinked and rubbed his eyes with his good hand.

"You don't remember any of it?"

"Any of what?"

"What is the last thing you *do* remember?"

"Going to bed, I think, sir. Although even that is fuzzy. Didn't we do a lot of harvesting yesterday? And then there was a watch and it started raining, very cold... See? I'm still a little damp, that must be real..." He squeezed his sleeve and smiled a little. "Then I went to bed and had bad dreams. Demons and monsters and fears and people turning to dust. A bit like what one sees in the worst mist, I suppose. Then you called my name just now and I woke up."

Sebastian pressed his lips tight and looked down into the man's eyes while he spoke. It was true. Connor really didn't remember anything about attacking him. "Do you remember anything before, um, before things started getting fuzzy, perhaps? Did anything unusual happen last night? Or the day before?"

"Last night," Connor murmured dreamily.

"Yes. Tell me about our watch last night."

"There were hardly any Shadows at the north side of the wall, not many at all. We weren't even fighting all the time..." His voice sounded a little distant, but he held Sebastian's gaze and wasn't lying. Sebastian's Sight wasn't strong, but no matter how tired he was he could always feel lies.

"True."

"Then the strangest thing happened." Connor smiled. "I know I don't have the Sight or anything, but you know how it's said the dead sometimes visit the living before they pass away, and with the Sight you can see them and all..."

"Yes." Sebastian had never actually experienced this, or knew anyone who had, but he had heard that it could happen.

"So, you see, my wife came to me last night. She died last month in my arms on the wall, you remember."

Sebastian nodded. He remembered. He wished he didn't, but he remembered.

"So, last night when I was sitting there between spells of Shadows, I saw her. I was right close to the place she died, and anyway, she came to me and sat beside me. She didn't say anything. I suppose ghosts generally don't, but she looked just the same and she held my hand and stroked my hair like to tell me everything would be all right, and it... it was so good to see her that I felt pretty dazed afterwards."

Sebastian knew the man was watching his face and so he kept it still and attentive, but inwardly he grimaced. It could not possibly have been any kind spirit that visited him last night. It must have been a Shadow in disguise. This was a new danger. He hadn't known before that Shadows could look like anything but Shadows. He didn't like to tell the man the truth. He looked so pitiful, and it would be so heartbreaking for him to know the truth, and yet in time he would have to know it. Everyone would have to know, and it couldn't be kept from him.

"Connor," Sebastian said softly after a minute. He sat on the edge of the bed, gently rubbing his left wrist, which had been strained in the fight. "Did the spirit give you anything? A gift? A pretty sphere of crystal perhaps?"

Conner looked surprised and confused. "Yes. How did you know?"

"We found it on the floor. When you took it in your hands did you not feel anything strange about it?"

"I didn't think about it. It was beautiful, and it was a gift from my Sally. It wasn't like anything I ever saw before and it *was* a bit chill, perhaps, now that you mention it, but it was a gift from a spirit. I suppose they would have to be different from ours."

"You know..." Sebastian said in an even gentler voice, "that spirits do not have physical possessions in this world."

"But she gave it to me!" He seemed a little upset, angry, and also worried by the grave tone of Sebastian's voice.

"You also know that spirits can be felt, but can only be seen by those with the Sight?"

"Yes, but I might have a trace..." He broke off and the slight defiance in his face cracked. His eyes went wide. "You know something. It—it wasn't her, was it?" His voice broke into tears.

"I'm so sorry," Sebastian whispered, feeling a cheese press closing down on his heart at the man's anguished expression. "But no. I'm afraid you were tricked. The thing that came to you last night must have seen poor Sally die and knew you were close to her. In some way, it took her appearance to trick you." Very softly, he told him about the object found behind his ear, and the sphere filling the room with black mist.

Connor covered his face with his left hand and wept for several minutes. Then he touched his arm and looked at his skinned knuckles. He reached up and touched Sebastian's face where a large bruise was darkening. "Something more than that happened," he said in a husky voice. "Tell me. I can take it. How did I get all beat up, and you...?"

"I'm afraid I'm the one who broke your arm," Sebastian said with a faint, crooked smile. Then he told him about the fight.

"By all the Stars," Connor exclaimed when he was done. "I'm ever so sorry. That's horrible. What a terrible fool I was..." He trailed off and turned his head away.

Sebastian stroked the man's hair. Healers got used to treating people, even those older than themselves, in a motherly or fatherly sort of way. "Don't torment yourself about it now. You should sleep." He whispered an Eldir spell for the healing and strengthening of mind and spirit, and held his hand on Connor's forehead. Then Sebastian stood. He was so tired, his hand and arm hurt, he was covered in bruises, and he thought one of his ribs might be a little cracked, but a glance at the clock told him it was a few minutes after midnight. He needed to get up to Joseph.

He started down the stairs but only got down one flight when he felt a faint touch on his shoulder, and a moment later another.

"What happened?" Helen's voice asked. "I felt danger, but I was on wall. Bad fight. Hard to get ahold of other captain. Then fear gone. Just off watch now."

"I same." That was Tatyana's voice.

Sebastian felt Helen's spirit form start a little at the other voice and then reach towards it. Since they also had a strong Sight connection, they could hear each other. It was a strange feeling, like having a conference with two invisible people. They must be tired and probably couldn't stay long. Tatyana likely couldn't say more, and even Helen seemed to be limiting her words as much as she could. "It's all all right now," he said aloud. "We had a scare tonight. We're all pretty tired, and I got beat up a bit, but it's fine now. I had better tell you all about it really quick though, if you can hang on. It is a new trick of the enemy, and you should be on the lookout for it too."

"Go ahead," Helen said.

Tatyana said nothing, but he could tell she was still there. He told them everything that had happened, speaking quickly while he walked slowly down the stairs and their spirit forms stayed close beside him.

When he concluded, Helen said, "Thank you. We will watch. Take care."

"You too," he said, feeling her kiss his cheek before slipping away. "I love you. I love you both, and Tatyana, give Mother and Father a hug for me, please," he couldn't resist adding.

He felt Tatyana squeeze his hand. Then they both were gone. He sighed, took his sword and bow, and headed up onto the wall.

Chapter 19

Hope

Efrian New Year's day (two months later), YA 1127

Aldor

ELISABETH SAT at the long mess table. The room was quiet. She had gone on some business to one of the smiths, Claudius of the Silver-tree house, when she came off watch. He was the best in the town, and she needed mail for a couple of her new recruits. Her watch was already in bed now, but she had not taken her breakfast to the guardian's room today. She didn't want to look at her paperwork.

It was new year's morning, or at any rate it would be when the sun rose, and she was having trouble mustering any hope for the new year. She glanced at the large, ornate clock on the wall. It was dusty and she could barely make out the face in the dim firelight from the hearth across the room. There was no oil of any kind to spare for lamps or candles. The golden hands glinted sadly in the faint light, and the inlaid gemstone birds around the face seemed like shadowy ghosts. It was seven o'clock in the morning. In an hour the sun would rise blood red over the forest in the east and bring in another year. She wasn't going to stay up to see it. What was the point?

For a minute, as she chased the last reluctant peas on her plate, she remembered the Midwinter festivals in Eldirad before the war. In those days, night wasn't so dark, and it held no fear, and every new year was filled with promise. She closed her eyes and pictured the crystal lanterns in the bare trees sparkling on the snow in the courtyard. The bright lamps that filled the windows of the royal ballroom, overflowing with music and laughter and the flying of silken skirts. Elisabeth had never liked the dressing up as much as some of her friends, and she didn't even always wear a silk dress, but she enjoyed the rollicking tunes.

She remembered the feast tables along the sides of the room and the ham and chicken and cider... and then to wander out into the sparkling night, especially on a clear night when the stars were like jewels, and to walk the streets where those who didn't fit into the ballroom, or took a break from the dancing, strolled and sang and laughed. The pubs were full of song, and people went in and out, and there was ale and stories and always music. There were funny short plays on the palace porch and people gathered, laughing in clouds of steam in the night air. The ball ended near two and many went to bed, but the pubs never closed that night. She would usually stay up, and there would be good food and drink and company. Then, at dawn, everyone rose and the whole city stood out on the east side by the river waiting for the sun to come over the trees, and when it did they cheered and sang. Couples kissed each other, and people danced about. Then the all-night revelers went to bed.

It seemed foolish and distant now. A myth from a different world. The cooks had given everyone a little precious sausage last night for the holiday, and there had been a half cup of spiced cider for each warrior, but breakfast was just peas and unbuttered potatoes. Last summer, with the new land, much more had been grown, but in spite of the work of the Efrim, the plants did not thrive in the faint mist, and they could do nothing about the stock animals sickening. Meat, eggs, and dairy had become very rare treats. Elisabeth tried to remember to be grateful for a relatively full plate of peas, but it was hard. It had been a very cold night, and the ice seemed still to cling to her. It wasn't really even the food that bothered her; she mostly forced herself to eat anyway. She missed the laughter and song. She was desperate to hear someone laugh. Not even children laughed in Aldor now. The town was frozen and still, waiting for a dawn that brought no hope. This was their fourth Midwinter at Aldor, and things only got worse. Colder, darker, less food and more sickness, and always more Shadows.

No matter what, she must never let anyone know her doubts. That was the duty of a leader, a place that was, by nature, a lonely one. She ate the last few peas without tasting them. Then she rose and took her plate to the kitchen for the dishwashers.

"May the new year bring peace," said the man who took her dish.

"Yes," Elisabeth said. She couldn't say more. She fervently echoed his prayer, but wondered that anyone could find the hope to say things like that after more than three years of fighting. The young, ambitious woman so excited at her new title and responsibility being sent here seemed another person in another life. Why had she wanted that? What made her think glory was the only thing that mattered—or that she was likely to find it? How had she been so blind? Her responsibility felt like a millstone around her neck now. She wished only to be done, to be rid of it, but she couldn't give up while people looked to her. She left the kitchen and went towards her room. She wondered if, tired as she was, she could go to sleep, or if she would just lie there and worry and try to figure things out, as she often did. She wondered if Helen had made any more of that sleeping medicine.

"Lady Elisabeth."

With her hand on the door, she turned and saw one of the village women had just come in the outer door. There was something in her arms wrapped in a blanket.

Elisabeth went back to meet her. "Can I help you?"

"I brought something for you, as a new year's gift... if you want it."

"What is it?" A tiny bit of warmth touched Elisabeth's heart at the thought of this lady bringing her a gift for the holiday. No one had done gifts in years.

"My cat had kittens two months back," she said. "I was pretty surprised when she got pregnant, and I worried about her, too, in these times—she's the light of my life, my Sally—but she did just fine. Two beautiful babies, and they're weaned now. They don't mind eating peas and are learning to hunt like their mother. Someone told me they had heard you liked cats..." She pulled back the blanket a little to reveal a tiny, furry face. "I didn't know if you'd want a kitten, but she's yours if you want her." She looked questioning, hopeful, as if she were not sure how her present would be received.

Elisabeth smiled for the first time since she had no idea when. There was no helping it with those big eyes on her. She wondered at the woman's uncertainty, and supposed she had a reputation for being hard and cold. Since she was a child, many had thought her nothing but a rough warrior without room for gentleness and love. Perhaps they had been right in a way; she wasn't sure now. She had been obsessed with competition and glory, but she didn't think that was all she was. Perhaps she had never known how to show love, or remembered to show it. She reached out a single finger that seemed too big and rough and ran the tip up the nose of the kitten. There was a strange new feeling. A gladness, a love that was painful in its intensity. "Oh yes, I want her. Very much. Thank you... you will never know how much this means to me." She held out her hands. "May I take her?"

"Yes of course, my lady. She is yours. She will likely be wanting to play. I just wrapped her up against the cold on the way over." The lady gently lay the bundle in Elisabeth's arms. The woman watched for a moment the warm smile that transformed Elisabeth's hard face and brought a surprising softness to her light-gray eyes, and she, too, smiled. Then she wished her happy new year and departed.

Elisabeth didn't take her eyes off the kitten as she slipped into the guardian's room. She lay the little bundle in the middle of her bed and bent to kiss its tiny head. She realized there were tears in her eyes. She had no idea when the last time she cried was.

The kitten looked up at her and, with one tiny paw, touched her cheek. She smiled and laughed a little. "You are a magic little thing, aren't you?"

When Elisabeth had taken off her mail and boots, she found the kitten sniffing around her quilt. Elisabeth ripped a string from her fraying woolen tunic and dangled it in front of the kitten's face. The kitten cocked her ears and leapt on the string with wild abandon. Elisabeth laughed again.

They played for ten minutes or so. Then the kitten curled up and fell asleep beside Elisabeth's pillow. Elisabeth lay down beside it. "I love you, my angel," she whispered, stroking the soft fur. "I believe I'll call you Thelma."

Just as the sun was rising beyond the curtains Elisabeth fell asleep, and she slept more soundly than she had in years.

19 January (a month later) to 13 February, YA 1127; Westtower

Joseph didn't like the hungry way his warriors looked at him when he unlocked the spice cupboard with Sebastian's key to take out the small ceramic salt jar. He felt them measure each pinch with their eyes as he went around the circle, and as much as he longed for salt himself, he felt obliged to be careful his own serving was smaller. He couldn't have anyone thinking his looked larger. He had come to care more about the respect of his people, to think of them really as *his people,* and even in his most carefree days he had always wanted to be trusted. He could never bear to be thought to be greedy or to have cheated.

He sat down with the others to eat his cheerless porridge. Sarah was still there, but she remained in the place of second captain, and even Joseph had ceased to feel strange about that. You just did what you had to do, after all. January was a cold, hungry month. In spite of all the work in October, the harvest was far from good.

Sebastian had shared his private room at the top of the tower with Joseph from the beginning, and since he had reclaimed his captain's star and had to go on a different watch, he had been sleeping there, too, sharing Sebastian's cot.

Joseph often helped with the medicines he had learned. He felt an ease and affinity for making medicines he had never expected. As a boy he hadn't liked botany much, but he had learned precision in the theatre and the army. He found it easy to measure and grind, and to learn the herbs Sebastian taught him. The magic element was similar. A lot of it was just precisely following directions, and even the spells, which had felt the most out of his league, were surprisingly easy. It felt good to be useful and to help Sebastian under his heavy burden. But he couldn't help seeing some of the papers on Sebastian's desk, and that just made him more worried about the food supply.

Some of those around him grumbled or made bad jokes about the small portions, but Joseph ate in silence and savored his bit of dry meat. He might once have laughed at the jests, and sometimes he tried, or tried to make a joke himself, but it was hard and usually fell flat. The fear would not leave his heart, and he was worried.

They had been dipping into the reserve storehouse, if sparingly, from near the end of the first winter, and it was depleted. Sebastian held the only key, so as to enforce rations on the hungry warriors, but Joseph could imagine what it looked like down there, not least from the grim look in his friend's eyes when he came up.

At the next watch change Joseph lingered, giving medicine to a sick woman, and went up to the prince's room, as people had started calling it, after Sebastian.

Sebastian looked up from his plate and a pile of papers and gave a ghost of his greeting smile. "Is something the matter?"

"Not really." Joseph looked at the floor and wondered why it was so hard to say this. "I just... I feel like we... I want to ask you something."

Sebastian smiled, but there was concern in his eyes. He could tell this wasn't about an herb or use of the mirror. "Anything. What is it?"

Joseph kept his eyes on the large gray stone tiles. "I just wondered how long the reserve stores will last at the rate we're using them."

Sebastian sighed and Joseph looked up to watch his face carefully. He noticed for the first time how thin Sebastian had gotten. He was strong and well-muscled still, but all softness was gone from his slim frame. He had been very handsome when they were young, but his face seemed harder, all angles now.

"That's what all these papers are about," Sebastian said in a low voice. "I calculate again and again. At present rate of gathering crops and assuming we don't use it in summer and are not obliged to aid the village much, it could last one more winter with tight rations. But if next summer's crops are worse, or we have to help the village, we might not even make it through next winter, and, of course, in that time we'll lose some people." He dropped his eyes to the desk and his voice became only just audible. "I hate putting that in the calculations."

"Over a year seems like a long time," Joseph said, but his smile was forced and his words lacked conviction.

"It does, and it is. Yet, we've had three years of this already. What do I have to make me think this will end by then?"

Joseph wanted there to be something he could say. Even something stupid. "You never know when a ray of sun will poke through," he said. He didn't believe it, but he felt he must. It was too frightening not to believe. Like a pit opening beneath his feet, or a door to a dark place in his mind he must slam shut before anything got out.

Sebastian held Joseph's eyes with a grave look. "It may, to be sure. I don't like to think of years more of this either." He dropped his gaze and his voice. "Sometimes it seems forever. An eternal torment beyond my strength."

Joseph went to Sebastian's side and put a hand on his shoulder. "Don't say that," he said. His throat was tight.

"I'm sorry." Sebastian sighed. "We have to go on. We have to prepare for the worst." Sebastian knew he could not let himself think of the real worst, but he needed to plan. If the tower fell the village fell, and there were not likely to be any survivors. No plan was needed for that. More hungry years, more of this endless torment, however, he had to accept and plan for. He put a hand to his face, rubbing his forehead. "I would be less worried if only we could find more food somehow, or if we had some Efrim farmers, but even if they could get here, Eldirad cannot spare the few she has, and I have no way to contact Efrim. There is nowhere closer than Eldirad, and they have nothing to spare even if we could get there."

Joseph thought for a moment with his hand still on Sebastian's thin shoulder. He had to do something for Sebastian. An adventure beyond the wall would at least break the depressing routine, and Joseph would like to be too busy to think for a while. "I could take a hunting party. We could go secretly and as far as we need to find the animals who have fled the fear of the Shadows."

Sebastian looked up. "You would lead that? I'm afraid it would be dangerous." There was a pained look in Sebastian's eyes.

"I would lead it if people will come with me. Sure, it's dangerous, but so is every day on the wall."

Sebastian moved papers on his desk without really looking at them. "Are you sure Sarah's willing to take your watch alone? Can she do it, you think? She hasn't seemed very confident since her illness."

"I think she'd be fine, not that I'm much judge. I could go at full moon when night watch is the easiest."

Sebastian was silent a long time. He took a bite of his porridge, but it was hard to swallow. Joseph absently built a stack of broken quills on the desk.

When Sebastian spoke, his voice was thin and cracked. "Perhaps it is best. You have permission to go with up to twenty warriors who volunteer of their own choice. You may not leave with less than six, though. I do not like it at all, but I see no choice." He dropped his voice to a broken whisper. "I just don't know what I'll do without you."

Joseph felt an uncomfortable tightening around his heart, but he took one of Sebastian's hands and made himself smile. "You'll get along fine," he said almost lightly. "We hardly see each other anymore anyway. Just drop a few of my socks on the floor now and then and you'll never know I'm gone." He nodded towards two mismatched socks that lay near the bed.

A smile flickered on Sebastian's face for a moment, and then he grew grave again. "I suppose that's almost true, but you don't fool me that easy, and I rely on you. Still..." Sebastian straightened his shoulders and pressed Joseph's hand. "To each his duty. We can only do what we have to do. Just take care of yourself, and good luck."

"Don't worry. I'll be back," Joseph said cheerfully. He hoped the words rang true to Sebastian. Joseph mostly believed it, and that was the best he could do.

Sebastian smiled. "I only wish I could come with you."

Joseph felt a surge of longing. The trip would be really fun if Sebastian could come too. But there was no possibility, and they both knew it. As captain, Joseph might be spared, even though he had come to act as second in command, but the prince could never leave the tower or the village now, no matter how important the mission, or how deeply they both desired it. "I wish you could, too," Joseph said.

Not long after that, Joseph went out to his watch. Sebastian remained staring at the wall for a long time before he was able to force himself to eat.

* * * * * *

Both Joseph and Sebastian spread the word of the mission to their watches. To Joseph's great surprise, volunteers flooded in at once. Before the end of the day, twenty men and women had found Joseph and pledged their service; as he was trying to go on for his watch, he had to refuse several.

"I'm sorry," he said to the third man. "But I already have as many as I can take."

"All right. I had hoped to go with you, but Stars bless you, sir," the man said, looking down.

"Thank you," Joseph said. He felt awkward. The man was about his own age, yet to have been called 'sir' in that tone—and by someone outside his own watch, no less. He didn't know what to think. For a moment he thought back to when warriors even of his own age called him 'boy.' Three years ago, at the beginning of the war, it had been standard, and it wasn't until he took his star back almost two years ago that anyone had called him 'sir.' Being called 'boy' had stopped sometime after that. He hadn't noticed exactly when. 'Sir' had become more common of late, but it still surprised him, and it was a moment before he turned and hurried up the steps to do his duty.

Joseph and his twenty companions departed at sunrise four days later. Sebastian stood in the snow to see them off at the south gate, but he said little and his face was like stone. Joseph tried to speak cheerfully, but in the end, it was too hard to part with Sebastian and he too grew silent. They embraced for a moment. Then Joseph led his people out of the gate and Sebastian locked it behind them.

At first, Joseph and his comrades had to fight Shadows in large numbers, and they went forward in a wedge with Joseph leading. It wasn't long, however, before they broke through the press around the wall. Joseph took extra care to kill all the Shadows that followed them, and they passed through the snow-covered land in silence. Of course, they left tracks in the snow, but they covered them as best they could without making themselves terribly slow. The snow was hard and the air brutally cold.

They traveled continuously, but they found they could run little even in the hard places where their feet left no mark on the icy snow. It had been years since any of them ran a long distance, and hard as the fighting on the wall was, it was not the same. They were all thinner, too, and the cold cut through their heavy clothing. When they could no longer run they trudged through the show, stomping and beating their hands to keep off frostbite. They rested only at the warmest hours of the day and huddled together, but that wasn't enough. Often they were obliged to build a little fire to thaw out fingers and toes, and although one of the women had the power to do something of a light shield to hide them, Joseph always felt uneasy until they were off again. So long as people were shivering, and their fingers and toes hurt badly, they knew they were all right. The snow made fighting Shadows easier, though. The dark creatures showed up easily against the sparkling white snow in the bright moonlight.

Early on the fourth day, Joseph's company came to the forest at the feet of the Narsi Mountains some sixty miles southwest of Obrin. On the lower slopes the trees were all oaks, maples, chestnuts, and beeches, with bare winter branches, but even that much cover seemed friendly. Of course, it also meant hiding places for their enemies, but they saw very few Shadows. Those they met seemed oddly weak, more see-through, and not as fast-moving. When they had hiked up through the belt of pines and crossed the bare snowy summit of the ridge there were no more Shadows. On the seventh day since their departure, they came down into the lower forests on the south side of that ridge and entered the basin of Lake Oslet, lodging between the tree-clad arms of the mountains.

Here they saw the tracks of animals again. Many of them. They were now some seventy-five miles, as the crow flies, from the tower, but they had found what they were looking for. They camped on the shore of the frozen lake for three days, and while some hunted, others fished in the lake. Those were a pleasant three days. The weather was calm, and they ate well.

Looking out at the smooth ice of the big lake on the second morning,

Joseph wished he had his ice skates. What fun that would have been. He did go out and slide about in his boots a bit in the moonlight that night and remembered skating parties back at home in the old days. He remembered when Edward had first taught him to ice skate, holding both his little hands and leading him around the edge of the skating pond. He remembered when he first learned to do tricks, and he thought about all his friends. But there wasn't time to play. They were here to work.

They cut and packed the meat, and it froze easily in the snow, so there was no worry about it keeping. By the time they set out, on the eleventh day of their trip, everyone was heavily laden with meat to take home. It was February by this time, but the cold and snow were no less. It snowed hard the whole time they were crossing the mountains and they had to use snowshoes. They had eaten well during their stay at the hunting grounds, however, and that helped. They didn't get cold quite so easily and were getting into better training. Joseph felt better than he had in years. Still, the loads were heavy, and they could not go faster than on the outward journey.

As they returned to the feet of the mountains they saw Shadows again, which became more numerous and powerful as they went on. They were obliged to fight hard several times on the tumbled snow field. The snow quite covered the short scrub bushes and grass that lived in that jagged, rocky land, but it did not make the land level or easy to walk upon.

On day fourteen, one man was wounded. His burden was divided up among the others, and they took turns carrying him on their backs. Joseph gave him basic soldiers' first aid and did his best with what he had learned from Sebastian and the medicines Sebastian had sent with them, but the man died in two days. They dug down and made a shallow grave in the rocky soil for their comrade, laying him out with respect and a few words of blessing. Then they stood together to sing over the grave.

The triumph had gone out of the journey after that. Joseph had felt strong, almost free in the hills and at the lake, but now he wanted nothing but to get back. He pressed his companions to long marches with little rest, and on the seventeenth day they neared Obrin.

Some of his people were getting hopeful again, and talk, as they ate and took their short rest in the shelter of a big rock, was cheerful, even if still in undertones. People dwelled mostly on the anticipated delight of Prince Sebastian and their fellows at what they had brought back.

Joseph didn't join in the excitement. He felt uneasy and stayed silent. After an hour, he rousted them and got them moving again.

They hadn't been walking long when a huge number of Shadows came on them from both sides. They saw them coming at a little distance, for it was daylight, but there was no escaping them. Joseph got his people in a circle with the packs in the middle. Then the attack was on them.

He called on his warriors again and again to raise their spirits for another stand. They had to hold, but several fell or fainted. Some fought with their weaker hand, or on their knees, but they kept fighting. For a time, all hope left Joseph and he thought only to keep fighting. They would all perish, and no one would know, yet they must go down hard and take as many Shadows with them as they could. Joseph's sword flashed back and forth before him, and he clutched his dagger in his left hand. This was the sort of last stand people wrote stories about. If only anyone would ever know. He dodged the blade of a Shadow and slew two more that went up in his face. The mist around them was getting thick, and for the first time Joseph could see dancing shapes in the corners of his eyes. They couldn't stand more than another a minute or two.

This had been his idea. Now he was paying the price, but it wasn't just him. The men and women who had trusted him were falling, and Sebastian... The flickering visions in the mist reminded him of when Sebastian had saved him from the land of nightmares when he was ill. In that moment he remembered Sebastian's words: "Take care... I don't know what I will do without you." And his own words, "I will come back." It was not just him and those who had made the mistake of trusting him. It was the whole fort, and he couldn't leave Sebastian.

Anger welled up in him. Not his usual light short temper, as swift to go as to come. This was a deep rage that was quiet but strong. A Shadow with a sword had pressed him to one knee, but he stood again now. The numbness in his left foot vanished, and his vision cleared. He made another charge. His blade flickered with white fire in the mist.

They were close. Not much more than a mile, he guessed. The wall was probably just over a rise or behind some snow-covered rocks or bushes. Somehow, they must get there. But they had their burdens to carry, and many couldn't walk. Joseph cried to Sebastian in his head and hoped Sebastian could see the mist of the battle from the tower if he looked, but no help could come in time.

Joseph caught sight of something crouching behind a little hillock. It was not a Shadow. It was dark green and solid, but it moved. Joseph leapt and grabbed at the creature. His hand closed on something skin-like that stung his hand, but he did not let go. He was now face to face with a vaguely human creature. It was as tall as he was, and heavier by nearly double, with dark green skin that had an oily shimmer. It had a little coarse black hair on its head and its eyes were yellow. Joseph met the eyes, and for a moment he was startled by the sheer wall of menace and power that seemed to crash into him. He staggered and wrenched his eyes away in time to counter a blow from a strange weapon like a sword with a serrated edge, which glittered with a foul, poisonous yellow light.

Joseph and the creature fought intensely for several minutes. Joseph's rage and defiance did not desert him but rose to meet the malevolent onslaught that pressed upon him, just as his burning blade met the weapon of his enemy. There was no time for thought. Joseph dove and stabbed and his sword went into the monster. It fell at full length, and Joseph dropped to his knees.

A shout from one of his people roused him just in time to duck another blade. The Shadows were still there. Yet they seemed less fierce and numerous. Joseph staggered to his feet and went back to his people. Seven lay dead or unconscious, four were groaning on the ground, and only two of the remaining eight were all the way on their feet and seemed to be able to see. The cloud was thick about them, and the phantom images were large and fierce in the corners of Joseph's eyes as they had never been before. It was getting harder to distinguish the phantoms from the real Shadows attacking. He used his will to push back the phantoms, and they receded a little.

He put on his pack and someone else's, and those on their feet followed his example while he defended them. Even some who couldn't walk put on two packs.

"Come, everyone. We're going to make it," Joseph said in the strongest voice he could muster. "We must get everyone out. Please, help me." He tied one man's hands together and slung him over his shoulders with his arms around his neck.

Others took the other six, and those who could not walk crawled with another on their back. Somehow, they got all the people and all the packs off the ground. Joseph could barely walk under the weight of the two packs and a man as big as himself, but he had to fight the lead through the Shadows. That was his duty. He also had to talk constantly to encourage his people and, most importantly, to lead them. Sight went before hearing, and the conscious all seemed to be able to hear him, although many couldn't see.

"Come on, this way, keep going," he said over and over.

He couldn't think. He gasped for breath, but he must go on. Must fight and not stop talking.

The Shadows seemed a little lost, as if there was less thought behind their motions. The green thing must have been their captain, Joseph realized as he and his companions staggered on a few more steps.

"Joseph?" It was Sebastian's voice.

For a moment Joseph thought he was dreaming, or starting to hallucinate, but he called back. "Here!"

A moment later Sebastian was there with some of his warriors. Those who couldn't walk and those they carried were swept up, and two unburdened men took rear guard.

* * * * * * *

It was almost five, and Sebastian had been in the sick room when he heard the call. Running up to the mirror, he saw Joseph attack the green monster. He shouted down to a warrior on his watch named Anna, who was working below, to keep an eye on the mirror. Then, running down, he gathered warriors to go out. Warriors in Sarah's watch on the wall spotted the rising mist of the battle against the setting sun, and Sebastian and his companions set out at once.

Reaching the incoming party, they saw a sorry sight, but there was no time for concern. The people who were crawling or dragging themselves along had to be carried, and so did those on their backs. When they were picked up, Sebastian sent two of his company to the back and took the lead, fighting back through the thickening Shadows near the wall.

When they were two hundred yards from the wall, Sarah released the sortie she and Sebastian had arranged and the whole party was swept into the gate together. Sebastian entered first because he had led, and he remained beside the gate to see everyone in. He counted every member of the expedition except one, but two were badly wounded, and a third dead, while even those very few still on their feet stumbled and leaned on his soldiers' arms. Joseph entered last, trudging doggedly. His face was ghostly white, and he didn't even look at Sebastian when he offered him his arm.

Sebastian did get Joseph to let him take the man off his back, but when he had, Joseph hurried off before him to the tower. Sebastian followed, and together they made sure all the meat was stowed in the ice room, and all the sick and wounded cared for. All had at least mild blindness and were put to bed with food and water if they would take it, but Joseph seemed to be able to see fine. Sebastian glanced at him often while he worked over the wounded, and Joseph gave out herbs and cleaned and bandaged a scratch on someone's arm. Sebastian was concerned about him, but he also wondered at his strength.

When at last everything that could be done had been done, Sebastian looked over again. Joseph knelt by a bed across the room. The torchlight shimmered on his bent head and glittered on his mail. He did not move. Sebastian thought of the moment he had seen him in the mirror and the flaming white light that had leapt from his sword in the darkness of the mist. That was amazing power. Joseph had a good blade with moonsilver decoration, but even with the moon in the sky it would not have shone like that without the use of extreme power, and now that Sebastian thought about it, the moon had set hours before.

Across the room, Joseph stood. He swayed, took a hasty step sideways, and put a hand on the wall. Sebastian was on his feet and at Joseph's side in a moment.

"You should rest," Sebastian said gently. "You have done very well, but you used so much power..." Sebastian realized it was half a question. Where had that power come from? Had Joseph known he was that strong?

"I... I promised I would come back," Joseph said faintly. He was so tired he wasn't sure how much longer he could stand.

"Yes, you did," Sebastian said. "And I'm so glad. But now, please let me help you to bed." He put one arm around Joseph's back and guided Joseph's arm around his shoulders.

"Thank you," Joseph whispered. He leaned into Sebastian's shoulder and let him lead him upstairs. He had made it. The duty was done.

Sebastian got him settled in bed and gave him some water. Joseph was asleep before he could offer dinner.

Sebastian stood watching him for a minute. He had been so afraid Joseph wouldn't come back, and he wasn't sure he could have kept going without him. When he turned away, he had to wipe tears from his eyes with his fraying woolen sleeve.

When he started down the stairs to check that everything was all right with the new stores before he went to bed himself, Anna stopped him.

"You know you left me to watch the mirror," she said, taking hold of his sleeve.

"Yes. I thought someone should see what was happening in case something went wrong and we missed them."

"All seems to have gone well enough, but I just have to tell you. You saw that green thing, right?"

"Yes." Sebastian shivered. It was the ugliest creature he could imagine.

"I judge it was very powerful, the look in its eyes—akk. It makes me shudder, and its weapon was horrible, but you should have seen how bright Joseph's blade was."

"I did for a moment."

"I just, well, I never saw anything like it, and his eyes were almost as bright when he faced that awful beast. He looked like a different person.

I mean, I knew he was strong and brave and all—not that he showed that either when we were younger, but this?"

"I'm just as surprised as you are." Sebastian smiled and almost laughed at the puzzled look on her face. "But it seems it is a good thing he did it."

"They never would have made it until you got there otherwise."

Sebastian thought of Joseph's white face and grew worried again. "I just hope it wasn't too much for him," he said, more to himself than to her.

"He didn't go blind like the others. Surely he'll be all right."

Sebastian nodded. It was hard to know what desperate duty, and overload of adrenaline, might do, but she was probably right.

* * * * * * *

The two wounded and one of the unconscious died and were buried with ceremony two days later, but everyone else mended. Joseph was quite himself again by the next day and took back his place on the wall. On the fourth day, they celebrated the meat. People spent rest time drying some for the storehouse, and they made lots of soup and put broth bones and pieces of meat to keep cold in the stone ice shed with plenty of snow and ice packed around them.

On the fifth morning, when the sun came up, Joseph left the watch to Sarah again and helped Sebastian take some broth bones and sausage to the village. They divided it among the people and, although it seemed a little thing, their gratitude was great.

Joseph and Sebastian walked back together from the village with their empty baskets over their arms. Joseph felt happier than he had in a long time, almost light on his feet, and Sebastian was grave, but a faint smile played on his thin lips.

When they had gone through the Prince's Gate, which was now always closed and required a touch of moonsilver to open, and were walking across the bare snowy fields, Sebastian spoke. "When you were gone, a couple people came to me and talked to me about making you a guardian. They had all voted, apparently."

"What?" Joseph stopped in his tracks.

Sebastian stopped, too, and a smile flickered in his eyes at the startled look on Joseph's face. "Don't look so surprised. You aren't blind. Think about it. You have really been playing that role for months now. You are second in command at the tower, you lead the watches on and off the wall, you have a key to the store cupboard, you tend the sick, what more could they want?"

"I don't know," Joseph stammered. He felt embarrassed, half frightened, and somewhere deep down, perhaps gratified. "Someone stronger, braver, nobler, more powerful, more competent..."

Sebastian shook his head, but his eyes still sparkled. "They won't find it. Not unless one of the great guardian angels themselves was to walk the earth, and I don't think that's likely."

Joseph laughed a little. "They were all up in the sky last I checked."

"They belong there. Anyway, I told them I'd talk to you when you came home. I couldn't think about it then. I was too afraid you wouldn't come home at all, but yesterday Anna came to me when you were on watch to see if I'd asked you. She's the one I left to watch the mirror when I went to you. She told me everything that night. By now I guess everyone knows about your battle with that green monster. Somehow you managed to hide it all our lives, but you have innate power, Joseph, and someday you'll have to admit it."

"I don't know." Joseph's cheeks flushed flame red, and an uncomfortable knot rose in his stomach. He didn't like the idea of being powerful or special; it frightened him. He didn't know why and had a feeling he didn't want to know. He felt that if that knot of fear came up, he would know, and that was something he had to prevent. "I only did what I had to," he said, swallowing hard. "I promised you I would come back."

Sebastian smiled with tears in his eyes and took Joseph's hand. He decided to let power go for the time. "Whatever else you are, you are the best friend in the world, and a responsible, noble person, and you are brave. I am so, so glad you came home, Joseph."

Joseph laughed, and it was genuine. The bubble of fear was suppressed, and his cares for the time lightened. "I am, too."

They started walking in silence again. Then Sebastian asked, "So, will you accept the title?"

Joseph thought a minute, looking at the glitter of the snow in the hazy sunlight. The people had voted him the honor and the duty—how could he refuse? He felt he wasn't equal to it, not a good enough person by far, but if they thought he was... He realized Sebastian was right; he had basically been doing a guardian's job, but it was not uncommon for a captain, especially one with seniority, to be assigned authority for a watch or a project. An unwelcome voice in his head reminded him that he didn't have seniority and, if he was honest with himself, he had gone much further than that common assignment of responsibility. His duties might actually change little, and yet there would be a new commitment, an added responsibility that came with those stars. Accepting them was a pledge. "I will," he whispered after a minute. "If they want me, all I can do is try my best for them."

Chapter 20

Death or Glory

18 April (about two months later), YA 1127

Northeast Efrim Wall

IN THE LITTLE more than a year since Aranin got his general's flower, and he, Analisia, and Yeven moved to the new post, nothing remarkable had happened. Aranin got used to commanding. It wasn't nearly as hard as he thought it would be. The captains were indeed glad to have him, and no one gave any trouble. The new post had come to seem like home, and in some ways, it was a relief to Aranin not to feel his father's watchful gaze over his shoulder. For her part, Analisia enjoyed being on the same watch with Aranin again, and she easily fell into the swing of being a captain at the new post. The pattern went on much the same as it had at Louranin's camp.

Watches took different hours here, since it was a strategy not to have any two neighboring companies keep the same hours. Aranin chose to take his watch from ten to four, judging them the worst, most hopeless hours of the night, and also the hottest and most unpleasant in heavy clothing on a summer day. Had he known, it might have given him a grim pleasure that he had made the same choice as Sebastian.

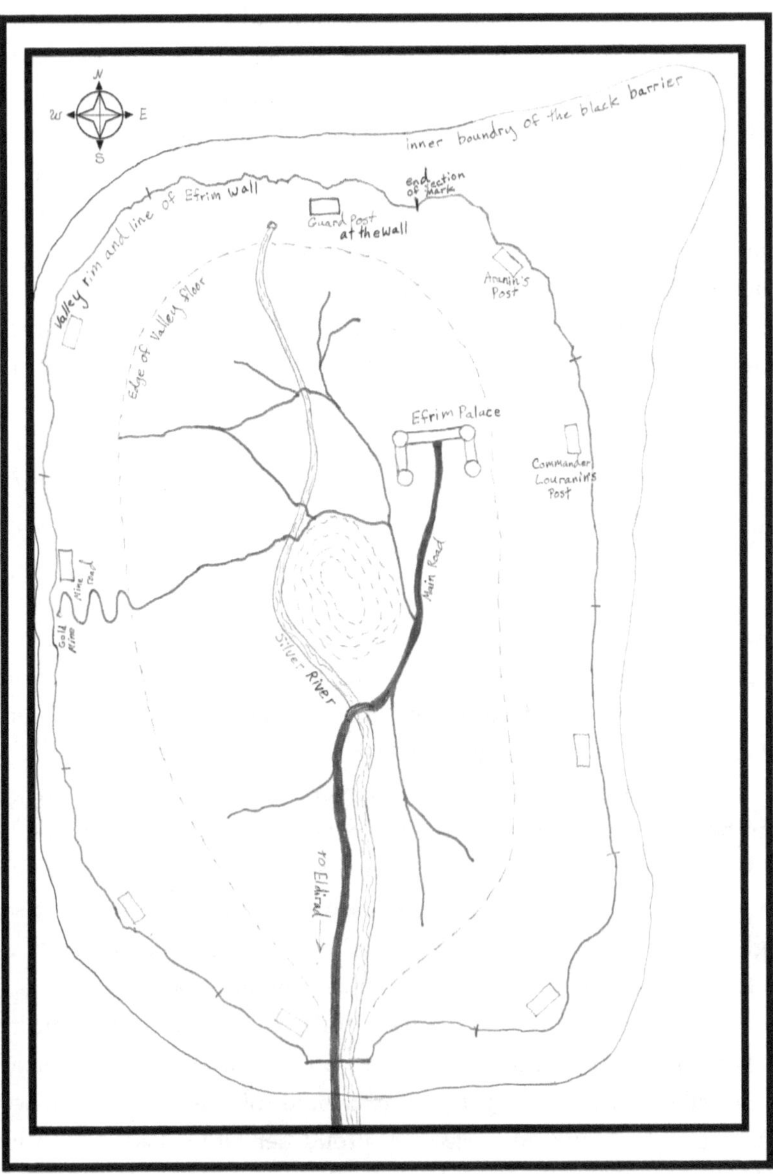

There were the hours on the wall, filled with the same hard work and horror as always, and then there was sleeping, eating, washing, and doing paperwork related to stores and supplies of various kinds.

Analisia retained her furious energy. She had to be always *doing* and couldn't bear the thought of an idle moment. She worked often at the cooking or washing, or fixing of weapons, and sometimes helped Aranin with the paperwork. He was still tired, and sometimes, especially when people died or he was forced to deal with papers and organization related to the sortie his father was planning, he got very depressed. When he couldn't bear it, or couldn't sleep, he sat at his desk and drew, and it was seldom that even Analisia knew. Once, he started a letter to Tatyana. He knew she would never get it, but somehow it helped to write it anyway.

✶✶✶✶✶✶

Now, the day for the attack had come. After a year and a half of speculation, training more warriors, arguing fine points with captains and generals all around the valley, and sending out a string of ill-fated scouts, Louranin had set a day—and what's more it had arrived.

Analisia woke that morning with something akin to joy. She had only slept two restless hours, or a little more, after her night watch when the bells rang to say it was seven and the assembling was beginning. Still, she felt like leaping out of bed, perhaps even skipping. It was a grim sort of gladness, of course, a hard battle thrill, perhaps, but today they were going to do something at last to make those Shadows pay.

Further, the attack was coming mainly from their corner, and the other two generals would not leave their posts far away on the other side of the valley, so Analisia got to lead a flank of the battle along with Aranin and Louranin. She was very proud her father had chosen her, and she was itching to begin. As she went out, people were already starting to gather. The whole of her and Aranin's watch was going, and some from the other watch at their post. Louranin, likewise, was bringing his whole watch, from his post to their right, and part of the other watch, too. A gray-haired captain marched in with an entire watch from the post on their other side, and closely upon each other came smaller battalions sent from all the other posts around the valley. The other leaders were all sending warriors in accordance with Louranin's order, though they could not spare as many since the sortie would not directly decrease the press on their sections of wall.

Analisia greeted every new troop with cheerful words and increasing hope in her heart. Her nation was mighty. They would not stand for the kind of treatment they had been receiving. It seemed to her that all the faces were smiling. Men and women met her eyes with optimism, and the sparkling of mail and swords made a glitter in the morning sun glorious to be seen. The sky above the touch of black mist was clear and blue. The sun was bright. The rising of hope was like sap in the trees, which somehow seemed greener than they had been in years. Huge trestles were set out, and two dozen women from the valley, who had come up specially, served a breakfast for all the gathered warriors. Analisia sat herself down between Yeven and a young captain from another station who was asking her enthusiastically about this corner of the forest and how the black barrier of the enemy was farther away here.

That was the reason this would be the corner to send the attack from. All around the valley of Efrimiel, a strange black barrier had grown up in the trees in the first year of the threat. In May of the first year of the war, messengers could no longer pass to Eldirad, and the barrier had thickened and strengthened since those early attempts. Even hardy soldiers who were sent in to scout it and try to figure out what it was never came back. They sometimes fell so close to the edge that they could be dragged out with effort and a good sortie of fighters, but only one had survived. He had been a recent scout during the planning stages, and he hadn't gotten into the barrier more than a few yards. When at last he came to himself, he had told that the blackness was much like that of the mist of the Shadows, only so thick it almost seemed to have a texture, a weight. Madness and fear walked in there, almost as in the dreams of the sickness, and the blackness choked and suffocated, sapping will, strength, and thought.

Louranin had given up trying to send scouts into it after that, and it had been confirmed that the only way for the offensive to go was towards the northeast corner. There, for a reason they were determined to find out today, the black barrier slanted away down the hill through the trees. It disappeared from view entirely, and scouts had not made it back with any information. Louranin had decided it was too well watched, and only an army would be any good. To get into that corner they needed numbers. They had also observed that most of the Shadows seemed to flow out of that area to spread around the valley, and the theory was that the enemy must have a camp or stronghold in that region.

Analisia helped herself to sausages and poured syrup over her pancakes. "There's something in that corner where the barrier is farther away, and today we're going to find it and destroy it," she said to the captain beside her with energy. "I don't know what a camp for Shadows would look like, of course, but they must have some headquarters. There must be some lord, or even creator, behind them. The Shadows themselves are clearly expendable."

"That's for sure. They are mown down in the thousands, and it doesn't seem to discomfit anyone in the slightest," the captain said with a touch of disgust.

"We'll find a way to discomfit them today," Analisia said decidedly. Then she reached for another helping of strawberries. It bugged her a little that she hadn't seen much of Aranin that morning, but it was such a crowd, and it was exciting to talk to new people from other posts. She glimpsed him at one of the other tables passing sausages to someone and hoped he was talking with someone nice too.

✶ ✶ ✶ ✶ ✶ ✶

Aranin was talking to no one at all. He had been much too agitated to sleep when he came down from his watch. What is the good? he said to himself against his will. I will be dead soon enough, and you don't need sleep then. Besides, it was quite hopeless. The anticipation was almost unbearable, and so he had risen and gone to his desk. He worked, with desperate energy, if little focus or conviction, on a picture of a unicorn. Then he wrote another letter that would never be sent, this time to Sebastian. He poured out his fear, grief, and the strange, surreal state of doing one's duty against all better judgement. Should he have tried harder to talk to Analisia? But it would have done no good. If he had questioned this lunacy, it would only have landed him entirely alone with no one on his side, disgraced, and likely as not kicked out of the army. And, these days, what else was there that was worth doing? He supposed he could be useful as a farmer's apprentice, but would any farmer have been willing to take him as apprentice in that kind of disgrace?

No. It was no good. His duty was his duty, even if he didn't agree, and since he couldn't get out of it, he had to pray he was wrong about the dire outcome. Perhaps they could make a worthy sortie and still return to the relative safety of the wall. Perhaps there was even some hope, as Analisia seemed to think. Perhaps he was just depressed and shouldn't be listened to after all. But the Shadows. There were so many. Nothing depleted them. Nothing dismayed them. They were without body or mind like humans, and yet they fought well. There was some mastermind behind them, surely, and no clever captain would leave a chink in armor as effective as the black barrier. Aranin was sure they would run into it if they went far enough, as sure as he was that no bird, squirrel, insect, or blade of grass could be seen on the edge of that barrier. When not even moss could survive, what chance had men, who were so easily put in fear, dark dreams, or madness by the mist of these beings?

When the bell sounded, Aranin had risen from his desk as one saying goodbye to life. He slipped the moonsilver charm his mother had given him deep beneath his undershirt. Then, with a face like a carven statue, he went out and greeted his father and the newcomers. He was careful to keep away from Analisia in the crowd that morning for a few reasons. First, he didn't want to have to talk, and she was sure to want to talk about the brilliant victory they would have. Second, he feared she would discover his ill mood and betray in the end his lack of faith, or be angry with him again on what so likely was their last day. Finally, he could see across the camp that she was happy, and he would not dampen that if he could help it.

So, he found a table a distance away and ate mechanically and yet a touch nostalgically. The black mist hovered threateningly over the camp, the sun seemed very distant, and many faces looked anxious or unhappy.

He wondered what choice these warriors had been given, little surely, about coming here to charge out into the very hands of the Shadows. He pitied them, but he, too, had no choice. The general's flower meant nothing except that it was his duty to try to convince his men of a hope he didn't believe and lead them forth, betraying their trust, to an end he dreaded.

Louranin called loudly for order. Aranin licked a last drop of maple syrup off his fork and stood. The time had come. To death or victory. Death was much more likely, but he would not give up. If he had to die, he would do so honorably.

Analisia leapt to her feet, and the other lesser leaders rose also. The army was soon formed into ordered ranks. Louranin's company went first. Then Analisia's would follow out of the gate and swing right. Aranin's warriors were gathered last to follow the others through the gate and swing left. They awaited only Louranin's word.

Louranin stood by the gate and raised his sword in the air. "Come, my warriors. Enough of cowering, enough of defending small walls, we are a proud people, and we will not be imprisoned or dishonored. Today we stride forth to take what is ours by right and to pay the Shadows for all the losses and indignities they have imposed on us. For the glory of Efrim! On, to victory!" Then he waved his gleaming sword, and half a dozen young men blew great trumpets on the wall. The sound rang in the valley and through the hills, proud and defiant.

With that, the gates were opened and Louranin charged through, followed by all his host.

The Shadow forces responded quickly to the place of the horn blast, but the numbers and ferocity of the Efrim attack overwhelmed them. The Shadows gave way. The Efrim were a fury coming down the hill onto the Shadows, a wall of shining mail, bright gems, and swords flaming with the fierce, deadly light of moonsilver, increased by the innate power behind the will and anger of those who bore them. Analisia and Aranin moved their flanks out smoothly as planned, pushing a tide of Shadows before them.

The hillside here was steep, although it was not so barren and rocky as the upper slopes farther north. Here, trees still clung, but at a tight angle, so their trunks reaching for the sky came often near to the ground, even ten or fifteen feet from the base. The Efrim had the advantage of the terrain, for, coming from above they plunged down upon their foes like the rushing tide of a waterfall. Both Aranin and Analisia found they were striving mostly to keep their warriors from flying on too fast. Athletic as the Efrim warriors were, they were mostly heavy, muscular people and used to fighting on a wall or level field. Never had the Efrim rivaled the Eldir for agility or woodcraft, while the Shadows needed scarcely any foothold whatever, and the leaders knew this, and tried to restrain their warriors from going beyond their limits. Still, some slipped, and a few fell badly down the hill.

Aranin slowed his flank a little, for this reason, and also because the glory of this assault felt false. That was a traitorous thought, perhaps, but it was too easy. He felt they were running headlong into a trap, and he commanded his warriors to slow and move in behind Louranin's company slightly so as to preserve the possibility of retreat. Louranin probably wouldn't have approved of this, but Aranin felt it was the only way. He was commanding alone, for all practical purposes. He had long ago lost sight of Louranin in the trees and bushes, and even if he might have heard him over the shouts, clashing of swords, and crashing of bushes, it was hardly wise to go shouting about battle strategy. No one knew how much the Shadows understood. In his year as general, Aranin had learned to take responsibility for his own post, and so he did his best, knowing the choice was hard and might be wrong. They were fighting Shadows on both sides and before them, and the hundreds or thousands that had been killed were filling the still, stuffy air of the forest with a horrible floating mist. So far, charging ahead, they were keeping in front of the worst of it, but some nearer the back of his company were feeling it.

✦ ✦ ✦ ✦ ✦ ✦

Analisia was caught up in all the thrill of the attack. The joy of battle rose in her heart as the Shadows fell in dozens before her blade. The mist did not bother her, and for the time, moving fast, her warriors seemed borne up also on the tide of hope. She didn't quite lose her head, and restrained her people from rushing to the point of overstepping their skill with hillside terrain, but she pressed forward as much as she might, and as the hillside became less steep she urged her warriors to a greater charge.

A sense of menace grew in the air, and the black mist thickened around them. Analisia felt her warriors lagging, losing heart, some stumbling a little, and she rallied them with a great cry. "We are close, my friends. This must be the stench of their camp. Come, do not falter, and we will be triumphant yet!"

Off to her left, she could hear her father shouting to encourage his people as well, rallying to a last charge.

Then it hit. The power that controlled the Shadow host sprang its trap and let go a Shadow army of immense strength. Thousands of Shadows poured out of the trees before them, while more battalions charged from the side onto Analisia's unprotected flank. These Shadows were of huge size and unusual strength, and many carried stolen Efrim blades. Only lesser blades, it was true, for they could not abide those with moonsilver, but shining with the reddish stain of poison. Her host gave way, caving in on itself before the power of the onslaught. She rallied her warriors and pulled them together into close ranks, protecting each other's backs.

Analisia was fighting desperately with three great Shadows with swords at once, but every sense was heightened beyond its customary measure. She strained for sounds that could help her piece together the action on the field of battle that she could not see through the trees. Her people had drawn close to her, and there were many dead, fainted, or wounded. The mist was getting thick even faster than seemed accountable by the number of Shadows killed. Off at her left she heard shouts, but more of fear than command. There was still the clashing of weapons, but there were also shrieks of pain and screams of grief or madness. All their triumph had turned to disaster, and honor to shame. She had to do something, and there wasn't a moment to lose.

"Urendina," she shouted at a young woman not far away. "You're fast. Take a couple companions and run back for the wall, now. It isn't flight. Tell the men on watch we will need carts for the wounded. The sort of small carts that men can pull on this steep slope. Also, prudence be hanged, we need three quarters of the remaining host to come down at once with those carts to help."

The woman nodded and started off, running up the steep hill with two companions who were likewise on the lighter side and swift.

Analisia got some of her people to collect and drag together the fallen into the center of her company's defense, and she moved the ring sideways, giving way from the Shadows on their right flank. Moving in among Louranin's host she found much valor remained, but there was little or no order. Here and there a captain held together a circle of warriors who still pushed back the enemy, but many fought alone, and many had lost heart and fled. Those who could still see fled up the hill, while some in blind terror ran wild, sometimes crashing into their fellows.

Analisia allowed herself no time in that moment to dwell on what this chaos meant. Shouting to the men, she brought them together. The scattered and disheartened force responded to the ring of her voice and the firm, unbendable will that led them on. They were brought into order and the wounded again gathered together. She could hear nothing in the forest further left and concluded that if Aranin's host had gotten that far they were pushed back—or utterly destroyed. This brought a clench of pain in her heart and an abject fury woke in her that no Shadow could stand before.

She ordered some of the warriors to begin dragging and carrying the wounded up the hill. They were tied on the backs of warriors or carried over their shoulders while still the swords had to be used, and some were dragged by their arms. But Analisia stood at the rear guard, and such was the power of her anger that none could stand before her. The desire of her heart was still to charge into the threatening cloud, but her men would not follow, and her duty now was to get them back behind the walls in safety. The offensive had failed, but she must save her land from total disaster, and the more men she got back alive, and the sooner they reached the walls, the better the chance that could be accomplished. They made slow progress backwards, but a few yards behind where they had been struck, near where the milder slopes turned to the steep pitch up to the wall, they came upon the warriors of Aranin's company. They were badly beset but still held some order. They had spread out into two lines, back-to-back, with their wounded in the middle, making thus a passage of some fifty yards in the direction of the wall.

At this place they were met by the second captain from the watch above with a hundred men and many small carts. The wounded were loaded haphazardly and pulled up the somewhat ragged path of safety Aranin's troop provided. However, Aranin was not to be seen, and although his men were holding onto their order and formation with bitter resolve, many here, too, had fallen. Analisia took the idea of the corridor at once and sent many of her remaining warriors to strengthen each side while the whole moved up the steep slope. The Shadows followed their retreat, undiminished by the thousands of their kind mowed down, and they picked up those swords that were dropped that they could use and continued the attack.

★★★★★★★

Half an hour later, Analisia stepped last through the gate and shut it behind her. The sun was still high, only a little past two in the afternoon, and up here on the ridge the breeze had blown away the black mists, but all the hope and light had gone from the day. She was very weary, and a poisoned scratch on her left wrist burned like fire and made her hand tingle, while blood soaked through her sleeve from a clean, but nonetheless painful, cut on her shoulder.

There was no rest yet. Of the leaders of this ill-fated and, it now seemed, foolhardy expedition, she was the only one left, and she had to organize things and get the wounded and dead accounted for and the wall remanned as soon as possible. There were no generals anywhere near, and precious few captains, and it never occurred to her to wonder if she had complete authority in this situation.

She did a man count; it seemed the first thing to do. She made all the unhurt stand in their companies and logged the missing by name. Then, those who knew them were asked to help her go over the dead, wounded, and unconscious, putting names on each and arranging for them to be taken down to the palace. Analisia didn't wish to do this duty. Knowing they were not among the conscious, she expected every moment to see Aranin and her father among the dead. Indeed, about halfway through the business, Yeven, who was helping her, rolled a man over from the cart and gave a choked little gasp. Analisia glanced up and saw her father. His sky-blue eyes were wide and unseeing, his gray face contrasting starkly with the dark red blood and green slime that smeared it from a festering cut on his cheek.

"Commander Louranin," Yeven whispered.

Analisia didn't speak, and those around them bowed their heads.

Analisia went to her father and took his hand, and her chest was very tight. A part of her was angry with him; this whole thing had been his idea. This disaster was his fault. She knew she had supported it too. She had believed, and that made her angrier. Still, looking on his unmoving gray face, and staring blue eyes, she could only feel grief and emptiness. She put a finger to his neck. There was still a pulse. "He lives," she said softly. There was no joy in the words, and no one said anything in response. With a wound, even a small one, the chances a person would live were so small.

Yeven helped her make him comfortable in one of the big carts that had been called up from the valley, and the company medic washed the wound. Analisia went on with her job. Many were dead, nearly three dozen, and half again as many wounded. Nearly a hundred were sick of the blackness, and as many had bad cases of blindness. It was a very sorry sight, and a sore loss. A dozen men were not to be found at all. Some of their friends were grieved, fearing what the Shadows might do to their bodies left in the forest, and others clung to hope, peering out into the trees in the hope they might come straggling in. For Analisia, though, there was no hope. Aranin was among the missing.

She remembered with a stab of pain and a sort of sickness what he had said to her when the plan first came up. How he had feared it. She had assumed he had changed his mind when he never spoke of it again, but even if he had... She thought of his grim face when speaking of the mission. It had certainly never inspired him the way it had her. And now, he had paid the ultimate price for this folly. Inside she felt cold and empty, but there wasn't time; she had to go on.

The small remnant of her father's troop she sent back to their post, where only one diminished watch waited for them, likely weary under the heavy press of Shadows, and with them she sent some of those who had come from the more distant posts. She sent back all those who had come from the post to the north as well. Although they no longer had their captain to follow and were sadly depleted, a full watch waited for them, and they would have to move people around and make do. She kept a few of those from other posts, who had all marched under her, for her post also. Aranin's company, keeping cautiously back, had received slightly lower losses than hers and Louranin's, but the post had sent forth nearly all its men. Those who had come at the end to bring back the wounded had mostly survived, and had gone back up to hold the hard press on the wall above, but that watch would have to be relieved before too long, and what remained of her and Aranin's watch couldn't hold so great a wall.

When she had ordered the warriors thus, and had seen that those now under her command at Aranin's post had food and went to rest, and that all the carts of dead and wounded had gone down to the valley for care or burial, then she sat down at Aranin's desk and wrote letters to the leaders of all the other posts. She asked some for the continued loan of those men they had sent, either to her or to the captain who now held Louranin's post, and also asked some of them to spare a few more men, for the press was still hardest on the northeast, and their companies still larger than hers. She worked mechanically, with dim eyes and a leaden heart. It seemed wrong, touching Aranin's things, using his pen; it was all a horrible dream that had no awakening.

She took some of her warriors up to relieve the watch at five. Those poor people had stood more than two watches since they last rested. She fought with a bitter fury up on the wall. There was no longer any fear or any hope. She was slightly ill and hadn't eaten since breakfast, but none of that seemed to matter. She couldn't even think of it.

It was one in the morning when the off-watch came up to take her place, and she walked down after her warriors in a daze. She didn't follow them when they went to eat, but went into the barracks and lit a candle on Aranin's desk. She sat down, thinking to write a report to her mother, but she began looking through the papers tucked into the desk.

There were pictures, beautiful pencil drawings of faraway times, and peaceful fantasy scenes. He had been drawing much more than she thought. She looked on each with love and growing grief.

Then she found the letter he had written to Sebastian dated the night before. In the flickering candle flame, she read with a sinking heart and her throat almost too tight to breathe, until her eyes overflowed and she put her head down on her hands. Into that paper he had poured out fears, and so much pain he had never told her of. To think he believed they were all marching to death and still put on such a brave face. The thought that he had died thinking that... She felt utterly broken. She was furious with herself for championing the ill-fated attack, and angry with her father that the whole idea had come up—and yet that thought was always followed by the thought that her father was wounded, and how could she be mad at him? She hated herself, remembering the time she had gotten angry at Aranin when he told her his fears. No wonder he didn't confide in her anymore after that, and how terrible it must have been for him with no one to talk to, writing letters to people far away who would never get them even if by some chance they were still alive.

She had no idea when the last time she cried had been, but she wept hard now. Eyes still streaming, she crept outside before her warriors came in for bed. She sat among the dead and dying trees nearby while slow tears streamed down her face, and she whispered brokenly to Aranin how sorry she was.

There, two hours later, Yeven found her. He knelt, thinking her asleep, and touched her hand. She shook him off with an impatient movement, but without looking up.

"Analisia," he said softly. "I understand. I know it's too terrible."

"He never wanted to go," she choked out.

"Perhaps. I never heard him say a word against it. Maybe he was just grimmer than you. He always has been more solemn. He... he did his duty." Yeven's voice broke. "He died well."

"I know, but he didn't want to go. He knew it was an ill-fated and hopeless errand all the time. He never spoke of it because I was cruel enough to be angry the first time he mentioned his fear right after Father started planning this, but I just found a letter he wrote. He addressed it to Sebastian, who I can hardly believe is even alive anymore, but it was like his last testament." She started to cry again.

There was nothing Yeven could say to that. His heart was sorely grieved as well, although he knew the pain must be worse for Analisia. Aranin was that sort of man, grave and quiet, never one to make a scene, but he hadn't realized how brave and strong he was. For a long time, he just held Analisia. Then he said, "Please, dear, will you let me get you something to eat? It has been so long since you ate or rested."

Mutely she nodded, and he went to find her some bread and jelly and sausage. Life had to go on.

✦ ✦ ✦ ✦ ✦ ✦

When at last the trap he had long expected sprang and Shadows by the thousands charged in on their flank, Aranin gave way as quickly as he could. No one would blame him for retreat now, and someone must try to see the others were not cut off from the wall behind. Many of his men fell to the mist that came thick about them, and some to worse, but he had them carried until he had his host on the slope behind the others. There he formed them into the corridor just as Analisia found them later.

"Listen, my people," he shouted with a strong voice so all could hear over the clash of weapons. "The day has turned against us, but we must not despair. Our commander, our future queen, and more than five hundred of our fellows are down there. Hold this corridor until they come. Keep shoulder to shoulder, and keep the fallen in the middle. No matter what happens, hold until they come. Only thus can it be said that we saved this day from complete disaster, and every one of you will be remembered in the tales of our people for your bravery!"

Men and women shouted and rallied to his call, and the columns that flanked the corridor were held firm and with a power that even the Shadows, especially here, farther up the hill where their power was slightly less, had trouble facing. Still, the fight was very grim. Aranin gave no more orders, but took his place at the outward end of one of the lines and hoped Analisia and his father would, and could, come soon for the retreat.

An onslaught of Shadows with cords came upon him, and his end of the line, before Analisia was in sight. There were thousands of them. The black mist came thick as they were mowed down, and yet they still came on. Aranin's sword glittered with white fire, and he slew several hundred in those first minutes, but the ropes came ever and anon, for him above all, and they tangled his hands and feet so that he stumbled, and his fingers began to tingle. Those nearest him were fallen or fled in blindness, and he could see no one as the darkness closed around him. He fought on, but the blackness closed in and suffocated him. There was only darkness, and a sense of space and emptiness. He was vaguely aware that he was moving but knew not why or where. He tried to stop or slow his step, and pain burned through him as though every muscle was on fire. He gasped, stumbled, and kept moving. He couldn't remember who he was, or where or why. He only wanted the pain to go away, and so he walked. Darkness and silence were everything, everywhere. There was nothing else. Never had been. Never would be.

Chapter 21

Broken Twice

2 May (two weeks later), YA 1127

Northeast guard station of Efrimiel

IT HAD BEEN two weeks since the disaster. Analisia had a duty to get on with, and she was learning to get on with it. The latest news was that Louranin was still very sick, but that some hope was preserved for him. It had been a very shallow wound and he was very strong. Nearly all the wounded from the 'fiasco,' as Analisia privately called it, were dead, and some of the sick, but some of the latter had returned to the wall. The day-to-day duties at her post were not changed much, save that she was now in sole command. She had reinstated the watch times after the disruption and taken the ten to four watch she had once shared with Aranin. There was one other captain to take the opposing watch, but she was in charge. It was now her duty to see that everyone was fed and had their clothes washed, and all that sort of thing. She was in charge of correspondence with the other post leaders and the accepting of new apprentices. Even with Yeven always ready to help her, she felt very alone.

At the end of the first week, she had gotten letters saying she had been awarded her general's flower by the officers of the army. At another time she might have been overjoyed. To become a general was an honor,

336

and it gave her great power and responsibility in the army. It was an important achievement in serving her people. If her mood had been brighter, she might have even thought how she had now earned her crown even by Eldir standards. As it was, however, the gratification was only slight, and there was no joy.

Three days ago, the older white-haired general from the southeast post, who was carrying temporary responsibility as high commander, had come and presented her with her flower. She felt there was a certain new respect many of the senior warriors showed to her now that she bore that badge, and there was some satisfaction in that. As a young woman and scholar, some of the warriors had looked a little askance on her when she first came, as a person of a world above but not connected with theirs. As a princess she had always received homage of a sort, courtesy, but also rules. People bowed and 'my ladied' her whenever she met them in the valley. But real, simple respect was something she had never experienced before.

The difficulties with the shortage of men had been worked out for the most part. Everyone was a little short until new recruits came, but they were holding steady. The Shadow press had not changed in the slightest. Four of the missing men *had* actually stumbled back, half blind and frightened, to a post a ways down the wall the evening after the attack, to great joy; but for the others, the rites of death had been performed. Songs were sung, candles burned in windows, and grave paintings done to be kept by the loved ones. Analisia had been allowed to keep Aranin's. A fine portrait of her brother, done by one of his friends in the bookshop, standing erect, holding his sword, as he had died, and wrapped in a white robe. White was the color of rebirth. She still kept a candle lantern burning beside the picture on her desk, although the mourning period was now officially over, and every morning she picked green leaves to set by it. There were no flowers among the sickly plants beside the wall.

She was eating breakfast with her watch when a great outcry went up on the wall. They were shouts of surprise and wonder, not of fear, and she did not go to see.

A young woman came running down the steps towards her, beaming.

"General," she cried. "There is a man coming out of the forest. He's far still, but I think it's Aranin!"

Analisia jumped to her feet with a gasp of disbelief. It had been two weeks. It couldn't be. And yet... if a man really was coming it must be one of their missing, and why not Aranin? He was strong. Perhaps he had been driven the wrong way somehow and hidden in the hills? The rest of his company had been so neatly together, and behind the rest of the force, and yet... She ran up onto the wall after the apprentice.

There was no question. A man was coming through the trees. He stumbled a little, as if weary, with his head down, and fought off Shadows with a crooked stick. He would be in trouble when he came near the wall, for he seemed unarmed. Analisia's eyes fixed on him, and her heart did several somersaults. Even with his head down there was no mistaking him. The shape of his broad, strong shoulders, the way he walked, the exact shade of his curly caramel colored hair hanging down uncombed about his face.

She ran back down the stairs and called to two dozen of her watch to follow her. "Aranin has come back. I can't imagine how, but I saw him. He looks weary and has lost his sword. We must go out to help him."

People cheered deafeningly. Among those who had served under Aranin, there was such a clamor to go that Analisia had to shout to make herself heard in choosing an appropriate number.

They went through the gate and fought out to meet the man who looked up as they approached. He nodded a little. "Thank you," he said.

The voice was like music to her ears—Aranin's voice, which she had thought silent forever—but there was no joy in his greeting. He must be terribly tired. "Come. Let's get you back to the wall," she said. She reached out to help him, to hold his arm, but he did not seem to notice.

"Yes. I have been in the forest so long. I was driven over the next ridge by the Shadows and had to creep back very weary. I am tired and hungry." He started walking towards the gate.

She reminded herself they were out in enemy territory, and besides, even behind the wall breaking down in tears of joy or throwing herself on him would be far beneath the dignity of her position as general. Anyway, he was tired and seemed grave and almost cold to her. The last two weeks must have been a terrible trial. Undoubtedly, he was angry with her for supporting the idiotic mission of their father's and not letting him even tell her his fears. She would never forgive herself for that. They came in through the gate, and she remembered the check. She didn't want to, but her people were watching, and it was policy.

"Let me just check your hair, very quick," she said apologetically. "You understand, I mean it was you who started the policy..." She felt herself flushing.

"Policies must be kept. Go ahead."

She quickly lifted the hair over his ear, running her fingers through it and checking behind the ear on both sides. There was nothing.

"All good," she said.

She led the way back to the dining table and made a place for Aranin beside her. He took the place without a word, and only a nod to the boisterous welcomes of the other warriors, and the cooks filled his plate. He began eating in a hasty manner that was somewhat sloppy and unlike him. She watched him for a moment. He must be half starved. Then she looked back at her plate and fussed with what remained of her now cold pancakes.

"I'm sorry about everything, Aranin," she said softly.

"That's all right. Don't think about it," he said with food in his mouth.

She felt abashed. Although the words were what she expected from him, it sounded more like a brush-off than forgiveness, and she didn't know what to say next. After a few minutes she tried again. "I really am sorry any of it had to happen. I... I found the letter you wrote to Sebastian."

"It's all right." His eyes remained on his meal.

She ate the rest of her pancakes. The five-minute bell rang, and she stood to get her sword and go on watch. "You should rest," she said to Aranin. "I suppose the high commander will want to assign one of us a new post now that we're both generals, but I think we could not tell him for a day or two. I would like to keep you here." She smiled and, reaching out, patted his mail-covered shoulder shyly.

Shrugging away, he half looked up. He returned her smile a little stiffly, but it didn't touch his eyes. "That is nice. I am tired today, but you know we should tell him soon."

"I know, but for now eat as much as you like and go sleep. I'll see you later." Analisia turned and went up on the wall. She felt strange, as if it were all unreal. She had wept for Aranin, buried him in her mind, and sung grave songs over his picture. She had mourned, and now he was back. That joy was somehow beyond her reach to comprehend. The sun shone brighter, the sky was bluer, and yet there was a rotten cherry in the box. He was so distant and strange, and that stained her joy with torment and regret. She reminded herself how tired he must be and how hard the last two weeks had been for him, but that just made her feel worse as hurt was overwhelmed by guilt.

About four hours later, a cart was due up to the post with the week's washing and some fresh supplies. It should have been routine. The washing was already sacked up to take away, and the supplies and clean cloths would be left, along with the mail, to be sorted out when the next watch got up. However, Analisia heard some kind of commotion. There were raised voices, and someone seemed to be crying. It was hard to hear over the noise of battle on the wall. She sent Yeven down to check it out.

What met his eyes as he ran down the steps stopped him for a moment in his tracks. The cart was loaded to leave. Aranin stood beside it, still in his mail, with a bundle of sheets under one arm and the neck of the young cart driver's tunic in the other hand. The boy was crying.

"What under the sun?" Yeven exclaimed, running toward them filled with shock and bewilderment.

Aranin let the boy go. "He refused to do his job properly," he said in a short, cold tone.

The young cart driver, no more than twelve years old, and a small lad even for such a young age, ran to Yeven, who knelt and put his arms around him.

"What happened?" Yeven asked softly.

"General Aranin came out of the barracks just as I was about to leave, with more sheets and clothes and such to add to the laundry, and he shouts at me to stop, so 'course I did, and I look back and see him, and I was so afraid, sir, you don't even know, because I... I was at the funeral for the prince, and now I see him. But I asked what he wanted, and he told me I had missed some washing, very sharp, too, and I said I took all that was set out, but if he had more he could put it on back. I thought that was right, wasn't it, sir?" The boy looked up at Yeven with wide blue eyes.

"Of course it was. I'm sorry you were frightened. We thought Aranin was dead until today, but he was only lost, and he is back now."

"Well, something happened to him," the boy whispered with a sniff. "I wish he had stayed lost. He used to be nice. But when I said he could put it on back he got mad and told me to get the bags down or I was not doing my job. I assured him it would be fine in the cart, and I'd see it all got there, and that's when he took my collar and started shaking me. I never knew the prince *really*, you understand me, but I've been picking up and such here for a year since my parents went into the army, and he was always gentle and kind before."

"He's had a very hard time lately and he's tired," Yeven said. "Please forgive him." Yeven went back to the cart with the boy.

"I am sorry I lost my temper, young man," Aranin said. "But you should do what you're told."

"I beg pardon, General," the boy said in a small voice.

Yeven jumped up in the cart and helped the boy pack Aranin's sheets into one of the full bags. He felt uncomfortable and uneasy, but his joy at seeing Aranin again was nearly gone. How could he be so cruel to a little boy? Aranin would never do something like that. Never. What had happened to him? A part of Yeven, which he hated himself for, almost wished, like the child, that Aranin hadn't come back. Something sent a tingling jolt up his arm as he pushed the last bit of sheet into the bag. He looked up to say something to the boy and caught a strange look in Aranin's eyes. A glint he did not understand. Yeven said nothing and finished packing the sack.

"All packed up," he said with a smile. "You really should try to sleep, Aranin, you don't seem yourself today. Don't worry, every last sock is inside. I'll just see Tommy off, since he had a scare."

"All right. I suppose it's been a strange two weeks. I don't feel quite right. I'll sleep now." Aranin turned away towards the barracks.

Yeven stayed by the cart.

"I am really fine to go by myself," Tommy said stoutly, although he still looked shaken.

"I know you are," Yeven said quietly as he watched Aranin disappear into the barracks. "But, you see, I didn't want to upset him after all he's been through, but I felt something strange in your bag of laundry. I know you're a brave lad, and I'd like you to help me a minute. Ask your horse to go, will you?"

"Of course." The boy hopped up into the cart and spoke softly to the horse, which started off down the road.

Yeven walked along beside the boy in troubled thought until they had gone down several turns of the road. Then he put a hand on the horse's flank and stopped it.

"Now we're not near anything. I think we had better unpack that one laundry bag. It's probably nothing, but you can't be too careful about black magic. I felt something that made my whole arm tingle. There is blackness in the very air up there, you know, and we can't wholly discount that a Shadow or two might get over the wall. They come up in such huge numbers."

"That's what Papa said when he wrote me. That they come thicker than ants."

"They do." Yeven jumped up and lifted down that last sack of laundry. Then he thrust his hands in the others, feeling around in them. "I don't feel anything in the others," he said cheerfully as he jumped down beside the boy who was untying the sack. "It may all be in my head, or I had some residue on my hands or something, but you won't tell if I'm making a fool of myself, will you?"

"A'course not." Tommy smiled. "So long as you don't tell that I cried back at camp."

"Deal."

Yeven shook the clothes out on the roadside among grass, small flowers, and last year's fallen leaves. Then, warning Tommy to be very careful, he started picking things up, feeling them, shaking them out, and putting them back in the empty sack. It was a large sack, filled with very smelly tunics, other people's underwear, and even smellier socks, so it was far from a pleasant job. Then Tommy picked up a tunic and made a small squeak as something fell out, something about the size of a large grape.

Yeven looked up at once. The thing that had fallen lay between a daisy and a clump of grass, but in just that moment they stood, startled, the daisy withered and the grass started to turn yellow. The mist coming up from the spot was thick and spread quickly. "Get back," Yeven ordered.

Tommy scrambled back several paces, holding his nose against the smoke. Yeven held his breath, pulled his tunic up over his nose, and stepped on the thing, trying to rub it out. That didn't help at all. A big cloud of the stuff went up suddenly all around him and spread out quickly on the wind. He coughed and his eyes stung, but the spot no longer smoked, so he bent to look at it. On the ground were fragments of something like very thin black glass, crushed beneath his boot. Well, that was stupid, he told himself. You just released all of whatever was in there. But what else could he have done? He looked at the boy, who was rubbing the corner of his eye and looking scared. "I don't know how that could have gotten in. Some Shadow must have stuck it in whoever's tunic that was while they were up on the wall, and they were too tired to notice when they came down. Shadows do things like that. Did you hear what happened to the head captain up at commander Louranin's post a little over a year ago?"

Tommy nodded. "We all heard the story, sir. Do you suppose that was it? What was that stuff? And why... why attack the launderers?"

Yeven looked at the shriveled daisy. Darned if he knew. It seemed like the black mist of the Shadows, at least more or less, but in that small a dose it wasn't likely to do damage to anyone. It had been quite a bit of mist for something so small, but still, most people weren't bothered much by one small cloud in the face, and as far as the Shadows were concerned, what would be the good of killing a launderer or two, even if it worked? Perhaps it was meant to go off in the barracks, or to kill the warrior wearing the tunic, or possess him... Yeven would never forget what happened to Lestius. "Only the Shadows know what they meant to do. I can't guess. It looks like black mist, nasty stuff, but I don't know..." he said, trying to hide a slight shiver.

He bent to pick up a pair of especially nasty socks, feeling sure they had gotten it, and now they should clean up quickly so he could get back to the wall. A sparkling black object flew spinning in the air. It turned and glittered, and with an old bat ball instinct faster than thought, he caught it. He felt the shuddering tingle of dark magic. He looked in his hand and, for a moment, saw something glittering like a faceted bead, black with traces of flame. Then the tissue-thin walls burst and a huge puff of mist went up. Tommy cowered and Yeven turned his face away. "That was another foolish mistake," he said with an attempt at easiness. "I didn't imagine there'd be more than one."

"How many do you suppose there are?"

"I don't know, but see here, Tommy. I think you had better take your horse and get out of this. You can take the laundry that is in the sack already. I'll deal with the rest."

"I will stay and help if you wish, sir. I'm not afraid."

"No. There's no sense in both of us doing it, and the poor horse can't tell us if he's willing."

Tommy agreed and, taking the three quarters full sack back up, rode away. Then Yeven went down on his knees. He moved every piece of clothing very slowly and carefully like he would have long ago in his shop if a bead went missing on the work table and he didn't want it to go rolling off. He was good at careful when he took the time, and when he found another one, he rolled it ever so gently into a dirty sock. He found three more before he had gotten through. Afraid to take the things any farther down into the valley, or back to the wall to get advice, he dug a deep hole with a piece of stick, carefully put the sock in there, and very gently filled the hole back up. He mounded it a little and made sure the soft soil was packed very firm. On top of the spot, he set three crossed sticks to indicate danger. When that was done, he bundled up the last of the clothes and headed down to the palace. Socks were always going missing. No one would care much. He hoped he had done no harm, accidentally releasing the first two, but they hadn't seemed all that bad, and at least it was only two of six.

By the time Yeven had found a girl near the edge of the valley to take the bundle to the palace, and run back up, there was less than an hour left in his watch. He was glad of that. He was tired anyway.

✳✳✳✳✳✳

As soon as Analisia was off watch, her thoughts turned to Aranin, and before eating she ran to the barracks to check on him. He lay in his bed, in the now empty room, fast asleep. She smiled. When he had rested, he would feel better, and perhaps he would forgive her a little and be glad to see her. She looked down a minute on his beloved sleeping face. She wanted to kiss his cheek or smooth the hair from his brow, but that would wake him, and he needed sleep. She left the room and found a place at the table beside Yeven.

"What was that commotion about anyway?" she asked as she sat down. "You were away a long time."

"It was a strange thing," Yeven said, fiddling with his greens. "Aranin apparently wasn't able to sleep. He brought out some missed laundry and was quite harsh to poor Tommy. He apologized, of course, and then he went to bed, and I hope he slept this time. He seemed very unlike himself, a strange look in his eyes, you might say." Yeven had nearly forgotten about the incident, after the other adventure that followed, but now it troubled him again. "Anyway, that was only a misunderstanding, but it was a good thing I went, and not only to break it up..." He told Analisia in a low voice all about the little capsules of blackness in the laundry.

"I will have to get everyone to check their clothes when they come down from the wall after this. It doesn't sound all that bad, and yet it must be, or the Shadows wouldn't do it. The launderers are mostly men of much less innate power than the warriors, but it doesn't make sense..." The whole thing bothered her. It didn't seem nasty enough for the Shadows, and that made her uneasy. Besides, how did no one notice something like that stuck in their clothes? But, without more information, what could she do?

The watch went to bed. Analisia worked at the desk a little while and then slept herself. She was troubled, but no matter what, finding Aranin had been a great joy, and she was very weary, so she slept well.

Yeven, on the other hand, could not sleep. He felt restless and uncomfortable. The events had unsettled him, and he kept hearing the boy's words when he said he wished Aranin hadn't returned. Aranin was Yeven's friend, one of the kindest, noblest, gentlest, and most practical people he knew. One of the best people he knew. And yet he had felt somewhere inside that he agreed with Tommy. Something had changed or broken in Aranin. He wasn't the same man. Sometimes a person's spirit just couldn't take it; Aranin had been depressed so much of the time over the last few years. Yet Yeven had always thought him too strong for that. He would never have guessed anything short of death could break him. To have that trust betrayed, that was worse for Yeven than having his friend die.

Yeven had been with Aranin during the disaster. As a member of his post, Yeven had fought in his company, and he had remained near him through it all. Aranin had been grim all morning. He had hung back in the charge, but that move had saved many lives in the retreat. He had held his head high and ordered his men to the last with power and dignity, just as Yeven would have expected of him, and far more. There had been no trace of fear or anger. Grieved as he was, Yeven had been content that Aranin had died nobly, with all the honor a man could have. Now, the idea that in the very end he had fled? It seemed strange, wrong. Yes, Aranin had been at the farthest point of their line the last time he saw him. In the melee, Yeven had not seen what became of him or the men near him, save those who were taken in dead or severely wounded, but it just didn't seem right.

Yeven rolled onto his other side. His back ached, his old sprained ankle from three years ago ached. Nothing was right. These thoughts went over in Yeven's head, as he grew more achy and uncomfortable instead of less. His head ached, and his very eyes hurt. He felt cold even under his blanket, although outside the curtained windows the May sun had not yet set. He got up to get himself some water and felt surprisingly unsteady on his feet.

He took a long drink, which did not quell his thirst, and rubbed his aching brow with a fretful hand. His forehead felt very hot. Was he getting sick? Why now, of all times, and who could he have caught it from? There were no flus going around the post. There had been little of that kind of sickness since they lost contact with the outside world, but it wasn't like the illness the Shadows brought. People who got that were always cold to the touch, at least at first, and more apt to be numb than achy. Also, as far as he knew, it always started with falling to the blindness, or at least a dimming of the sight. Besides, there hadn't been anything unusual on the wall today. He went to one of the windows. The sun had set now, and an evening breeze came cool on his face. He leaned his head in his hands.

The dusk was deep when a small clock beside a bed chimed eight and a woman sat up and rubbed her eyes. She stuffed her feet in her boots and walked over to rouse the two youngest apprentices who, not having night watches, were obliged to help with all the cooking.

"I'll help if you want to let one of them sleep," Yeven whispered. "I can't sleep for anything."

She smiled. "All right. Cecilia has worked very hard lately on arrows. I'll let her be." She woke the other apprentice. He was the youngest, a boy of eighteen. In the old days, someone of that age never would have been allowed to apprentice, but the need was very sore. The three went out together. The other two got out pots and pans while Yeven got wood and stoked up the cooking fire in the kitchen and lighted the torches around the big tables in the camp. Ill as he was feeling, it was better to be working.

They were just starting the chopping when Aranin came in. "I came to help in the kitchen," he said. "I am so hungry. What should I do?"

"I do think three cooks is enough," the lady said. "Have an apple if you can't wait. You were so tired no one wanted to wake you at last meal."

He looked about the kitchen in the bright lamplight as if he had no idea where to get an apple, which made Yeven even more uncomfortable. Yeven set down the knife he was chopping potatoes with and reached up into a box to hand Aranin an apple. When he looked back Aranin had taken up his work cutting the potatoes. Yeven was angry for a moment, and his already hot cheeks flushed. "Oh, have it your own way," he snapped. He left the small shed in a hurry, feeling ruffled and a little lightheaded. He sat down beside the well and watched the light of the kitchen door with glazed eyes. What on earth made Aranin butt in like that? He had never done anything like that before. Yeven drew some water and washed his hot face. He was shivering a little now, and had goose bumps, but he was sure he wasn't really cold. He wondered if he shouldn't try to lie down again for the half hour or so left before his watch was called to eat.

"Yeven?" The voice was high and boyish, and although not loud, it was urgent and anxious.

Yeven looked up to see Malinar, the boy apprentice, silhouetted against the kitchen light and running towards him. Yeven stood swiftly to greet him, wondering why boys in trouble always seemed to be running to him lately. "What's happened?"

The boy panted up. "General Aranin's acting strange, sir, and it frightens me. He bumped into Lady Caracia and she burned herself badly in the fire. He apologized, of course, but the tone of the voice was wrong. He didn't sound like he meant it. She is nursing the wound, natu-rally, and he is still in there cooking, or trying to, but he seems to have forgotten how. He salted the fruit I chopped for him and doesn't seem to know where anything is or what we're making, and, and he yells at me when I don't find things for him fast enough, however strange they are. He keeps sending me on errands that don't make sense, and the last time he looked at me..." Here the rush of words slowed, and the boy shivered a little. "He... he... his eyes didn't seem right, and *so* cold. I'm afraid he has gone mad, and you... well, I know you were friends, and with Caracia binding her burn you're the only other one awake."

Yeven closed his eyes for a moment and took a deep breath. It was all the fears he had hardly dared to think, and felt disloyal thinking, confirmed. He stood. "Run, quick and quiet as you can to the barracks and get General Analisia. I'll go deal with him as best I can."

The boy nodded and ran. Yeven walked over and entered the kitchen. Aranin looked up from the fire and answered Yeven's forced smile with one even less natural.

"So you were having trouble getting on with Malinar?" Yeven asked in a quiet voice.

"I don't know what it is with the boys around here," Aranin said. "They don't do as they're told." There was a faint tone or accent in his voice that sounded wrong.

"I'll help you," Yeven said. Aranin was stirring something into a kettle of beans. Yeven had only to hope it was bacon or molasses, and not milk or vinegar or a cup of ginger or some such. From what Malinar had said it could be anything. Yeven picked up the potatoes that still lay on the cutting board and carried them to the smoking pan. He took a sidelong glance at Aranin and felt his unease grow. Aranin seemed to be looking for something, opening cupboard doors. Nothing had moved in the last two weeks. He ought not to have trouble, but he seemed lost.

"What do we use not to burn our hands around here? It is a disgrace not to have it!" His voice was sharp.

Yeven reached into one of the cupboards in the corner and handed him a quilted hot pad. "They're right here where they always were," he said gently. Tears were rising in his eyes as he watched, and they stung.

"Of course. I have been through so much," Aranin muttered. He took the hot pad and lifted the beans off the stove.

To Yeven's eyes the beans looked rather watery, and he doubted they were done, but when he ventured to say so Aranin yelled at him.

"Don't you question your superiors!"

That was when Yeven went from uncomfortable and grieved to really scared. General flower or no, Aranin was as likely to say something like that—even to a child he didn't know, let alone a friend—as turn into a dragon. Yeven dropped the cutting board and clutched Aranin's wrist. "What under sun and moon is wrong with you?" he exclaimed.

At that moment, Analisia, who had been roused by Malinar in great haste and told everything in a deluge of words as they hurried out to the kitchen, stepped through the door. In a heartbeat she looked from the shock and genuine fear on Yeven's pale face to the distorted anger of Aranin's as the two struggled. Then Aranin saw her.

"General," he snarled. "This man questioned me and made fun of me."

Why under the moon would he call her 'general'? He must have entirely lost his memory. She had to swallow hard before she could speak. This man looked like her brother, but he acted nothing like him at all. "Yeven. Let go. Aranin, come here and tell me all about it in private."

Yeven let go at once and Aranin came out with an admonishment to the others to see the meal was served on time. He would not take her hand, and for the moment she did not press it but led him away to a place beside the wall at a few yards' distance from the barracks and the kitchen, and just on the edge of the torchlight. When she looked at him, Aranin began a long and complicated explanation about how he tried to lend a hand, and the lower ranks would not obey him. That just because he didn't remember where they had put a bunch of worthless stuff, since he had been away suffering alone in the hills, they had looked at him strangely and questioned him, and the man named Yeven had laid hands on him and should be punished. Analisia listened in rising horror. It was a coherent narrative, delivered in an even tone. She thought it worthy of one of the cruel commanders she had read about in books from Ikkik. She had heard of some Efrim generals, too, who could be very stern— her father was rather demanding, for that matter, but not this cruel. Certainly, nowhere in it was there a trace of her brother.

When at last she could get a word in edgewise, she asked, "Do you know me, Aranin?" Her voice almost shook.

"Of course I do. You are General Analisia."

"More than that, forgive me, but what else am I?"

She thought she detected a touch of panic. "You are... are princess— crown princess."

"Yes, and...?"

"How should I know? I don't keep track of other generals. That is the high commander's job," he snapped.

Her heart broke again at that, right down the fissures so recently put together, but she was too strong to show it then. Something very wrong was happening. "You are not at all yourself, Aranin," she said gently. "I am going to have to send you down to the healers, and until then, I'm sorry, but you are going to have to be kept under guard."

He nodded and followed her without protest, although his expression looked strange and bitter in the torchlight, but when she reached out to take his hand he flinched away.

"I won't hurt you. Is there something wrong with your hand? Did you burn it?"

"Yes, it hurts."

She looked at the hand as they walked. There were no red marks, no sign of a burn. Something here was all wrong. No, wait. Everything here was all wrong. She stepped right in front of Aranin and looked up into his eyes. He tried to get away and she grabbed his arm in a quick motion. They were among the tables now and near a torch, and as she looked into his eyes, she saw something wrong with the lake-blue iris. It wavered, almost snakelike for a second, and it wasn't quite as blue as it should have been. They were not her brother's eyes. When he came he had not let her meet them, but now she held him in her gaze and would not let him go.

She slipped her free hand into her tunic and grabbed the moonsilver pendant from her mother, which she always wore on a chain around her neck. With one swift move she drew it off over her head and pressed it to his neck. He screamed, a shrill shriek of pain and anger, and kicking at her knocked her to the ground. A red welt rose on his neck where the silver had touched. She leapt at him, whatever he was, and brought him to the ground. This was not Aranin. Aranin had died, as she had thought. This was too cruel. To mock her grief like that. A fury rose in her, greater than she had ever known in her life, and her eyes blazed like living blue flame. There were several minutes of fierce struggle on the dusty ground. Her rage had great strength, but the being she fought was powerful, and Aranin's form was bigger than hers. They were locked together, and he was trying to get his hands on her throat, when rolling near one of the long trestle tables she saw a glitter of silver in the torchlight. She grabbed it without looking or thinking and stabbed. The power of her anger made a flicker of fire in her weapon, and it pierced the throat of her opponent. He pitched backwards, gasping, and in a moment lay still.

She sat trembling. The fury drained away, leaving her shaken. She was sitting on the ground in the dust, half on top of a dead man who looked exactly like her beloved brother. In her right hand a silver fork dripped with red blood. It was too much. All of it. Shaking uncontrollably, she stood and turned. There were people. All the people of her watch had been roused by the noise and they starred at her in surprise, some in horror and fear. That was the last straw. Already sobbing she turned and fled into the dark trees, and there she threw herself onto the leaves with the deadly fork still in her hand.

A moment later, Yeven was kneeling beside her. He put a hand on her heaving back. "Analisia, I'm so sorry," he whispered. He was half horrified, but he wouldn't ask her what had happened.

"It wasn't him," she choked out. "I know it wasn't. It... it looked like him, but the moonsilver burned it. I'm... I'm sure it wasn't him, but to kill him all the same..." She burst into a passionate flood of sobbing.

Yeven held her shaking shoulders for a minute. Then he thought about her words. The thing was not Aranin. He had to believe that. It made more sense, anyway. Aranin had died with honor as he thought. But if it wasn't him, what was it? And what was it trying to do? And did it do it? Why did it want to be in the kitchen? He stood. He felt terrible. The tears that leaked from his eyes burned. He ran back to the camp.

"Everyone, check every crevice of the dorms and the kitchen. That was no one we know, and whatever it was, it was trying to sabotage us."

The people stirred. A group went into the barracks to search. Some still stood around, horrified. Yeven went into the kitchen. He smelled the beans. They seemed to have a lot of ginger in them. He took down a fine moonsilver ribbon that one of the warriors had hung there. It was custom to have one in a kitchen. He dipped it in the beans and the ribbon flared hot in his hands. No fire could warm moonsilver; the beans were poisoned. He went out and quietly told several of the people what he had found.

"You look like a ghost," one woman said. "Let me take that. I'll see something else is made for people to eat."

He handed her the moonsilver ribbon. He wasn't very hungry and didn't care much about whether the meal got done or not. He went and looked for a moment at Aranin's body in the torchlight. It looked so horribly like him, yet, as he watched, it was changing. The skin was darkening and losing its warm color, and the form was growing larger, more muscular but less graceful. In one place the monster's swelling arm had already ripped the cloth of Aranin's tunic, and the caramel colored hair was simply melting away. Yeven tried unsuccessfully to swallow in his dry throat, then he turned and went to look for Analisia. He took a small torch this time.

He found her still prostrate on the ground, still crying, if not with so much force. The fork she still clutched was now stained in dark blue blood. "Analisia," he said softly, sitting down beside her. "Look at the blood. It's not red anymore. The body looks less like him by the second."

She sniffed, and looked. She rolled over and sat up. "That's better," she said in a broken whisper. "But I thought I had him back, and now... all over again... and it looked like him when I killed it. I will never be able to forget that."

Chapter 22

We Must Live

14-30 April, YA 1127

Eldirad: Aldor Forest: East Efrim fort

TATYANA STOOD LOOKING out her bedroom window at the square below. There were very few people visible in the streets this spring. She thought things were getting bad last year, and yes, provisions had been short then, and hope starting to wane. The last ten months, though, had been much worse. Just three weeks after the birthday party, in the beginning of July when it was unusually hot, her father had collapsed on the wall from heatstroke. It was an unfortunately common malady among the warriors in their heavy clothes during the hot months, and Edward's afternoon watch had it the worst. They still made ice, in the town square now that they couldn't use the river, and they tried to make sure everyone had some in their shirt when they went up. But it could be hard, especially if one was running up to their watch at the last minute from the hospital, to get enough to keep from overheating in the heavy clothing all the warriors had come to detest.

Tatyana remembered the day too clearly. She had felt the sudden call and had run outside in her summer nightgown. When she saw two warriors helping him off the wall, her heart skipped a beat and sank into her shoes, fearing he was wounded. She had run forward and taken one

353

of the warriors' places to help him back to the palace. She was so relieved when she realized what the matter was that, in spite of the fact it was a serious situation, she almost felt like crying from relief. They laid him on the living room couch and she and Clara stripped off his heavy clothes and cooled him off with ice. He recovered quickly after that, but after years of not enough food or sleep, and way too much work and worry, Edward was already on the point of exhaustion, and he was weak and ill for three weeks. It hadn't been until September that he had been able to safely take the afternoon watch in the heat again.

Tatyana shivered. That had been a very bad time, even on her scale of bad times, and then it got infinitely worse.

During those first three weeks, when she was in sole charge of the city, one of the captains came to her. He told her everyone was worried about food, which she knew, and that he had twenty warriors willing to make an attempt to reach Efrim to see if they had enough to share, which she didn't want to hear.

It had been her first time making a decision as acting ruler, and she still had nightmares about how wrong she had been. Of course she had thought she was doing right. Her father had still been quite ill, and with heatstroke she knew he'd be heat sensitive for a while. She didn't know how long it would be before he could take a day watch, and until then she could not go with the warriors. She should have known that for a mission into an unknown threat a captain wasn't enough, but he was a strong and reliable man of middle years who told her without a trace of a lie that he had never been bothered in any way by the mist on the wall. All the soldiers going with him said likewise, and she knew none of them were lying.

The mail to Efrim had stopped very early in the war partly due to a nasty mist that had been getting thick around the valley, and partly because the Shadows between Eldirad and Efrim had been thick and it had never seemed worth the risk. But it was only two miles, and with their magic gifts if the Efrim still lived they were likely to have a lot more food. Her people were hungry. How could she not even try to reach a place two miles away? The party would be back well before night.

So the next morning before her watch she had gone to Sebastian with the Sight. It hadn't been easy, but it only took three words to ask if

Efrim still stood, and he had told her that it did. She had been delighted to know they still lived, and although she hated making the decision she had decided to let them men go. If she had had any sense she would have made them wait until Edward was well whether they liked it or not, but she hadn't.

Only one returned from that party. One young man, who raved and cowered in his corner bed in the hospital for two weeks before it could be gotten out of him that they went less than a mile before they encountered a wall of blackness that made their oxen panic. The warriors tried to pull the carts themselves, but they, too, began to go mad or collapse to the ground. All those people had died just trying to get to Efrim. It had haunted Tatyana ever since.

Now, she watched a thin child in a much-mended linen dress far too short in the sleeves knock at the palace door and, after a long discussion with Clara, go away looking sad with only a small sack of oats. Tatyana blinked back tears. How could her nation have come to this? She couldn't try Efrim again. She tended to believe, as most of the city did, that they must have been crushed during the couple days between her asking Sebastian and the mission. They all knew such things could happen in war, and somehow it seemed like just their luck. She had not felt Aranin and Analisia die, yet she was tired and they were slightly weaker connections. There were times she could have missed it, and she had mourned for them. She saw no hope that Efrim still stood now, after nine months, and even if by some miracle it did they were beyond reach. She had to do something else.

She pulled on a pair of socks and her right big toe stuck through the end. She had more darning to do. They did still have some wool, and socks and woolen clothing could be replaced, but not as fast as they wore out. The sheep flocks were much reduced, and the shortage of time and hands to make the yarn and fabric, now that so many civilians had gone to the wall and those who remained were so busy making arrows and trying to keep the city alive, was almost worse than the shortage of wool. With the soldiers wearing two or three layers of tattered wool clothing on the wall, even in summer, it wore out fast. The linen undergarments, and summer clothes for children, suffered even worse since there had been no flax for years. She sighed. They had once been such a proud, civilized people. Now they were just a bunch of starving raga-muffins.

In that state of mind, she went downstairs. Her mother was making soup in the kitchen for the patients in the hospital. Her father was on the wall. She slipped out and went to the old gymnasium. This had once been among her favorite places. She started gymnastics because all future warriors were recommended to take the basics, and she had kept it up until the war because she loved it. Swinging and flipping on the bars, climbing ropes, doing flips and the like and handstands, sometimes on someone's shoulders. It was fun. Now the gym was a last desperate hope to feed people instead. The windows were all closed to keep out the mist, but early afternoon sunlight poured in on rows of ceramic and wooden planters full of large, healthy plants.

Tatyana hoped to find Yevenia here at this hour, and sure enough she spotted her bending over a long box of beets. When Tatyana approached, she could hear the spells Yevenia was softly singing as she stroked the leaves with her thin fingers. Nothing remained of her plump, rosy comeliness, and her long golden hair was turning white, but when she stopped her chant and looked up, the kindly smile in her dark blue eyes was just the same.

"How are things going?" Tatyana asked.

Yevenia wiped sweat from her brow with the back of a much-worn linen sleeve. "As well as can be hoped. Efrim power only goes so far in speeding up growth, although we can guarantee everything in here will get as big as permitted by its kind." She looked down at the beets and felt the top edge of the curve of the roots with a skillful finger. "The roots won't be ready for a few weeks yet on these, but we could pick some leaves if we're sparing. We can regrow them pretty quickly."

This was a project Tatyana had spearheaded last summer after the tragedy, and she consoled herself that it, at least, had been a success. One day last summer, she had gone to where Yevenia was working in her garden, over plants that were sickly even under her powerful hands, and talked to her about the farming situation.

Tatyana had loved Yevenia since she met her at eleven, but she had never discussed serious things with her. Perhaps because Yevenia was such a gentle, friendly person Tatyana had thought of her just as the nice, motherly woman who helped with homework and served dough-nuts and cocoa to her daughter's friends. Yevenia didn't have the Sight and didn't always understand Helen's fears or wish to discuss grim matters. Her house had always been a happy place for Tatyana, away from the serious concerns of the royal family.

Farming, however, that was Yevenia's area of expertise, and she took it very seriously. Tatyana had found that in a pinch Yevenia was a strong, serious person and very ready to address the problem in any way she could. Together they had planned this and gotten people to convert the gymnasium, which was mostly abandoned, into an indoor garden. No one had even tried to plant outside the wall since that first year, when next to nothing survived, and now gardens in the city were sickly. However, indoors, away from the black mist, Efrim power could still grow luxuriant and productive plants, even in the winter. It had been a blessing, and had gotten the city through the cold months, but it wasn't enough. Efrim farmers were terribly few, and this garden couldn't feed the whole city.

Yevenia gestured to the large room with one thin, dirty hand. "We have every pot filled, and between the barrel makers and the potters they have made us enough nice pots to cover every surface." She smiled. "I find Ericka's idea of putting pole beans on the climbing ropes especially pleasing."

Tatyana turned to look. For all it made her a little sad seeing the unused gym equipment, she couldn't help smiling too. The row of long climbing ropes in one corner rose like columns of broad green leaves. Two of them were bursting with white blossom. A swinging ladder hung beside them from which a young woman with dark brown hair was leaning out, tending the leaves with a soft song and gentle touch. That was Ericka, one of the few Eldir with the Efrim gift. Her grandfather had been an Efrim farmer and, thankfully, she had inherited the power.

There were three men in the room, too, varying widely in age. One was white-haired and likely over a hundred. The youngest was about Tatyana's age. They all had a similar story. They were sons of farming families. They had sisters who inherited the family farm and, instead of marrying into another Efrim farm family to use their gift, they had come to Eldirad and married Eldir women. Tatyana was grateful. Unlike property and honor in Efrim, their magical gifts came to both men and women alike. Some said that because of its nurturing aspect the plant power was often strongest in women and cited that as a reason for the original orientation of the society the way it was, but Tatyana wasn't sure. That might be true, or it might be that because the society was that way people thought that. Her observation of the world had not convinced her that people needed any reason for a society being how it was. It usually just *was*.

What she did know was that these male Efrim farmers, treated so disrespectfully by their own nation, were a blessing to her. They most certainly had the gift, and, although Yevenia was the chief member of the team, they had worked tirelessly by her side for the last nine months to great effect.

"I like it, too," Tatyana said, nodding to the columns of beans. "What you and your team have done here is wonderful, and we've gotten through another winter, but what do you think our prospects are? This is very labor intensive, is it not?"

"It is." Yevenia sighed, and the light in her eyes dimmed. "We have put our hearts into this, and all hours of the day, and we are proud of it. I venture to think we are deservedly proud. All the same. Indoors, the coming of spring will not help us as much as it would outdoors. More daylight will help. The room at least has decent windows, and we won't have to warm it as much, but plants do not really like living indoors. It takes power to keep them healthy in here, and to make them grow and produce in the way we have. Although it is nothing to the power we would have needed to make our gardens thrive like this outside in the mist. The Eldir farmers will plant all the outside space within the wall, of course, they always have, and it is possible we will find time to plant our own outdoor gardens, too, but I know it isn't enough. The outdoor harvest is bound to be worse again. It was nothing close to enough last year, and even with this place, we drew on the emergency storehouse and had a hungry winter. We will have the whole summer to use this space this year. I venture to hope that with the outside gardens it could prevent us from using the storehouse until fall, but without the outer fields there will be no grain, and we simply cannot grow enough to store much."

"That's what I thought." Tatyana's eyes were fixed vaguely on the young Efrim man who was working over a bed of peas. "No grain, and the herds of animals are in terrible shape. So many have died, and most of the females just won't reproduce, so there we are for meat. Next to nothing, in spite of me and my soldiers' trips out during off-watch to collect fodder for the beasts. Most of our cows that are still alive are dry, and our herds of goats, sheep, pigs, and chickens dwindle. There's no grease to be had, and we can't live that way, and no candles or lamps made with tallow. Most of the honeybees have died, too, so there isn't any honey or beeswax. Some of the hardier bumblebees still pollenate what flowers the outside fruit trees manage to make, but not well. I've seen lots of people sending their children up in the trees to pollinate with their fingers."

"That's what we've been doing here. I've thought about trying to find a hive somewhere in the city with a queen alive in it and bringing it in here, but in the meantime, I've hired a team of young kids, five and six years old, who were getting in the way at home. They do well enough once I train them to be gentle with the flowers. I get to sing songs with them, too, and tell them tales. They want tales of the city festivals before the war the most. These children don't remember a time before the wall, or only dimly."

"That seems so strange," Tatyana whispered. Then she gave a crooked smile. "But I admit, sometimes I think that time was all a dream."

"I suppose so. Such a different world. Telling stories to the children brings back the memories, and it is fun singing songs with them I haven't sung since you and Helen were little, but the disbelief in their big eyes when I talk of the festivals and the feasts and the music and pretty clothes, or even swimming in the river, well, it does make it all seem very far away." Yevenia sighed and picked up a watering can. She carefully sprinkled the beets.

Tatyana shifted her feet. She grew deadly serious again. "It is worse now, though. In spite of everything we did, people were really hungry last winter. We have been hungry for years, but this was worse, and..." She dropped her voice to a whisper. Technically it was a secret of the royal house, who had the only key. "The storehouses, even the new emergency one, they're just about empty."

Yevenia paled a little more. "Empty? The grain and salt and everything?"

"Everything. It echoes in there like it was newly built, and the salt is terribly low."

"I'm afraid there's nothing I can do about that. I certainly can't grow lard or salt or grain. Potatoes and beets can go a long way, there are a lot of good things in beets, and we have beans and peas, but none of it is as good for people without some sort of fat, and it will be hard to go without grain or meat when people are already so hungry. What are we going to do, Tatyana?"

"I wish I knew," Tatyana whispered. In spite of all their hard work, she could tell by walking down the street that people were weaker than last fall. Warriors, because of their strenuous physical efforts, were allotted a somewhat larger ration than civilians, but she could see the weakening in her people on the wall, too. They didn't have enough food. Some people complained about the limited rations Clara doled out in Edward's place. Some even complained that the king ought to do it himself. King Edward had no time for that, and neither did Tatyana, besides Clara was good at organizing and lists and such. They let the people complain for the most part, and they didn't tell them that the reason for the strict rations was that when it came to grain and meat, there was next to nothing left. That was too frightening a thought, and they didn't want it to get out. People were demoralized and frightened enough. The problem was, in another month or two it would run out and they could keep the secret no longer. "I'm going to have to do something," Tatyana muttered under her breath.

"I'm afraid there is little more we can do," Yevenia said with a tired sigh. "I have been trying to plant high-calorie foods, and things high in vitamins, but I can only grow so much. If we had several more big buildings and three or four times as many Efrim farmers we might be able to meet demand, but as it is we never can."

"There's no choice. Somehow, we're going to have to get food from outside the city."

"Not Efrim again?" Yevenia looked alarmed.

"No. It's no use, but what about the coast? Perhaps there is nothing as terrible as the black barrier in that direction. Aldor is no good, of course. They are hard up, too, but on the coast, assuming they are still there, they will have trade and should still be able to get anything."

"You think there's a chance anyone could make it through the forest with all the Shadows?" Yevenia looked doubtful and her fingers fluttered distractedly over the pail of compost she had gotten out.

"I don't know, but I think we will have to try. It doesn't look like our efforts inside the city are going to be enough."

"I suppose not. We could try harder, perhaps." Yevenia looked up at the ceiling. Maybe if we hung some pots from the rafters, too..."

"That might be a good idea." Tatyana knew that wouldn't be enough either, but she wasn't going to discuss it any more just now. She needed to think. Besides, Yevenia's expertise was gardening. If Tatyana wanted to plan a mission, she needed to talk to her father.

She took a little tour of the indoor garden. A couple of the men showed her, with evident pride, the fine bed of peas hung thickly with ripe pods, and another displayed the large and important herb beds used for medicines. As desperate as the need for food was, they must grow herbs for medicine in some of that ground. It was a beautiful and even hopeful place, but none of it was enough, and the thin hands and faces and threadbare clothing of the gardeners were a constant reminder of that. After a time, she left and went back up to her room. She slept until her alarm went off.

She ate her dinner of greens and mashed potatoes. Not real mashed potatoes like those she had once loved. This was literally a potato that was mashed, without any of the milk, butter, or salt that made it really good. The greens would have benefited from butter, too, but at least it eased the ache in her stomach. She went out to meet her watch, but asked one of her captains to take charge for an hour and went back to the palace to await her father.

She met him in the hall when he came in. Mother had gone to the hospital. It was the day to change sheets.

"Is everything all right?" Edward asked as he hung his sword by the door.

"As much as usual," Tatyana said, forcing herself to smile. "I just wanted to talk to you while you have dinner."

He gave a tired smile. "I welcome the company, but likely not the subject. Come in the kitchen and tell me all about it. I promised to take an hour shift in the hospital after I eat, and I want to be quick so I can have time to sleep."

Tatyana followed him in and sat down opposite. She tried not to watch as he ate his share of undressed potato and greens. They might not be delicacies, but her mouth watered, and she couldn't help longing for the food, even though she would also have liked to give him some of hers. He had always been slender and wiry, but it was different now, and his sea-gray eyes looked large in his gaunt face.

"So, what is it?" he prompted when she didn't speak.

"It's about the provisions."

"We are certainly in a grim way. If the warriors on the wall lose any more strength, the Shadows will be too much for us."

"And the poor children," Tatyana said softly. "Father, our city is starving to death right before our eyes. The indoor garden is helping, but it will never be enough."

"But what do we do? Do you have any ideas?" Frustration gave a hard edge to his words. "Efrim is near, and a few more Efrim farmers might save us, but we cannot reach them, and I don't really believe they live. Obrin is in trouble, and so is Aldor. We can't grow enough in gardens. It takes too many warriors trying to protect the flocks outside the walls. Collecting forage for them is almost as bad, especially now that so much of the undergrowth is dying in the forest. Besides, the animals are dying. I thought of hunting, but the parties that gather wood have gone twenty miles in dangerous forests without seeing any sign of animal life of any kind."

Tatyana took a deep breath. "I've been thinking about Selna."

"It's a long way, and the Shadows are bad in the forest."

"Yes, but there is a chance a party could get through," she insisted.

"I'm afraid it isn't a good chance. It would be very risky, and if we met with a barrier like the one to the north, we might have another tragedy like the last."

She shivered a little, feeling the pain of that failure and the guilt clenching down on her heart. "Not necessarily. As I see it, now that we know about the barrier, a strong person could go close enough to it to know what it was. If they were sure that was what they had encountered, then they would just have to turn back, but if there isn't one, they might make it through, and the coast markets probably still have all the things we need."

"I suppose there is a reasonable chance they are far enough away that things aren't bad there." Edward was silent for several minutes. He finished his meager dinner and took his plate to the sink. He stood a minute looking out the window and seeing only the faces of his hungry people. He thought of the colorful kingdom by the sea, and of the dark, forbidding forest between them. At last, he said, "It is very dangerous, but I suppose you are right. We've gone over all the other options and in your plan only lies a trace of hope. Without more food our warriors will weaken. I cannot give us six months before the Shadow force becomes stronger than ours." Turning, he came to stand beside her. "You don't fool me with your *they*. I feel the lie, and know you much too well. It is true this is the last hope of our people, and we must rally our warriors for a dangerous mission. It is the duty of the ruler to lead them. But it is also the duty of the ruler to remain in the city, so I'm afraid we can't go together."

"No, of course not." Her tone rose a few notes and she stood, too, feeling her chest constrict. "Last time I let them go without me because I was in charge of the city. I have hated myself for that ever since, but I don't have to stay home now that you are better."

Edward swallowed hard. "You should stay. I will go."

"No, I won't— I can't..." her voice rose sharper.

Edward put his hand on her shoulder, and when he spoke, his voice was husky although he fought to keep it steady. "How do you think I feel about you going?"

Tatyana felt bad about that, but tears were pricking her eyes now and that made her both ashamed and angry. She shook away from his hand. "I'm sorry, Father, but please. It has to be me. You can't go. You're the king. You should stay with the people. Besides, I'm stronger than you are!"

"I'm not sure that's true." His words were sharp, but then they softened, and an anxious look came into his eyes. "Your Sight is stronger, yes, but I'm worried about you. You don't look well."

"Neither do you."

"Perhaps. No one in this city looks well. Then it's beside the point, but that doesn't mean you are stronger than I am or better able to make the journey."

At that moment, Clara walked in with a basket of damp sheets to hang by the fire. She looked from Edward's hard face to Tatyana's flashing eyes and their stiff posture as they faced each other.

"What is this about?" she asked sharply. "Why is there a journey? Neither of you are fit for a long journey, and I won't let you go if I can help it." She set the sheets on the table and came over to take a hand of each.

Edward explained the idea of going to Selna for provisions. "It is our only chance, dearest. I have to go. I can't let my people starve to death."

"No, you don't." Tatyana said. "*I* have to go. I have suffered every day since I sent that last mission out to their deaths. I can't live with myself if I don't go now, and I couldn't bear for you to go." Anger and stubborn pride fought in her breast, but the tears were coming. She tried to force them back and think of a real argument.

"The deaths weren't your fault. I... You—" Edward stopped himself and looked down at the white stone floor for a moment. He hated himself as much as she did for that tragedy. He felt he should have gone, that maybe he could have saved at least some of those men. He cursed his weakness and his mistake in getting overheated. He took a deep breath. "You had good reasons to let them go, Tatyana. I would have done the same."

"Thank you. I still feel I have to go, though. It is what I owe my people."

"You think I do not owe them as much?"

Clara cut in. "Please, both of you. This is too dangerous. You can't leave the city. I know we are desperate for food, but I'm worried about you. Are you sure you can even walk that far?"

"Sure I can," they said, almost at the same moment.

Tatyana met her father's eyes and, in spite of everything, they both smiled a little.

Edward sighed and took one of Tatyana's hands in both of his. There was great pain in his eyes, and his voice when he spoke was broken and husky. "I'm sorry, Tatyana. Go if you are determined to. Perhaps you are right. You are younger, and maybe faster, and I suppose it would look pretty strange if I showed up in Selna at a time like this."

"It would, and you have to stay with our people," Tatyana said. "They count on you."

"Perhaps that's true, but remember, they look on you as a ruler, too, or near enough. The city will miss you while you are away." His voice dropped and got a bit thicker with emotion. "But not as much as I will."

"I'll miss you, too, but I promise I'll be careful, and if there is a black barrier I will turn right around and come home."

"So be it." He squeezed her hand and then, without another word, turned and left for the hospital.

Tatyana looked at her mother and cut in before she could protest. "You can't stop me, Mother. It is the only hope."

"Perhaps," Clara whispered. She was worrying her skirt in her hands. "But please take care."

"I'll do my best. But for now, I must go to my watch." Tatyana gave her mother a quick hug and left the room.

* * * * * * *

Thus, it was decided. When Tatyana wasn't on watch she spent time organizing. There were provisions and carts to arrange for. The money was easy. Edward unlocked the bottom drawer of his desk and took out the chest that held the royal treasury of trade coin collected from tax on the foreign sale of goods, to be given to farmers, theatre people, and such folk who provided for the community in ways that did not earn them any trade coin for their outside purchases. He took nearly all the money out, and she hid it in a couple bags she could wear under her clothes. Gathering trade goods from all the Eldirad craftspeople was more time consuming. That was the greatest part of the wealth of the nation, and the craftsmen and women, even if they hadn't made anything intended for outside sale in many years, all had things to send.

As it turned out, the hardest part was getting volunteers. It appeared that the people had been badly frightened by the tragedy of last fall, and they were also tired, weak, and starting to despair. Tatyana couldn't blame them, but it worried her. When three days had passed with no volunteers, she began to doubt herself. Would they have trusted more if it was her father who was going? Did her people not trust her after all? And should they? Edward convinced her to go up to the porch herself and make a speech telling the people of her plan and her hope.

That seemed to help. That afternoon, when she was going out for her watch, a young man stopped her and said, "Princess Tatyana. I am loyal, I swear. Where you go, I will follow, be it to hope or death."

"Thank you," she said. The grim nature of the vow chilled her a little, but the sincerity she could feel behind the words touched her heart. "Stars bless you and bring you hope."

After that, people trickled in. They were mostly her age or younger, although there were a couple older volunteers. She chose thirty who looked strong, or at least better than the others, and they set out at dawn on the twenty-first of April with twenty wagons pulled by most of the remaining horses and oxen in the city.

They set out with trepidation, but though there was mist in the forest they met no wall. Nothing like the black barrier to the north. The forest was horribly silent, and Tatyana felt sometimes as though she didn't dare breathe. They jumped if a cart or harness made a loud noise, and without any special reason they all spoke in whispers, as if they were in the chamber of a dying person. They had to fight Shadows many times each day, but they kept going, and passed round the skirts of the first mountain ridge early on the third day.

The dark and breathless feeling in the forest weighed heavier on the hearts of the party with each passing day. A few strange, distorted creatures seemed to flit in the trees at times, but they made no more noise than the Shadows. Tatyana didn't mention them, and few others admitted to seeing them. She had no way of knowing if they were really there or in her mind. They made some ten miles or so a day. The progress made Tatyana impatient, but with fighting and keeping pace with the oxen they couldn't go faster. It was a struggle as it was to keep the animals from bolting or running mad whenever there was an attack. The worst attack came on the fourth night, when they were camped. There were ten people on watch, but mist hung in the trees, and none saw the Shadow force coming until it was on top of them.

The first sign was the fear among the animals, but it only gave a few seconds' warning. Tatyana leapt up out of half sleep and charged to where the attack seemed the worst, but the Shadows were everywhere. Some people went to the animals, but there were too many Shadows, and arrows flew. Two horses fell to the black arrows and the others cried in terror. Three bolted, and one of the oxen stampeded in terror, knocking down the man who tried to calm it. Meanwhile, the press was hard. It was dark, and although torches were lighted, they seemed to be swallowed up in the all-consuming inkiness of the forest. All the warriors fought as hard as they could for more than an hour, and it was all Tatyana could do to keep them organized around their carts and to keep the blackness of fear and despair from her mind.

When at last the cords ceased to come from the darkness, and enemy blades no longer sliced the air, Tatyana fell to her knees and sat a moment, breathing hard.

"Well, we got through that," a woman's voice said cheerfully beside her.

Tatyana looked up to see the woman offering her a hand. She took it. "I guess we did. We had better look at the damages."

It wasn't good. Six had the blindness, three had fainted of the sickness, and two men were dead. Two horses and an ox were dead also, and three other horses had fled, leaving three carts without a single animal to pull them. Tatyana's heart felt like a stone, and she had to blink back tears, but there was work to do. She made the blind sit in the wagons with the sick; graves were dug and the dead buried. She said the appropriate words and led her companions in the appropriate songs, but the weight in her chest only got heavier, and she couldn't help thinking that the tragedy was not as swift as it had been for the party sent to Efrim, but it was still coming for them.

There would be no more sleep that night, and they plodded on down the white stone road in the dark without speaking. Two people at a time took turns pulling each of the carts left without horses.

After that they only rested in daytime, which Tatyana realized they should have done all along, and a full half of the party kept watch at all times. The light increased, and the mist in the trees lessened as they went on. They still saw Shadows, and had to fight them, but they became less numerous and less fierce, until on the ninth day they saw only one.

They came to the edge of the forest that evening, cresting the last hill and looking down into Selna. With a fresh breeze from the sea full in their faces, they all stopped and stood still. A dozen yards to their left, the East Fort of the Efrim guard rose majestically. Three stories of white stone trimmed with silver, and sparkling glass windows looking out from the upper stories. The whole thing glittered pink and gold in the light of the setting sun. Below them, the green hill sloped down a dozen feet to a sturdy gray stone wall with an iron gate and two bright flags on either side with the yellow and green ship on blue of the republic of Selna. Beyond the wall they could see green fields, orchards, and flowers sloping down to the crowded buildings of the city, and beyond that, the glimmer of sun on water. The sun was setting over the sea, right between the high, dark peaks that guarded the entrance to the bay of Selna.

They were shaken out of their reverie by a gruff voice from the wall before them. *"Who are you and what do you want?"* a man's voice shouted from the wall in Selnese.

Tatyana saw her companions looking at her and realized many or most of them probably never even learned Selnese, and besides it had been a long time. She had once been fluent, but after four years she was very rusty, and it was a relief that she understood the man at all. She had tried to practice over the last couple weeks, but it took her several minutes before she could formulate a sentence.

"We come from Eldir. We greet Selna as friends, and come to trade. Peace and friendliness look on our people." She could see the man standing above the gate now, and she looked at him and bowed slightly when she finished speaking.

The man spoke in a low voice to someone near him for a minute. Then he said, *"We beg your pardon, but we do not trust strangers just now. I've heard tell all Eldir is a wasteland populated by evil ghosts, and Efrim is worse. Something grows inside them, and they turn evil, becoming monsters. We will not be fooled again. The state of affairs is sorry, indeed, but the old treaties are no good now."*

Tatyana felt her pride bristle a little, although a fear filled her at what he said about Efrim. She took a deep breath and thought of what words to use. This was important. It was diplomacy, even if only with the gate guard, but thinking of words herself was much harder than understanding them. *"I am sorry to hear that. I hope to show you that Eldir is not a wasteland, and that our treaties may remain. Our countries have lived long in peace, and we want only friends. I am Crown Princess Tatyana of Eldir, and I hope to speak with the council before I go. I want to know more about what you hear. For tonight... tonight we will not... annoy you. We go to the fort of our sister country to rest."*

The man conferred with his fellows again. *"What you do on that side of the border isn't none of my business. Go up there if you will. That Efrim monster is gone, we think."*

"Can you tell me what you mean?"

"I s'pose. Five days ago it is now, I think, an Efrim came to the city. He stayed up at the fort and came down during the day, and we let him in. There were rumors, of course, that shadows and ghosts had taken over all that land, but we've always had good dealings with the Efrim at the fort. They treat us well, are very good for trade with their nice goods, and the men are known for always being polite to ladies. Besides, they helped us a time or two when the coast was attacked.

"Anyway, after we'd let the man in, and he didn't speak that good Selnese I'll say, but be that as it may. He was rude, and he stirred up trouble. The matron of our best inn thinks he tried to poison the soup, and he was downright mean to the serving girl. He stole a thing or two also, or so we think. We don't want anything to do with them anymore. They've been taken over, I tell you.

"One of our merchants, a very respected citizen, he came up to the fort just two days back when the man didn't come down. Looking for some reckoning for what he had been doing, he was. Well, he says he went up there and saw the man trying to hide from him. The monster ran for the forest, but our man swears he saw him and that he didn't even look human anymore, sort of human, mind you; we're sure it was the same man, but he was greenish, and rather larger than he had been, and his hair was shorter and turning darker.

Our man, he threw his knife, but the thing got away. I don't know what you have to say to that, or why I should be trusting in old treaties now."

Tatyana felt shaken and wondered if she could have heard all that right. It sounded terrible. She wondered if there was any way she could get them to trust her. But, more than that, she wondered what could have really happened to the Efrim. The green thing sounded a bit like the monster she had heard Joseph fought, except, as she understood, that one had shown no sign whatsoever of being human. *"That news hurts,"* she said at last. *"It is sad, but I thank you. We will return in the morning."* Then she spoke to her companions, and they walked towards the fort.

As they walked, she told them what the man had said, since it turned out only three had understood at all. Everyone was grim and worried, and arguments broke out as to whether it was really possible something like that could have taken over an Efrim, or if they were all long dead as most people thought, and this thing was pretending. Tatyana didn't join in the argument. She couldn't believe that the Efrim could really be turned into something that terrible, but the explanation of the event unquestionably included magic with which she had no experience, so who knew?

She had felt an intense sensation of fear for Aranin—how many days ago was that now? It had been during the week of preparations before their departure, and the feeling lingered. They had been good friends, very close, but not close enough for her to go to him. If she had power like Helen she could have, but her gift wasn't strong enough. It was strange. She had given him up for dead last summer. Now she wondered and worried.

She led the way into the stable at the fort. It was a large, spacious building with more than a hundred stalls, and it smelled of stale hay, but also of something else. Something that made her uneasy.

"Open the shutters, someone," she whispered. "And keep back. Keep the animals outside."

One of her women opened the large wooden shutters that covered the stable windows. Gray evening light spread across the stalls. Tatyana lit a lantern and walked slowly forward. The smell was nasty as she neared the far end. Old blood, sickness, and something worse. She came to the last stall with two others behind her and looked in. In the hay on the far side of the room a form lay sprawled. It did not move, and she could sense that it was quite dead.

Swallowing hard, she handed the lantern to the man beside her and, going cautiously forward, knelt by the body. The man on the floor was certainly dead, by something like two days, she guessed, and he was certainly Efrim. He appeared to have been ill for several days and to have died in great pain. She was sure he couldn't have been the man they saw in Selna, in spite of the similar timing. He would have been quite weak and unable to eat or walk during that time. There were bad burns on his wrists and ankles, and strangest of all, a row of cuts on his arm. They appeared to have been made in succession with many hours, perhaps even as much as a day between. The first cut was partly healed, perhaps some four or five days old at the time of death. The last had no blood and had clearly been made after death.

"What happened to him?" the man with the lantern whispered as he bent over the body.

"I don't know," Tatyana said. "The wounds would have bled badly, but they didn't kill him. He died of sickness or pain."

"What's that?" a woman close by said with a note of distaste in her voice.

Tatyana looked. Not far from the body lay a strange black vial, a box, and a bowl. The bowl had the residue of something reddish black dried to it. The vial, when she touched it with one finger, burned and tingled like black magic, but looking at it she was sure there was dried blood on it.

"Something's been measuring out blood and mixing it with something," another woman exclaimed in horror.

"So it would seem," Tatyana said. She felt a chill go through her. "Something in that box, which feels too evil even to touch, is put in the blood. Some kind of potion, I suppose, and there's no doubt where the blood came from." She looked at the body. "It was his." She wanted to get out of there that minute. "Someone cover the poor wretch. We'll bury him in the morning. For now, let's get into the fort and see if it is safe for the night, and if they left anything to eat."

Chapter 23

Selna

30 April to 18 May, YA 1127

Selna: Aldor Forest: Eldirad

THE SPELL that held the moonsilver latch on the door of the fort was pure. When Tatyana let them all in, the large hall echoed, and there were thick spiderwebs in the air and dust on the floor. Nothing appeared to have been touched. Tatyana and most of her companions made a thorough search of the building, while the others made supper.

Of course, after three and a half years, what perishable food had been left was little more than dirt on the shelves, but there was plenty of flour and baking soda and salt, and even sugar, and canned preserves. Tatyana's only problem was keeping her companions from eating too much, after so long on starvation rations, and making themselves sick.

Then they went upstairs. They were all weary, and as soon as Tatyana had made sure the two who were still recovering from the Shadow sickness were comfortable, she lay down as well.

In her dream she saw again the scene in the stable, but the dead man's face in the lantern light changed to Aranin's, and it was contorted, marked with pain. He lay splayed out, his arms and legs tied, but his head moved slightly, and blood dripped from a cut on his arm, a cut just like the ones on the dead man in the stable.

Tatyana woke with tears on her cheeks and cold sweat on her palms. She stood and went to the window. She could see starlight shimmering on the waves of the far ocean. She told herself it was only a nightmare. She had so many nightmares these days that sometimes it made her wish she could go without sleep altogether. But some part of her wasn't sure. The image was very vivid. She got a drink of water and then made herself lie down again, but it was a long time before she slept.

She woke to bright sunshine streaming in the window and cheerful voices. Someone laughed. Clear voices singing wafted up the stairs. For a moment, it was like waking into another world, or as if the whole last three and a half years had been a bad dream. She smiled and, jumping to her feet, went to the window that looked out over Selna to the sea. The city below shimmered with color. Silken flags of every bright shade she could imagine flew from the buildings in the morning sun. Tatyana had to think for a minute before she realized today was the cross quarter day. May first. The beginning of the sunny months. The May festival was a really big deal in Selna. Selna was known for a love of good times, and their festivals were grand, but May was said to be the best. Aranin had gone to the festival once when he was stationed here at the Efrim guard post in the old days, and he had told her all about it. It sounded wonderful. She had quite forgotten about the existence of holidays. Her people celebrated this day, too, but they hadn't celebrated anything in so long.

"We might get to see the Selnese May Festival," Tatyana said to the others in the room. "If we can get the guard to let us in."

"He just has to see sense," one woman said impatiently.

"You have to admit, his story sounded pretty bad," said another.

Tatyana agreed with both of them. The man had a right to be careful, but she had some theories about what had actually happened. The theories were not exactly comforting, but it was better than the idea of a sort of magical infection that turned people into monsters. Of course, there had been the strange control from that black thing behind the ear that had been used on that man who attacked Sebastian, but this was different and, if anything, creepier.

After a breakfast of more biscuits, jam, and canned fruit, they made their way to the gate again. Tatyana had to talk to the guard for a long time, and keeping a straight face while she spoke was far from easy, since the man was wearing a short cloak of vivid red, blue, yellow, purple, and lime green over his blue uniform and a pointed hat with six brightly colored feathers in it. She had heard that the wilder one's costume at this particular festival the better, but it made it hard to concentrate. It also made her painfully aware of the mended state of the linen trousers she wore, and the subdued and ill-fitting nature of the silk blouse.

She told him about what they found in the barn the night before. *"I believe the green monster was using some kind of sinister potion, the nature of which I do not understand, but as a healer I can swear to you that the man I found could not have walked in your city as recently as you say you saw him. I don't believe he entered at all. It was the monster all along, but he was using the man in some way to make himself appear like him."*

The guard nodded, and his feather plumes bobbed. *"I suppose a potion could do that, but what are you trying to convince me of?"*

"Only that whether they are alive or dead, you have no quarrel with the Efrim and no reason to dishonor them. As for me and my people, we are of the Eldir, and while we are beset by Shadows, we certainly are not conquered. Do we look like shadows, sir? And do you think this many of us could be monsters using a disguise potion?"

After looking each of them over for a while and asking Tatyana what seemed like an endless number of questions about the laws of Selna, he decided to let them through, provided they left their weapons at the gate. They walked down across the meadows and, crowding a little closer to each other, entered the noisy, bustling streets of the city.

There were people everywhere dressed in jewels and the wildest silk costumes imaginable. Everyone had five or six bright colors, and there were outlandish hats with heaps of flowers, or sometimes merpeople or sea monsters, on them. Silk bunting hung from every building, and there were flowers along all the streets. People were laughing and talking, shouting and singing. They were mostly Selnese in appearance, men and women of medium height, notably shorter than the Eldir but not as small as the people of Ikkik. They had smooth, golden-brown skin and shining jet-black hair that set off the bright silk of their costumes. Some of the poorer people, whose costumes were of wool or linen and had few jewels, were of darker or lighter complexion. It was a wonderful sight, but the Eldir felt very out of place. They were taller than everyone, and paler of skin than nearly all, but they stood out worst of all in the subdued tones of even these nicer clothes they had brought to wear in the city.

Tatyana had just begun to wonder if it would be possible to find any normal market venders amid the carnival games and party stalls, when a parade came down the street. People swept to the sides and a band marched down playing a rousing dance tune. Behind them were horse-drawn wagons decorated with flowers and fantastical scenes of sea creatures, some of which must reside in Selnese myths she had never heard of. The first float threw chocolates at the crowd, and some threw pastries or flower petals. Tatyana couldn't help herself. For the moment, she put aside cares and marveled at the beautiful floats and joined the crowds in picking up the treats.

When it passed, and she stood sucking on a piece of chocolate and watching the parade trundle into the distance, she thought about Helen. How she wished Helen could have seen this, and Analisia. Analisia would have loved this. Father and Mother, too, and Sebastian and Joseph. She was sure it would do them good to see something like this. It would at least have made them smile, and she realized more than ever now that smiling really was important. She thought of Aranin, how he would have loved some of the more artistic floats, and of the sketches he had made for her the last time he was here. For the moment, however, she tried to stick to good thoughts of him and not to think about the dream or wonder if Efrim still stood.

Tatyana and her companions drifted apart after that. In the festival air, no one seemed worried about limited language abilities, or anything else. She was pretty sure enough Selnese merchants spoke at least pidgin Efrian that her people would manage. For her part, Tatyana wandered all morning among the festival stalls. She talked to some of the people. She bought herself a few treats and a nice lunch. The streets of Selna were safe enough, but mild flirting was common and had always been a nuisance to Tatyana when she came before. Now she was a little surprised not to be the focus of it at all. She supposed the last three years had changed her a lot. Some people looked at her a little suspiciously, but most seemed glad to see someone who wore the stars of Eldir.

Everyone hoped her people would come back, and one merchant

where she stopped to buy some linen fabric confided to her, *"Everything looks fine and glad today, as of course it should, but I don't mind telling you we miss your trade sorely. Things have been tight, and trade's not half so good without the business of your nation and Efrim. We counted on that, and the fine work you brought was important to our oversea trade too."*

"I have brought some of what you are hoping for," she said, fumbling in her bag with a smile. *"I can't say when we'll come back for sure. Times have been hard for us lately, but we will establish proper trade as soon as we can. Here, how much good sturdy linen will this get me?"* She held out a jewel-inlaid leather handbag from one of the leather workers of Eldirad.

"A good deal, and I'll take as much more like it as you wish to give." He looked downright eager.

In the end she also gave him a knife with an inlaid handle Clarence had made, and a bracelet of green jewel leaves. In return she got a good deal more good linen and woolen fabric than she could carry. The linen would mostly be for underclothes and summer things for children, the wool for warriors, and she chose pleasant colors she hoped people would like. Yes, starvation was the real issue, but their clothes were in tatters, and she decided room could be spared in the carts for some new fabric. The merchant sent his two assistants to help her carry the cloth until she found some of her people. That didn't take long.

As much fun as it was, Tatyana was worn out with the noise of the party and glad to go back to the fort, and she got some people to come with her. She saw to the burial of the Efrim man, and then she rested for a while.

Wandering around the dorm in the late afternoon, she found an easel up against one wall with a cloth over it. Softly, she lifted the dusty cover. Beneath was a mostly finished seascape. It showed the harbor of Selna at sunset with pink and gold light catching on the water and tinting the hulls of the ships at anchor. In the center was a great ship in full sail, greater than Tatyana had ever seen. But it had never been finished. The hull was half painted, and only white silhouettes showed where sailors should have been. She could not mistake the hand, sure and clear, with soft, almost invisible brushstrokes. The dream came back to her, and the fear and feeling of unease that still lingered when she thought of Aranin. She was next to sure it was not just her own fear but a feeling of the Sight.

She ran a finger along the line of one of the graceful boats in the painting, and tears filled her eyes. She had always liked Aranin a lot. He was a good friend, grave, kind, thoughtful, and so talented. He had seemed so young last time she saw him, but she realized if he was still alive he was nearly thirty-two now, well into manhood. She wondered how he had changed, and she missed him intensely. She sat on her bed and made an attempt to reach out to him with the Sight. The connection was there, she could feel it, and it sang with a discordant note of pain, but when she tried to go to him, just for a moment, it was no good. Her Sight was not strong enough. He was alive, that was something, but the sense of pain and danger was strong, and that horrible dream would not fade as normal dreams should.

✶ ✶ ✶ ✶ ✶ ✶

At dusk, nine of her warriors still hadn't returned, and some who had were rather ill. They had partied more than was good for them. When she went and hunted down the others, she found this wasn't uncommon. The festival had been too exciting for many after the years of hardship, and wine flowed freely at Selnese festivals, especially as evening approached. She guessed several of her companions had quite misjudged how much of such things they could handle after so many years of privation. She didn't really blame them. Coming from the grim world they did, even the colorful streets were intoxicating. She didn't let them stay into the evening, though. She apologized for any unconscious rudeness on their part, paid any bills that remained, and bundled them all home. Three had passed out and had to be carried. At the fort, she made them all take baths and go to bed. They had enough provisions in the fort for convenience now, and Tatyana cooked dinner for those who wished it. Then they went to sleep early, and this time she had no bad dreams.

The next day, they simply rested. There was no use going into the city. Nothing would be open the day after a festival. It was nice to rest. There were a few books on a shelf in the fort, and a good many games for quiet evenings. Tatyana found a story she was fond of and read for most of the day.

The day after, she had to go in early to have her audience with the council. The gate keeper had sent someone to inform her the evening before. The young man had looked frightened to come near the guard station, and had run away as soon as he gave the message. The story of the green monster played on people's imaginations.

Tatyana wore her best silk dress, which she had brought for this purpose. Her mother had taken it in to fit her thin form. It was still in good shape, unlike all her other clothes, since she had no cause to wear it. She pinned her guardian stars and the heir star to the front and did up her hair with a jeweled pin. Then she went to the gate and let the guard lead her to the grand council chamber near the harbor. She was nervous. During the four years of her adulthood before the coming of the Shadows, and especially the two years after she became crown princess, she had gone on ambassador missions alone, but nothing as important as this. Besides, that seemed part of another world. It was hard to face rumors that your nation might be desolate and peopled with evil ghosts, and your allies were turning into green monsters, especially in a language that seemed more ill-fitting after years of disuse than her dress had been before it was altered.

At the bottom of the great marble stairs, she took a deep breath and lifted her chin. She hoped she looked like a queen, and indeed, in spite of her extreme thinness, she made an imposing and elegant figure. She stood before the council for four hours answering questions and trying to be patient and not let down her guard. They were the heads of the thirteen great households of Selna and were, as a rule, very old men, with a few very old women for variety. They argued with each other over a great many things. Some seemed very suspicious, and others were very anxious to know the state of things in Eldir and Efrim. Tatyana knew she could lie to them. There was nothing like the Sight in the magic of Selna. No matter what, diplomacy called for mild lies all the time, and the Eldir forgave foreign diplomats even though they sensed every one. Still, she did not like to lie if she could help it. Selna had never been a nation of conquerors, and they had never been a threat to Eldir. So, she told the truth—or most of it. It was the best way to get them to believe her.

She told them that she could not vouch for Efrim, as contact had stopped more than three years ago, but she also told them about what she had found in the stable and her feeling that there were at least some people alive in Efrim. She told them of the hard press at Eldirad, Aldor, and Obrin. She did, perhaps, paint things a little more stable and less grim than they were, but on the whole, she was as frank as diplomatic courtesy allowed.

It was a trial, but in the early afternoon, they finally concluded by deciding to believe her.

"We are very relieved to hear that Eldir still stands," said one of the men. *"We acknowledge that Eldir and Efrim have been the great powers of this part of the world for many centuries, and we feared, when we heard they had fallen, that there was no hope for any of the other kingdoms such as ours. We have long counted on your trade, and the goodwill of your nation, and even more so that of the Efrim at the fort."*

"We would like to know about the Efrim," a thin, white-haired lady added. *"But with your nation our treaties stand, and you shall have any help you ask for. You are a fine young woman, and I hope you will be a great queen someday. Take our message of friendship to your father."*

Tatyana thanked them and promised she would. Then the youngest member of the council, who was about the Selnese equivalent of her father's age, took her to their school of magic to ask her questions about the potion the monster was making.

It was a large, rambling campus on the east side of the harbor surrounded by a high, ivy-covered stone wall. It would have been fascinating to explore if she had been allowed and had the leisure. A woman with very bright, dark eyes met them at the door of the main hall, and the council member explained what Tatyana wanted.

"Come with me, princess," the woman said. She was brusque and businesslike and made even the lyrical and drawn-out language of Selna sound clipped.

Tatyana followed her into a little building beside the main hall. There were shelves filled with jars and a row of small kettles on a stove along one wall. Tatyana explained again everything she had found in the barn.

"*So, you think the monster was using some kind of potion, do you?*"

"*Yes, I am guessing. It must have somehow made itself to look like an Efrim. I am sure that man wouldn't have had the strength to walk within the last six or seven days before he died.*"

"*Very likely, very likely...*" The woman got a book from a shelf and flipped through the pages written in the clear, square letters of Selna. "*I trust an Eldir judgement on that, especially one who wears the flower.*" She nodded to the small pink jewel flower on Tatyana's waistband that indicated a healer trained at the Eldir school. "*It would also make sense of the half transformation the merchant claimed to see. You said the last cut didn't bleed?*"

"*It was made after death.*"

"*And that was the same day Mr. Vincenti saw the monster?*"

"*I believe so.*"

"*Our main focus here at the Academy, as I presume you know, is weather magic. Therein lie most of the gifts of our students. However, all learn potions a little, and we have scholars who have made a deep study of such matters. We, of course, do not teach any potions of this sort, but living blood has powers. I'm sure that is why it brought the man with it, and when the man died, the monster could no longer use his blood to take on his form. What the monster may have had in that box I cannot tell you, although I'm sure they were magical ingredients of some kind.*"

"*That makes sense. Can you give me any advice concerning the nature of this threat? How to detect it? Or prevent it? Or break the spell?*"

"*Perhaps...*" The woman tucked some gray hair behind her ear and flipped through the book again. "*As anyone used to the principles of transformation knows, the eyes are always the hardest. A man may transform himself into an animal, but his eyes usually remain recognizable. I admit no one appears to have noticed this creature's eyes being unusual, but perhaps they didn't look hard enough. Sometimes it takes a clear eye, or one that is prepared to see differences. If you have any sort of charm or magic object that is intolerant of evil, that should not be able to be fooled. Also, I would guess that a*" *revealing spell would work at least enough for the eyes to revert to whatever the monster's eyes look like. Do you know any revealing spells?"*

"I'm afraid not. We learn to break spells, and we learn charms of concealment and light weaving, but not revealing. And our charm breaking has no effect on potions, which are a foreign art to us."

"I believe I could teach you that, if you will teach me something in return. As for prevention, the only way I see is to be sure such enemies get no one alive."

"What would you like to know in return for the spell?"

The woman looked thoughtful. *"Your healing powers are like wind calling, inherited rather than learned?"*

"The power is, although the skill is learned."

"Could you teach me to make the herb to aid fever that you sometimes bring to market?"

"I can."

"Then it is a deal."

Tatyana stayed for the rest of the afternoon at the school. First, she taught the lady, who turned out to be the director and potions teacher, her recipe. For in Eldir, potions were only used in healing, but in those they excelled above all other lands. Then, Tatyana practiced the revealing spell until she could reveal every time the true form of an object the director had concealed with magic.

The sun was low when they parted with words of friendship on the school steps. That evening, Tatyana spent a couple hours teaching the new spell to her companions. It could be very useful in the future, and Tatyana hoped she would be able to teach it to Helen and Sebastian over a Sight connection. That would be hard with her limited ability to talk. She would probably do best to try to get Helen to come to her and listen, and then hope Helen could explain to Sebastian. She thought again of Efrim, wondering if the valley still stood or if only a few tormented prisoners remained. She wished she could tell them about the spell, too, but even if she, or perhaps Helen, had the power to contact anyone there with the Sight, there would have been no one with the ability to hear them.

✶✶✶✶✶✶

The next two days were spent mostly shopping for supplies. Now that they were honored in the city, they could come and go as they wished and bring in their carts and horses. They concealed the fact that three carts were without animals to draw them, not wanting the Selnese to know the full extent of their weakness. This was easy since they only brought a couple carts at a time. The shopping was kind of fun but also overwhelming. The merchants were all eager for her trade goods and her money, and, with the added incentive that the council had told everyone to help her, people swarmed around her. Every way Tatyana turned, merchants, farmers, or craftsman were trying to get her attention or tempt her with some luxury or delicacy. A few of her warriors gave in, in small ways, to the tempting foods, but she forced herself to stay practical.

She bought all the salted meat and lard available and many sacks of grain. She bought barrels of honey, since it was high in nutrients and calories and delicious as well. She also bought several big blocks of chocolate and a good deal of salt. She did allow herself to be temped into some small sacks of spices. They would make food so much more enjoyable, and they didn't take up too much room. She had realized over the last few days that making people smile was the most important thing after all. Without hope, no amount of food would do any good. So, she got a few carefully selected frivolous things, too. Some pretty new buttons for the new clothes, colored ribbons for the children, tubs of butter, baking powder, and sugar.

One evening, a couple of her warriors convinced her to go to the theatre. She didn't understand more than three quarters of the words, and she doubted her companions understood even half, but it was a slapstick comedy and they all enjoyed themselves. It made her think of Joseph, and she wished he could see it. Tatyana laughed so hard she cried. She wasn't sure when the last time she had laughed like that had been. Had she been this happy since before the Shadows came? Had anyone at home? No. She wished she could put the laughter and bright

382

colors of Selna, and the clean sea air, in a barrel to take home to her parents.

* * ★ * * *

On the sixth morning since they arrived, the carts were all packed tight, and everyone's packs were full. They ate a good breakfast at first light and were standing on the hill looking out over Selna by the time the sun rose. Everyone turned away from the sea with a certain reluctance. They had eaten and rested well, and breathed the clean air of the coast for five days, and they felt stronger than they had in a long time. Still, the road ahead was dark and dangerous, and Tatyana was sure hers was not the only heart filled with foreboding. They had to hurry home. Their friends and families were waiting, anxious, and hungry. Tatyana had gone momentarily with the Sight to her father the day after they arrived, so the city knew they had reached the coast, but that was unlikely to make the people less anxious for their return. A part of Tatyana wanted to linger a few more days, just to put off the journey and the dangers and griefs it might hold. But that was no good. They had to get back.

She roused herself and gave the word to start. The thin horses and oxen strained at the heavy carts, and the carts pulled by people required five or six to get started, although four at a time could pull them once they got going. It was a blessing the road was paved smooth and nearly level. They changed people on the carts every hour, and sometimes people helped the animals as well. Thus they went for most of the day. They rested briefly in the afternoon and went all night. They did not move fast, and there were many short halts as the next couple days went on, as well as a longer rest and sleep by turns in the lightest hours. Tatyana felt a growing unease as they went, and she desired speed, but they couldn't push too hard when they had so far to go.

Shadows increased, but fighting wasn't too bad for the first few days. On the fourth night, near where the worst attack had been on the way out, they were assailed again. Tatyana had been at a turn pulling a cart, and she ran to the aid of the guards, but the battle was nearly as bad as the last time in this place. Once again, they were successful in beating them off, but not without losses.

Another ox and a horse were dead. Even harnessed to the heavy cart, one horse had run mad, bucking and running into things, so that one wheel on its cart was cracked and several barrels had to be resecured. One warrior was dead, too, another wounded, and a dozen temporarily blind. Tatyana tried not to think that out of the thirty she brought with her she had already lost three. She tried not to think four, but although she cleaned the man's small wound carefully while one of her warriors fixed the cart's wheel, and gave him every known medicine, it was hard not to count the wounded man dead. Next to no one had survived a wound before the moonsilver trick Helen discovered a year and a half ago. Even with it, the outlook still wasn't good, and his chances would have been better in the hospital away from the mist. And indeed, two days later, he died.

They were fighting most of the time now, which was difficult with four carts now under human power and only twenty-six people left. There were very few to guard them and any bigger attack meant the carts had to be stopped while they fought it off. Such bigger ones came several times a night as they neared home. Everyone was exhausted, but it was hard to rest. The black mist, and the oppressive stillness of the forest, weighed heavier at every step, more so, it seemed, even than on the outward journey.

It was like a force that made every step harder. They seemed to be walking through silence as thick as jelly. The breathless forest felt cursed, and it grew slowly harder to think. Tatyana felt ill, but she needed to work hard to rally the spirits of her people. Sometimes in the depths of the night she tried light weaving to help conceal her party, but that, too, was exhausting.

In this way they came to the night of the seventeenth of May, eleven days since they left the coast. They were very close now. A distinctive stone at the side of the road told them they were only a mile from Eldirad, and Tatyana pushed her people to greater speed, putting all her strength into the cart she was pulling. They were so close, but great fear and need for haste filled her. She was sure a terrible attack was coming. That last mile would be the most dangerous, but the closer they got to the city the better their chance that help could come if they needed it.

The thought of home lit a flame in the most weary and dispirited hearts, and the carts charged along. They passed the half mile marker. Another few minutes and they would be in sight of the bridge.

Out of the forest on both sides of the road before them came veritable walls of Shadows. Their path closed like a slamming door, and the Shadows surrounded them. People struggled with the animals, which were wild with terror.

"Keep together," Tatyana shouted.

The carts were put in the middle, as had become habit, and the warriors spread out around them. They all fought hard, but they seemed pitifully few. "By the Stars, Father, help!" she screamed in her mind. "Anyone, help!" Should she try to weave a shield, or join the fight?

One of the leaping and bucking horses broke the harness and bolted, knocking a woman to the ground. A Shadow bent to stab the woman in the back with its poisoned blade. Tatyana grabbed her dagger and threw it with all her might. It flew through the Shadow, making the poisoned knife clatter to the road, and pierced half a dozen more before sticking into a tree. Tatyana made up her mind. She had to fight; she didn't have the power to make an effective light weaving. She went to the front lines, but she was tired, and her people were faltering in the black mist. She stumbled and struggled back to her feet.

She felt a light touch on her back and a new strength. It was Helen. She shouted again and again to her people, pulling them closer together so they were right around the wagons. She could keep her footing now, and a faint flicker came to her blade. The troop of large Shadows seemed to be almost spent. Perhaps there might be some chance to make a few more yards forward?

Another battalion of Shadows crashed into their line like a breaking wave. Her people stumbled, and she tried to weave a small shield with Helen's help. Fighting would not work. At that moment, she heard the clashing of metal and light feet running on the hard stones. Voices drew nearer. Helen had gone, and Tatyana's eyes were growing dim, but she struggled back to her feet.

People. There were warriors all around her. The fallen were loaded up onto the carts, and the carts were being pulled. Tatyana went with the rear guard. She just had to keep fighting. There was hope now, and hope brought her strength so long as she could cling to it.

They were across the bridge. There was a terrible press of Shadows, and then they were at the wall. They stood and fought hard while the carts got through the gate, and at last they were within the walls.

Peace. Safety. She was home. She had made it, gotten her people home.

Tatyana staggered, dizzy and blind, and fell to her knees. There were hands on her shoulders. She was lifted in strong, kind arms. She lay her head against the silky coolness of a mail shirt.

She was in a dream, somewhere between sleep and waking nightmare, but always she felt she was being held. Someone was holding onto her, whether with real hands or spirit ones she could not tell, nor did she think, but it was an anchor.

When she woke up, she felt her soft bed and warm quilt. A large, bony hand held hers in a firm, warm grip. She clutched at the hand and, with an effort, opened her eyes. She looked up into her father's face. He smiled, and his sea-gray eyes were moist with tears.

"Good morning," he said.

Memory flooded back to her. "Did I...? The others... the provisions...?"

He smiled even more and took her other hand. "Don't worry. We got everyone who was with you. Nearly all of them had collapsed by the time we got there, but there was only one dead and two wounded, and at least one of the wounded will be fine. I think it was just from a frightened horse. She has several broken bones, but nothing that can't be healed. The rest should pull through, and the provisions are all safe. The boxes and barrels are well made. I had some people check. Nothing is contaminated."

"Did you see all the things I got?"

"Not exactly." He gave a half smile. "When I carried you up here you didn't even seem to know me, and I wasn't about to leave you until I was sure you were all right. But I have gotten many reports since yesterday afternoon. You did very well, my dear girl. For the time, at least, you have saved our country."

Tatyana smiled then. She was tired, but comfortable, and she had done it. She had set out to do something truly important for her people, and she had actually succeeded.

"You should rest now," Edward said gently. "I'll tell your mother you're awake. She'll be up any minute to sit with you, and she'll bring you some food or water if you wish. I must go try to sleep a little before my watch.

Glossary of Terms

Aldor: Aldor is a town in the kingdom of Eldir. It is on the Silver River and south of the capital on the trade road to Ikkik. Its population is of both Eldir and Efrim descent, and it is known for its trade fairs where people from the Eldir and Efrim capitals come, as well as merchants from Ikkik and other kingdoms farther south.

Black barrier: A thick barrier of especially powerful black mist that the Shadows erected around the valley of Efrimiel.

Captain: The second rank in both Efrim and Eldir armies, until the creation of head captain by the Efrim. Captains are lower-level officers. A captain can be in charge of a watch or sometimes even a smaller scouting or border guard company.

Efrim: Both the nation and the ethnicity of the Efrim people. Efrim people are tall, but not as tall as the Eldir. They are usually stocky and broad-built with golden to light brown hair and blue eyes. Their magic power is the Plant gift.

Efrimiel: The valley that is the central point of the Efrim nation. The valley of Efrimiel is where nearly all the Efrim people live and where the royal palace stands.

Eldir: The nation and ethnicity of the Eldir people. The Eldir are very tall and slender of build, with long, straight black hair sometimes varying to dark brown, and gray to gray-blue eyes. Their magic gifts are the Sight and the Healing gift.

Eldirad: The capital city of the nation of Eldir. It stands on the Silver River, two miles south of the south end of the valley of Efrimiel and on the crossroads of the north-south road running from Efrimiel to Ikkik, and the east-west road that runs from Westtower and Obrin to Selna on the coast.

Equinox: The date when day and night are equal. September 21 and March 21, or thereabout.

General: The highest rank of the Efrim Army besides the High commander. There are never more than half a dozen at a time, usually fewer. They have authority over captains and sometimes command several captains and many warriors.

Guardian: The highest rank of the Eldir army besides the ruler, a king or a queen, who is the supreme commander. A guardian is equivalent to an Efrim general in authority, taking command over captains and often large groups of warriors, but there is something different in the mentality. A guardian is supposed to be selfless and a protector of their warriors and their nation. They are expected to lead rather than command.

Head captain: A rank created in the Efrim army by High Commander Louranin during the Shadow War to give some captains authority over others.

Healing gift: An exclusively Eldir magical gift usually linked with the Sight that runs consistently in the royal line. It gives a person the ability to use magic in healing, strengthening a person, lowering their fever, reducing pain, and even dramatically speeding up healing.

High commander: The highest rank of the Efrim army. There is only one high commander, and he is the ultimate military authority beneath the queen. There is an ancient tradition of the high commander being the consort to the queen, as is the case in the time of this story, but since arranged marriages stopped in Efrim shortly after the coming of the Eldir, it is no longer required. The high commander now is only the consort if he happens to be a general. Otherwise, a general will be appointed to the post by the queen for the duration of her reign.

Ikkik: The kingdom to the south of Eldir. They are patriarchal, and very feudal, and relations with Eldir are diplomatic but not exactly friendly.

Innate power: A person's inner power or spiritual strength. It is their core power. It affects other powers, as you cannot be powerful in Sight, the Healing gift, or the Plant gift, without substantial innate power, but innate power is independent of all gifts, and a person with great innate power can be without other magic or have only a small gift for it.

Obrin: A village at the west of the territory of Eldir. The people have different heritage and history, and different language and religion than those of Eldir and Efrim, but long ago they came to the queen of Eldir for protection and ever since have been a protectorate of Eldir, largely autonomous but watched over by the prince or princess of Westtower, to whom they owe allegiance and to whom they turn in trouble.

Plant gift: The magical gift of the Efrim. It is not common, running in the farm families of Efrim for the most part. It gives great power over living plants. The gifted can heal plants of sickness and make them grow at a rate far greater than their unassisted nature would allow, although the latter takes much exertion. They can make a plant stronger and healthier with just a touch and a song, and they can also make a sort of plant concealment charm.

Receiving level: This designates the lowest level of the Eldir gift of the Sight above trace amounts. A person with this level of the gift can sense lies with no effort and can hear others speak when they come with the Sending. They may also have visions and dreams, although with less regularity than those with stronger levels of the gift. They can feel danger to loved ones, although this is not entirely reliable with any other than the very closest connections.

Selna: The republic to the east of Efrim and Eldir. Selna is a coastal nation, fertile and prosperous, that relies heavily on the sea for fishing and trade. They are known for fine festivals and wine.

Sending: Sending is the second level of the Sight gift. Those who have it can sense lies and hear others speak with the Sight. They have Sight visions and dreams and can feel danger to loved ones with great reliability. On top of that, they can send their spirit out to one of their connections, visiting them in spirit. There are levels within the gift of Sending, and while most can only go to first-degree family, and one or two others, some very gifted people, like Helen, can go to any close friend.

Sight: Along with the Healing gift with which it is often linked, it is the greatest magic of the Eldir. The Sight gives a person dreams and visions of the future, which is the element of prophecy, useful but difficult to interpret. The other side of the gift is connections. There is a web of connections between people. Someone with the Sight can feel these almost like threads. Some connections are stronger than others, based on how close the bond is. The strongest bonds are family, mother/father, brother/sister, parent/child, and true love. True love can be platonic or romantic so long as it is of sufficient intensity. For most it is only these strongest connections that can be relied upon, and with which the Sending, and Speaking level parts of the gift are possible. The Sight has three levels, Receiving, Sending, and Speaking, and each person born with the gift is born with a level. They can overstep the level they are born with if they have power, but they cannot do so for long without risking serious consequences. Sight at all levels, like any use of power, is affected by a person's mental state and physical weariness.

Sight/Power overuse: There are physical consequences to overuse of innate power, whether through the Sight or otherwise. These include bad headaches, temporary blindness and, in the worst cases, fainting. Barring some extreme overstepping of power, all symptoms other than a general weariness will fade within an hour.

Solstice: The longest night in the winter and longest day in the summer. The winter solstice is the Efrian new year's eve.

Speaking level: This is the highest level of the Sight gift. For most attributes, see **Sending.** Speaking level means that when a person goes in spirit to another person who also has the Sight at any level, they can speak to them inside their head. This gift, too, varies in its strength so that for some going beyond a word or two is risky and exhausting, while for others speaking is relatively easy unless they are already weary.

Westtower: The western guard station of Eldir and headquarters of the prince of Westtower, who watches over the protectorate of Obrin.

About the Author

Morgan's Cummings lives in rural Northern California with her family, her beloved cat Emil and her chickens. She enjoys gardening, and is passionate about all things fantasy. Her work is characterized by the themes of nobility of spirit, the strength of friendships, and a struggle of good against evil.

Visit her website at https://morgannacummings.com to see more, and check her latest releases.

If you'd like to follow her writing journey, see more about her worlds, or simply want to see cute pictures of her cat, find her on Instagram @morganna_cummings_author or on facebook as Morganna Cummings.

A review of this book at your favorite retailer or book tracking site would be much appreciated.

Also by Morganna Cummings

CHRONICLES OF THE GUARDED REALM: THE SHADOW WARS

The saga continues with:

Facing the Shadow

Times are dark in the sister kingdoms of Eldir and Efrim. The war with the Shadows has already stretched for four long years, and still even the most powerful of the Eldir healers have found no real cure for the deadly poison of the enemy weapons. Now a plague born of the same evil magic, impervious to all their arts of healing, and carried in the very air, is sweeping the Eldir nation.

The battle against the Shadow armies has been terrible, but worse is coming. When the great monsters behind the armies of Shadows step forward to fight, every life will hang by a thread.

A prophecy may contain the clue to a cure for the poisonous magic of the enemy, but time is running short. Without it no one will survive, yet it will take more than a cure to win the coming battles.

The friends who have risen to lead both nations will have to give all they have, or more, to protect their people, and everything they love.

This battle could end an era, but will there be a new dawn?

The third and final book in the trilogy, *Lord of the Shadow,* will be coming out in 2027